COACH'S MIDNIGHT DINER:
THE BACK FROM THE DEAD EDITION

A COLLECTION OF INTERESTING AND ENJOYABLE
STORIES WHICH WILL UNDOUBTEDLY EXPAND
THE READER'S IMAGINATIONS, AND MAY CAUSE
INSOMNIA DUE TO THE INTENSE NATURE OF SOME,
AND THUS IS NOT RECOMMENDED FOR CHILDREN
OR THOSE WITH WEAK CONSTITUTIONS OR HEART
CONDITIONS

COACH'S MIDNIGHT DINER:
THE BACK FROM THE DEAD EDITION

Editor-In-Chief
Coach Culbertson

Diner Editors
Vennessa Ng
Michelle Pendergrass
Mike Duran

Layout Editor
Melody Graves

Story Editors
Robert Garbacz
Matt Mikalatos

Reader
Keving Lucia

Cover Artist
Adrian Rivero

Coach's Midnight Diner is published annually by ccPublishing, NFP, a 501c3 organization dedicated to advancing Christian literary writing. Mail can be sent to 60 W Terra Cotta Ave, Ste. B, Unit 156, Crystal Lake IL, 60014-3548. Submissions are not accepted by mail.

COPYRIGHT

SUBMISSIONS

Submissions are only accepted online at http://www.themidnightdiner.com via our Online Submissions System. This is the 21st century. Submissions received by mail will not be read, looked at, returned, or reviewed in any way, unless the author is Stephen King. Otherwise, get with the program.

TABLE OF CONTENTS

BOX

DANIEL G. KEOHANE

She awoke in darkness. Whether it was morning or evening didn't matter. Such concepts were lost to Xing-chi. Even her name, which had meant something to her father and mother, no longer had significance. She was *she*, with occasional labels and epithets spat by the men who came to her in moments uncountable. No light meant only that no one was coming to pull her small, cramped body from its home. And this *was* her home, an acceptance which had long ago crossed the threshold of her mind. Any hope of the world turning back to its proper shape had long fallen away, crushed under her sparse weight inside the box.

Time passed. Light gradually blossomed, vague and gray. She moved slowly in the tight space, long-practiced at silence to avoid attention, rising until her right eye aligned with the imperfect circle in the second-highest slat. Once a rough knot, it had fallen loose many months ago when her crate was lowered unceremoniously onto a platform much like the one on which it now rested. She stared through the hole, a surrogate Eye through which Xing-chi could view the world. She raised her left knee, bit down on her bottom lip as a sharp pain cut upward along her side from the neglected muscles, and held herself aloft on tips of slender fingers. Eye to Eye, looking into the gray.

This world was larger than the previous, wide and spacious with air that was at least cleaner than the damp shipping hold which served as the first of many worlds she'd traveled to after the leaf and tree of her childhood home had been ripped away forever. Other boxes like her own filled the cavern. Many would contain lifeless cargo, books or machine parts, jumbled straw entombing a single expensive vase. Sometimes, in other places, she would watch men opening the crates as they followed a list on clipboards, adding items or taking them away. Always, if their puffy, sweaty faces turned her way Xing-chi would fade from the Eye, drift into the shadows of her home and hope she had not been seen either by the men, or their thoughts.

There were moments, however, when the box felt too tight and angry around her, when she welcomed their attention, rough and violent as it usually was. It served as confirmation she was not dead, was not mere spirit once drifting in the wind now caught in a net and caged, never to see or touch the trees of the Next Life.

Her mother talked of a place like that. A world of joy and music and warm breezes. *Tian Tang* was its name, the point all must travel toward but never reach, not until the time they were lifted by the Light and delivered to its bosom. Her mother would sing of this place and read from her book. In those long-ago moments Xing-chi understood little but savored the woman's tone, the sound of her hope. She had forgotten her mother's voice now. There had been a father, too, a stern rock of a man. His gaze rarely fell on Xing-chi. She remembered he had smiled once, but the reason for it was as elusive as her memories.

Maybe what she was remembering was *Tian Tang*. Perhaps she'd already passed from her old life and reached its perfection, only to lose her footing and fall backwards into this box.

She raised herself higher until her head touched the top. Her small nose poked through the Eye. Xing-chi breathed in, quietly pulling into herself what smells she could draw from the room. Wood of course, so many crates. Something else, wet and greasy. No food, not yet, but this consideration sent saliva to run like a fever over her tongue and teeth. She licked her lips, swallowed, turned her ear to the hole as a distraction. Silence, the sound of *waiting*. A sniffle, far off from one like her, never too close, never a word or gaze to share with another.

There, a soft whimper, perhaps a yawn. All like her were careful with silence. Perhaps this girl had been inside too long and wanted to draw the men to her, if only for that craved attention, that confirmation of her *being*. All of them, trapped spirits. Flies in amber.

CLANG!

The sound was so abrupt Xing-chi curled onto the bottom of the box, away from the sudden light washing through the Eye. Tight, low voices uttering unknowable words. Their tones told Xing-chi that no new books or lamps would be unpacked this day. They had come for her, or another. The voices grew no closer, moved at a distance towards some other part of the world. The voices rose sharper, accompanied by the sound of wood being pulled free of its nails, a crate being opened. A girl's voice, high and delicate like broken porcelain. Xing-chi once understood the words she spoke, or those like them. If there was understanding now, it was trapped outside the box, never to be reclaimed. She did not *want* to know, because there was no room in her dark place for another's pain. The voices passed back the way they'd come. She uncurled slowly, keeping to the shadows far from the Eye, saw shapes flitting past in the distance. One man, apparent by the hair on his large face, moving too fast to discern detail. Tangled black hair followed, its owner lower than the hole. Xing-chi suppressed the urge to move forward, to see who it was. The broken porcelain sounded again, but was hushed into silence. Another clang echoed in the cavern a moment before the light died. Xing-chi did not move, non-existent once again in the sudden dark, and waited for the gray to return.

She eventually curled back onto the floor, the top of her head resting on the wood, bare feet pressed to the far wall, knees bent and stiff. She thought no more about what had happened, simply let the activity, which had come and gone like lightening, drift about as a new shape in her shape-less world. They would return. They always did after one was taken. They would open her box and lift her out, let her wander in some far corner to stretch and defecate. If she was fortunate they might spray her with a hose and for a joyous moment remind her she was alive. Because if she was still in this First Life, shattered as it might be, then *Tian Tang* may still be waiting, may still be a hope.

Xing-chi closed her eyes. She was hungry, but would eat when food was offered.

☙

A RIPPING SOUND. The shaking of her world. All was falling and lost. These thoughts stampeded through her brain as Xing-chi awoke. She tried to curl tighter but her movements were too sudden, the pain too sharp. The top of the box *cricked* open, angles of light widening as the top was hefted against the many nails holding it fast. Large, gloved hands pushed up and up.

The men had returned but she'd been sleeping, hadn't heard, could not prepare.

A pockmarked face mostly hidden in a thick, wiry beard loomed over her—the man she'd glimpsed earlier. His smile was lost in hair and cratered flesh, eyes narrow and wet. He spoke words and Xing-chi waited, still curled tight in the small space. A second head peered over the top of the box, long and thin with wide eyes. He licked his lips twice and they glistened in the artificial light.

"One of our finest," the bearded one said. Xing-chi understood nothing except the tone. The thin-headed man would be taking her for a time, touching and maybe hurting. That was all right. Her existence was now a truth revealed in the trembling, expectant gaze of both men. The thin man said something. The beard replied with, "Twelve or thirteen. Can't tell with this kind. Look like babies no matter how old, right?" He laughed. Thin-head did likewise, without humor, glancing across Xing-chi's bent and naked body.

She kept her eyes open, looking sideways at the men, listening to words familiar from past conversations like this one. Would the thin man choose another? Did they not see her? She wanted to move, do something to attract his attention so he would lift her from the box and *see* her.

He nodded. The beard did as well and his head rose higher as he lifted the top free. His chest was wide and muscular, like her father's only much, much bigger. He was going to lift her out like the lamps and books. She was here. She existed. The other man would have her for a time in some cold and distant corner. Xing-chi was both excited and terrified. She wanted to smile, *and* wanted to die. *Tian Tang* was again a hope, but the road was hard.

Rumbling thunder of a dozen shouting voices. The large man had been reaching down but now he stopped and straightened, turned in unison with his companion towards the noise. He barked short words then was gone, the platform rocking back and forth with his departure. The thin-headed man looked down at her, fear and need swirling about his nose and lips like Autumn leaves. His arm snaked into the box. Tears ran down his face as he gently touched her leg. More shouting, closer, one word repeated over and over, "Now! Now!" Then, "On the floor now!" He continued to touch her as Xing-chi stared into his lost and defeated eyes. She tried to speak, tried to thank him for the contact. She could not, no more than she could move more than a few inches in such a confined place. Even so, she savored the proof of her existence in his—

A black-gloved hand grabbed the man's collar and pulled him away from the box.

The word, "Now!" was repeated with such venom Xing-chi curled against the pain of her muscles and closed her eyes. The box shook. What came next would not be good. Demons and anger. A new word was shouted at her from the top of the box, "Miss?" making no sense, the tone too tight and wild. Xing-chi bent her arms about her head, forced herself into the wood, became the grain. Like the world of her birth, this terrible place was crashing, turning over, and if the one which replaced it was worse than this, she did not want to be anywhere. She understood with constricting clarity that she had, indeed, fallen from the Next Life. It would be best, then, if she was no longer here or anywhere. Only patterns and swirls in the wood inside a box in a lost cavern of gray light.

When the man's voice returned, it was softer. As all around her, shouts and frantic words filled every corner, the soft tone of Black Glove's voice dominated her small world. "Miss," it whispered, like a warm breeze, "can you understand me?"

She did not understand. Her spirit was pattern and swirl, no more substantial than a lost memory.

THE ROOM WAS warm, filled with light. *Warmth* was a concept long forgotten. Xing-chi wondered how cold it had been inside the box. Without choice, things simply *were*. She curled on the bed in the same position as when the soldier had lifted her out, wrapped her in a rough blanket, and carried her away. She understood those moments with clearer thoughts now. The soldiers had come for her and the others, brought them here. She dared not venture further in her mind with these considerations, nor their implications. For if the tiny world in which she'd lived for so long was the same as that of her lost home, her mother and father...the meaning was too much, too terrible. She pressed against the mattress, tried to disappear into the sheets like she had done when the thin-headed man had been pulled away. Too much. All, of everything, was wrong.

"How long?" A new voice in the room. Not the yellow-haired woman who often came and spoke to her, touched her, shined lights into her eyes. Her long face was like the man above the box but softer, prettier. This new voice was also gentle, another woman. Xing-chi could not see the face it belonged to, nor did she care to. She closed her eyes tighter and pressed her face hard against the bed.

"Best we can tell," the yellow-haired woman said, "two and a half, three years."

A sudden intake of breath. "Oh, my God. How...why did...." Staccato words, but Xing-chi found comfort in their rounded edges, and the hope that they were speaking about her.

"She's been like this for hours. Won't acknowledge anyone, but she probably doesn't speak much English, either."

"Can't you put some clothes on her?"

"She won't let us. Not yet. Try to talk to her, Sue. Please."

Xing-chi let their voices lull her. So much like her mother's, especially this new one. Light footsteps, leaves across stones. "Miss?" That word again. Would it be her name now? A cool touch on her shoulder. Xing-chi flinched, but the fingertips remained, hardly there at all.

"Ni ming bai wo shuo shen mo xiao gu nang Ma?"

Every muscle in her body froze—not tightened as they often did at the sound of men approaching. She merely became motionless, fearing any twitch or movement would make the light filling her chest fade away.

She'd understood the words the new voice had spoken. *Do you understand what I'm saying, young girl?*

The touch remained, patient. Xing-chi had to show she understood before they gave up and went away. She opened her eyes, did nothing else, not yet. The mattress stretched out before her in a soft, white landscape. A figure moved like a cloud in her peripheral vision.

"Ni ming bai Ma?"

Emotion poured into her, drowning her. She turned her head and a woman like her mother, but not her mother, sat on the edge of the bed. Her face was round and flat and loving. It smiled and spoke and Xing-chi died in her gaze. The world filled with water. She could no longer see, felt an arm curl around and lift her up. Xing-chi's own arms and legs remained curled, but she allowed the contact and knew it would not hurt. She cried against the stranger's dress, understood her own nakedness for the first time. She was an infant reborn into this world of warmth and light and perhaps she had made it...no, she would not think this, would not hope, only let the angel hold her and hold her.

❧

XING-CHI SAT ON the bed. The woman remained, one arm around her shoulder, always touching, always this contact. She'd tried to wrap Xing-chi in a blanket but the moment she felt its confining embrace a black terror sent her curved, angled limbs flailing until the blanket fluttered to the floor. She was happy the way she was, body open to warm air and the woman's arm, always around her shoulders, connecting the two of them like a newborn to its mother.

"*Ni zhi dao ni ming zi Ma?*"

The woman wanted to know her name. Xing-chi wanted to tell her, knowing that it was not *Miss*. She wanted to say *I am Xing-chi*, not knowing *why* she was called this. When she tried to remember the fear crept back. She wanted to tell this woman, this angel, something, wanted to *speak*.

She tried to say her name, but her mouth was broken, tongue disobedient.

"That's OK," the woman said in that strange language. The yellow haired woman said something equally alien before she crossed the room to a wide glowing wall. A thin, bamboo-like shade covered the window. She pulled on a chord and the veil was lifted.

Sharp daylight, so bright it was almost painful. Xing-chi needed to squint, but she kept her eyes open, needed to see what lay beyond the glass. When she saw, understanding and joy flooded into her again, like sunlight filling her body. She gasped and tried to straighten her arm and point.

The woman said, "*Ni xiang qu chuang kou Ma?*"

Do you want to go to the window? Xing-chi reluctantly looked away and stared at her face, so much like her mother's. She could not say the word, but thought, *Shi, shi, shi!*

The woman nodded, helped her off the bed. Xing-chi's legs would not straighten, would not hold her weight.

"Let me help." The angel lifted her with both arms. Xing-chi leaned against her chest and held tightly to the woman's neck. Always, though, facing the window. When they reached the glass, brilliant sun poured over her. She reached out her fingers and they curled against the glass. She continued, letting the back of her hand bend, then her whole arm. She could not reach what beckoned from outside. So close.

"She's trying to reach the tree," the other woman said behind them.

Xing-chi accepted the futility of what she was trying to do, and instead pressed her palm flat, fingers splayed. Wide green leaves filled the world beyond, edges red and yellow. They were perfection, like the story of the first woman and first man from her mother's book. The outline of her hand spread like fog across the glass.

Xing-chi tried to speak but her lips bent funny. She ran her tongue along them, soothing, calming. She swallowed and focused only on the single word she wanted to say.

"*Tian Tang*," she whispered. The joy hearing it spoken aloud, and its truth, gave her lips strength to say it again.

And again. And again.

NOWHERE

SIOBHAN SHIER

I had no idea who the man across from me was.

I found myself sitting in a small coffee house, the ones you rarely see anymore. Always cozy, filled with couches and a menagerie of furniture, board games, and newspapers, these types of local joints were vanishing from the face of the planet, overpowered by the unyielding force that is human progress.

The man placed his hand on mine. It was hot; a dry heat that you find in people whose mean temperature is above the norm. It wouldn't surprise me to find that he faked fevers when he was a child, and got away with it. Lucky bastard probably got to play hooky a lot.

"Are you alright, Yuri? You look a little dazed," he said, his voice soft.

The man was striking, but you wouldn't notice it right away. You would never see him on a billboard, face flushed and pouting towards the world as he pulled his brand name boxers low. He had hair that looked like an absence of light, and a face that belonged in a porno. His shoulders were broad in an unnoticeable way and his eyes were a dim shade of gray.

He also knew my name and I still didn't recognize him. It was getting harder and harder to identify people each time the world changed, and it was getting stressful. It would be pretty easy to slip up.

I played it cool.

"I'm fine." I said, leaving my hand where it was. I could feel calluses as his fingers traced along mine. No one I dated in the past had ever made small expressions of affection like that. One fellow wouldn't even walk next to me. He was always three feet ahead of me, not even bothering to look back to see if I would keep up. It made me feel more objectified than any demeaning comment ever could. The relationship did not last long.

The man smiled a light expression that didn't touch his eyes. He stood, pulling me up with him.

"We need to get back."

I followed him out of the coffee house, admiring the fit of his suit. It was silk and clung to him like plastic wrap.

We walked in silence for a while, in an area designed for foot traffic. The sidewalks were wide, leaving barely enough room in the street for cars to drive. The stores were quaint and well lit, bakeries, restaurants, novelty shops, and the occasional antique store. There were a few pedestrians walking around, window shopping or just chatting with one another. They all smiled at the man as we passed, moving to the side almost unconsciously to let him pass. It was eerie.

The man reached over and caught my hand, lacing his fingers with mine. It was a sweet gesture. At that moment I wished that this were my life, that I was living it with this affectionate, handsome man instead of being just a visitor. It was the first time I didn't want to go back home. That feeling chilled me, and at the time I didn't know why.

We stopped in front of a small diner. It was decorated in sheet metal and red leather, an effect most likely an attempt to mimic an idealistic vision of the 1950s. The metal was crinkled in concentric patterns, playing tricks on the eye when looked upon. The sign on the outside said: Yankee Rose. It was a weird name for a 1950s diner. Normally you would expect to see Ruby Cafe, or Rocky Road, or something with an over alliterated title.

The man caught my other hand, turning me to face him. He squeezed both my hands gently as he gazed at me, a gentle expression on his face. I wanted to kiss him.

"Are you ready?" he asked, his voice still so soft.

I smiled at him, too distracted to give any other response.

"Just remember," he continued, "this is a war. Every word must be chosen with care. No leniency for the enemy, no compassion, and no remorse for what we must do."

What?

The man pulled me after him into the diner, the door swinging freely on its hinges behind us. I trailed in his wake as he brought us deeper into the bright red with a determined stride, mind still trying to make sense of his words.

The people in the diner were lively; the place was ringing with laughter and smiling faces. One table had a ring of waiters standing around it, beaming and clapping their hands to a birthday song.

We arrived at a booth, deep in the back, almost hidden around a corner. The man gestured for me to sit down and so I did, sliding sideways into my seat. He sat next to me.

Across from us were a man and a woman.

The woman would have been hard to pick out of a crowd. Her dull brown hair was a little greasy and there were dark circles under her eyes. She was dressed in off white sweats. Her eyes were unfocused, and she slouched, her head drooping to the side, lax and unsupported.

The other man was difficult to look at. My eyes ached and watered as I forced them to gaze at him, fighting every instinct that wanted to let them slip away, to look at anything else. He was an old man, white beard covering his chest; he was a young man with a wreath of leaves around his forehead. He had six arms, than only two. His head was an eagle, a jackal, and a cat. He was a woman, pregnant and than simply young. He was beautiful, hideous, old and infantile. He was invisible, on fire, covered in shadow, or made out of mist. He had wings, scales, fur, and was naked. He was horrible to behold and I felt fear.

My legs began to tremble and I looked down at the table.

The man I came with placed his hand on my thigh and the terror fled, replaced by a deep calm. I glanced over at him and he smiled again, this time showing his teeth.

"Greet them," he whispered.

I turned back towards the couple. I stared at the limp woman for a moment before discomfort forced me to look at the table.

"Good afternoon," I said.

The woman's head lifted, tilting upwards as if it were pulled by a string. The terrible creature at her left leaned into my field of vision. All I could hear was a faint murmur of sound.

"Good afternoon, Yuri and Luc." The woman's mouth moved, producing sound. "Let's get right to business. Yah wishes to discuss the surrender of Hollywood. We are willing to release them in exchange for the withdrawal of troops from Hong Kong."

The man I now knew as Luc snorted.

"Firstly," he said, "you can't surrender what you've already lost."

I glanced at Luc and he raised his eyebrows, nodding his head slightly at the two sitting across from us.

I repeated his statement, word for word.

"Secondly," he continued, "I thought I was here to make some progress instead of taking insults. It appears that I was mistaken."

I repeated what he said, finishing just as he began to stand.

"Wait, wait," the puppet woman said, words stumbling out of her mouth in haste. "We apologize. Please sit back down."

The man hesitated, and then lowered himself back into the booth.

"We offer to fix your voice's little problem. Is that worth something to you?"

Luc reached out and touched my cheek, sliding his fingers backwards until he tucked a loose strand of hair behind my ear.

"That is worth nothing," he said and I repeated.

As the words left my lips my mind caught up with the conversation. That horrible creature could fix my problem. At least, maybe it could. They might have been talking about the me that was before, the one that knew everyone's names and what the hell was going on.

There was only one way I could find out and it wasn't by blending into the background of another person's life.

"Are you talking about me?" I asked Luc.

He nodded, stroking his hand down my arm.

"You know I'm not who I'm supposed to be?"

"Of course, Yuri. It was obvious the second you arrived. We can talk about this later though, right now I need you to focus and tell Yah this."

I said the words to the two across the table with haste and turned back towards the man. I couldn't let this drop. I couldn't just hide and let the world wash over me while I cowered out of sight. This might be my only chance to stop this madness.

"Why won't you let him fix me?" I said, raising my voice so that everyone at the table could hear me.

Luc glanced over at the two across from us. They were silent and the hairs on the back of my neck rose as they looked at me. I didn't take my gaze off of the man with the light absent hair.

"Let me ask you this," he said. "Are you so weak that you can't solve your own problems?"

The woman across the table coughed. It was a stilted and purposeful interjection.

"We have another proposal for you," the creature said through her.

"Everyone deserves some help," I replied to Luc.

He frowned and the earth rumbled beneath us, causing pictures to rattle on the walls and one waitress to loose her balance, dropping her load of plates to the ground.

No one else in the diner seemed to notice.

"If you believe that nonsense, you belong with them, not with me," he said. "No one deserves anything. You have to work for it, earn it, and demand it. Only fools expect the world to be handed to them on a plate."

"Speaking of which," the woman said, her voice carrying a little further this time, "our proposal is an unconditional surrender of Great Britain and India for your current voice."

"What?" I said. What the hell did countries have to do with anything?

Luc glanced over at me, an expression I couldn't identify flicking across his face. He hesitated a moment before he spoke.

"Give me a day to think about it."

I said nothing.

The two of them vanished with a pop, leaving behind a faint smell of olive leaves. I stared at the empty space they left behind.

"That went very well," Luc said, standing. He grabbed my hand and pulled me to my feet. I didn't resist.

To be honest, I don't really remember what I was thinking at the time. I suppose I was in a state of shock, I mean, I had just exposed myself as a fake for the first time, been told to fix a problem I didn't even understand ,and sold off for some countries. I wasn't sure if I should be scared, annoyed, or pleased.

Luc tapped the table and it folded up. The floor slid away to reveal a set of stairs leading down into darkness. I glanced around again. No one in the diner seemed to notice.

"Lets go home, shall we?" he asked, his tone bright and cheery. He began to pull me down into the darkness.

I took the first few steps down the stairs and I stopped, resisting his firm grasp.

"I don't think I..."

The floor snapped shut above me, catching the back of my head and knocking me forward into the waiting black.

~

I WOULD LIKE to say that when I awoke the world changed, and that it was different from before. That was not the case.

There were stars. When I opened my eyes all I saw were brilliant specks of light against a black drop. *The night sky,* I thought.

I dragged my hand across my face, trying to rub the stars out of my eyes and make sense of what I was seeing.

I was looking at a black ceiling speckled in florescent paint. It was a high, domed ceiling. To get that effect a person would need to climb a ladder and fling paint up into the air with reckless abandon.

The room I was in was a bedroom; I was lying on a large queen sized bed with a gray duvet and large, overdone pillows. There was a small dresser and a table. On the table were several picture frames.

I slid my legs across the silky bedspread and stood, walking over to the table. The pictures were frame after frame of myself... and Luc. The two of us were eating lunch in the park, rocking out at a concert, dressed up and attending a late night Rocky Horror showing. In each picture I had a smile plastered across my face, toothy and genuine.

My life I knew before contained no pictures of me as an adult looking that happy. There never was a person that touched me like that, and even if they existed, I wouldn't have let them get close enough. Looking at those pictures my life seemed so distant. It was a past life that flew farther away from me with every second I spent without it.

I needed to find out why the person who made me happy in all of those pictures would trade me like an unvalued object. I couldn't leave this life without trying to fix it for her, and for me.

As I turned towards the single door of the room, another picture caught my eye. It peeked out from behind the dresser, down at the floor. It must have fallen. I pulled it, wiggling it with some force to free it.

The picture was me, just me, no Luc. I was lying on the bed that stood behind me, the sheets and pillows all the same fabric and color. My eyes were open and my mouth was slightly ajar, a strand of drool peeking out of the corner of my mouth. My eyes were unfocused, face lax. It reminded me of the woman at the diner.

I put the picture back where I found it, wedging it in just as firmly as it was before.

☙

I OPENED THE door into the color red.

I froze, blinking at the sudden change in color scheme, overwhelmed by the shades of the carpet, the drapes, and the furniture. There were two red oak desks against opposite walls, facing inwards into the room. On them, flat screen monitors with wireless keyboards and mice. Behind them individually, a man and a woman, both dressed in shades of red so dark they could have been mistaken for rust.

The woman glanced up as I entered the room, pushing her horn-rimmed glasses back up the bridge of her nose with a solitary finger. She took that finger and pushed it down against a small black button that protruded ever so slightly out of the desk. I never would have noticed it at all if she hadn't touched it.

"She's awake," the woman said, eyes still fixed on me.

The woman nodded.

She didn't have any ear piece that I could see, and there was no sound, so the motion made her look a bit mad.

"You can go in," she said, gesturing to the double blood red doors at the other end of the room. She looked back at her computer screen and her fingers began flying across the keyboard. The man never looked up during the exchange.

I didn't argue, ask questions, or demand answers. Just because Luc seemed to know who and what I was didn't mean that I should let anybody else on to that little secret.

The doors opened, moving on silent hinges.

Luc was waiting.

He sat at a large desk, the kind the villain mastermind would hover behind in any B rated movie. Papers were strewn across the worn surface. His head was resting in his hand, elbow placed in the middle of a disorganized pile. His eyes were closed.

The doors shut behind me.

"Hi, beautiful," he said, his eyes still sealed.

I bit my lower lip. It was one thing making the decision to stand up for her and another actually finding the words to do so. There was a pressure in my chest as my heart raced against my brain: the prize, a construction of a sentence.

"I don't want you to do this to her." I said, weakening my position with ineffectual words.

"I wouldn't be doing it to her."

It took a moment for the nuances to sink in and for me to believe the meaning. I gaped, sputtered, and waved my hands in the air. My surprise and I were alone together. Luc did not react.

"You can't trade me." I said, finding strength in my indignation. Anger filled me. I was not a possession to be bartered away.

Luc opened his eyes.

They were brilliant. Pits of black where galaxies swirled, time rushing forward with an abandon only written about in the most hedonistic of poems. The world was in flames and it had frozen over.

"I wonder, can you even find a reason why?" he asked, his voice a liquid that melted the room away.

It was hard to think. The visual and audio display was disrupting my thoughts, throwing them off track. I couldn't look away.

It stopped.

Luc's laugh pierced through my confusion. His eyes were normal, dull gray and containing only the minute changes in color that you would find in anyone with irises. In front of him was an old card table, papers strewn across the surface. The desk was gone.

My mouth was open, and I felt like I was about to speak, but I couldn't for the life of me remember what we were talking about.

The only explanation I could think of was that she had taken a hallucinogen before I arrived. That or the always possible option that I was insane.

Luc took my hand.

"You're not losing your mind," he said. "But you are losing something else."

He drew me to the back of the room.

"Time for a tour," he said.

The wall vanished.

I followed him forwards into the dark shadows that replaced it. I don't know why I didn't panic, scream, and run away like Goldilocks at the end of her story, but I was calmer than I had ever been since this shit started happening to me.

The darkness opened into a well lit office area. Men and women sat in small desks, flimsy walls of brown plastic fabric separating them from one another. The tops of their heads poked out of each of their cages, a sign of life in an otherwise barren environment. A cacophony of voices filled the air, none of them speaking to each other.

"We'd like to tell you about..."

"You're in luck, there's a special offer..."

"Give me one moment while I..."

Luc walked down the aisle between the cubicles. I glanced behind me and saw a blank wall. The only place to go was forward, after him.

"No, sir, that is not what we..."

"Two for the price of..."

"May I speak to Ms..."

The room was long, and it was several minutes before I reached the other end where Luc was waiting. On the wall behind him was a large white-board, lines of purple drawn on it to form a chart. There were two categories, L and Y, and underneath, numbers.

"Do you understand?" he asked.

No chance in hell, I thought to myself. How was I supposed to understand anything that happened in this place?

"Don't give up so easily," Luc said. "What does this *mean* to you?" He gestured at the board.

I gave it a second glance. Side by side numbers were usually a comparison in the world I came from.

"A score," I said.

Luc nodded. "And if I traded you for Great Britain and India, this is how the numbers would change."

I didn't see him move. The numbers on the board melted away, swirling together in a multicolored blob. Within seconds they rearranged themselves. The result was obvious.

"Why haven't you said yes?" I asked.

"I'm going to," he said, teeth glinting. "Just waiting on the timing."

My mind twisted around that before giving up, and going onto my next question.

"Why am I worth so much?"

Luc threw his head back and laughed. The sound came deep from within his belly and filled the room with its spontaneous expression. The rest of the noise in the room ceased, and for a moment the only sound was Luc. When he fell silent, the background chatter resumed.

"Yah wants to end the disturbance your traveling is causing," Luc said.

"So he would send me home," I stated.

Luc shook his head. "No. There's a much simpler way to end the problem." His eyes did not connect with mine.

Before I could open my mouth a large man ran up to Luc and handed him a small slip of paper. Built like a lumberjack, the tweed pants the man wore looked ridiculous.

Luc took a long look at the paper before crumpling it and tossing it on the ground. "Show time!" he said, his voice bright and cheerful.

The white board slid to the side and the wall opened up, folding against itself like baker's dough to reveal a spiral staircase.

I heard a gasp behind me.

The large man's eyes widened, his breath coming in short, quick bursts. His eyes darted in between Luc and the stairs. His muscles tensed, veins pulsing visibly in the light. Luc's back was to both of us.

The man's eyes came to a stop.

He lunged forward. Body springing into motion, every muscle engaged to take him towards the opening.

Luc's hand lashed out.

It sunk into the man's chest, delicate bone and flesh vanishing in the expanse of muscle with no visible effort, impaling him like a fish flopping on the end of a spear. Luc didn't even look over his shoulder.

The man's eyes rolled into the back of his head, the whites staring up at the ceiling as his skull flopped backwards. His face was frozen in a silent scream, teeth bared and tense as his lips pulled away from them.

Luc twitched his hand.

The body flew, limp as it crashed into one of the cubicle dividers. The flimsy brown material crumpled from the impact and weight of him, folding on top of the desk behind it. The woman sitting at the desk was knocked out of her chair, sprawling onto the floor.

A silence held the room in its grips. Faces turned but no one moved.

Luc put his hand on the small of my back, pushing me forward and up the stairs.

"We don't have much time left," he said.

The steps were a pearl white color with smooth rounded edges. My feet slipped a few times on the surface, unable to find traction. Each time Luc caught me, grabbing my elbow and half carrying me upwards until I found my footing again.

We exited the stairwell.

The walls were a dirty blue, as if an expectant mother anticipated a boy, painted the walls, and then miscarried to such a degree that she became infertile. Shutting the doors, she would have left the room closed and unused until someone, or something, caught a glimpse and stole the faded, dusty color to smear on the walls of this drab and unappealing place.

It was a diner, different than the one where I first saw the creature.

The waiters looked like they had invisible weights strapped to their shoulders. Not one of them smiled. The customers were subdued, staring at their drinks and food with only the most casual and inane comments passed between them.

We came to a booth in the back, holding the creature and the woman from before. Luc sat down. He patted the seat next to him and flashed his teeth at me once more.

I remained standing at the edge of the table, hesitant and indecisive. My instincts were telling me to flee, but my mind wanted to know what had happened to Schrödinger's cat.

"The deal is for this person only. My previous voice..." Luc's voice hesitated before he continued, his tone indicated a correction of his words, "...her body...must remain intact and unharmed."

"Agreed," the woman replied.

I don't know what I was expecting, but it certainly wasn't that the conversation would be finished without a moment for me to think about what was being said. The creature reached out with a finger, claw, talon, and touched the back of my hand.

Pain exploded in my head. The diner spun away as dark spots ate away at my vision like a deadly virus. A voice, indescribable in its depth and volume spoke.

"Greet your end with rapture, Abomination."

The sensation was like a vice, pressure trapping me and confining me with the pain. There was nothing physical about the sensations, nothing that would make me think that my body was in any danger. No, the excruciating stabs were related to me and my sense of self.

In those moments I understood death more clearly than any other point in my life.

The creature was killing me.

The unmistakable sound of Luc's laughter pierced through all of it.

The voice, the pressure that was hurting me more than any physical attack could, screamed in an anger that echoed around in my mind. Boiling clouds of rage fell short of me and I felt myself slipping out of its trap, slipping out of this world.

I opened my eyes.

It had changed again. The diner, Luc, the puppet woman and the vengeful murderous creature were gone.

I recognized the man in front of me.

PAINT IT BLACK

M. L. ARCHER

A composition in six movements

I. Molto Grave'

When a loved one not only dies, but races to death's dark embrace as if it were a prize or reward it cuts us to the core. The heart is left with a single agonized cry of *Why?*

That question became my own last March when my brother took his life. The discovery was unbelievable. But he didn't die alone. My brother was a cultist. He and twenty-seven others took knives to their own throats and they did it because they thought space aliens were coming to take them away.

I could almost handle believing he was unhappy and distraught over his divorce. But...space aliens?

I am, by profession, a violinist with the Dallas Symphony. My brother, Rick, and the others took their lives after spending time in a group called 'Heaven's Temple,' based out of Santa Fe, New Mexico. For many hours, I researched this group, hunting to see if, among other things, it still had a following in Santa Fe. It did.

Here's the core of the 'Heaven's Temple' entire belief system: mankind is about to be recycled and the Ascended Masters are coming to help a few chosen souls shed their mortal bodies and raise them up to heaven. "Hey Rick, the aliens want you! Kill yourself!"

I didn't buy it.

That summer, I decided to leave Dallas and take a summer job playing for the Santa Fe Opera because then I could further investigate them without alarming my family.

The Sunday before I left, I played the special service music at my parent's church, and then went to their home for supper. It seemed to cheer mom up for a little bit. She'd been awfully quiet since the funeral.

When it was time to leave, my father walked me outside and shook my hand. "Well, son, thanks for playing the service. Your mom needed a few braggin' rights."

"Thanks, Dad. You think she'll be okay?"

My father shook his head. "I don't know."

I leaned back against my little Tercel. From sheer habit my violin case was tucked under my arm.

Dad gave a small laugh. "You remember all the crap Rick used to hand you about taking up the fiddle instead of playing football?"

"Yep." I said feeling the wetness start down my cheeks. "I still can't believe he did it, Dad. I miss him."

"I know you do. And you know what bothers me? I don't think he did anything crazy as suicide."

I looked up. "You think he was murdered?"

"I don't know. I just know in my heart, there's more to the story. You do, too. That's the real reason you're going to Santa Fe."

My father kept a step ahead of me all my life. I wasn't surprised he had me figured out now. I wiped my eyes and nodded.

"Thought so," he said. "I'd do the same thing if I didn't think it would upset your mom. Find out whatever you can, but be careful. Call me if anything strange happens. Your mom couldn't stand to lose another son." His voice broke, "Neither could I."

We stood on the driveway and embraced each other until he gave me a light whack on the back and said, "I'm proud of you, son. You're a damn fine musician."

II. Allegretto con Brio

Santa Fe is an artsy town in northern New Mexico. It is populated by Native Americans, Mexicans, white guys, cowboys, and plenty of folks who simply didn't get enough of the sixties.

A man decked out in full blown Indian regale sat at a picnic table beneath a tree. I thought he looked like a chief in one of those tourist re-enactments. Since we were in the town square, that made sense. I walked over and took a seat.

"Afternoon," he said to me.

"Hey."

The Chief peered at the luggage I hauled with me and the violin case in particular.

"You with the opera company?"

"For the summer. I heard I could learn a lot here."

"Oh, yeah. Santa Fe is a real education," the man said. "Sometimes good, sometimes not so good. But I like musicians. Music is a wonderful gift. It summons the gods to us. I'm glad you share it. You have a place to stay?"

"Yeah, I'm supposed to meet an old friend any minute. Hey, if you don't mind my asking, what are you dressed up for?"

"Oh, this?" the man said tugging at his shirt. "These are my pajamas. Can't you tell I'm asleep?"

My jaw sagged open as I studied his expression. No, he wasn't kidding.

❧

STEVE WILCOX IS my best friend. He's a little guy our high school bully population used to torture with names like Steve Smallcox, Won'tcox, and Nocox. But he had a dusty voice and could lay down a rhythm and blues riff that was pure gold. He moved to Santa Fe, started a rock and R&B band he called Soul Catcher. They had opened for some fairly major groups like Nickelback and were catching the eye of the larger record labels. I wanted to see him make it big. It was a just a matter of time.

A station wagon, large enough to hold a drum set, pulled into the square. Steve hung out the front window, spotted me, and waved.

"If it ain't the fiddler on the ground! Hop in, man!"

I opened the back door, tossed my stuff in, but kept my arm around the violin case. Riding shot gun was a black guy with spidery dreds poking out from underneath a wool hat. Steve introduced him as Samuel.

"Louis is a *real* musician. He's a concert violinist."

Samuel turned. "You can play that thing, then?"

"I do my best."

"You can do rock?"

"Well, yeah, I need a microphone, but sure."

Steve glanced at him. "He can make that violin do anything. I heard him do this piece once where he had to hit all harmonics. It sounded like he was playing the friggin' flute."

Samuel suddenly gave Steve's shoulder a swat. "Then forget about talking to Admar."

"No. Don't bug Louis. He's here doing opera."

"But...Admar is a pain in the ass. He can't play sitar worth a damn."

"No, shut up!"

Frustrated, Samuel turned around in his seat and pointed to my violin. "Dude, could that thing imitate a sitar?"

I shrugged, "Sure."

Steve hauled his car off the road and hit the brake. "Damn it, Samuel!"

Samuel looked as confused as I felt.

"Is there a problem?" I asked.

Steve ran and hand through his hair. "Man, I didn't explain anything to Samuel, I didn't think this would come up and I sure as hell didn't think it would be our first topic." Steve looked at Sam, "Louis's brother was a Heaven's Temple member."

"Oh damn man. Did he..." The silence in the car proved answer enough.

"Damn, man," Samuel said, "I'm sorry."

"There's this gig coming up at the end of the month." I caught Steve's eyes in the rearview mirror, I'm pretty sure he was gauging my reaction. "Some civic organization put it together about a week after..." he stopped. "Anyway, it's turned into a big deal. Well, locally at least. We're doing a concert out in the desert, kind of weird, but kind of cool. It's like a fund-raiser for some of the families. Everyone figured the area Goths would be out en masse and it would be a big success. They're calling it Goth the Desert. Anyway, we're on the roster. Everyone has to do at least one dark song and we can do the old Rolling Stones number, 'Paint It Black' like no body's business. Except for the sitar. Sam's right, Admar sucks."

"I'll do it."

Samuel, who seemed so gung ho before, eyed me carefully. "Are you sure? You don't think that's some bad mojo, do you?"

After a moment, I said, "No, I'll do it for Rick."

"Well, here then," Samuel said rifling through a stack of music pages on the front seat. "Got to admit, I think it could be cool as hell on violin."

I sat back and read the black specks on the page listening to them translate as tones in my head. Samuel was right, it would work on violin in an excellent way. The dissonance, the glissandos, and throbbing rhythm conjured images of the devil sawing away on a cursed fiddle beneath a pallid moon.

That's when I felt it: a sense of being watched, as if I surfaced on somebody's radar. I shivered despite the summer heat.

III. Andante

"You still got the Amati?"

"Hell yeah, why do you think I keep the case practically handcuffed to me?"

Steve laughed. "I would, too. Damn. That thing is worth it."

Among violinists, three common makes of instruments you hear of are the Stradivarius, the Guanerius, and the Amati. The Strads and Guanerius are instruments for big sounds, romantic concertos, large concert halls, that sort of thing. The Amati is more suited to chamber music, crisp and clear. I decided a long time ago I didn't want my career to be as a soloist. I wanted a place in an orchestra doing what I enjoy. Anyway, I'm more of a technician than a showman. So when I came across this Amati six years ago, I snagged it. Not to mention I lucked out and, by a series of extremely fortunate events, purchased it for a mere ten grand. Last time I checked, it appraised for forty.

"So," Steve glanced at the ground, embarrassed, "I was pretty sick about your brother. When I saw his name on the news, I couldn't believe it."

"I couldn't either. In a way, I still don't." Folding my arms, I peered down at him. "Do you know anything about the group he ran with? Because, I'm telling ya, from the little I know, I don't understand how they got to Rick, let alone all those other people."

"The month before everything happened, those cult guys were swarming the place," Steve said. "You saw their slogans everywhere. One of them gave me the creeps, especially when the offer for this desert gig came up. On the alley fences, everywhere, their people wrote, 'Music summons the gods.'" A worry line instantly split Steve's forehead. "Dude, what's wrong?"

"There was a guy in the town square who said those exact words to me. An Indian chief."

"He's one of them! I'd see him around town, but he was gone when the crap hit the fan. He's only been back the past few days." Steve tapped his temple, "Watch it though, he's loco."

"I'm going to talk to him. I want to know how those bastards got my brother."

IV. Allegro Resoluto

Work began the next day. I showed up at the rehearsal hall and received my assignment as first violin, chair seven. My stand partner, chair eight, aka, Julie Simmons, was a dark haired, wide-eyed college girl. Very cute. The Maestro was Haruka Watanabe, who conducted the St. Louis Symphony during the regular season. He had a good smile, and an excellent sense of humor. Any other year, I'd say my summer was off to a wonderful start.

Since it was our first day, we ran through the music, marked bowing changes, the usual stuff. At the end of the morning Maestro Watanabe was pleased.

"Wednesday we start rehearsing with the singers," he said with his quick, Asian accent. "But I don't see a problem. You people could make my singing sound good. Nice work."

During break I pulled out a blank sheet of music paper and the sitar part for "Paint It Black." I needed to do some transposing. The version Samuel handed me was written roughly in the key of B minor, but at the garage rehearsal last night I knew they were looking more at B flat Ionian. No biggie...I just needed to translate it into something I could read, get it under my fingers and then take it from there.

Julie took an interest. "'Paint it Black?' You play rock? How cool!"

"Yeah, I'm doing that Goth the Desert thing with a friend's band. I'm supposed to be a sitar."

"What've you got so far?"

I put down my pencil and placed my violin under my chin and tried a bit. I couldn't help but think of Rick whenever I played the song.

From behind, the Maestro's voice snapped me back into reality. "Wow, you play that well," Haruka said. "Rolling Stones on fiddle, who'd have thought? Sounds more gypsy than Middle East, but yes, very good."

"Thanks."

Julie said, "He's going to be in Goth the Desert. I'm jealous!"

"Well, you're a concert musician so at least you already have something black to wear."

At that, even I had to smile. But then some pristine fellow in the flute section muttered to his partner, "Oh, that whole Heaven's Temple thing... Who in the name of God could be that stupid? I mean, really!"

I walked over to the guy and said, "My brother."

For moment, he stared, "I'm so sorry," he whispered. "Please accept my apology."

"Thank you." I returned to my seat, but a tepid wave of depression washed in. My thoughts dragged, my heart...listless.

At the end of rehearsal I didn't stop to chat with Julie who must have mentioned her favorite coffee place two or three times, but I packed up my instrument and headed out the door.

Cloud hanging over me, I headed to the town square and took a seat at the picnic table hoping for a chance to see the Indian again.

I waited, he didn't show. I took out the music sheet and finished transposing. He still wasn't anywhere to be seen. Annoyed, I took out my violin and started practicing for garage rehearsal that night. People began pausing to listen. After awhile I looked up and realized I had trouble seeing through the small crowd that gathered. The Indian stood in back peering at me.

Immediately, I quit playing and called, "Hey, Chief! I gotta talk to you!"

There came a smattering of applause and the people wandered away. I turned to put my Amati back in its case and saw the bottom of it was filled with money, ones and fives. The chief walked over. "I knew you'd look, I knew you'd seek me. Tell me your thoughts."

"You don't want my thoughts, pal," I said, my lip curled. "I want to know if you belong to that Heaven's Temple cult."

"'Cult' is such a harsh word. It's my belief system."

"Screw you. Yesterday you said you were also asleep."

"I am. You are merely part of my waking dream world..."

"You crazy..."

"Crazy? If I'm crazy, how do I know so much about you?"

I stepped back. "You don't know me."

He stepped forward. "*Louis?* I know your brother left on the mother ship with the Ascended Masters. I know you're here because your heart is broken and you want answers so much it's practically killing you. It will, if someone doesn't help you. But don't worry, I'm here."

The guy stared at me as if I was the only thing in the whole creation that mattered. I knew only two things about him: he was completely convinced of everything he said and he was out of his freaking mind.

"You're crazy," I turned and started to walk away. "You keep the hell away from me..."

"Or what, Louis? You going to kill me?"

The very suggestion shocked me to the point that I spun around. "What! I never said..."

"Don't worry, Louis. It's going to be all right. The Masters, they'll take you to your brother.

I turned and started to walk again.

"Music summons the gods and you call them everyday," the Chief called to my back.

෴

THAT EVENING THE garage rehearsal went well. I made it to bed by one feeling tired, but happy. Julie came to mind, and I thought what an idiot I'd be if I didn't get to know her a little. Tomorrow, coffee. Yeah.

My eyes barely closed when I heard a knock at the door.

"C'mon in," I muttered into my pillow. I heard the door open, but otherwise, silence and in that silence, coldness walked down my spine. I rolled over and sat up. Someone stood in the doorway.

"Hey, who's there?"

A dark silhouette swayed back and forth. Alarmed, I climbed out of bed and grabbed the music stand I'd left set up near by.

The figure was too black. I should have been able to make out a face in the moonlight. "Hey! Who are you?"

A raspy, dead voice whispered, "It's me, Louis."

"Me-freaking-who?"

Into the moonlight stepped an apparition that made me drop the music stand and stumble back. "...No..." I whispered. It was Rick. His throat was a black gaping hole, his shirt red from his own blood. My brother lifted his hand and shambled forward.

"Come on, come with me."

I could barely breathe. "G-g-get out! Get..." Rick lunged for my throat. I screamed.

The house was dark, my door was closed, the stand stood at the end of my bed. I sat up.

"Louis! You okay?" Steve called, tossing open my bedroom door.

His entrance caused me to yelp again.

Holding a hand over my heart, I took a deep breath. "Aw, jeez...I'm sorry, man. I had a really weird dream."

Steve leaned in the doorway. "Sounds more like a nightmare. You sure you're okay?"

I bobbed my head, "Yeah, yeah. I'm fine. "

V. Molto Romantico

The next morning I decided I knew why my brother died. The cult-types, like the Chief, got a hold of him and spun his thoughts around until he didn't know what he was doing. I felt certain that even the nightmare was the result of letting the Chief mess with my head.

I could understand how my brother got involved. Scripture filled the cult's website, so after his divorce he probably looked for a Christian group to join, except these guys only borrowed the name. Certain I now understood, I took measures to try and focus on living rather than on my brother's death.

Before heading to work, I stopped off at a coffee shop and picked up a gift mug and a small sack of gourmet coffee. They even put it in a decent looking bag.

I gave this to Julie before rehearsal. She peeked in the sack, drew out the mug, and then smiled upward, "You got this for me?"

"Well, I was thinking that if you don't have a coffee maker we could just go get some after rehearsal."

"I'd like that."

Julie proved to be not only a fantastic distraction from my problem, but I could also see myself falling for her.

"You know what I really want to do?" she asked one night while we were at a club watching Steve's band play.

I gazed across the small table basking in her presence. "What's that?"

"Well, I love the idea of joining an orchestra, I'll probably do that first, and do some teaching, but I want to write new music, too. I want to write a symphony," she said as she stirred her icy drink. "And I'm fascinated with how much music affects our spirituality."

"In what way?" I asked.

"Look at the Old Testament," she said. "David kicked a demon out of King Saul just by playing his harp. What is it about the vibration and frequency of certain tones that would make that happen? Exactly how much does music effect the human mind, and why?"

Despite being brought up in church, I wasn't sure how strongly I believed, but I wasn't put off by people who did.

Julie told me all about her dad who used to sing 'Jesus Loves Me' every night at bed time and how it kept her from feeling alone.

I can't say I feel the same.

Steve's band began to play. It was the Queen stand-by, "Somebody to Love."

I offered her my hand. "I bet we could dance to it."

The next night she took my breath away. It was the opening of La Traviata and Steve asked me to score some tickets for the band. No problem. I had sent my tail coat to the cleaners to get it pressed and stopped to pick it up along with a little opening night gift for Julie. By the time I came back and finished dressing, the rest of the band had gathered.

"Lord, have mercy!" Samuel cried. "Look at you, boy!"

Amy bustled around in her concert finest straightening collars like an excited den mother. "Oh, my gosh, you all clean up so well! I'm so proud! And look at you, Louis, coat and tails, down right dashing!"

Steve shot her a glance. "Settle down, woman! Hey, Louis, I think we just found your 'Paint it Black' costume."

"Huh?"

"How about when we do the desert thing, we just put you in a Grateful Dead t-shirt and then you wear your tails over it."

"I'm there, man."

At the concert hall, I headed back stage to tune up and find Julie. I didn't see her right away, so I got down to business rosining my bow, until from behind, I heard, "Hi, Louis!"

I turned and almost dropped my Amati.

I guess Amy was right. We all cleaned up good. Julie wore a long black, dress, that showed off a fine curvy form that made me think of a violin. I couldn't help it, I wanted to play her.

"You look great!"

I plunged a hand into my pocket and drew out the tiny box I picked up for her. "Since it's opening night, I bought you a present."

"Oh, you didn't!" She lifted the lid and gasped, then to my dismay, a tear trickled down her cheek.

"What's wrong?"

"Pearl earrings. I saw a pair like this in the store downtown I wanted to get, but I didn't have the cash. And the girl I'm staying with, she was teasing when she said, it, but told she me, 'If that Louis guy really likes you, he'll know to get them.' Which is crazy, because how did you know?"

"Julie, I love you."

For a second we could only gaze at each other, love struck dumb. The next moment we hurried to the orchestra pit, set up our music, and she fumbled to put on her new earrings. Once we were ready for the Maestro to step out, she leaned over and whispered in my ear, "I love you, too." Then her warm, soft lips brushed against my cheek. As for the performance, I don't remember a single note.

VI. Presto Fucco con Spirito

I realized my brother's memory was already fading. I asked myself if I was letting him rest in peace, or merely ignoring him.

The thought bothered me enough that on the morning of 'Goth the Desert' I walked through the town square hunting for the Chief. "Are you tired of running, Louis?"

"This is what you damn people did, isn't it? You played head games."

The Chief squinted up at me. "You think that? He made his decision to join the Ascended Masters based on the evidence. You should, too." He tossed his arms to either side. "The gods, you summon the gods every day..."

I reached out, grabbed his shirt, and hauled him over.

The Chief stared right into my eyes. "Why do you think you have no peace? The gods are calling and your soul wants to answer. "

I turned him loose with a slight shove.

"You will see. The evidence is coming to you. Open your heart, let your heart call to them, then play your music. *You* will summon the gods."

His presence felt like finger nails on a chalk board. Standing there, I wanted to hit him. "Get the hell out of here,"

I spent the rest of the day preoccupied over the words he parked in my head. *Let your heart call to them.*

I thought of Julie and worry knotted my belly. Did I *want* to see this evidence?

That night, 'Goth the Desert' turned out to be as noisy an event as we all thought it would be. An ocean of black-frocked groovers made their presence known on the desert floor. I've been a fiddler for a long time, but until that concert I never realized how much of a religious experience musicians create. Julie was right.

One guy, the leader of a group called Casket, sauntered up to me. He wore his jet black hair down to his shoulders, his eyes were artfully outlined in black, his lips glowed in blood red, and when he spoke it was with a serpents hiss.

"Hey, concertman, I see an aura around you..." he said. "We've all been waiting...waiting for you..."

Trying not to sound rattled, I raised an eyebrow. "Yeah?"

"Yeah...the demons made you our conduit. When they knock, let them in." The Snakeman stared so hard into my eyes, I felt hypnotized.

I glowered and told him, "Let's not."

He continued his snake gaze another minute, hissed, "Feel it, baby," and walked away.

Steve appeared at my elbow. "I see you've met our resident psycho."

"A regular Chuck Manson."

The words of the Chief, now the Snakeman, the dreary setting, and everywhere, everything was painted black. Fitting, yet disturbing. The dark music began. I could feel my heart protesting against the unnatural strains. I don't mind "downer" music, once in awhile. But this was non-stop and with my mind parked on Rick and everything else, yes, it was affecting me. The atmosphere became thick and I kept tuning my violin, thinking it must be getting humid, but it wasn't really. It was something else.

When Julie showed up I thought she would be a bright spot, but she was quiet. She brought a jar of eye black I had talked about getting. I thought I'd put some around my eyes, play the part a bit. I had joked that I'd look like a six foot raccoon, but now, I wanted my eyes to look black. I wanted to be dark.

"You didn't tell me your brother died in Heaven's Temple."

"How'd you find out?"

"The first flute told me."

When she stepped away, Snake slithered over and whispered, "When you're gone, I'll look after your woman."

We went on around midnight. Steve wearily shook his head and said, "Let's end this with some real music." We walked onto the stage just as the concert FX department sent lights flashing across the sky to thunderous applause. They took the shape of huge luminous orbs hovering over us. Some might have been a hundred yards across, with smaller, glowing circles racing around their perimeter. Craig, the drummer, looked up at the balls of light and muttered, "Man, never seen a light show like that."

Neither had I.

The black, leather clad MC stepped up to the mike and announced, "It's the witching hour, boys and girls! Time to paint it ALL black! Welcome Soul Catcher!"

Craig's drumsticks beat the opening tempo and we took off. Steve began to croon, "'I see a red door and I want it painted black...'" There must have been five thousand people surrounding the stage and showing no signs of slowing down. I thought I could hear them howling. I tightened my bow.

I kept hearing the Chief telling me over and over to "open my heart and call to them."

My solo started and at first I played according to the way we rehearsed. But something happened. I suddenly had these brilliant ideas of musical improv. The band looked excited and changed to keep up with me. My melody glided into some thing totally wild, gypsy-like and crazy. People in the audience were dancing like dervishes and that made me push even farther. Pure, unfettered, white-hot, power surged through me and my fingers moved like lightning strikes. The Chief said music summoned the gods and even as I played, I wondered if they were indeed being summoned.

I remembered a music theory book I read by John Cage. In one chapter he said, "The purpose of music is to quiet the body, the soul and the mind, thereby making it subject to divine influence."

The idea clicked in my head so fast and hard I could almost hear it. They were right. The cult bastards were right. When the last chord was struck I lifted my arms in the air and bellowed into the microphone with a voice I no longer recognized, "MUSIC SUMMONS THE GODS!"

A huge roar went up from the crowd. I closed my eyes, not wanting to see the look I knew Steve had to be wearing on his face.

But there was no time to worry because the lights came on. Giant beams blazed down on us from the orbs overhead. I could see the white made-up faces of the Goth crowd looking up in shock and then delight... and then pure terror. Out of the largest orb came smaller light streams, like laser beams on steroids. They blazed down burning anything in their path.

The screams became deafening, but I was filled with a strange calm. The whole band hustled off stage and while they grabbed guitar and equipment cases, I carefully found my violin case, placed my Amati inside and carried it with me, like I always did.

"Louis!" Steve cried. "C'mon! Let's get out of here!"

"I'm right behind you," I lied. I stepped from the platform onto the desert. The main orb produced a light that was more like a thick cloud. I headed for the center of it. From somewhere far behind me I thought I heard Julie call my name, but by that time, I didn't care.

The light grew heavy and I felt it envelope me with suffocating weight.

I was scared, but I was angry, too. I threw my head back and shouted, "What are you?"

I heard my name, over and over.

They droned on and on, like the music. I wanted to scream. Finally I shrieked, "You killed my brother!"

The voices stopped so suddenly it was like stepping off the edge of the world. Then, out of the silence, a single voice spoke.

"No, Louis, I'm not dead."

The voice came from behind me. My brother stood there. Again.

Rick was now a glowing figure, his face smiling and exuberant with glory. "Louis, it's alright," he sounded wispy, but happy. "I've never felt so much joy! I came to give it to you."

I was on my knees in the sand, unable to look away. "No...no..."

"Look at me!" Rick glided steadily forward. "I've been given more power than anyone can imagine."

My mouth didn't want to work; I began to quake. I could feel these creatures in my mind, my body, pulling me, drawing me toward them. I was an off balanced man clinging to the edge of a cliff. "They-they made you...you-you killed yourself..."

"No! I experienced liberation! My soul is free! I've come to set you free, too."

I couldn't move, I could barely think. Tears ran down my cheeks and all I could do was sit there and beg, "Rick, no man, no..."

"C'mon...I'll help you. We'll do it together."

He bent a knee and knelt by my side. A dagger appeared in his hand and he placed it in mine. The knife pulsated in my hand, like a warm, live thing. I wrapped my fingers around the hilt. Lights from the orbs sparkled across the blade. "I'll help you. They made me whole."

I was exhausted, emotionally beaten. I could only stare as this figure of Rick picked up my hands and aimed the knife at my throat. Like a lamb led to slaughter.

Rick wrapped his arms around me and whispered, "It doesn't hurt, we'll do it on three. One..."

I glanced to one side and realized I could see the body of the Chief lying near us. I recognized bits of his clothes, the rest of him burned to a crisp.

"Two..." My eyes hunted for help and I caught a glimpse of the knife and the reflection of the thing next to me. Its face was missing.

"Three!" I hurled the dagger to one side.

Its face was missing. There were was nothing but strange gray flesh covering huge bumps and swellings. "Louis," it said, taking on my brother's appearance again, "You know it's the best way."

I couldn't answer. I didn't know what to do. I slowly grasped my violin case and began crawling away.

The pull was stronger than ever. It took every ounce of will power not to scream.

I couldn't get away, I knew it. My arms and legs were like misfiring pistons. But out of all my confusion, like an answered prayer, Julie's Old Testament story spoke to me. If music summons the gods, then it can send them away.

I opened my violin case.

I couldn't use my bow, I shook too much. Kneeling in the dirt, my violin in hand, I slowly, very slowly, began to pluck the only song that came to mind.

"...Jesus...Loves...Me...

Rick shoved his "face" into mine. "YOU'RE GOING TO DIE!"

I took out my bow and drew it over the strings, over and over until the song set the demons howling and the orbs danced over head. Suddenly, the desert was quiet and empty. For a moment, I stood staring at the blanket of stars, now unobstructed, wrapping the sky with their comforting light. It seemed reasonable to sit down and play some more.

That's where they found me.

Sitting Indian style and playing Jesus Loves Me.

-In memory of my brother-

HINKY JENKS

CHRIS MIKESELL

Hinky Jenks, Madelyn Argent, and me, we could've changed the world. Now I'm here alone with the envelope from Maddy's father, and the priest with a *click-clack* heel on one of his shoes is walking the cellblock toward me.

Damn you, Jenks.

My death warrant expires in nine hours. No chance of a reprieve.

But I'm getting ahead of myself.

ARGENT SAID HE won Hiram Jenkins in a poker game against Primo DeAnza, head of the upstart gang cross-town. Said he won the hand legit and Primo was worming out of his marker. My crew, we didn't care. When it came to laying into those flatheads, reasons weren't needed—like Queensberry Rules at a knife fight, they just get in the way and turn the fun into a piece of work.

So we grabbed one of Primo's boys outside a little mom-n-pop by the train station and beat him 'til he told us this guy Jenkins was a driver for one of DeAnza's heavy guns, Diego Marquez. Then we beat him some more for being a snitch.

One night while Marquez was paying a call on a skirt, we went in and removed Jenkins from behind the wheel of his Sixty Special. Left a couple sticks of TNT wired to the Caddy's ignition just to square things. When DeAnza realized we not only collected on the debt, but extracted interest too, Santa Rosa got her introduction to the art of mob warfare.

To look at the town, you'd never expect it would have its criminal element professionally run. *Hell, what criminal element?* you'd think. Then again, you'd never expect our sleepy little place an hour north of San Francisco to grab Hollywood's interest, either—but it did. The mob war and the movie biz and Jenks and Maddy and me. You wouldn't believe any of it if it wasn't true.

Hiram Jenkins—Hinky Jenks, we started calling him—came to us a driver. A good driver, maybe even as good as Benny Pullman down state. Up until we lifted him from behind the wheel of Marquez's Caddy he'd never slipped up. Never let a man get pinched. Always managed to get his boys away before the heat showed up. Of course his goof getting boosted and then DeAnza's vendetta against us meant he wasn't safe out on the street. Which meant he spent a lot of time at the Wexler Granary, playing cards in the back room and learning what ropes there were to learn.

Which meant real quick we knew half of why DeAnza kept him out in a car: the boy was just wrong.

Most troubling was his habit of eating everything with gelatin. Not as a side dish or salad, but everything he ate had to be covered in the stuff. Peas and carrots, that we didn't mind too much. Kinda looked like the stuff you might serve a kid with cut up pears inside. Vienna sausages, though—or worse, sardines. Most of us went down the road to Agostino's Bakery & Meats whenever Hinky Jenks brought out his lunch pail.

The other troubling thing was the way Jenks watched you. Always had his eyes on the door when you'd come in. Always had his hand out to take something from you, sometimes even before you'd half a mind to hand it to him. Hell, even if you were coming up from behind him he'd see you somehow and step aside.

Then one day—the day Jenks rushed us all out of the back room right before a grenade flew through a window—somebody, Fingers maybe, or his brother Shank, figured out the real reason DeAnza kept Jenks behind the wheel. Kid was clairvoyant or somnambulant or some other word that ain't even English—whatever, he could see the future. Near as we could time it, about ten seconds before of the rest of us caught up. So anytime the cops swooped in when Jenks had been driving for DeAnza, he gave the word ten seconds early and whoever could piled into his Caddy, and whoever couldn't faded out the back. When the police finally came they wouldn't find nothing but a couple stripes of rubber smoking by the curb.

Ten seconds doesn't seem like much, I know, but take your thumb and put it in a vise grip. Spin the crank a quarter turn past conversational, and you'll discover just how long ten *Allegheny's* can be.

Jenks said DeAnza never figured it out for sure, and stupid flathead he is, that makes sense. Just trusted the kid's intuition, which built into reputation, which while it never advanced him past wheelman, meant a comfortable life for a gringo in DeAnza's outfit. Said he almost drove off when we came to collect, but figured being among his own he might do better for himself. Plus, Marquez was a prick.

So we discovered this and were thinking how we could use it to our advantage—a trip to one of the Long Beach casino ships, for instance—when Jenks looked up at the door and the sappiest smile melted across his face. Eight seconds later Madelyn walked in. The boss's daughter. My girl. And Jenks was grinning at her like a kid at the bijou before the Hays Commission set up shop. Would've pasted him one right there, but by the time I turned back from gawping at the girl myself, he was out of his chair and hiding behind Pinky Magrew, big hulk of a guy.

I forgave him for not being able to help himself. Easier than walking all the way around Magrew.

Madelyn came over and whispered her dad wanted me up at their house on Park Street. I said so long to the boys who didn't hear me over the sound of them making plans to score big with Jenks's secret talent.

Salvatore Argent had always been like a father to me. In a town of izzes and ain'ts, my neighborhood was one of those with bad grammar. Argent changed things around for me, though. Like a father. Like a father-in-law, we'd hoped at one time, too. That was before he announced "the plan" and everything started going to hell, though not even Hinky Jenks could've foreseen the disaster then.

Argent's idea was to take care of DeAnza for good: frame the bastard and run him out of town, maybe even get him lynched. The West Coast premiere of Alfred Hitchcock's *Shadow of a Doubt* was a couple weeks away and would do fine. The movie was filmed locally, about the biggest thing to ever happen in quiet Santa Rosa—second only, maybe, to what we had planned. When I told Argent about Hinky Jenks and his seeing the future business, he re-evaluated the plan, added a couple touches, made it foolproof.

And so far as we could see, it was: Jenks lifts one of DeAnza's cars and takes me to the premiere before the stars arrive; then we get out—skin darkened and hair flat—and rob the looky-loos; finally, Madelyn plays her part and DeAnza gets scandalized in the process. No way the cops can turn a blind eye to that. And Santa Rosa returns to the well-managed town it used to be, with yours truly running DeAnza's operation.

While we waited for the big night, Jenks went to work with Fingers Patelli cracking safes. First night they went out Fingers showed him how to listen with a stethoscope to the tumblers falling into place. After the next job, Fingers—pale as a celery stick in gelatin—told the story that Jenks had no sooner fitted the earpieces and the safe was open. Hearing the tumblers click ten seconds before it actually happened, Jenks had spun the dial left, around once to the right, back to the left, and *zip-zing-zoom!* five grand and a pile of Santa Rosa-Sonoma Rail stock certificates.

The Tuesday before the movie premiere Jenks accompanied Argent to his usual poker game. Stood behind the boss with me and Magrew, tapping the back legs of Argent's chair once for bluff, twice for get out while you're ahead. Magrew spent the night shoveling pistachio after pistachio into his yap, dropping the red shells on the floor. Me, I just glared across the table as if I didn't know better. DeAnza was none too happy to see his former driver, but kept his mouth shut. He wound up losing five or six hundred, though he stopped short of sinking any more of his boys in the pot. The boss walked away even, let the mayor and chief of police go home winners. "Next time," he said, clapping the mayor's shoulder as they got up from the table. DeAnza left thinking there would be a next time. Hell, even we thought there'd be a next time, too.

The action that Saturday went down like clockwork. Magrew drove Jenks and me across the railroad tracks west of town. DeAnza territory. If he'd been more reasonable he'd have been welcome to it. Bars and the odd cathouse and cardroom for the migrant fruit pickers from Petaluma to Sebastopol. Business Argent didn't need, but of necessity expected a cut from. DeAnza, he had expectations of his own. Like he's equal, a rival maybe. You don't have to be no mindreader to know that push is gonna come to shove, and shove is gonna come to a shallow grave sooner or later.

Jenks knew of a fence behind a certain garage that slides open on oiled skids. Said DeAnza's boys used it when the cops were on their tails. Drive down the alley, honk as you speed past, and someone slides the fence out of the way after the cops go by. Around the block once and through the alley again, cutting your lights before you reach the gap, which disappears once you're through. Jenks figured it worked for getting a car in, it'll work for getting one out. He wasn't wrong. Axle grease on our faces, hair styled so we looked like goons out of Dick Tracy, and no one inside the garage came out to ask who we were or why we were taking the Lincoln-Zephyr.

We reached the place, the California Theatre, right on time. The chief of police gave up the schedule for the night's events during the poker game. When exactly Hitchcock and Teresa Wright and Joseph Cotten and the mayor were set to leave the train station—recreating some scene from the movie for a *Life* magazine photographer—and then drive with police escort over to the theater. With the chief and his men across town, waiting for their little parade, it was a sure thing there'd be no cops at our end. Again, things ticked along perfectly.

"Nobody panic!" I shouted, stepping out from the rear of the Lincoln. "Nobody fights and nobody gets hurt." Jenks got out from behind the wheel and made a show of his Thompson M3.

There were a hundred, maybe a hundred-fifty, fretful peacocks in their Sunday best and sparkliest, but nobody squawked. Jenks handed me the grease gun and began collecting plumage. Madelyn stood a third of the way toward the gilt-edged double doors. I don't know how good Teresa Wright looked in the picture, but she had nothing on Maddy. Low-cut black dress with ruby accents, fur coat, high heels, blah, blah, blah. Could've been in the movie, for sure, if her mother hadn't disapproved of motion pictures not being dignified. I dragged my eyes away and made another heavily accented threat.

Jenks was doing fine. Nobody talked back and the bag filled up. He had gone up one side of the crowd and was coming back the other when he reached Madelyn and she dropped her earrings and ruby choker in the bag. Behind us a car rumbled by, dragging its tailpipe. Magrew's signal that the police escort had started. Two minutes.

"Okay, everybody, we're done here. Nobody be a hero, okay?"

Jenks passed by me, toward the car. I glanced at Madelyn.

The Lincoln driving off was her cue. She stepped out of the crowd, stood in the middle of the mosaic entryway. "You cowardly bastards, how dare you—"

I brought down the muzzle of the submachine gun. Surprisingly easy. Pulled the trigger. And all the gears fell out of our little clock.

Somebody ran up from the street, jumped in front of Madelyn. Hinky Jenks. The bullets meant for her shredded his coat black and red. Jenks staggered, spun, fired a shot from his waistband revolver that clipped my leg. Then he fell backward into Madelyn's arms. She collapsed beneath him and cradled his shoulders.

I swept the nose of my gun across the crowd to keep them back. They disappeared into a gray, cotton-muffled world as I turned back to Jenks. "What the hell, Hinky?"

His eyes opened, looked at me and then up at Madelyn. The two of them—Jenks stretched across Maddy's kneeling lap, his head lolling behind the crook of her elbow—looked like a china thingummy my Aunt Olivia kept on a shelf above her fireplace.

Maddy opened her mouth, but Jenks spoke first. "Can—?" Blood bubbled over his lips from the coughed question.

Madelyn swallowed, whispered the words Jenks already knew. "The doctors say the cancer, there's no cure."

"It was this or a slow, painful...miserable..." My words dropped off as he nodded. "I'm sorry, Hinky." Jenks nodded again and smiled before his eyes rolled up white.

Madelyn and I remained frozen as Chief McHenry's far-off demand broke through the silence. Statues. Our fates sealed as certainly as Hinky Jenks's.

From that point on time sped up. While I got dragged off to the back of a police car and Jenks to a useless ambulance, the bag from our car was retrieved. After the jewelry, wallets, and watches were returned to their owners, the movie premiere—take two—went ahead as planned.

I was on my way to the gas chamber at San Quentin before the trial even started. No way the district attorney was going to let the case slip through his well-manicured fingers. Even if Argent had been inclined to overlook my failure—Primo DeAnza became even more powerful in the wake of our fiasco—the situation was beyond his control.

৵

THE PRIEST STOPS his click-clacking outside my cell. A guard leaves a wooden chair and retreats to his post at the end of the hall.

I sit on my bunk, arms draped over my legs, eyes fixed on the floor. From the knees down, the priest steps into my field of vision. He sits in the chair, puts a boxy black case on the floor. After crossing his legs, the priest picks at something on his right heel and flicks it through the bars.

A woman's fingernail, painted red.

I blink.

A pistachio shell.

I look at the priest's hand still resting on his shoe. The fingertips are stained pink.

"How's life treating you, Johnny?" The voice goes with the fingers. Pinky Magrew.

I look up at him. His face is faintly plum colored from the tightness of the shirt collar. There had been no anger in his voice.

"Not who I was expecting, Pinky."

"Weren't gonna squeal on your family, were ya?"

Was I? Had I been? When the letter from Argent came that morning, the morning of my execution day, the letter with Maddy's obituary and a photograph of her wasted body in a hospital gown, thin and fragile as a scattering of winter sticks, I had been—what? Angry. Afraid. Alone. I'd wanted revenge, absolution. Just someone to talk to.

"Tell me about it," Pinky says. "Your old father confessor."

I look into his eyes. Hard. Cold. Nothing like the pain and sadness of Madelyn's in the photograph. In Jenks's, lying in Maddy's arms.

I'm sorry, Hinky. He had nodded before I'd had the words out.

"I ain't got nothin' to say to nobody."

"Ahh, I'm just hassling you, Johnny. Let's do this communion thing so I can get out of here." He tugs at his collar, so whether he means out of prison or out of the disguise, I'm not sure.

Magrew opens his left hand and starts reading the words he's written there.

Agnus Dei, qui tolis peccata mundi, miserere nobis.

He stops and unlatches the box at his feet. Something gray and wet falls from beneath the lid. After uncrossing his legs, he smears it into the concrete floor with his right toe. The lid peels away slowly from the sticky, dark maroon-stained interior.

Magrew continues reading from his cribbed notes. *Ecce Agnus Dei, ecce qui tollit peccata mundi...*

He removes a silver plate with several white wafers on it and a small red bottle. When the stopper is removed I catch a whiff of almonds. Amaretto ...or did the wafers come from Agostino's Bakery?

"*Domine, nom sum dignus et intres sub tectum meum,*" I respond from childhood memory. "*Sed tantum dic verbo, et anabitur anima mea.*"

I receive a wafer on my tongue. Bitter. Probably not from Agostino's.

When I take the cup, it's bitter too.

The ritual that used to offer comfort, offers only sadness now. A farewell communion. Family, together—not anymore.

Magrew finishes. Assures me that a real priest will be around to do last rites later that night. That it's been good to see me one last time. That the boss don't hold no grudges any more. He makes the sign of the cross and drags the chair away.

I lay back on my bunk, thinking of Madelyn. The angel, not the blasphemy in the photograph. Did she find redemption in the end?

A stiletto of pain twists in my gut. I bend over the edge of the bed, panting, and then stumble to the steel toilet. The scent of almonds comes mixed with the stench of bile.

I fall on my knees, shuddering, as the knife turns again. Hail Maddy—Mary. Oh, hail...*oh, hell*. The second mouthful of vomit burns more than the first.

No more grudges, Magrew? Maybe being delivered to hell by the damned will count in my favor when the scales are balanced. The sound of my laughter comes weakly from somewhere and the cold cement floor caresses my cheek.

Me and Mary and Jesus, we were gonna change the world.

My head doesn't bother to lift itself the next time my throat heaves. My eyes sting, but they're focused in the past.

Jenks, he nodded that second time, smiled just before—less than ten seconds before... Is there hope?

My hands roam around my body, trying to stop the pain. My throat. My belly. They rake across my heart.

Is there anything else?

I lie on the floor gasping for air. Then I just lie there.

Madelyn smiles down on me before the world goes gray and quiet. And then silent. And finally black.

FLOWERS FOR SHELLY

GREG MITCHELL

Morning comes and the first thing I think is:
I'm going to buy Shelly flowers today.

No special occasion or anything, I just like buying her flowers from time to time to break the typical male stereotype and remind her how much she means to me.

Shelly is in her final semester at college and has spent the last fourteen weeks as a student teacher at Williford Elementary. Children are her passion, though we don't have any of our own, and yesterday she told me that the principal is already thinking of hiring her on full-time, assuming that Mrs. Halbert finally gives up the ghost after two hundred and eighteen years of teaching second grade. I'd never seen Shelly so happy. Never one for meandering, my wife always needs to feel as though she's working toward something. Now instead of ambling on until graduation, she's looking at a bright future as Williford Elm's newest second grade teacher, securing *my* reputation as "Mrs. Brightwell's husband!" Actually, I'm excited at the thought of accompanying her to the peewee football games and being introduced to all of her students. I'm proud of my girl and I can't wait to see her shine.

I roll around in bed, relishing the fact that I get to sleep in till eight, whereas Shelly has to be up and off by seven. She blow-dries her hair in the other room, giving me a few more minutes to sleep. But it never really works. I always hear her getting ready. Sometimes I just lay there pretending to sleep, watching her get dressed, brush her teeth, put on her little "I'm a Student Teacher, Ask Me How" nametag. It makes me smile.

She's beautiful. We met at a friend's desperate attempt to recapture the 90s by throwing an all Grunge party, B.Y.O. Kurt Cobain tattered lime green cardigan. During Everclear's "Santa Monica" Shelly saw me across the room and knew she had to devour me.

Okay, I'm pushing it a bit. But *she* noticed *me* and made the first move. We talked the entire night, long after the party ended. I was nervous. She was really hot and I wanted things to work out, but there just wasn't a thing in the world we had in common. I never pictured myself marrying someone like her, and maybe that's why it was so perfect when it happened.

I watch her now, thinking of how far we've come since that first night, as she puts away the blow dryer and starts to pluck her eyebrows. Yes sir, I'll buy her flowers and have them sent to the school. That should warrant some "oohs" and "aahs" from the kiddies in her class. Then Shelly will get all embarrassed and have to get her class back on topic, and I'll know that for one moment, time stood still and she thought of me.

"Hey, you better get up," she speaks as she exits the bathroom.

"I'll get up," I moan. On second thought, "Why don't you come back to bed and we'll just snuggle all day?"

"Sure, okay," she nods. "We can keep each other warm when the bank forecloses on our house and the sheriff and his men with shotguns come and take everything away."

"Ha ha. One day won't kill us. You skip school, I'll skip work. We'll just lay around."

Shelly comes over and sits on the edge of the bed, fully dressed while I'm still sporting bed-hair and boxers. "Caleb, you'd really better get up."

Another moan as I wallow around in the covers, burying my face in the pillow like a grown, responsible man.

"I'm serious," she laughs. "Don't you dare go back to sleep."

Exasperated, I reach out and pull my lovely bride into bed with me, gripping her tight.

"Stop it!" she screams, laughing.

"Stay here!"

We roll around and she tugs, but I won't let her go.

"You're gonna wrinkle my clothes!"

"What terrible fate!"

But, alas, Shelly breaks free of my tickling clutches and stands, straightening out every horrible wrinkle. Just when I think she's won in the Most Mature competition, she picks up the nearest pillow and bashes it into my face.

"Now, will you get up and give me a kiss?"

I shake my head and hold out my arms. "Come to me."

"No," she pouts with a funny whine. "You tricked me once; you won't do it again. If you want me, come up here and get me."

I rise up and stretch the few extra inches to embrace her, but she backs up.

"Come on," she entices.

I stretch a little more, but she backs away again, still holding her arms out to me.

"You're almost there, just a little bit closer."

Seeing where this is going, I groan and finally give in to her feminine wiles, getting out of bed and throwing my name in the hat of life, ready to accept whatever the day offers.

"There," I state for the record. "Happy now?"

She kisses me.

I have Shelly. And everything is all right.

❦

WORK SUCKS. IT'S 9:30 a.m. and I want to go home, lie in bed, and wait for Shelly to return with less pressures. And, preferably, less clothes.

It's my lot in life to screenprint those shirts with cheeky sayings like "Hottie" or "Your Boyfriend Wants Me" that you see on the underdeveloped bodies of fourteen-year-olds. It's not a glorious job, and the fact that I'm contributing to the already swollen head of adolescence does nothing to redeem my place in the world. Luckily, the Good Lord has spared me from monotony in the day's work by providing the divine invention that keeps my equally upbeat co-workers and myself from falling asleep. The television set.

So, we're flipping through channels, giving me a much-needed break from screen-printing the three-hundredth round of "I Make Bad Look Good", when I realize that I was going to order some flowers for Shelly today. Despite her earlier efforts to use sexual attraction to woo me from the bed, I did indeed return to sleep for another fifteen minutes and forgot about the flowers.

Abandoning my post, I move over to the wall phone by the window. I take a nearby phonebook, looking for the florist.

That's when the ambulance passes by.

Our shop faces the main highway that leads to town, so seeing emergency vehicles is nothing new or shocking. Hot on the heels of the ambulance are two deputy cars with their sirens and lights whirring.

I find the listing for *Rachel's Flowers* in the book and cradle the receiver between my chin and shoulder as I dial. A fire truck passes.

"Must be some wreck." Kevin, my co-worker, takes notice, pausing in his channel surfing long enough to look over my shoulder.

I nod. The nice lady from *Rachel's* picks up and I order Shelly's flowers. Orange roses. Her favorite.

"Do you want a card?" the lady asks.

"Sure," I shrug. I proceed to tell her that Your Little Love Muskrat is thinking of you and to make sure the flowers get to Shelly before lunchtime. The lady assures me they will. I thank her for her time, she thanks me for my credit card number, and when I hang up and look to Kevin...

He's frozen. Mouth open. Staring at the TV.

"Did we get the scrambled channels in again?" I joke.

"Check it out."

On the TV is not some scantily clad co-ed, as I'd expect to garner so much of Kevin's attention, but the news. He turns it up for my benefit, though the bottom crawl says it all.

"...some kind of bizarre phenomenon," our enlightened anchor reveals, "...it seems that graves everywhere are emptying and..." He breaks off in a chuckle, trying to maintain a semblance of professionalism as he finishes, "...the *dead* are coming back to life." The newsman's words are accompanied by presumably live footage of a cemetery suddenly animated, its former denizens marching sluggishly forward in search of some unnamed goal.

Kevin's hand tremors on the remote. "No way."

"Come on," I drawl.

"This is a joke, right?" Kevin asks, still looking at the TV. He snaps out of his reverie and, taking aim, clicks through channels. Different faces all give the same news.

My stomach churns and I can't suppress a maddening grin. "Well...isn't that something?"

"Don't joke, man!" Kevin turns to me, his eyes wild. "This is messed up!"

He pushes past me in a frenzy, fumbling for the phone.

"I gotta call my parents!"

I stare at him numbly as he dials. Is this really happening? I want to laugh at him for acting like an idiot, blubbering all over himself, but I wonder...is he onto something? I think of my own parents. Harry and Claire. I spent most of my childhood in foster homes, and they were special enough to pick me at age thirteen when there were far cuter and less sarcastic three-year-olds available. They raised me in a stable Christian home and taught me the things I still believe. I think to call them, but...

Shelly.

I need to get Kevin off the phone. The thought is quiet inside me. I don't think I've completely realized what's happened. The dead are coming back to life? This is insane. Stupid, that's what it is. Impossible. Please God, I want to talk to Shelly.

I'm pushing Kevin out of the way.

"HEY!" he protests with red, teary eyes.

"I need the phone."

"Get away! I'm not done!"

We struggle over the receiver. My heart is pounding and I want to hear my wife's voice and convince myself that this isn't happening.

Screeching tires outside. I let go of the phone and look through the window to see a police car headed right for the shop. I can't even breathe a word of warning. I jump clear as the car busts through the wall, crippling Kevin and his precious phone. Screams from the others as they rush to check on Kevin, but I know he's dead.

Stuck inside our shop now, the car dies and the smoke settles. But there's still a struggle inside. I stand on wobbly knees and look through the glass to see one cop in the passenger seat, his throat pried open. The driving cop has a gash on his forehead but still wrestles with someone else. The back-seat cage is peeled back by strong hands and I see the thing fighting the cop. Its face is missing flesh, eyes are sunken and hollow, mouth hanging open in slack-jawed stupor. It lets out a soul-sick moan as it descends on the cop's bald head. He yells and bats at it, but the diseased thing comes down hard, sinking its yellowed teeth into the cop's head. The man screams and flails, and the others in the room holler and gag.

I find myself laughing. This isn't real. I'm not really seeing this man die. Kevin's okay. I'm still in bed. I dozed off after Shelly left and I'm still dreaming. Yeah, I'm going to wake up. Shelly is going to...

The cop stops screaming and the zombie slurps up the last of the guy's scalp. Then the thing catches sight of me. It stares, turning its head from side to side. I want to run, but I'm still standing there, transfixed, looking at a dead man. But the most terrifying thing is that the dead man is looking *back*.

The thing inside the cop car starts to howl and twitch violently, banging its head and hands against the glass. It roars, throwing its weight against the door. The sound echoes throughout the remains of the shop and my co-workers take off in the other direction, screaming. But I'm still standing there, and the dead man still wants out.

Suddenly, I feel a cold sensation around my ankle and see a bloody hand reaching out from underneath the car. Pulling. *Yanking*. Moans rise up like phantoms from the depths of hell and I look into the still teary eyes of Kevin as he lures me in. At first, I think he's somehow survived, but then it hits me. He's dead, too.

I can only watch as the door to the cop car bends outward with a squeal. The thing inside shambles out. He moves awkwardly, still ridden with rigor mortis, but he wants to feed. I can see that in his drooling face. He wants to eat me. I'm petrified. I struggle for my life against Kevin until I fall back on the concrete floor and stare up at the lumbering monstrosity that steadily moves my way. I know I'm going to die. And the only thing I can think is...

Will Shelly get her flowers?

SPLURCH!

There's a *boom* and suddenly my face is covered in warm red and the zombie above me slumps over. I glimpse a smoking bullet hole in the dead thing's head. A shadowed figure steps into view, aims a pistol at Kevin's wrist and fires. Bone and tendon snap and I'm freed, with Kevin's hand still dangling from my ankle. I gasp and kick the twitching member off.

"Caleb, are you okay?"

I look up to meet the gaze of my savior. He's wearing a McDonalds uniform.

"Come on," he says. "We gotta go."

❧

IN THE BIBLE, the apostles James and John were dubbed "The Sons of Thunder" due to their over-eagerness to get themselves into a scrape. In my life, I have my own Sons of Thunder. Their names are also James and John.

James and Johnny McTiernen have been my best friends since fifth grade. They were always the quiet kids in the back of the classroom, doodling monsters on their homework and passing the latest issue of *Fangoria* between the aisles behind the teacher's back. They were the kids voted *Most Likely to Be Found on a Water Tower with a High-Powered Rifle* in high school. They are unparalleled in their inability to join society; at age twenty-seven, they both live with their mother, surrounded by empty pizza boxes, computer parts, and more action figures than you can shake a stick at.

James, the go-getter of the two, joined the Air Force fresh out of high school and became part of Military Intelligence. He served in the Armed Forces for seven years and now faithfully tends the fryer at McDonalds. Johnny, on the other hand, makes his living by walking into the other room and asking his mom for twenty bucks every week.

Yet, in a world where the dead are returning from the ground to feast on the living, the McTiernens are heroes. Right now I'm riding in the backseat of their late father's faded yellow '69 Dodge Charger, the words "Bite Me" freshly spray-painted on the back window, awash in a sea of loose ammunition and fully automatic weapons. Johnny drives the snub-nosed beast, the roar of its engine rattling the cab and ringing in my ears. At Johnny's behest, R.E.M.'s "It's the End of the World As We Know It" blares from the speakers, and the lug has the nerve to bob his head to the beat. James is sitting in the passenger seat, loading bullets into bandoliers strapped across his chest. I stare at all the guns occupying the backseat with me, the empty Coke cans and crumpled McDonalds bags, and I'm awed by the absurdity of what is occurring. Finally, I'm able to ask—

"What *is* this?"

Johnny is the one to lay it out for me. "I saw it on the news and I knew that if we didn't think fast, we wouldn't last long. Graveyard's next door to our house, remember?"

My breath leaves me. "That's right...Did they...?"

"They were already on top of us. I got all the guns. Started shooting. Mom...she didn't..."

Johnny grows quiet.

"I'm sorry."

He pushes forward like a soldier. "I dumped everything in the car and headed over to get James and you."

"Why?"

Johnny looks at me as if I should know the answer. "We love you, man. You're our best friend. We couldn't leave you behind."

I smile, genuinely touched, but recognize that this isn't the best time for sentimentality. The shop where I work(ed) is on the exact *opposite* end of town from Shelly's school. Out on the outskirts, things aren't so bad, but I know that the epidemic will grow worse as we get closer to town.

"What's going on?" I ask.

James turns to me, excited. "Zombies, Chief. Whole world's overrun by zombies."

"But that's insane!"

James shakes his head, as if he's about to break some very grown-up news. "Nah, man. There's things going down in the government that you wouldn't even dream of. I've seen it! I was NSA!"

"You're telling me the government made zombies?"

Johnny shrugs and leans over his shoulder. "Don't sound so surprised. Could be some bio-weapon gone bad."

The brothers share a reaffirming nod, and I see something in the Thunder Twins that I'd never thought I'd see: purpose.

In a way they were always preparing for this. Conspiracy theories and video games aside, they have always been soldiers in need of an apocalypse, and that apocalypse has come.

"I have to call Shelly."

James plucks his cell phone from his belt and tosses it to me. I dial Shelly's cell phone and wait. It rings an agonizing three times.

"Hello?" She sounds scared.

My heart breaks and I plug my other ear with my finger to drown out the Charger. "Shelly!"

She cries out on the other end, "Caleb! Thank God! I tried calling the shop, but there was no answer!"

"Where are you?" I ask.

"Still at the school. We locked ourselves in. I'm here with all the kids. I tried calling the police, but I can't get through yet. Where are you?"

"With James and Johnny. We're headed your way."

Johnny turns to James and whispers, "We are?"

"Yes, we are. Head to Williford Elementary. Now." Turning back to Shelly. "Are you okay?"

I can hear her relief, like everything is going to be okay. It *will* be. I'll get to her and we'll be together and everything will be all right.

"I'm fine," she says. "Just scared. Caleb...what happened?"

"I don't know. But..."

Before I can finish, we hit town. James is the first to say what we're all thinking.

"...They're everywhere."

They are. Zombies. *Everywhere.* Johnny slows down to coast amidst the wreckage and chaos. Fires burn bright and firemen fight to put them out while police shoot into the descending hordes of the undead. Men, women, and children scream and claw to get away as they are pulled into the awful sea of rot and decay. Blood is everywhere, and even over the noise of the engine, I can hear that hollow wailing.

"Caleb, what's happening?" Shelly.

There are hundreds of them. Like locusts. Climbing over everything. Toppling power cables. Pushing cars aside. Stupidly moving forward, just like on the news.

Shelly again. "Caleb?!"

The plague to end all plagues has just hit us and I know that in a week, there won't be anything left. We're all going to die.

Taking in the sight, Johnny's awestruck face slowly forms a mad grin. "Cool."

I come to my senses and return to Shelly. "Stay inside the school. Lock the doors. Cover up the windows. Don't let them see you. I'm coming to get you, okay?"

"Okay. I'll keep calling the cops. Caleb..." She drops to a whisper, "What about the kids?"

"We'll find a way to get them to safety, okay? I promise. I need to go. We need to—"

Ker-Clunk!

A zombie repels off the grill of the Charger and Johnny laughs maniacally. "Yeah! Ten points!"

"Shelly, we need to go. I'll be there soon, okay?"

"Okay. I love you," she beats me to it. She sounds desperate. As if she's afraid she'll never have the chance to say those words to me again.

"I love *you*." My stomach churns. It feels like good-bye.

I hang up and fight the urge to vomit all over the weaponry. Was that it? Was that the last time I'll ever talk to Shelly? Why didn't I tell her how her arms always felt like home? Why didn't I tell her that the smell of her skin was soft and right and true? Why didn't I—?

"You okay?"

James is looking at me, concern on his face.

"We have to get to Shelly."

"We will, Chief." He means it. He knows what she is to me. They both do.

"What are we going to do once we get her?" I ask, trying desperately to form a plan.

But it seems the Thunder Twins have already thought it through.

"Fort Meeks is about two hundred miles from here," James announces. "That's sure to be the closest fortified place. That's where we're headed."

"What about all the kids at the school? We have to help them, too."

"Maybe we can take a bus," James suggests.

"Like the Partridge Family!" Johnny exclaims, mowing down another jaywalking zombie. "Ten points!"

"We have to hurry."

"Don't worry," James assures me. "Williford will hold for a long while."

"How can you be sure?"

"When we were nine we made a model to scale and, using G.I. Joes, tested the integrity of the complex," Johnny states.

"You guys are starting to wig me out. You'd think you were planning for this or something."

"Vampires, actually," Johnny corrects. "But, hey, zombies are close enough."

I sit back, watch the carnage unfold on the other side of the window. Aside from a few stray zombies wandering into the middle of the road, we seem to be under their undead radar. They seem perfectly content to chase down and render asunder the smorgasbord of pedestrians.

"What do they want?" I ask.

"Isn't that obvious?" Johnny retorts, a hint of mirth in his voice. I'm not sure if I should be comforted by his apathy or disturbed.

"But when will it end?"

"When there's no one left to eat."

There is silence in the Charger, and I think of Shelly. Of our song "Santa Monica":

We can live beside the ocean
Leave the fire behind
Swim out past the breakers
Watch the world die.

Here it is. The end of the world. We felt so safe. We built our movie theaters, cheap restaurants and amusement parks, and we entertained ourselves for awhile. Sidetracked ourselves from the horrors that were waiting one day away.

I recall what I did yesterday and wonder if I wasted it. Shelly washed the dishes and I watched TV. Then she went for a jog around the block and I played around online looking for replacement blades for my electric razor. Precious moments that I could have spent with her. We could have talked. We could have sat on the couch in silence, holding each other, feeling our heartbeats. That's what we used to do when we dated, but we've been doing less of that lately. I wish we could...

It suddenly enters my mind that we'll never have children. I won't get to see what our babies look like. I won't get to feel their hands squeeze my finger. I won't get to complain because they keep us up all night with their crying. I won't get the chance to take them for granted. I won't see their first days of school or their first loves or be able to worry about them when they get their driver's licenses and take the car out. I won't get to fight with Shelly over how to raise them. Oh, I want to fight with her again. To shout and raise hell and hate each other and then to stop and listen to each other and realize how much we love each other and make up and make love. I feel like a lead weight has dropped within me.

No, I refuse to think that. I've seen the movies. There's always a small band of fighters that manage to survive the initial attack of the zombies, and they fortify. They stand their ground and are somehow able to rebuild a fraction of civilization. And if ever there were two people who could get Shelly and me to a place like that, it's the two slackers-turned-commandos in the front seat. I *will* get to Shelly. I'll rescue her and Johnny will drive us to Fort Meeks and I'll hold her close all the way there. We'll gaze at the drooping liner of the Charger and feel our heartbeats and know that we're alive. We'll fight again. We'll make love and have babies. It'll be hard raising them in a world of the dead, I know. But Shelly and I can do it. We can make it work.

"We need to stop," James tells me.

"*Why?*"

"If we're taking a bus, we need gas. We can't be certain how much is already in the bus, and we don't have any idea what roads might be closed or blocked."

"In other words," Johnny picks up for his brother, "we might have to go the roundabout way to Fort Meeks."

"And that burns gas."

I don't like the idea of stopping for anything but Shelly, but for the kids, I agree with the Thunder Twins.

❧

I'M AIMING A shotgun over the Charger's hood. James is beside me, wearing bandoliers and confidently holding dual .45s. The shotgun shakes in my hands and I wish that Johnny would hurry.

He fills the third gas can and I think that's all we'll safely be able to get now. The abandoned convenience store is our own slice of quiet in an otherwise tumultuous world. The road ahead is filled with crashing cars, shrieking victims, and that God-awful moan of re-animated monsters. It suffocates my soul and I'm ready to be back in the car where the engine drowns out most of the noise.

"Almost there," Johnny says, still fueling.

"Do you guys have money for this?" I ask.

Suddenly, both brothers look at me with raised eyebrows.

Right. Stupid question. Dead clerks don't care if they get paid. Right. "Sorry."

James nods, going back to his watch, and Johnny's back to gas-duty.

"If they come," James speaks quietly, but with great authority, "aim for the head."

"They teach you that at the NSA?"

A shrug. "No. It's the Romero Rule."

He's speaking insanity, but I'm thinking insanity is the new normal.

"I got it!" Johnny holds up the gas can.

It is knocked from his hand and sent pinwheeling to the concrete, splashing gasoline everywhere, and the zombie who did it now has hands on Johnny's shoulders.

"AHH!" Johnny screams.

"HEY!" James charges forward, using the butt of his gun to beat at the zombie's face. The brothers struggle against the monster and I can only stare. The moans grow closer and I look around in dread, seeing their hungry attention turn to us. They approach, their disfigured maws stretch wide, tendons popping, bone dust unsettling, and maggots rolling out.

"Help us!" James screams at me. I aim my shotgun at the zombie attacking Johnny and fire.

"Stop shooting!" James yells. "There's gas EVERYWHERE!"

I'm shaking all over and hating myself for not being the kind of monster-hunting idiot savant that my friends are. Not knowing what else to do and already feeling the grave's breath on the back of my neck, I flip the gun over, taking firm hold of the hot barrel and I swing. James pulls Johnny out of the way in time to narrowly miss the deadly arc. The butt of the shotgun cracks the skull of the zombie, dislocating the jawbone from the brittle flesh. The thing swirls and wobbles, but is not defused. Its hands stretch toward Johnny.

The monstrosities are swarming the car and the Thunder Twins know it. Using what little time we have left, we reach into the backseat and gather as much weapons and ammunition as we can, then stand there, looking at each other, with nowhere to drop our gear.

"What do we do?!" Johnny has to yell to be heard over the reverberating moans closing in on us.

Luckily, I spot the movie theater where I used to work in high school. I start running. I can hear the brothers cussing after me, but they soon catch on and follow. We push past the zombies and race toward the theater. We make it to the glass double doors before the zombies even have a chance to start turning our way, so I know we have a couple of seconds.

"Great idea!" James shouts. Johnny rushes at the doors and pulls.

"It's locked!"

Still mid-morning, it's a long time before the janitor would show up. Somehow, I'm thinking this place is going to be locked until the end of time. Johnny rears back with his foot, ready to kick in the glass, but I stop him. "Wait!"

"What?"

"Don't break the glass! You'll leave the door wide open!"

James divides his attention between the impending hordes and me. "What do *you* suggest?"

"There's a door on the roof." I examine the building. Large jagged rocks jut from the concrete of the theater's sides, leading all the way up to the roof. It won't be easy with the equipment and a few hundred pounds of soda and pizza weight between the Thunder Twins but—"We can climb."

James thinks it over for a split second and nods.

I sling the shoulder straps of the rifles and shotguns across my back and start the climb. Below, I can hear James opening fire with cold precision. Johnny, on the other hand, takes out an AK-47 and sprays the landscape with lead.

"Eat *this*!" he screams.

The climb comes easily to me and I dump all the guns on the roof. I rush to the door and jiggle the handle. Locked, of course, but we could open it with a few well-placed shotgun rounds. With my burden shed, I run to the edge of the building and start climbing down for the second load.

"I'm empty!" Johnny cries.

James nods and removes another clip from his stash. He tosses it to his brother and the sounds of machine gun fire hurt my ears. I grab more of the guns and ammo and make my second trip up the building. The next time I head to the edge, I make the mistake of looking out over the city. As far as the eye can see, there is nothing but death, destruction, and an enemy as numerous as sand. Truly, this is hell.

"Caleb!"

My attention is stolen from the insurmountable task before us, and I see that the zombies have made it within a few feet of my friends. Suddenly, I worry that climbing up here was a bad idea. If the dead things have any kind of motor skills or coordination at all, they could follow us. But it's too late now. I've either bought us time to get to Shelly or I've led us to our deaths, but we're here and we have to make the best of it. I grab a gun and hang it over the edge of the building, opening fire.

"Come on! Hurry!"

James scrambles up. "Cover me," he hollers over the escalating death howls. Johnny nods and throws his head back in wild laughter, giving James opportunity enough to join me on the roof. I try to shoot as many as I can. Bloody scalps explode backward and the dead things finally fall down. But they never quit twitching. Not entirely.

James makes it to safety and shouts to his brother. "NOW!"

Johnny slings the smoking gun over his shoulder and starts the climb, but all those years of watching cartoons in his underwear have ill-equipped him for the task. He stumbles and slacks. James is about to go over the side again to help him up, but I know he'd be better at covering us than I would.

"Wait," I hold him back and hand him my gun. "I'll go. You're a better shot."

He looks worried. My best friend or no, he doesn't seem to trust me with his brother's life. But right now, trust is all we have. James nods and takes careful aim, blowing out the back of the zombie's head nearest his brother. With adrenaline coursing through me, I climb down and drop to the ground below.

"What are you doing?!" Johnny screams at the top of his lungs.

"Leave no man behind, right?"

All smiles have left him, but he understands. I help him up and he starts to climb.

"AAGHH!"

My ankle is torn open and I feel blood soaking my sock and filling my shoe. I look down and meet a zombie face to face. Blood, skin, and the better part of my lower pants leg dangles from his mouth. I kick my attacker, turning his jaw sideways. He falls back and the others climb over his body.

"Go, go, go!" I shout above me, furious that I came down here.

James reaches down and helps Johnny over the edge, then turns to me.

"You're bleeding!" he exclaims, voice shrill.

"I cut my leg on the stone! Get me up!"

He does and I'm safe. Johnny looks down at the cannibals as they start to cool and mindlessly paw at the building, as if fumbling in the dark for a light switch. He whistles. "What a rush, huh?"

An entire life's worth of rage blazes like wildfire inside me. I grab the nearest gun and start firing blindly into the crowd below. I want them to feel pain. I want to kill them.

&

IN THE BATHROOM of the deserted theater, I break down.

We managed to shoot off the lock and took careful survey of the theater. No one is here. All the other doors are locked. We're safe. Johnny and James took liberties with the soda fountain and candy and they're back up on the roof, snacking and retelling their adventures. I can hear gunshots and the accompanying *thuds* of penetrated dead-things hitting the pavement. The glass is holding out front and I know that they haven't figured out that we're in here. I told the Thunder Twins that I would go and bandage my wound, which led me to the bathroom floor.

I may not be a post-apocalyptic Rambo like my compatriots, but I'm not an idiot. I've seen enough movies, and whether zombies run or shamble, can think or are completely brain-dead, eat brains or just eat flesh, one thing is terribly certain: Anyone who is bitten *will* be turned.

I don't know how long I have. A week? A day? An hour? I'm not sure, but I know it's coming. I can already feel the fever. My leg is numb where the wicked thing bit me and my stomach feels heavy, despite the fact that I've thrown up three times already. I haven't told the others. They'd probably shoot me and, realistically, that's probably the best thing for everyone involved. But I think of Shelly.

I can't stop crying. My body is convulsing and it hurts deep in my chest. I want to see Shelly again. To hold her. To kiss the tip of her nose again. I want to bury my face in her neck and breathe her in. But I won't get to. I'm already degenerating into some flesh-eating...

It's not fair! Why me? This is Johnny's fault! Why couldn't he get himself up?! Why did I go after him? Why did I even go with either of them? Why didn't I just say a big thankya to James for saving me and get in my *own* stupid car and drive straight to the school by myself? I could be with her right now!! We could be together and the Thunder Twins could go on their way wreaking havoc, listening to their stupid songs and relishing the fact that their secret boyhood desires have come to fruition. But I don't want that!! I don't want to fight! I don't want any of this! I want Shelly. Why did I go with them why didn't I drive myself why didn't I stay in bed why didn't Shelly...

Whoa... Stop.

I'm losing it. Thoughts running together and everything is blurry slip slip slipping and I don't know why I can't think, but Shelly needs me and told her I'd see her again, told her I'd come for her...

Stop.

Cold sweat now, and I'm shaking. Got to get hold of myself. Things are becoming really confusing and I feel tired. I want to sleep. My brain is on overload and I wonder if maybe that's its way of fighting death. I wonder if the plague is killing my mind and it's gasping for life. I'm dying...but only to be born again. And that cursed part of me that the thing put in me...it *wants* that. Wants that peace and that—

No. Not yet. First...I have to do it. I don't want to, but I know that there's no other way now. This is it. My only chance. I pick myself up off the sticky floor of the theater bathroom and take to the lobby. I find the phone. I duck behind the counter to make sure that the things don't see me and I make the hardest call I'll ever make. I call Shelly.

There's a moment where my heart beats so loud that my head hurts and I can feel bile rising in the back of my throat. I wait, thinking in that silence that she's already dead.

"Sergeant Roth?!"

She picks up. My heart stops.

"No, it's me."

"Oh, Caleb! Where are you?! I've been worried to death! I got through to the police and talked to a Sergeant Roth. He said he's trying to get to the school. He's coming to help us. Where are you?"

"I got bit, sweetie."

The world halts. "What?" she finally asks, the breath leaving her.

"I'm sorry," I wail uncontrollably. "I was trying to...I'm so sorry, Shelly."

She's crying, too. Through the static of the phone, I hear her and it only makes me cry harder. I feel so cold and alone, and I miss her so much.

"No," she tells me. "No, you're lying. You're playing a joke...Shut up! SHUT UP! You didn't get bitten! You're okay! You're coming to see me!!"

"No, I'm not, baby. It's—"

"I don't want you to die." She breaks down and sounds like a little girl we'll never be able to have. Children are Shelly's passion, you know. She always wanted...

Everything becomes silent and I cling to the phone. This is the closest I'll ever be to Shelly again and we both know it. My throat loosens. I feel like I can speak without my voice cracking again. "I bought you flowers today," I tell her.

"Yeah?"

"Yeah. The really expensive kind—"

"I love you." She cuts me off.

"I love you, too."

"Nothing can change that."

"I know."

She trails off. Then, "Caleb, will you still come for me?"

"Shelly, I can't. I won't..." I'm starting to cry again, but I make myself stop. "I won't be the same."

"I don't care. I just want to see you."

"It's not safe."

"But if you come now, maybe you'll have time to get here before... before it happens. Maybe you'll still be you and I can hold you and we can...God, I can't believe we're doing this..."

"I don't know how much time I have. All we have is right now."

"Caleb—"

"Stop it! We're out of time, Shelly! This is it! I'm *dying*!"

She starts crying again, and I'm starting to think God did the merciful thing by not letting us see each other right now. It would only be harder. But the need...I need to

[*Eat*]

see her.

"Okay," I give in. "I'll come for you. I'll find a way. But don't wait for me. If the cops get there, go with them. If I'm not there by then...I won't be coming. Do you understand?"

"But you'll try?"

"I'll try. Until I can't anymore."

❧

SHELLY AND I talk more, about the good times and the bad and then...we talk about the times we'll never have. In a single phone call, we have five children and name them all, giving each one a voice and personality. But sadly, my worst fears come to pass as Shelly says the three most ugly, hurtful words I've ever heard.

"My battery's low." She cries hysterically. "No! It's not enough time! We're not done! Please, no!"

But it's done. Rather than being cut off by some insensitive machine we force ourselves to hang up. All we say is, "I love you, and I'll see you soon," and my time with my Shelly is over.

❧

I RE-ENTER THE bathroom and do something I never thought I'd be doing under the circumstances. I pray. I've always considered myself a faithful guy, but when faced with the reality that my time on Earth is almost over, I find that there is so much more I could have done. I marvel at all the time I let slip by. What did I *do* with my life for all those years? It seemed so important at the time, but now, I suddenly can't recall the point of it all.

I grew up believing that, when I died, my soul would go to heaven. Where will it go now, when I change? Will it be like falling asleep? Will things go black and then I'm up in heaven, ready to meet the Almighty? Or will I be a prisoner inside my own body while it does unspeakable things? Will I know what horrors I'm committing?

It's time to set things right with God. I pray He forgives me for all the kind things I never said, the generous things I never did. The times I could have been more like Him, but chose to stay like me. Mostly I pray that He forgives me for what I'm about to become, and gives me the strength to see it through.

❧

AFTER A FEW moments to collect myself, I am resolved to go find Shelly, assured that it is the last thing I will ever do. When I come to the rooftop, Johnny and James are kicked back, drinking Big Gulps, and Johnny is enlightening his brother.

"Alien colonization."

James pauses in serious consideration.

"Yeah," Johnny says. "Alien colonization. Think about it. The aliens release some kind of spore, the zombies kill everyone off—sort of like a Scorched Earth tactic, only with people—and then the aliens move on into their newly fumigated habitat."

I interrupt. "Jesus tells a parable of the Rich Man and Lazarus in the Bible. The Rich Man is in hell and asks if he can come back to earth to try and convince his loved ones to turn to the Lord so that they won't end up where he is."

James and Johnny jump, paranoid, and spin with guns aimed. "You scared us, man."

I continue. "But Abraham tells the man that he can't. He says that the people didn't believe the prophets or the Word of God and that they wouldn't even believe a man returning from the dead."

James and Johnny watch me, intrigued, as I walk to the edge of the building and look down on the ever-increasing multitudes of damned souls. Not just *one* man down there...but a *million*, all come back from beyond.

"Maybe now they'll get the hint."

It's quiet for a moment, but Johnny breaks the silence. "I like that theory, too. I say Caleb wins for originality."

"Shut up," I reprimand. "Just shut up."

James asks, "What's wrong?"

No use lying to them. It won't help anyone now. "I'm bit."

They both look to my bandaged, bleeding wound.

"But you said—"

"I lied. I'm bit and I'm changing. I can feel it."

James stares at me, brow furrowed. Johnny, however, all sense of enjoyment and mirth leaves his face and his eyes are wet and shiny. He starts to...is he crying?

"It's my fault," he weeps. "You were trying to help me. Now it's my fault that you won't get to see Shelly again..."

A moment ago I hated Johnny. But now I move to him and give him a hug.

"It's okay."

James paces.

"I can't stay with you guys," I say. "I gotta go find Shelly."

Johnny wipes his eyes and turns to me. "Uh...that's not a good idea. You'll be one of them before you get to her."

"I don't care. She doesn't, either."

"What?"

"I called her. We've decided. This is what we want."

James turns to me, angry. "You'll kill her. Is *that* what you want?"

It's hard for me to hear, but I love him all the more for saying it.

"Maybe I won't."

"Bull."

"Hey!" I'm coming undone. Tired of talking. Ready to

{*Eat*}

do something besides talk! "I'm going and you can't stop me!"

He raises a .45 to my head.

Johnny protests, "James, don't."

"I'm doing the right thing. We all know it."

Johnny moves between the gun and me. "Don't. There has to be another way."

"There's not."

"There is," I say. "I can help you."

The two swivel to face me, ready to hear what I have to say. Now that I have their attention:

"I have a plan."

&

THE PLAN IS simple. I'm going to climb down, march over to the Charger, and bring it and the canisters of gasoline over to the other side of the building. The Thunder Twins can hop down, load up, and head over to the school to save those kids, help whatever parents made it, and back up the police, assuming any can be spared to the scene.

"They'll eat you alive down there."

I remind them, "I'm *not* alive, remember? I'm like them."

"Not yet. You haven't turned."

"Not entirely, but maybe enough for them to leave me alone."

"We can shoot our way out," is James' idea.

"And waste your ammo."

"Shut up."

"I'm trying to *help* you. Let me go get the car."

Johnny now. "What then for you?"

"I'll walk."

"The school is five miles from here. We're smack in the middle of the friggin' town. You'll *absolutely* be changed if you try and walk the whole way."

It's James who finally gives in. "We can drive you."

I know it's hard for him to say that. He doesn't trust me anymore. I can see it in his eyes. But he *does* pity me. "You don't have to do that," I say.

"I know. But we will. *Part* of the way. As soon as you start up with the moaning, we're dumping your zombified carcass on the side of the road."

Johnny turns to his brother and protests, "We owe it to him to take him all the way."

It's to me that James answers. "It's not that we don't want to help. We know how much Shelly means to you. I wish...I wish I had someone like that to miss and to worry about. I envy you, man, but John and me aren't going to be good for anything if you bite us, too."

"He got bit for *me*!" Johnny.

"Which is why we're taking you part of the way."

I nod, accepting that as a miracle. But we're wasting time. My mind is slowing down now. Not frantic or racing. Calm. Quiet. Focused on

[*Eating*]

finding Shelly.

James takes a deep breath, then releases it, "Let's go."

❧

THE SUN GOES down on the Day the World Ended as I set my first foot upon the concrete below. Glancing to the rooftop above, I see James and Johnny, locked and loaded, ready to back me up. The zombies are all around me, milling about absently, bellowing their inane gibberish at no one in particular. Maybe they're just realizing that they're alive after being dead for so long. I'll know soon enough.

I inch through the mob, grasping the fact that, aside from the zombie-speak, it's quiet out here. The screams have all died down, and the unsettling thing is, I appreciate it. It's peaceful and it relaxes me. My mind has decelerated and I feel a lot more at ease about things, ready to accept whatever fate is before me. Even if it is just a bullet from the barrel of James' or Johnny's gun. Just as long as I get to see Shelly one last time.

Across the street are the Charger and two remaining gas cans. I make my way slowly, keeping an eye to either side of me, studying the zombies. They notice me, that's certain. Their vacant eyes search me out and stare on, but their jaws remain closed and they keep their iron-cold grips to themselves. I'm not a threat to them. Or a meal. I'm a new recruit.

In the middle of the road, a pack of them share supper. A woman, I think, but there's honestly not enough left of it to make an accurate distinction. One of the cannibals turns to me, stares without emotion or reason, then just goes back to his dinner. I watch them eat and my mouth waters. I think I might vomit, but realize it's not disgust I'm feeling but...

No. Don't think that. Just keep walking.

I turn back to the theater and am a little surprised to see how far I've come already. Swimming out to the deep end without any floaties on. James gives me the thumbs up and I resume my mission. It doesn't take me long to get across the street and I find the Charger undisturbed. I gather up the cans and throw them in the trunk, then take my place behind the steering wheel and...what now? The car is off. I need to turn it on but how don't remember losing knowledge too fast now and hands feeling stiff and—

Stop. Think. Key. Right.

I put the key in the ignition and turn it over, hearing the familiar rumble of the high-performance engine. I put the car into drive and carefully pull forward, giving the herd time to bump and wander out of my path. No need killing

[*My brothers*]

them and getting them all riled up if they don't need to be.

I pull up to the movie theater where I used to work in high school eating popcorn watching movies talking to girls girl girl girl Shelly girl with long dark hair and wide thoughtful eyes and want to kiss kiss

[*Eat*]

her and hold her close and—

"Ah!" I force myself to focus, banging head to steering wheel. It's getting hard hard to think. Thoughts are slipping through fingers like sand through hourglass and time is almost up. My stomach growls and vision is getting darker around the edges.

In a few moments, I'm on a lesser-populated street corner on the opposite end of the theater where I used to work and talk to Shelly-girl. James and Johnny carefully lower their bang-bangs to me and I take them and put by yellow car. James is the first one down and I see him look at me and see something different.

"Caleb? You okay, man? You're starting to look a little—"

"I'm fine. Let go."

"What?"

"I said 'Let's go'."

"O-okay."

He turn to Johnny brother that I saved to die and says, "Come on, hurry."

Johnny climb down and takes bags from me. I start coughing and feel like I can't breathe and he stop and stare at me like I'm a monster.

"Hey..." he say to me. "You don't look so good."

I cough. Cough cough can't breathe mommy where medicine no medicine going to die to save Johnny to see Shelly.

James takes Johnny brother aside like I don't notice. "We have to hurry," I hear him whisper. "He's getting worse and fast."

Twin Thunderbolts help me in yellow Charger and put me in backseat with McDonalds bags am really hungry wish I had

[*Flesh*]

burgers to eat.

"I'm hungry," I tell them and see them look at each other scared.

"Just get us out of here," Johnny say to James.

Car takes off vroom vroom fast and I wave to my brothers behind me. I think I see one wave back at me. They are very nice at dinner time.

I feel lump in pants and "Uh oh" I tell my friends.

Johnny wrinkles his face. "You smell that?"

James turns and looks at me and I feel shamed and embarrassed. "He just soiled himself."

I think Johnny is starting to cry. "This is all my fault. I'm so sorry. I'm so—"

I pat friend on shoulder saying, "Don't worry, Caleb getting better."

"Don't touch me!" he hurt Caleb, hitting hand away and pointing shiny thing at my nose.

"Calm down!" James is nice. "He's doesn't know what's happening. His body is dying and his mind is breaking down. It's not his fault."

"I want to see Shelly," I tell them ever-so-niceties kindly.

James won't look at me like used to he did but he sounds happy. "I know, Caleb. We're almost there."

"This isn't happening. This isn't fun anymore."

"Shh, he'll catch on. You'll upset him."

"I not upset, okay to be born."

"You're not being born, dummy! You're dying!"

No, that is mean. I cannot die, I have to see Shelly who holds my hand when I sick and scared. Shelly needs me to have her to be there need to see that Shelly of mine.

"Pull over!" Johnny is yelling and I getting scared. "This is freaking me out! He's gonna turn and he's gonna bite us!"

"I no bite you, Thunderboy."

"Shut up! SHUT UP!"

Car stops fast too fast and I hit my head on back of seat. James is getting out and opening my door and bright light hits my eyes don't like it too bright to see anything.

"I'm sorry, Caleb. We can't take you any farther. I'm really sorry."

I smile and feel tooth fall out. Shamed again but James looks nicer than I've seen him in a long time. Always a funeral to bring out best in people.

"Listen to me." He tells me, looking close into my eyes that are getting darky dark. "If there's anything left in there, I want you to know that we love you and we'll miss you and we'll take care of Shelly."

"Shelly needs me."

"I know, but we'll take care of her. We're going to the school to get her and the others and we're going to Fort Meeks just like we planned. She's going to be okay."

I smile, nodding and hear creaking in my bones. "I know. I'm going to eat her."

James steps back, looking horrored at me. "Caleb, man..."

"What?"

He doesn't say anything more to me. Only gives me fast hug and gets in car. I wave but they do not wave back. Just drive away in yellow car. I wave and wave, but know they must go. It's time for me to go see Shelly.

⁊

CAN'T STOP. LEGS heavy. Arms numb. I lost friends. Have new ones now. They are behind me. We go to school. Shelly teaches at school. Walked long long way. Here now. Friends with me. Lots of cars in parking lot. On fire. Crashed. Blue lights and red. Hurt eyes. I hear Charger somewhere. Shouting. Gunshots. Children screaming. Hurt ears.

Oops. Trip over. Look down see hand. Lady hand. She belong to truck. *Rachel's Flowers*. Orange on ground.

"Hey..." I smile.

Pick up flowers. Little trampled, but still pretty. Card inside. Open it up. Love Muskrat. Thinking of you. Flowers for Shelly. I take them. Money well spent. Move for school. Stomach growling. Time to eat. Almost there now. Promised Shelly I come. Caleb keep promise to her. Always. I will meet her my new friends. We will play and she will like them. We will all

{Eat}

play together.

I miss Shelly. Big yellow bus here. People getting on. Where is she? Look everywhere. Can't—Ha ha. There is she. In front of me. People running away. But she stay.

"Hurry! Hurry!"

Men with bang-bangs. Blue uniforms. Thunder brothers.

"Shelly, hurry!"

Smile. Shelly. Her eyes wet. But she smile, too. Hold out flowers.

"...Flowers for Shelly," I tell her.

She cry.

"They're beautiful."

"...your favorite."

"Shelly, hurry! They're here! We have to go!"

She look to James. Then to me and I feel

[Hungry]

warm. Hold out hands to her. "...don't go. You skip school. I skip work. We stay and snuggle. Shelly stay."

"Shelly, no!"

Shelly nod. Take hand. "Okay, Caleb. I'll stay. This time...I'll stay."

James yell, but don't care. I take Shelly and

[*Eat her*]

hold her. She scream. We're playing again. She happy she with Caleb now. Am happy, too. Have Shelly again.

And everything is all right...

THE DENIAL

MAGGIE STIEFVATER

You can't deny your nature, that's what they all said. But they were wrong. The moment that I wanted Lily Gable, wanted her like wanting to be *with* her instead of wanting to be *in* her, I had denied my nature.

She was an interesting girl, Lily, which I suppose is how it happened. The denying my nature and becoming one of one, instead one of many, I mean. She lived in an apartment just off campus, by herself. Well, she had a hamster, as well—damn ugly thing it was too, because someone had thrown hot oil at it before Lily took it on. Anyway, aside from the fugly hamster, she lived alone, and she was putting herself through college writing bumper sticker and t-shirt slogans and selling them online.

I remember the first time Lily made me laugh, watching her outside her window on a dull, rainy night. She was sitting on her bed, her laptop on the vintage quilt, knees folded up on either side of her face like a grasshopper, and she was thinking about her unpaid electric bill. There weren't any lights on in the room, other than her laptop, because she wanted to save energy.

This was a waste of effort, by the way, because it was actually a miscalculation on the part of the power company, but she didn't know that. I thought about making it right, fixing the problem and erasing the frown-lines from over her fine light eyebrows. I think that was the beginning for me.

Anyway, she was trying to write a bumper sticker that would sell well enough to pay the bogus electric bill, and finally she swore and typed *Honk if you're hotter than me.*

And I laughed.

Then I became human.

No, that's not true, really. Wipe that from the record. I wasn't quite human. But I was a hell of a lot closer than I had been before.

God, that's funny. *Hell of a lot closer.* Sorry, I amuse myself.

So of course I wanted to get closer to her. I was too chicken-shit to actually talk to her at first, so I followed her. I waited outside in the shadows, watching her come home from her classes, shoulders bundled up against the cold, backpack covered with beaded rain from the walk. And I was there in the morning too, an anonymous figure on a bench, one of hundreds she passed everyday. As she walked by me, I could see her peering at the cars that went by, reading the bumper stickers. Every so often her lips would move, and I would know that she was trying one out.

Everything in life was funny to Lily. She always had a grin on her face. Not a Pollyanna sort of grin. What, did you think I would do this to myself for a nice Pollyanna girl? No, she laughed at things like people on painfully obvious first dates—the ones that weren't going well. She grinned at middle-aged women scrubbing the alloy wheels of their husbands' BMWs on the curb as they parallel-parked. She smirked when high-powered businessmen stepped in melted ice cream on the sidewalk and tracked it into their offices.

I loved it when she smirked. Her eyebrows got all pointy and her mouth got small. Like she was blowing out birthday candles.

Anyway. It took me a long time to actually follow her from her apartment, and the day I chose to follow her, it turned out she was going to church. Well, spank my ass and call me Jesus. I hadn't ever thought of her as a church-going type, probably because one of her best-selling stickers was *In Case of the Rapture, Can I Have Your Big-Screen?* But there she was, in a skirt that was probably a bit too short to really be chaste, heading into St. Michael the Archangel's on Grass Street, not at all awkward.

I followed her in. It was weird to enter a church under my own steam, instead of riding on someone's shoulders. Inside St. Michael's, it was dim and too-warm, smelling of many bodies, some of which were wearing adult diapers. Lily took a seat up front, and I took a cautious seat on the edge of a pew, waiting to burst into flame or become a pillar of salt or some other crap that ought to happen to me in a church.

"Mommy," a voice whispered beside me.

"Shhh."

"That man's not a Christian."

I looked to see who was talking. It was a little blonde boy. I'm bad at ages, but he was old enough to not smell like the people wearing adult diapers but not old enough to drive or swear.

"Shhh," his mother whispered in his ear. "People with tattoos can be Christians too."

I had tattoos? I hadn't realized. Oh, shit, yeah. Look, there was one on my arm, a dragon eating its own tail or something. That was wicked cool.

The little boy leaned towards me. "Do you believe in God?"

"Hell, yeah," I told him. Far more than he did.

The mother gave me a hard look; I looked back with half a smile. She was hot, and the deep V-neck of her top showed me the edges of her breasts. I finished my smile so she'd know that I noticed. She slid a little further down the pew.

In front, Lily stood when everyone else stood and kneeled when everyone else knelt. Her lips moved the same way everyone else's did. Damn. Of course she was Catholic. Whatever. I could handle that.

But after learning of her mad skillz with holy water, it took weeks for me to approach her again. Weeks during which I learned about hunger and work. My tattoos hadn't come with a trade, so I fell back into old habits to make money: deceiving people. It was not quite giving into my nature as I deceived for entertainment rather than for the pleasure of it.

And so when I finally showed myself to her, I was not a nobody. I was not a somebody yet either, but I had a name: Nick Bishop, and some people knew it.

Lily came down the stairs of her apartment, backpack slung over her shoulder, and she paused when she saw me standing on the sidewalk at the base of them. Her eyes lifted up and down me and for a moment I wondered what my shaved head, my black eyes, my black coat would get, if they would get a grin, or a laugh, or a smirk. They got none of those. Instead, her eyes narrowed, studying me as I stood there, a black blot on the white sidewalk.

I spread my arms out and then brought them over my head, fingers reaching towards the sky as if I could claw heaven down. Doves burst from my sleeves, wings beating against my fingers in their struggle to vanish up into the steel gray morning.

Lily's mouth pulled up on one side and she made a grudging noise of approval. Her eyes finally dropped from my face to my feet, where there were some coins and bills from the tricks I had done while waiting for her. Stepping to the bottom of the stairs, she began to rummage in her pockets for change.

I smiled at her. Friendly but approachable, not too much teeth. I wanted to befriend her, not eat her. See—denying my nature. "Just your attention is enough. May I have it?"

She raised an eyebrow. It was pointy. "You have it."

"Besides," I added, wanting to turn the one pointy eyebrow into two pointy ones, "You already gave me something."

I opened my hand and showed her a delicate gold cross on a chain. Her hand went to her neck, pulling down her turtleneck. Goosebumps raised immediately as her bare skin touched the frigid air.

She made a face, though she didn't reward me with a full smirk.

"But—" I took her hand, touching her for the first time in a millennia, and cupped the cross back into her palm. Her eyes were on the back of my hand, on the blue and green star tattoos that disappeared into my sleeve. "—I already told you I only wanted your attention. So thanks. But no thanks."

She smirked, now that she had her cross again. "You're good."

I grinned.

Lily went to class. After she had gone, I stayed on the sidewalk in front of her apartment for a long time, imagining being invited in, sitting on her bed and watching over her shoulder as she typed bumper stickers.

While I loitered, a few passersby eyed me, and I did some tricks for them. One of them was a little boy with a yellow puppy on a leash. In the old days, I would've turned his puppy's skin inside-out to make the boy cry and then would've slid away into the cracks of the sidewalk like beads of mercury. Instead, I made dog biscuits appear in my cold-numbed hands and underneath his father's ridiculous hat. The father gave me a twenty and led the boy and the dog away.

The weeks went by, and each day, when Lily came out of her apartment, I was waiting. One day, I turned pebbles into rosebuds. Another day, I levitated her backpack and made her pass her hand underneath so that she could see that it really floated. The next week, I made a puddle of water appear on the sidewalk at her feet, and spat a small boat into it. Both vanished when she stepped into the water, grinning.

"You're good," she said, and went to class.

One frozen day, when she came out of her apartment, days before her winter vacation, I clouded the icy air with my breath until the mist birthed a butterfly.

Lily made a soft noise and clapped her hands around the insect, making a cage for it with her palms. "Asshole," she said, but her voice was fond. "It'll die. It *is* real, isn't it?"

I hadn't thought of its fate but I supposed it would freeze in this D.C. winter. It didn't seem that important. Butterflies died all the time. "Real as you."

"I have to bring it inside. Unless you can magic it someplace warm."

But she was already half-turned towards the door as I shrugged. She looked over her shoulder. "Will you freeze as well, in this weather?"

I tilted my chin up, held out my arms in my long black coat, a giant dark bird. "Anything's possible."

"Come inside and have some coffee."

I gestured down the sidewalk. "Don't you have to hurry hurry to your classes like always?"

"I have made them magically disappear," Lily said. "Like you would. Get the door for me."

So we went inside the studio apartment that I had watched for so many months, where I had first heard her laugh at her own jokes, all alone in her room, with only my invisible presence as company. It was brighter than I remembered, the light all white and blue from the icy white sky out the windows. There was her laptop, sitting on the faded plaid couch, a bumper sticker stuck on the back of it. I turned my head to read it: *Veterinarians Do It Doggy-Style.*

Lily walked into the center of the living room, the light from the tall windows illuminating her slender form as she uncupped her hands.

The butterfly lay still in her palms and she moaned. "Oh, dammit. I think I've killed it."

I walked over and looked into her hands. She hadn't killed it, but it had fluttered against her hands so hard in its fear that its wings were ruined. Worse than dead, it had been drawn down from a creature of the air to no better than a roach or ant. I looked up at her eyebrows, drawn down low over her coffee-colored eyes, and at the line of sad frustration that her mouth made.

"Silly girl," I told her, and laid my hands over the top of her palms. Beneath my fingers, I felt the butterfly's lace wings kiss my skin, moving faster and faster. I lifted my hand from hers and the butterfly flew into the air, a small patch of her quilt rising over our heads and dancing in the light of the window.

Lily's eyebrows drew together for a second as she watched it fly through her apartment, as out of place as I was, and I thought that she would call me out, tell me that what I had done was real magic, not sleight of hand. But then her fleeting frown became her easy grin as she fell into the willing suspension of disbelief that all magicians relied on. I wouldn't have to lie to her about the ridiculous kindness I'd done for her, though lying was something I was even better at.

"I'll leave the magic to you." Lily went on the other side of the counter to make coffee, and I sat on a stool on my side. "Milk? Sugar?"

"Black," I said truthfully.

"Hope this isn't too strong," she said, and slid a mug over. She leaned against the counter towards me, boobs pushed together, but I was looking at her hands, imagining her reaching out to take mine. Imagining what it would feel like, touching my cheek softly just before she went to sleep. "So. Nick Bishop." She said it as if she was trying the words out in her head, like I had when I'd decided on the name in the first place. "That's a name everyone's saying these days."

"Is it."

Lily held up her mug to her lips without drinking it. "They say that you're going to be the greatest magician of our generation."

I grinned at her. "Who's they?"

"People."

"People who know what they're talking about?"

Lily smirked. "Not generally. But a lot of people are saying it anyway. They say you came out of nowhere."

"Nothing comes from nowhere," I said. I drank the coffee. It was too strong. It tasted like battery acid.

"So where did you come from, Nick Bishop the magician?"

She didn't mean it seriously, but I answered that way. "Hell." No one could say I had lied to her. No one could say I denied what I was.

"Wow, it must've been pretty bad if D.C. was a step up," Lily laughed. "Remind me not to visit."

"Don't visit." The idea of her there, the demons scratching their nails on her skin, pulling her mouth into a scream, was so physically painful that I shuddered, bile in my throat. The memory of my nails in flesh, my teeth ripping hair—

"Coffee's that bad?"

I looked at her and for a moment I couldn't remember what language she was speaking. Then I laughed. "Like oil. Like dirty oil."

"Sorry. Want a fresh cup? I can try again. Second time's the charm."

Friggin' get it together. I smiled, no teeth at all. "No, thanks, I could use the protein."

Lily smiled at me. "I like you, Nick Bishop the magician."

The winter passed us by, Lily and I. Her butterfly did not die and neither did she. Soon I couldn't wait outside her apartment for her, because the crowds to see me were too large. So Lily told me to stay in her apartment, and I did, sleeping on her couch, and doing magic for ever larger audiences who brought their willing suspension of disbelief in their pockets and purses. I had earned enough money to move out, but I didn't. I had earned enough of Lily's desire to move into her bedroom, but I didn't.

I made doves appear on stage, pouring out of vases of flowers that had been nothing but coat hangers a moment before. I poured rainbows from my hands and pulled keys from my mouth; rainbows from far-away rains and keys to doors that would never open again. And the crowds shouted that they loved me, and that I was God, and I denied that I loved it, that I loved being lifted above everyone else and wielding power far beyond them.

I denied, too, that I brought darkness to Lily's apartment. I denied that the shadows were deeper in her living room than they had been that winter, that her eyes were dimmer, that I was slipping from one of one, to one of many again, and that the many were hungry.

By next autumn, Lily's grins were gone, so too her smirks. Her laughs hurt my ears, because they denied her nature.

I returned to the apartment one night after a show and found it dark. So dark that even I could not see through the blackness of the night. The light over the oven was on, but it seemed dim and faraway, like a ship bobbing distantly on an ocean.

"Lily?" I called, and the darkness ate my voice.

I moved through the kitchen, found the couch, saw that it was unoccupied, and moved towards the bedroom door. I had never been inside. I could not allow myself to want her, because what else would I want?

But behind the door, I heard water running, and that seemed wrong. I didn't waste my breath saying her name again. I just pushed through the door, into the drowning darkness of the bedroom.

It was ten thousand times worse in this room than it had been in the darkest of the shadows of the living room, and now I heard the silent voices laughing at me. Laughing that I shouldn't have thought that I was an individual, that I shouldn't have singled out a human for my peculiar brand of love. I'd never thought that they would've emerged for the unique pleasure of tormenting one of their own by tormenting her.

I burst into the bathroom, and found Lily laying in the bathtub in a tank-top and jeans. The water covered the tiles, the soles of my shoes, her mouth. Her hair floated out around her.

"Lily," I said again. I didn't know if she'd magically made herself disappear, like her classes, if she was dead in my hands like a butterfly, or if she had merely beaten her wings useless in her fear. I reached into the water, lifted her from the tub, and lay her across my lap.

Movement in the tub caught my eye, and I saw the butterfly—our butterfly—floating slowly by on the surface of the water, dead. She'd drowned it.

"Fuck, Lily," I said, clutching her to me. I wanted her. I wanted her to be mine. I wanted her to hold my hand, damn it, I wanted her to love me. I wanted her alive. I wanted her to touch my face.

Her eyebrows were damp and sad, so far away from the smirk that I had loved that it was hard to imagine it was the same girl. She was supposed to have made me happy.

I bent my head and touched her forehead with mine, her nose against my nose, so close that my lips almost were touching hers, mine hot, hers cold. The darkness pushed in against the florescent bathroom lights, urging me to take her if I wanted her, to destroy her and take her into myself. To throw off this human form I'd taken, to bear her soul back home with me, to *make* her touch me and force her brows into the smirk I liked.

But.

I can deny my nature.

The voices laughed wildly, too many and too varied to count.

I put my hand on Lily's face, on her cheek, and then I kissed her, like I had wanted to for months.

Suck her out, the darkness said. *Take it out.*

I pulled my lips away from hers. "Lily," I said, "I think I want you to be happy."

The darkness was silent.

Lily took a breath. I carried her back into her bedroom, and I turned on the lights. They pushed back the shadows, but not completely. I was one of many. I laid Lily on the bed and watched her pulse in her neck for a moment. Then I went back into the bathroom and scooped the limp butterfly out of the tub.

When I went back into the bedroom and opened the window to the night, her eyes opened. "Nick. *Nick.*"

"Lily, I love you," I said. I laid my hand over the top of the butterfly, waited until I could feel the soft fluttering of wings against my fingers, and then I opened my hands.

Lily propped her body up and watched my stolen body fall to the ground. I lifted up into the air, my lacy wings fluttering in the light breeze, and I flew out the window, dragging the shadows behind me.

And she began to laugh, tears running down her face.

EN ROUTE TO INFERNO

MIKE DURAN

Ragged asphalt bled from the vast obsidian night and rushed under our headlights like the Styx out of Hades. The desert air, tart with sage, sent Jax's curls lashing about his face. "They call it *el curativo*." He held the Polaroid print aloft and smirked. "*The healing.*" Then he flicked the picture at me with the coolness of a card shark. "See fer yourself."

"She's a witch." Casey grimaced and kept kneading his gut with his fingertips. "I'm telling you, it's white magic, some kinda pagan sorcery."

We were ten hours past the border, sunburned and sleep deprived. Our research had turned into cerveza and bottomless tacos, Ensenada just another watering hole along the way. How we'd been chosen to document the enigma was, shall we say, circumstantial. Yet every mile seemed to blur our mission.

"The leg looks new." Jax turned around and stared blankly out the windshield. "But like I said from the start, on the backside of the calf there's, without question, an eyeball."

The picture levitated on my lap, buoyed by the night air, before arcing about the interior of the van. I snatched it mid-flight and turned on the overhead dome. Casey winced at the light and wedged himself further into the corner, now a miserable shivering cocoon. An oily imprint marked the spot where he'd rested his head against the side window the last two-and-a-half hours.

I angled the print under the light and peered at it, as if one more look would help. The more I tried to disarm the mystery, the harder the fuse burned.

The pictures had made the rounds, harvesting coffee stains and fingerprints along the way, eliciting debates and denunciations. Well before the age of pixels, from a distant pre-digital world, the three snapshots had arrived at our school and immediately become legend. A nameless missionary, they said, traveling down the Baja interior, happened upon the village. Supposedly, a woman lived there, levitated and glowed in the dark, attracted a following of sorts. Fugitives and vagrants probably. *Infierno*, he called the place, and attached a map and a warning. *Guárdese de fiel*, it read. *Beware the faithful.*

How the seminary had acquired the photos remained a mystery. But after years of speculation and late night dorm deliberations, we'd agreed to invalidate the devilry. They drew lots, as the sailors did before flinging Jonah overboard, and the four of us were chosen. Dub put 50 we'd never find the place, that it was all a hoax, and Erwin Locke matched him. When we left, the pot was pushing 400 bucks. That we became sidetracked reinforcing our commitment to Christian liberty, one tequila shot at a time, was another story.

I'd studied the photo a hundred times but now again, under the pale yellow light of the cargo van, the mystery re-emerged. The gloss had long since tarnished, but the image remained unmistakable: the lower half of a male body, clad only with a urine-stained pair of briefs, with two different appendages. The new leg—the one alleged to have sprouted at the command of the healer—extended unblemished, flushed pink like that of a newborn infant. But behind the calf, barely visible, rose a nodule of flesh and beneath it, what looked like an empty eye socket.

Sykes adjusted his wire rim glasses and watched me from the rearview mirror. Could he detect my growing disconcertion? Perhaps the most stable of the bunch, he had been at the wheel non-stop. Yet his steady gaze did not belie fatigue. He spoke loud enough to be heard above the onslaught of night air pummeling us through the open windows. "We're not far, maybe fifteen miles out." And then, "We'll find out soon enough."

I nodded and passed the picture back up to Jax, who maintained his diabolical smirk. He took the Polaroid and said, "Oh, we'll find out all right."

Suddenly, Casey doubled-over and moaned. Then he clambered over me, stinking of sweat and vomit, grappling for the door handle. "Pull over! Hurry!"

"Here?" Sykes was already navigating the vehicle onto the torturous shoulder.

Casey flung the door open as we ground to a stop. He scrambled out of the vehicle and went retching into the night.

A frail kid who seemed far more inclined toward the arts than ministry, I'd met him in Ethics and immediately liked him. Shy but affable, he was reluctant about the campaign from the start. On the eve of our inauguration, with unflinching, devout candor, he proclaimed that chance shouldn't play a part in a venture like ours. *Nobler men*, he intoned, *died of lesser presumptions*. Casey—as tightly wound as a viper before striking. Of course, Jax mocked him. But knowing Casey's trepidation—or *premonition* one might say—and now his sudden peculiar ailment, unnerved me. We'd already stopped twice for him, so he couldn't have much left. Yet there he was, wringing his insides. The entire desert seemed to pause and listen as he pitched his guts into the Sonoran scrub.

I climbed out of the van, as much to stretch as help him, and glanced back at Sykes who sat staring out of the windshield at some distant point. Cricket song resumed, peppering the desert with its bloodless vibrato. The smell of cacti and creosote startled my senses, expunging the surplus alcohol from my brain and reawakening me to the terrain. A smooth ridge rose in the west, cutting a black swath into the constellations. By the looks of it, we had entered a narrowing canyon. As my eyes adjusted, I could make out Casey straddling the earth on all fours, panting.

I turned to my comrades and said, "He's bad."

But Jax had a bottle of tequila out and was hammering another shot. He winced and drew the back of his hand across his mouth. "I warned 'im 'bout the beef."

"I had the beef," I said flatly.

"Then it was the water." Raising the bottle in a mock toast, Jax said, "Shoulda stuck with this," as he bit back another swallow.

A coyote yapped in the foothills and another, nearby, answered. Sykes remained fixated forward.

"We gotta go back," I said to no one in particular.

"Go back?" Jax shoved the bottle under the seat and glared out the window at me. "We're one day and one miser'ble border crossing 'way from gettin' him any decent help. He's gonna have to soldier on. We ain't come this far for nothin'."

As much as I hated to admit it, he was probably right.

"Besides," he added, "we're seeing a *healer.*"

"There's lights up there." Sykes rejoined the conversation. "Maybe it's a village."

"...with a 24 hour pharmacy and a freezer fulla ice cold beer," Jax quipped.

Something rustled in the brush and I lurched at the sound. Casey stumbled from the darkness like a cast member from Night of the Living Dead. He stood, rubbed his hands up and down the front of his thighs, and said sheepishly, "I think I crapped my pants."

"Damn!" Jax leapt out of the van. "You ain't gettin' in here like that."

I turned to Jax, purposely blocking his view of Casey, and uncomfortably close to the fledgling M.Div. student. "He's sick, dude. Lighten up."

"Your breath stinks."

"And I suggest you lay off the liquor."

"Is that a request or a demand?"

Insect chatter rose in between the tenuous silences.

Night creatures inhabit many legends—whether it's banshees keening on the Scottish lowlands or shape-shifting Hyaenas, stalking the desert for men to mimic. According to Talmudic myth, Lilith was the first Eve, the dark feminine side of the divine, the Black Madonna or Queen of Demons. One legend said they found the floozy copulating with fallen angels near the Red Sea. The name "Lilith" was often translated as "night monster." Jax knew this, but at the moment, I doubted it mattered. Nevertheless, these arcane facts had been rattling in my brain since sunset and made what happened next even more unnerving.

Sykes choked out some inarticulate warning, wrenching us from a potential scuffle. We turned in the direction he pointed to see a mule loping up the road, bearing a rider with empty eyes, and a lantern hovering before them.

కా

WELL PAST THE witching hour, the old man on the mule pulled up on the far shoulder and swung his lantern our way. A jerry-rigged harness with a splintered fiberglass fishing pole stretched atop the beast from which hung a guttering kerosene lamp. The whites of the rider's eyes glistened from the flame, revealing pale gelatinous pools.

"What the—?" Jax leaned into the hood of the van, puzzling over the visitor. "Where'd he come from?"

Casey plopped onto the running board with a groan, apparently unconcerned about his feces-stained khakis or the stranger who regarded us.

Sykes nodded toward the man, who did not acknowledge him.

"He ain't got pupils," Jax hissed.

Sykes motioned for Jax to can it, and greeted the stranger in stilted Spanish. Then he said, "Infierno."

Shadows of suspicion and disquietude lapped at the edges of the old man's features. After a brief, ponderous silence, he began speaking, drawling out words in robotic precision, from which I culled parts: "...door...light ...dogs...meat...devil." I knew just enough of the language to inflame my ignorance. His tone went from cautionary to somber, compounding my discomfort.

"What's he saying?" whispered Jax.

Sykes brushed off the query and remained intent on the stranger's admonitions, nodding and occasionally soliciting further info, until the man stopped speaking and swung the lantern to its original spot, bathing the mule and rider under its halo.

Starshine speckled the cerulean sky, a gulf of twinkling radiation, silhouetting night birds in their spiral orbits. An arid breeze whorled a dusty specter across our headlights, rattling the old man's lamp and flinging grit into the van.

Jax wiped his eyes and then peered at Sykes. "So? What'd he say?"

But Sykes gazed into the desert, squinting in thought. Finally, he drew his fingers through his hair and turned to us.

"There's a village between here and there, a last stop before Infierno. But this canyon, it's a dead end. There's no way out, only back."

We exchanged glances of uncertainty, which ended upon Casey who now sat hunched forward, knees drawn into his chest, trembling.

"So who is he?" I asked, gesturing toward the old man.

"He's a watchman of some sort."

Jax snorted. "A blind watchman? You gotta love it."

"He watches the road, turns the faithless away. Says the devil roams this place looking for flesh, and that only those who believe can survive hell."

"Hell? I've survived eighteen hours in a car with you guys, that's hell enough."

"Infierno means *Inferno*." Sykes turned and said coolly. "Or *hell*."

"We're en route to hell." Jax nodded to himself, matter-of-factly, and then pawed under the front seat and produced the tequila. "It's the story of my life."

I scowled at him. "Haven't you had enough?"

He ignored my remark and said to Sykes, "If he's blind, why does he need a light?"

Sykes cast a sideways glance. "Maybe it isn't for him."

Casey moaned and stumbled to his feet. As I turned to steady him, he bolted into the night dry heaving.

"We gotta do something." I did not attempt to conceal my anxiety.

Jax opened the tequila. "Ya got that straight," he said, and chugged.

"The village is just up ahead." Sykes stared after Casey, whose profile had vanished in the black expanse. "Maybe we can find help."

My silence was concession enough.

Jax belched and the fumes wafted my way. He repositioned the bottle under the seat as I went in search of Casey. I found him hugging himself and mumbling in Latin. "*Indulgeo n-nos,*" he sputtered, "*nostrum m-malum.*" I'd barely passed Latin but knew enough to decipher Casey's plea. We returned and I assisted him into the van. Crawling onto the seat, still muttering, he looked at me with waterlogged eyes and said, "You ain't taking me to that witch."

I patted his shoulder and shrugged. "I dunno, Case. Maybe she really *can* heal."

The watchman had his ear cocked toward heaven, making his empty orbs glisten in the lamplight. As if sensing our decision, he prattled something to Sykes.

Jax climbed back into the front seat. "What does he want now?"

"He said we should turn back—" Sykes gazed grimly between us. "Unless we believe."

But, having come this far, believing was our only option.

**

SOMEWHERE ALONG THE way, asphalt yielded to gravel and the van rattled its way toward a cluster of lights in a basin of black. Despite the turbulent ride, Casey lay curled next to me drained of movement. The canyon narrowed, becoming immense pitch curtains on both sides, drawn upon some yet unrevealed tragedy. A vibe was brewing that I could not put my finger on.

Several jackrabbits scampered through the high beams as we approached a dry wash. The road, growing less navigable, spread cloven from some bygone deluge. We idled at the precipice before Sykes issued a benediction and maneuvered our vehicle into the gulley. Gravel spat as the van descended and then crested the bluff. On the other side, an emaciated calico dog greeted us, loping alongside like a hapless escort. Wooden shanties with corrugated metal roofs rose along the way. Behind lightless windows, eyes stirred and watched our arrival. Up ahead, several lanterns blazed, demarcating the gateway to a ramshackle village.

But it was the luminous scarecrow that occupied our attention.

Gripping the front seat, I peered forward as we approached the effigy. A tortured amalgamation of ruddy clay and palm husks sculpted into humanoid likeness, it stood lashed to a post by barbed wire and faced the road, its arms extended in mock appeal. Herbal wreaths and amulets draped its sandblasted torso. An over-sized gourd served as the head and inside the hollowed cranium burned two vigil candles, blinking and bleeding wax. Blocks of incense, articles of clothing, jewelry, and fleshy objects were heaped in reverent disarray around the icon, a teetering altar of sacrifice to the goddess of the wasteland.

We sat gawking at the hideous mannequin as our dust cloud caught up and drifted past, blushed crimson by the brake lights. Casey groaned, wrenching us from our trance. Fearing he would puke again, I scrabbled to the side door, flung it open, and leapt out.

The air had chilled and on it, a trace of desert lupine and poppy; the moonless canopy stretched above the canyon like a godless void, leaving us adrift in an existential ocean. As I stood, momentarily overcome by the solitude, Casey rolled over, craned up at me and croaked, "Water."

Just then, something skittered from behind the van and bristled against my leg.

With images of night things already riffling through my noggin, I immediately envisioned Lilith, seductress of the night, grappling at my thigh with her inescapable talons. I stumbled backward to avoid her clutches only to glimpse the calico dog brushing past. Unable to regain my balance, I tripped over a clump of withered agave and careened into the shrine. As I struck the earth, objects scattered in every direction and the scent of tallow erupted. Spinning onto my hands and knees, I stared up into the incandescent eyes of the clay goddess.

"You all right?" Sykes sprinted around the van, leaving it idling while Jax sat hooting.

I clambered to my feet, hastily brushing debris from my hair and shoulders, and scanned the contents of the altar I had profaned. Sykes stopped at my side and we stood squinting in the lantern light, straining to identify the peculiar items spread at our feet.

"What the—?" Sykes adjusted his specs and peered forward

Sprinkled amidst the menagerie of charms and assorted trinkets were things cruder, more unsettling. Small animal carcasses and mummified body parts interspersed the items along with a withered fetus, a skull bowl and what appeared to be a freshly cut human ear.

For a hefty fee, we had learned how to articulate Calvin's TULIP and trace eschatological timelines. Yet in the presence of this witchery, textbook theology seemed impotent. A sickening realization of utter helplessness yanked my stomach into a freefall.

"Uh oh." Jax stepped out of the van, shorn of humor, and motioned toward the village. "Now you dunnit."

We turned to see figures of disparate shapes advancing from the village. Jax joined us and we huddled, breath notched in our throats, gaping at the approaching forms. The arrogance and reckless presumption that had fueled our quest evaporated as the silent shadowy crowd shuffled toward us. If we had a plan of attack, it went unuttered and, most assuredly, would have proven futile.

Sykes cleared his throat, stepped forward, and called out what we all felt but dared not speak. "We need help! *Ayuda. Necesitamos ayuda.* Can you help us?"

Moths pattered against the headlights, the beams of which stretched along flat earth and scrub, and forced the landscape into immense obtuse shadows. Yet there was no response from the villagers. They came to a stop, one by one, just outside the fringe of lamplight and stood motionless.

Jax leaned into me and whispered, "They're pissed." He reeked of alcohol. Then to Sykes, "Tell 'em we're sorry 'bout—"

I nudged him with my elbow while remaining fixated on the welcoming committee.

The light was enough to make out an elderly woman at the forefront, skin stitched with wrinkles, hunched over a walking stick. She hobbled forward and stopped under the oval swath of light. One need not ask for an exposition of her tale; sorrow etched her features. Tightly drawn lips and unwavering gray eyes testified to a sadness graven into her being, a weight that no word or act of kindness could ease. She muttered something in Spanish, a brief, incoherent string of words that Sykes strained to interpret, then she drew her shawl over her shoulder and gazed longingly at us.

As Sykes shook his head in incomprehension, a boy stepped out of the gloom. He had fair skin, gentle features, and a withered arm. He said in broken English, "We are the faithless, those who bear their sin."

The little dog circled the duo before sitting at the woman's side. She spoke again, this time with added urgency, and then shuffled forward and used her stick to scratch a line in the gravel, a barrier that now stretched between them and us. As she settled back, the boy interpreted. "The magic, it cannot enter here—only the unbelieving. Do you seek entry?"

We exchanged puzzled glances. Then Sykes turned and spoke directly to the boy. "Our friend is sick. *Enfermo*." He motioned to his stomach and mimed pain. "Very sick. *Sí. Entrada*. We seek entry."

The boy peered skeptically before responding. "There is no healing here, only the *bearing*. We are the faithless."

As we pondered his words, a figure emerged from the darkness behind us and stumbled through our headlights, slashing the beams and roiling dust into a gritty fogbank. It stood swaying, silhouetted inside the shimmering cloud.

The woman staggered back, gripping a fistful of her shawl.

Having extricated his bedraggled frame from the van, Casey sloughed toward us and slurred the word, "Water," before collapsing in front of the vehicle.

The old woman began chattering, a monotone incantation that rose into a warble, as Sykes rushed to Casey and huddled over him. The shadowy crowd of onlookers remained motionless, silent witnesses of our unfolding plight. I quickly joined Sykes and knelt beside him.

Casey's flesh had turned cool and taken on a rancid grey appearance. As I felt for a pulse in his carotid artery, I saw his tongue lying swollen between flaccid lips. Sykes leaned over him, then looked up and said, "His breathing's real shallow. This is...crazy."

Lurching to his feet, Sykes ran his fingers through his hair, and then pleaded with the villagers. "He's sick! D'ya hear? My God, this is serious!" An uncharacteristic panic laced his words, which only served to drag me further into the chasm of despair. Then Sykes flung his hands in astonishment and turned me. "Who are these people?"

The boy pointed the nub of his malformed arm at Casey and said dispassionately, "He must endure the evil. It is the way of healing."

"Endure the—?" Sykes gaped at the boy, varieties of rage sweeping over his features like a desert thunderstorm, threatening to explode. "What're you talking about?"

"It is the way of healing," said the boy. "The *bearing*. We can witness. We cannot help."

"Ya mean, you *won't* help." Jax glared at the resolute natives.

"You seek the *mundunugu*—the white one." The boy stared up the road, into the hills, and we followed his gaze. "Infierno. It is her dwelling, the place of magic."

A jagged black ridgeline loomed before us, marking the closure of the canyon, the end of the road. A single beacon winked in the foothills like a portal in a starless firmament, beckoning us onward.

"C'mon." Sykes motioned for assistance. "Let's get him into the van."

"We're not—" I took Casey's other arm, recoiling at the stench of infirmity, and we bore him to the vehicle. "He said he didn't want to go, that she was a witch."

We hoisted him on to the seat and his body lolled into the vinyl. Sykes shook his head, then looked at me and said, "It'll take us two, three hours just to get back to the main highway. And from there—?" He shrugged. "We don't have a choice." He put his hand on my shoulder, then summoned Jax and jogged around the van to the driver's seat.

We don't have a choice. Is that what it had come to? What started as a game of chance, a haphazard investigation into thaumaturgy and heathen hoodoo had become shipwrecked on the shores of predestination. The inevitability of a collision with forces much bigger than us loomed, like the dead end canyon, on every side.

I rummaged through the gear in the back of the van and retrieved a bottle of water from the ice chest. For fear of choking Casey, I poured single capfuls onto his lips, which he lapped at before becoming unresponsive. I looked nervously at Sykes, but he gazed up into the canyon towards Infierno.

Jax remained brooding at the villagers who stood huddled under the glow of the lantern in silent obstinacy. He mumbled something, and then staggered toward the shrine, apparently unconcerned about trampling the offerings. Rearing back, he spat in the face of the pagan deity. It returned the favor, sputtering hot wax in reply. For a moment, they squared off, man against myth, flesh against spirit. But in this battle, I feared we were outmatched. Jax cast a final sneer at the villagers, and then wove his way to the van. He crawled into the passenger side, yanked the tequila bottle from under the seat and said, "To hell it is."

IT HAD BEEN our destination all along. But instead of juvenile curiosity, necessity drove us forward and fate sat shotgun. Somewhere up ahead the *mundunugu*, the white one, waited, speaking forth legs with eyes in them and drawing the haughty by the cords of their own mischief. Now we were the ones being studied.

As the road climbed, it turned to hard clay and ragged clumps of brush encroached upon our path and clawed the vehicle. The high beams announced our approach, through rut and gulley, into the dead-end canyon. God only knew when the last civilized folk had ventured this far. Casey's breathing remained shallow and he passed from catatonia to a restless lethargy. I leaned over him with my hand on his shoulder in silent prayer. But the image of the young boy, his withered arm aimed at Casey, haunted me. *He must endure the evil.* Yeah, musn't we all.

Dust and insect residue had smattered the windshield with an opaque film. Jax leaned out the passenger side window and slurred occasional warnings about approaching logs or boulders. An herbal pungency clung to my clothing, reminder of the pagan totem, and mixed with a smell of burning debris that had tainted the night air and grown increasingly acrid.

The single light of the village dropped in and out of view, swallowed by ominous mounds of rock and cacti, growing brighter with our successive rise and fall.

I continued my mental skirmish with the boy from the village; his withered arm blazed in my brain like a gavel of condemnation, banishing us into the bleak expanse. Sykes watched me in the rearview mirror, his bloodshot eyes chiseled with uncertainty, but left me to my tortured supplication.

Finally, we surmounted a ridge and the village opened before us. It sat in the wedge of the canyon, a sheer cliff with a district of caves bored into its face. Pockets of fire and smoldering rubbish burned in a crater at the base of this rocky terrace, a derelict landfill in the middle of nowhere. Its orange glow lapped at the surrounding precipice, washing the confines in an eerie toxic haze. Several car chassis lay overturned, rusted and blanched by the sun, and tumbleweeds and trash clung to the crevices like muddy snow at spring's thaw. We had reached the end of the road.

"It's a flippin' dump." I sat enthralled at the vaporous pit.

Sykes maneuvered the van upwind of the smoky gulch and turned off the ignition. "Either that or a nuclear test site."

The engine had been running non-stop and, without its sturdy hum, the stillness rushed into the vacuum. The motor cooled to metallic pings as we sat taut, surveying the village of Infierno.

Unlike the last stop, there was no welcoming committee, no dark horde lumbering out to greet us. Were they unaware of our arrival, or simply unconcerned? Even worse, were they lurking in the shadows preparing to swarm our vehicle and incorporate us into their next pagan ritual?

Jax gazed absently out his window, his head bobbing without rhythm on some invisible ocean of tequila. Sykes looked at him, then slung his arm over the seat and lowered his voice. "How's Casey?" He studied the shadowy form sprawled on the seat next to me.

"He drank a little water."

"Good. Maybe he was just dehydrated."

"Yeah. Maybe."

Something screeched outside the window and passed overhead—an owl most likely, making its final rounds before dawn. Sykes cocked his head toward the sound and then said, "It's late."

I nodded and we sat there, studying the field of embers and the hazy glow it cast across the sandstone coliseum. Finally, I asked, "So whaddya we do now?"

But Sykes had turned around and slouched into his seat.

His observation about the hour seemed to awaken a biological urgency, for a sense of great fatigue swept over me and I leaned into the side window with a sigh.

My eyelids fell, impenetrable shutters, and behind them burst grey corpuscles in abstraction. The faint crackle of the fires became a surreal metronome, tick, tick, ticking in my head, drawing me into a subconscious netherworld of night things and latent fears. Those two worlds merged as if the illusion was not in their union, but in the waking separation...

...and there, Lilith waited for me, stealth and catlike, the toxic dump her lair. It seemed she'd been here all along, on the periphery of consciousness, gorging herself on the souls of men and shitting out their remains; nails and nerves and gristle flushed into the draught of society, bleached of life, of hope, by the she-thing. Were we anything but the waste of her machinations? As I gazed upon the feeding, her mouth grew, a gaping unhinged orifice, belching stench and threatening to swallow all that looked upon it. Yet I watched.

Sheol and Abaddon are never full, or so said the Poet. *And the eyes of man are never satisfied.* Was our appetite any different from hers? Insatiable. Ruinous. Drawing us ever further into the hinterland of delinquency. Yet I watched. And just when I should fall into the pit of my own making, she looked upon me, re-composed, and again became the seductress. Lilith—eyes without end, exile of heaven. She swaggered to me, proud feline that she is, and began to speak. But instead of words...

...she barked—a distant, guttural yapping that was so discordant from the vision, it compelled me to cry out.

I started from the nightmare with an infantile yelp.

Cool. Damp. Lightless.

Where was I? How long had I been dreaming? Unable to gauge my surroundings, I began fumbling about until I recognized the interior of the van. Sykes jerked to attention in the front seat and spun about at the sound of my panic. But I was staring at the empty seat next to me and the open van door.

Somewhere up ahead, a dog barked—sounding altogether like Lilith's nightmarish voice—and its frenzy battered the canyon walls.

"Casey!" I cried, scrambling to exit.

Jax groaned, intoxicated into immobility. As I stumbled out of the van, his head lolled toward me and he surrendered a glazed lethargic stare, but he did not attempt to rise. Meanwhile, Sykes had jumped out of the vehicle and stood with his hand on the door, gazing toward the sound of the rabid animal. As I started forward, he said, "Wait!" Then he reached inside and turned the headlights on.

The sandstone amphitheater lay awash in the bleak glare giving me a better, if not more unnerving view. Hovels and holes of various sizes dotted the canyon wall like buckshot. Within them, forms slouched and myriads of glistening eyes shrunk from the obnoxious light. Perhaps 80, 90 yards away, in the furthest corner of the canyon, rose a crevice, a massive rip in the wall of rock. A thin trail of blue smoke meandered upward from the chasm and filtered through the branches of an arthritic grey mesquite tree that stood sentry. In the mouth of the cave was a tall figure, gaunt and spectral, clothed in white. Before it, standing bent and unsteady, was our friend.

"Casey!" My cry ricocheted off the surrounding precipice.

As the sound erupted, the dog barked even more frantically and the ghostly giant drew Casey into the cave.

Without a word, I bolted after him.

Overhead, a frail turquoise luminescence rimmed the canyon, and in it shone the morning star, heralding the coming dawn. We had survived the night only to be summoned into further dark. Sykes called after me, his footsteps pounding the earth as he followed. The headlights splashed our flailing images against the cliff face like massive shadow puppets in a dance of death.

I stopped at the entrance and Sykes pulled up next to me. We stood panting, dwarfed before the archway, and only then realized how tall the robed figure must have been. The cave of *Polyphemus*, Homer's mythic cyclops, sprung to mind. That the one-eyed monster would huddle below dining upon succulent human flesh only enkindled the discomfiting memory.

We stood peering into the chasm, frozen by dread and apprehension.

"It's a trap!" Sykes hunched with his hands on his thighs, gulping air.

I looked sideways at him, puzzling at his observation, and then gazed into the shaft.

The entry sloped gradually, twenty perhaps thirty feet, before opening into a chamber. A pale glow, its source unrecognizable, thrummed the smooth walls of this subterranean room. There was no sign of movement.

"A trap?" I was shaking my head in bewilderment. "Well what're we—? We can't just leave him." Then I leaned into the tunnel and bellowed, "Casey!" eliciting a flurry of yapping from the unseen canine.

We stood poised, but again no response came—just threads of smoke coiling through the fingers of the dead mesquite.

Sykes turned to me, his lips drawn in a tight bloodless line, and nodded. "Okay then—" And setting his jaw, he walked defiantly into the chasm.

As he drifted into shadow, I teetered there. *Beware the faithful.* Yet who exactly were the believers here? And would faith be our asset or our undoing? But much like Lilith's cavernous mouth, the archway seemed to draw me toward it. I inhaled deeply, as a diver before a titanic plunge, and flung myself into the throat of the earth.

Immediately a claustrophobic panic uncoiled in me, forcing my breathing into short, irregular gasps. A thick musty smell, like ages of aromatic sediment, clung to the chilly corridor. Root, flower and fire had coalesced into a hallucinogenic ambience and now entangled my senses with its dreary spell. Our footsteps padded the stone as we navigated the descent toward the chamber.

The tunnel narrowed on all sides, which left me wondering how the stilted white specter had managed its entry. Lightless passageways branched off into unseen burrows and crawlspaces. My eyes burned from the stench of incense, but I stayed fixated upon the warmly lit chamber we approached.

When suddenly a shadow unfolded on the opposite wall.

We stopped in our tracks, looked at each other, and then bolted into the subterranean room.

"Shhh!"

I skidded to a stop and turned to face a squat, dark figure, clad in a white gown, which stood guarding the entryway.

"Shhh!" she repeated, glaring at us, a stumpy finger to her lips. Then she motioned to Casey, who lay curled on a stone slab in the center of the room, lifeless.

But for the moment, my intrigue rested upon this woman. Shorter than I, she wore a white habit and dress, looking for all the world like a Sister of Mercy transported into this cyclopean underworld. However, her skin was black and scalene, like that of a great venomous lizard. Sykes stood at my elbow now, equally captivated by the reptile nun. Her eyes softened, and she said, "*El curativo*," with a type of hushed reverence. Then she waddled back to her spot by the chamber entrance.

Only then did I notice the giant, clothed in the same white garb, perched on a ledge nearby with her knees drawn up on either side of her body like an immense crab. Burning on the wall behind her were perhaps a dozen candles in soot-blackened clefts draped with waxen stalactites. A fluted chimney curled its way upward and disappeared in the ceiling above. But the woman's elongated face was not turned toward us; instead, she watched another drama.

For standing over Casey was a girl—a nymph-like figure robed in a silken girdle. She had milky white skin and eyes of captivating innocence that fixated me with a most unsettling gaze.

My first reaction was one of embarrassment, as if we'd barged into the chamber of a princess. In this reeking wasteland, she seemed so completely out of place that I stood gaping, unable to comprehend what I was seeing or how to respond. She possessed an elegance, an aura of life that shone in her features. Her eyes glistened like dark rubies against her alabaster flesh, and she watched us with wonderment, the edges of her lips curled in a faint, inquisitive smile. Had I ever encountered someone so brimming with mirth?

Yet even though I stood enthralled by the elvin youth, I sensed something ancient, almost inhuman, dwelt there. She was far too young to be the healer—the Polaroids were said to be twelve or thirteen years old, and she couldn't have been much older than that. Yet her eyes possessed an ageless quality, as if her winsomeness was the result of some profound detachment that left her altogether untouched by humanity. Perhaps we had stumbled upon some primordial intelligence, a superior race that had survived solar flares and ice ages. Or was this cherub even of terrestrial origin?

Casey moaned, and the sound shocked me into the present. For a moment, I feared he would vomit on the sprite, splatter the place with his malady. I winced at the thought. Instead, he groaned and attempted to rise before slumping back onto the table.

At this, the girl cocked her head, and without the faintest movement from her lips said, "El curativo?"

The words seemed to emanate from the air, muffled, guttural, entirely unlike the frail white child. Was she speaking telepathically? Or had someone else, a troll or cave creature, uttered the words?

Her gaze bore down on me, as if warranting a response. *El curativo?* Yeah, right. *The healing.* That's what we'd come for; that's why we packed the bags and followed a screwy old map to some landfill in the asshole of the world. We were here to witness the healing, to examine the one who spoke limbs to life, to invalidate her sorceries. Yes, it was *el curativo* that we sought.

As I was about to answer in the affirmative, shuffling footfall awakened me from my stupefaction and I spun around to see Jax at the entrance of the chamber, swaying and blinking in befuddlement, grasping the empty bottle of tequila. He steadied himself, squinted, and pointed across the chamber, slurring inaudible words.

"Good God!" Sykes followed Jax's gaze and stood gaping.

Only then did I notice row upon row of bunks carved into the chamber walls, narrow cells wherein dark forms huddled, slithering, sniffling, and watching us with jaundiced eyes.

The healer acknowledged our shock with a slight nod. Then she placed her balled fist over Casey's stomach.

The same muffled, throaty voice said, "Do you believe?"

Believe? Someone coughed in one of the bunks and I saw an appendage, something winged and spindly, pass through the shadow. *Believe in what?* Just when I should ask, she opened her hand and extended it over Casey. But in her palm, I glimpsed something that sucked the air out of my lungs. It was an orifice, a fleshy cavity lined with serrated teeth that moved in utterance as it settled upon Casey's body.

Guárdese de fiel, the note had read. *Beware the faithful.*

"No!" I lunged toward the altar. "We do *not* believe! The faithless! We are the *faithless!*"

At this, the crab woman stepped off the ledge and in three loping strides towered over me, her lean face pinched into an icy glare. Underneath her gown, something roiled, a bulbous growth clamoring for exit.

Sykes pushed between us on his way to Casey and hoisted him off the slab. The white one withdrew her alien hand, its mouth now frothing in garbled expletives, and she watched us with a bemused puzzlement.

"C'mon!" Sykes wrestled Casey onto his shoulders, unconcerned, perhaps oblivious, to the second nun's lumbering approach. "We're outta here!" He lunged back toward the tunnel.

As I followed Sykes into the passageway, a rustling sound filled the chamber behind us. I barked at Jax to flee, but he was drooling, frozen with dread. I dare not turn to witness the object of his horror.

Daylight framed the entrance of the cave in predawn gloom. We spilled out of the tunnel and fell into a gasping heap under the decrepit tree, a sulfurous grey sky dropping soot, and a distant horizon now rimmed with fiery gold. Casey lay moaning, mumbling in Latin again, as Sykes struggled to lift him. However, I rose slowly, because a large shadow stood between the van and us. Seeing my paralysis, Sykes turned.

The watchman had extinguished his lantern, and sat motionless on his mule. As we looked upon him, he tilted his head in our general direction. "*Purgatorio,*" he said, motioning back down the road from whence we'd come. "*La aldea detrás allí.*"

I looked to Sykes, but his eyes were vacant, as if the watchman's words had rendered him mute, torn something vital from his marrow. Suddenly, he heaved Casey from the ground and plummeted forward with a maniacal burst of strength.

"What—?" I scrambled past the watchman and caught up with Sykes. "What'd he say?"

"Purgatory!" he panted. "The last village. It was purgatory!" Then he stopped and stared wild-eyed into the heavens. "We passed up purgatory for hell!"

As if on cue, we both looked behind us.

Out of the crevice, hobbling and limping, dragging tumors and tails and organs aplenty, poured the believers. Jax was scattered amongst them, assimilated into their company. The canyon walls yielded up their occupants, pitiful parasitic grubs tumbling to earth, and together the offspring slouched toward us, wave upon wave, stitched with nonsensical body parts and swollen bowels, hauling the baggage of their own belief.

We had been warned. *Only those who believe can survive hell*. But there, believing was its own hell.

Then they fell upon us, the gnawing, hungry horde, but we did not relent. Our resolve did not waver. So there we remained, in parts, the faithless.

TIM'S HOLY HAMBURGERS

BRIAN JOHNSON

After leaving Denver, Thompson, Utah was where my money ran out. There wasn't much there: a local theater, a Shop-and-Go, a Ma and Pa grocery, three churches of various denomination, and a burger joint. Most of the burger joint's business came from a community college up the road and from the highway. It was one of the only places to eat on I-70 for 50 miles in either direction.

When my luck ran out five years ago, I took up washing dishes for Jack Boejay, A.K.A. old Geezer Brown. An old country boy in his sixties who didn't care to wash his hair or beard much; and working in the joint with the grease had long since turned it honey brown.

Jack up and died from a "massive coronary accident" about 3 years after I came here, or so the hospital's doctor told me. I could have and should have moved on after that, but I had made a few friends in this town.

Jack was a stern boss, but he gave me decent money for what I did. He let me live in his basement, and pushed me to get my Associate's Degree from the community college. He wanted help with the bookkeeping and his other business ventures.

When he died, I helped an older sister go though his stuff. I had enough to bail, and for that matter go back to school, but his sister found his will.

It was a folded napkin that read:

Hello Tim-

If you're reading this I guess I've gone to meet my maker. Either that or I'm going to kick your ass for going through my stuff when I find out. If I'm dead please continue... This is my last Will and Testament decreed on this date April 17, 1998. I hereby leave all of my estate and worldly possession's to Tim Struthers. He has been a constant companion and friend of mine for two years, and by the time this is read, if he is still around all my stuff is his.

Jack's signature glowered at the bottom of the napkin with the notary signed by the bank's president in Crescent Junction, where Jack kept the business account.

His sister took what she wanted and the bank's president, Steve Harper, helped me switch the account over without paying inheritance tax, which seemed the stupidest tax in the book, especially since the lost money would've closed the burger joint.

One month after Jack's death, I reopened under the name "Tim's World Famous Food".

I kept ole' Geezer Brown's memory alive by hanging his last picture above the deep fat fryer.

After selling one of Jack's rental houses, I bought a couple large neon signs and deposited them on the highway. The house went to Mrs. Mary Glasgow and her fifteen-year-old son, Randy. Randy was retarded and Mrs. Glasgow worked next to the bank at the community hospital in Crescent Junction.

So, one day she walks in to the restaurant with Randy, gives me a twenty and says feed him whatever he wants, if he gets rowdy send him home. Before I staggered a reply, she's gone. Randy didn't do much that day, he just sat staring out the window, rocking back and forth. Business was slow, so I tried some conversation. Even setting across from him, he wouldn't acknowledge me.

I threw a burger, milkshake, and fries together and set it down before him. No response.

I pulled out the accounting and started running figures. I have a bad habit of saying numbers when trying to calculate them, something that got me expelled from the first test in college algebra. As I worked up the profit and loss margins, I noticed Randy calling out numbers. I didn't think much of it until I wrote down what he called out. The kid ran numbers faster than my adding machine. I tested him the rest of that afternoon, and he didn't miss once.

His mother came to retrieve him as the supper crowd was geared up.

"Your son's got a way with numbers, Mrs. Glasgow." I yelled as she tried to leave.

"I'm so sorry Tim, I got called to work at the last minute and didn't have anyone to watch Randy. I didn't mean to put you on the spot like that." She replied, "Here, take another twenty, I figured he would've walked home earlier. He can take care of himself, I just hate him being alone all day."

"What's with the numbers though?" I asked.

"Randy's autistic, and sometimes numbers are really easy for him."

"Listen, if you're afraid of leaving him alone, just leave him here," It's one of the nicest things I've done but the kid intrigued me. Later that night I looked up his "condition" in my old "Abnormal Psychology" textbook. It talked about having a strong dissociation with the world around you and every one in 100 have some extraordinary ability in Math, Art, or Linguistics. The top one percent hung out in my burger joint.

Mrs. Glasgow took advantage of my offer. Randy came in on Tuesdays and Wednesdays, I usually saved my accounting for those days. Other days, he drifted around town.

On Sunday I'd run 40 miles West to get the week's supplies while the joint was closed. Randy'd stand by the highway rocking back and forth like he waited for the starting gun to go off.

One Sunday I found him waiting in front of the joint. It wasn't a good day for me. On the drive west I noticed the framed embodiment of a new fast food restaurant going up.

"Pray for a Taco Bell," I thought.

The truck shuttered to a stop next to the joint, Randy stood there oblivious to me or anything else as trucks kicked dust up in his face as they drove by.

"It's a bad day Randy. Go home."

He rocked, watching straight ahead.

"GO HOME," I screamed into his face. No reaction.

The keys clanged against the door and the lock turned heavy. As I unloaded the last of the groceries Randy somehow slipped inside.

"Randy, I planed on doing busy work today, not playing babysitter. The grease on the walls and glass are chasing customers out. If you stay, you clean."

I threw him an old rag and a bottle of grease cutter. With my luck, he'd drink it.

I went to the back and packed hamburger patties, marking dates on their containers; when I heard a loud thud out in the restaurant.

I found Randy on the floor with the rag and cleaning solution in hand. He'd ran into the glass front door, leaving an imprint on the grime that covered it.

"Randy, are you okay?" I walked up to him as he sat rocking Indian style looking at his imprint on the door. Hell, he looked okay.

I picked up the cleaning solution and sprayed the door. His image slowly ran as I started to wipe it off.

"Noooo," he screamed and pushed me aside.

"What is wrong with you kid?" It seemed useless, he stared at the gunk sliding down the door.

"You need me, I'll be in back." I had enough of this. Any more annoyance, and he was back out on the highway.

I shook my head and went back to work. An hour or so went by, I looked out front a few times to see him clean the front window. With the grease and grim built up on it, I could see it taking some time.

I rearranged the fridge and cleaned up.

"Get ready to go kid, I'm on my way out." I took an extra malt out of the fridge for him, feeling bad about screaming earlier.

"Alright, get up Randy." Once again, he sat cross-legged staring at the door. The door looked clean except for some greasy stuff that probably wouldn't come out.

"Let's go, buddy," I could hear him mumbling something as he rocked back and forth.

"Jeessos, Jeessos, Jeessos," he repeated softly.

"What about it?" I asked staring at the door. The answer stared right back at me.

A large rig kicked up dust as I opened the door. The dust settled onto the grease giving the image contrast.

I let the door shut and looked at Randy through the door's image.

I could make out what he mumbled.

"Jesus."

The glass door of "Tim's World Famous Food" beheld the graven image of Jesus Christ straight from the "Shroud of Turin".

Religion spooked me as a child growing up a strict Roman Catholic. Graven images of Christ were one thing I knew.

"Go home Randy, go home!" I opened the door and grabbed him. Randy stood outside with a puzzled look but I had to get someone to see this.

I drove to the nearest hardware store, 20 miles to the East. Joe Gardner, one of the few people who worked Sunday in a Mormon ran community, owned it.

"Joe, you got to come see this, I've never seen anything like it myself!"

I grabbed a roll of tinted foil from the shelf and some instant film.

"You look like a man possessed, Tim. What's up? Did aliens come looking for a burger?"

"Close the store and come with me, you got to see it. Come on, man. You never see anyone on Sundays anyway."

I ran and started the truck up like a kid going to his first kegger. Joe strolled after locking up the store to start our pilgrimage.

For the next twenty minutes Joe listened to me ramble with this half-believable, half-you-gotta-be-drunk look on his face. As we neared the restaurant, the Sheriff and three other cars pulled up to the building. Randy stood in the middle of the group pointing to the image with a rare smile plastered across his face.

After I left, Randy ran into the church. With Sunday evening service in full gear, he knocked over the holy water as he stumbled into the sanctuary. The congregation thought he'd seen a ghost, and it was close to the truth.

The priest helped Randy up and got pulled from the church to the burger stand. I heard the priest kept adjusting his glasses while looking at the door. When he figured out what it was, he called the Sheriff and the other churches, telling them to come as soon as possible because "A miracle occurred".

That night "Tim's World Famous Food" opened for its first Sunday night business.

Baptist, Mormon, and Catholic all stood together staring at a strange religious icon stuck to the glass of a burger joint.

I ran through a week and a half of groceries in one night. Joe and Steve (the Bank President) flipped burgers and cut fries till one in the morning. Old man Tillman, who owned the Ma and Pa Grocery, helped me restock and even ran to the next town to get what he didn't have.

It's amazing how miracles and disasters can bring a town together.

Mrs. Glasgow showed up crying as we started cleaning. I couldn't tell if it was the shock was from seeing the image in the window, or hearing her autistic son say "Jesus" and point at the door, but together we cleaned and closed at two.

I moved everyone outside and closed up the register. Finishing up I heard soft singing. There were over twenty people holding candles, singing, praying, chanting, and every other type of religious communion known to man. I knew right then that the next few weeks were going to be very busy.

The next morning the crowd grew. News trucks from local stations, Denver, and Salt Lake City showed up. I had to fight to get through the door.

"I'm the goddamned owner, let me through." The sound-bite played for the nightly news across the nation.

Business was great. I tried to take orders, talk to the press, people, religious leaders, and whoever else came in. But by two, I had ripped the phone out of the wall thanks to all the reporters that called.

The sheriff finally showed up and forced a little order as people trying to get into the restaurant fought with people outside as they opened the door.

"Tim, I think it's probably in the best interest if you shut down for a couple days." I had already made enough money in two days to cover two weeks of business, but I decided to close up the front and let people come to the back for orders. That evening, I ran through all of the groceries and decided to give up. The reporters tried to get through the back door for an exclusive profile of the owner of this building. The deputies took them back up front. I just didn't have time for this. I did a few interviews and said the image hid underneath a lot of grease and dirt for who-knew-how many years. As I gave the interviews, I thought of ole Geezer Brown's picture up above the fryers. I wished he was here to help me with this, his answer to the problem would be to "properly clean that damn window".

The crowds of the day forced me to the highway that night. I wanted to just get away and drive. As I left the restaurant, I watched Randy across the highway staring at the door as if the highway held him back. It wasn't, it was all the people.

I drove and listened to the radio. The radio found an AM station out of one of the unidentified local transmitters that hosted a paranormal talk show.

"Icons and the weird places they dwell. We have a call from Thompson, Utah.

"Caller...please turn down your radio."

The caller went into some really heavy talk about the body of Jesus, as another caller screamed about the apocalyptical significance of the shroud. Someone even called about the appearance of strange lights in the sky in the area, and a government cover-up."

After driving for three hours, I went back to the restaurant, cleaned out the fryers and fridge, and posted a "Closed until further notice" sign. I then headed to meet the Sheriff.

"Buddy, not only should I close down for a couple of days, I'm getting the hell out of town." I passed the keys to him as a fight broke out among a couple of people screaming at each other.

I stayed at the Glasgow's that night and thought about going to Salt Lake City the next morning. At sunrise I passed the restaurant. So many people spilled onto the highway that the Sheriff's office closed half a mile of interstate. The sheriff frantically attempted to get some control with a small perimeter set up around the building. Most of the locals stayed away from this native miracle, and from the crowd gathered I could see why.

The true believers had shown up in their full garb. Billboards proclaiming the current point of view on evolution, abortion, and the sport fans favorite "John 3:16". From the vantage point I had more than 5 blocks away, I heard screaming to make some point over a loud speaker. I watched until the early afternoon when more police arrived from the neighboring counties.

It was getting far too crazy and I needed that vacation. I made it to Provo, Utah when the news came on the radio.

"Holy Hamburger Shrine's owner has criminal past."

I slammed on the brakes making a family of six tailgating me fly past. I watched a five year old in the back flip me off as they drove past. Someone had checked up on me and found the trail of trash I left in Denver.

Finding an open Four Seasons hotel, I checked in and headed straight for the bar. The bartender glanced up from the waitress and started giving me the hairy eyeball. To make it easy for them all I sat at the bar.

I hadn't watched professional basketball since the strike, but it was the only thing available to fall into. The game ended and I had almost finished the bottle of bourbon that sat just out of reach. The news came on as the bartender decided to make some small talk.

"So whacha doin in Provo?"

"The same thing I did a few years ago in Thompson."

"Isn't that the place they found Jesus?" he sneered.

"Yeah. Somewhat."

The news was coming on and I wanted to lay down and cry. The first story was, of course, me. The bartender watched the screen as it flashed an old faded picture of me from Denver. It was the Christmas before I left, taken at my parent's house. My long beard and haggard looks reminded me about how hard things were. A few buddies of mine had dragged me into stealing credit cards and some other information type crimes. We were spending money left and right and living like life didn't matter. Someone caught up to us; two of the people in the ring were caught at Dillard's trying to buy a big screen for Superbowl. Trick of the trade, when you do something illegal, keep it small or you'll get caught. They were arrested, prosecuted and spent some time in jail.

The rest of us knew it was only a matter of time. The night before I left, I set fire to all the documents, credit cards, loan slips, and any piece of incriminating evidence found. At sunup I left Denver and went as far as Thompson before realizing I had nothing left. Hell, if not for old Geezer Brown . . .

"That guy in the picture looks kind of like ya."

"There's a reason." I looked at the bartender and slipped a hundred on the bar. "Now hand me that fifth of bourbon you've been skimping me on ...and act like you have no idea who I am."

It was a stupid move, by the time I was looking for the little blue man at the bottom of the bottle, two of Provo's finest were asking me questions.

There was an outstanding warrant for my arrest and the bartender kept my change.

Two hours later in the confines of the local police station while waiting for word from the Colorado District Attorney, the second chapter of my life came to a close.

The police captain pulled me from the cell and sat me down in the visitor's area. No one came to visit me, he just wanted to see the expression on my face.

CNN had live coverage of the riot that broke out a few hours before. The crown had grown steadily out of control, and when news broke of my past, they rioted. While I drowned in a bottle of bourbon, 33 people were injured, 4 seriously, as police from 3 counties, the sheriff, and as many deputies as he could find attempted to move the devout off my land. Today's sound-bite came from a woman in her mid to late forties, toothless, and 300 lbs. overweight screaming "charlatan" at the top of her lungs, while being arrested by the police. God bless the Press. But that wasn't the worst of it. The next scene was replayed on the nightly news across the nation for the next three days.

Apparently Ms. Charlatan's husband had a history of mental problems, and more than one occasion believed that God had spoken directly to him. Usually telling him to burn something.

I remember seeing the leer from this guy by the second day of our little miracle. He headed a local backwoods militia and born again Christian army, even had a show that aired on the local UHF station. One sleepless night I came across it, he stood in front of a shaded map of America screaming, "Are you going to wait for the Apocalypse, or are you training to slam Satan's disciples!"

As his wife was being pulled away for attacking a cop, he took his barely running 1962 Ford truck and with some 100 pounds of TNT in the back, ran it into the restaurant. The TNT was triggered on impact. Mr. Christian Soldier, a sheriff's deputy, and Tim's World Famous Food were gone in a fiery instant.

After watching the footage for the 16th time, left alone with my thoughts in the visitor's area of the police department, I broke down and cried like a little girl.

Someone had pity on me. Apparently Colorado has a statute of limitations on the charges that were filed against me. I had passed it by 1 month,

4 days, 11 hours, and 21 minutes. I was released on my own recognizance, and told to go home and clean up my mess. I grabbed my stuff from the hotel and threw my key at the night desk clerk as I walked by.

I drove back to Thompson with the radio off. Four hours of near silence with the road flying by can make a man think about his situation. The old familiar neon sign called out a few miles in the dusk "Tim's World Famous Food", and after passing it, I came to the smoldering restaurant.

A few news crews were doing reports in the area, and the familiars of the community stood around talking like it was the town fair. I stopped the truck down the street and walked to the fire-chief.

"Total loss for you son," he said as the smoke wafted into my eyes. I tried to blame the smoke for the tears spilling down my face. Mrs. Glasgow knew better and led me away. We drove by my house and found a few reporters waiting in front. I ducked under as she drove by, waving.

"Well looks like you're staying at my house. Hell, I'm going to start charging you rent."

"Mary, I think it's time for me to leave."

"Are the stories true, Tim?"

"I had a bad past Mary, no crap. Ole' Geezer Brown brought me up all over again, and re-taught me how to live. He forced me into school, taught me to make an honest living. For a while, I'd completely pushed out my past life, and it took a miracle to bring it back."

All night I tossed and turned. Even through it was a decent pull-out couch in a basement, I just can't sleep in someone else's bed, plus I had too much on my mind.

I heard the front door of the house slam at 2:00am. I got up and looked outside. Randy sat there staring up at the moon. By the time I got back to bed, I decided to sleep for about 2 hours then go home and pack.

When I got up, Randy was gone. I figured he went back to bed. I snuck out to the truck and let it roll down the driveway before starting it.

One thing I like about this time of morning, no one is up or on the streets. The newsmen must have given up on me coming home, since no one was waiting when I reached the house. I looked around and couldn't find any damage, thank God. I knew the people of this town were good folk but the outsiders worried me, and I was in the phone book.

Gathering what I wanted took less than 30 minutes. I was once and still the king of quick escapes. Someday I might even come back.

With my things tucked into the truck, I took my leave of Thompson. I always go west when I get into trouble. Fifteen minutes down the road there was the new fast food restaurant. What had been a skeletal building a few days before looked ready to open tomorrow. Randy sat on the cement step leading to the building, I wanted to drive by and just go, but I felt the need to say good-bye. Randy barely looked up as I pulled in.

"Embers aren't even cold on the restaurant and you've found a new hangout."

I don't know what's in the mind of an autistic child, but a kid that adds numbers faster than a calculator can tell when a friend's leaving.

"I've never been great at good-byes, squirt. That's why I usually leave in the middle of the night. But you've been a pain in the ass and I'll miss you for about the first 100 miles. Tell your mom thanks." I wanted to go and was just about to my truck when I heard him say my name.

"Tim, no, Tim." It was soft enough to be lost out there on the highway, but it turned me around.

Randy looked at the glass door in front of him, ran into it at full speed, and bounced off.

"Randy, I can't go back." I looked for a phone to call his mom, but there wasn't one installed here yet.

"Tim, no, Tim." Randy walked back up to the door and smeared his face across it.

He moved across the glass as if he was attempting to paint.

I though he was trying to hurt himself when an image began to appear on the door. I grabbed a rag out of the truck and handed it to him. He used it to smooth over the grease and dirt.

He worked for an hour before the first rays of light came across the Utah desert. As the sun struck the door it became apparent that the town, news, and religious factions had fallen to the artistic abilities of a fifteen year old autistic boy. I stood there and laughed myself hoarse.

Randy regained himself and walked to the door about to wipe off the image.

"Randy, let them deal with it. Come on boy, I'm taking you home."

The town of Thompson, Provo, and even Salt Lake City had reports that year of Jesus popping up in the strangest locations. I just always made sure I had an alibi before they showed. Usually it was, "I was with the autistic boy. Couldn't have been me."

I stayed there for about three more years; I tried a couple of businesses on the side with help from the locals, but nothing really took off. Even had some visits from old friends from Denver. I was sure to move their asses though as fast as possible.

Randy and Mary ended up moving to Kansas. The State sponsored a study on autism, and Randy had been specially picked to attend. We keep in touch, but without Randy around I wanted to move. I did think about Kansas, but that's as far as that went. I'm thinking about opening a Baha taco joint down in New Mexico. Hopefully without a religious theme, but we'll have to see how business does.

SCHADENFREUDE

TOM BARLOW

Megan's waiter brought her a jug of the local Huerigen wine, and poured her a glassful. She sipped it slowly, content to wait quietly for her long-estranged aunt, and take in the streetscape of this tiny Austrian town, so different from her home in Arkansas. She adjusted her chair slightly to bring her face into the shade cast by a canopy of grape leaves over the restaurant tables tucked into a narrow courtyard. Not for the first time, she wondered why she had wagered every penny she owned, and the wrath of her family, to seek out a virtual stranger. Except that she was the only relative that had ever successfully broken free of the family, a family whose embrace, for Megan, had become a stranglehold.

A few minutes later, a woman appeared in the entryway, silhouetted against the backdrop of the 17th-century Hainburg town hall across the road.

Although Megan did not remember her aunt, she realized immediately that her mother had been right when she said Megan would recognize her family resemblance. The woman had the Hauser family hips, rounded shoulders, and large head. As soon as her Aunt Rebecca stepped into the ambient lighting of the restaurant, however, those familiarities became caricature.

Megan stood, fighting to maintain her composure, as her aunt approached the table. If this was a family resemblance, Megan thought to herself, she might throw herself in front of the next train.

She had never encountered anyone as ill-featured as her aunt. Rebecca's hair was sparse, with bare patches showing through like moth-eaten holes in a wool sweater. Profound wrinkles scored her face. Her enormous nose twisted to one side and both of her eyes protruded; the left seeped an alarming yellow puss. Her ears were red and scaly and a wen the size of an egg overwhelmed her chin.

Her aunt smiled, liverish lips parting to expose stained teeth set askew in her jaw, and extended her hand in the royal manner, palm down, wrist limp.

"Megan?" Her voice was raspy, breathy.

"Aunt Rebecca?" Megan replied, trying to recapture the enthusiasm she'd felt when first deciding to seek her long-lost aunt, an ocean and a continent away.

As they air-kissed, she caught a whiff of her aunt's personal stench. Megan sat down abruptly and poured herself another glass of wine.

"Wine?" she asked, pulling her aunt's glass toward her.

"Please."

To Megan's relief, her aunt still knew and practiced the protocol of small talk, allowing them to size up one another. They discussed Megan's journey and her aunt's train trip from Vienna, as they both downed glasses of the wine.

"Jesus, that's good." Rebecca slid the glass back to Megan for a refill.

"Mom says hi," Megan said, as she poured.

"I doubt your mother sent you here to say hello. I would imagine she was appalled that you would even consider visiting me. I've had twenty-five years to think about what to say when one of my family finally decided to talk to me again, but I'm still at a loss for words."

Megan's mother had warned her about her sister Rebecca's bluntness. "She didn't have much say in the matter. I paid for the trip myself." Megan tried to keep from sounding too prideful.

"I'm flattered, I think. Or maybe not. Why would you come all this way to see me?"

"Discovering a long lost aunt? Are you kidding? Who could resist?" So much for small talk, Megan thought.

"People disappear for a reason," Rebecca replied. "A lot of people like being lost."

"Mom wouldn't tell me what it was that drove you two apart."

"How old were you when you first learned I existed?"

"Fourteen. I was floored when I saw your name in the family Bible."

"How old are you now?"

"Twenty-four."

"Why are you here? Why now?"

"Why won't anyone talk about you? What happened?" Megan removed her glasses, which caused her aunt's image to blur enough that she could tolerate glancing at her politely from time to time.

The waiter reappeared at their table. Rebecca discussed the menu with him, in German, although, as she explained after he left the table, he was Slovakian. "They've taken all the menial jobs. But they're lazy. What can you expect, though? They grew up as good little communists."

Rebecca ignored Megan's last question, and went back to asking about all the family members that she had known or cared to know, a pause between attacks. She showed little reaction when Megan told her of the ones that were dead, and how they died. They soon fell into an uneasy silence.

"You're probably wondering," Rebecca finally said, waving her fingers at her face as though chasing away a fly.

Megan feigned ignorance.

"Horseshit," Rebecca said. "We share too many genes; you'd have to be an idiot to not be terrified you could end up looking like me."

"Mom said there was a strong family resemblance, but I don't see it."

Rebecca opened her purse, removed a photo, and slid it across the table. Megan put her glasses back on in order to study the picture. In it, her mother stood next to the boar statue Megan recognized as a landmark of old-town Munich.

"That's me," Rebecca said. "Six years ago."

"Oh." Megan paused as the words, my God, went through her mind. "What happened?"

Rebecca waved to the waiter standing at attention by the kitchen door. When he looked her way, she pointed to the jug. He brought a refill and poured them each a glass. Megan noted that he stayed at arm's length from her aunt as he poured.

"I guess you won't open up unless I do. Your mother was always the same way. So, the reason your mother hasn't talked to me in twenty-five years, is that I'm vain and selfish."

"What do you mean?" Megan asked.

"I was a jealous child, especially where your mother was concerned, probably because we were so close in age and appearance; we were occasionally mistaken for twins. Your mother was always more accomplished. She was smarter, and you know about her music. That's where your talent must come from.

"When I was sixteen, a young man took over the milk delivery to our father's store two or three times a week. I worked the counter after school each day. He was an incorrigible flirt, and I became very enamored of him.

"However, it seemed that every time I thought I might have the opportunity to talk to him alone your mother would show up, in her best dress, with a bit of mother's makeup on. I soon became convinced he was smitten with her.

"That afternoon, I lied to him that your mother had taken another girl as her lover. He told several friends, and soon the rumor had spread through the entire town. Back then, people were more small-minded about such things.

"Your mother and I ended up in a huge row, bringing up every hurt, real or imagined, that each of us had suffered at the hand of the other. Among us six children, she had always been the golden child, and after this, she gathered the others tightly to her, forming a pact against me. From then on, I had no peace at home."

"Why didn't your parents step in, stop them?"

"Our father did step in when he learned what I had done. He beat me until I could barely walk. I couldn't go to school for two weeks, until the bruises faded. I suspect he was pleased when I ran away."

"Where did you go?"

"I followed a man to St. Louis, then another man to New York City, and another to Paris. I finally married a gentleman from Vienna, although he left me five years later. By then, I had no other home, so I've been here ever since. Arkansas would seem like a foreign country to me now, I suppose."

The waiter interrupted them to present their meals. Rebecca picked up her fork and knife as if to eat, but stopped her hands above the food. "After Franz divorced me I became even more obsessive about my looks. I tried everything I could think of to recapture my youthful appearance: facials, a lift, stylings, Pilates, even aromatherapy, for Christ's sake."

Megan mechanically cut her veal, her potatoes, and her asparagus into bite sizes, trying to digest what her aunt was saying.

"It was the night of the opening of the Vienna opera season—I remember it perfectly, a wonderful production of *Aida*. We were invited to a friend's apartment on the Ringstrasse for drinks afterward. I was standing by the gas fireplace, looking at myself in the mirror above the mantle. I remember how the light of the fire cast shadows on my face, highlighting all of the wrinkles I thought my foundation had disguised. He walked up behind me, but I didn't know he was there, because his reflection did not appear in the mirror. When he touched my shoulder, for a moment, I wanted to cry."

"How could someone not appear in the mirror?"

Rebecca jabbed a piece of potato and brought it to her mouth, chewed, and swallowed. "Because he was the devil."

"The devil? As in Satan, the devil?"

A half-hour earlier, before Megan had seen her aunt's face, she would have laughed at anyone claiming to have met the devil. Yet now she could not help but consider that her aunt's appearance was supernatural.

"What did he want?"

"He said he wished only to see a sad woman cheered. He said the opera had broken his heart with its tragic beauty, and in response he was of a mind to grant a favor to beauty."

"What did you say?"

"I was drinking a great deal in those days, and that night was no exception. I laughed at him, told him I thought him a silly man, and that if he was in a generous mood perhaps he could return my lost beauty."

"What did he say to that?"

"He said that he would be most pleased to do so, but that, since he was the devil, I had to agree to his devilish terms."

"And?" Megan leaned forward, wine glass in both hands, her food forgotten.

"He said that I must accept a condition; there is always a condition. He said that with every charitable thought I had, or good deed I performed, I would grow more beautiful. With every negative thought or deed, I would grow less beautiful."

"That's all?"

"That is the exact thought that went through my mind; that's all? Even in my drunken state, I saw it as an elaborate joke, although there was no one around to witness it. He was handsome, though, in a very hard sort of way, so I saw no harm in playing along."

"And?"

"He disappeared as soon as I turned my back for a moment to fill my glass. I left the party soon after.

"I hailed a cab for the ride home. I distinctly remember thinking that the driver was another one of the damn Slovakians. When I opened my compact to check my makeup, I saw that I had ruptured a blood vessel under the skin of my nose.

"I passed our new doorman on the way into my apartment building, and I remember thinking that if he didn't start bathing regularly, I was going to ask the manager to have him replaced. When I entered my apartment, I had a new wrinkle across my forehead."

"That must have been frightening."

"I was too drunk to focus on it that night, but the next morning, when I saw myself in the mirror, I remembered everything."

"What did you do?"

The waiter interrupted to ask if there was something wrong with their meals. Megan's aunt said something to the waiter in German: she caught the words 'family' and 'talk'. He smiled and backed away.

"I phoned a friend of mine, the man with whom I most often dished dirt about our friends. I sat before the mirror as we talked, watching myself as I made catty remarks about our mutual acquaintances."

"And?"

"And with each comment, my face and body would change a little. Warts, wrinkles, blisters, boils, wrinkles, age spots, my face changed as we talked. I hung up on my friend after a couple of minutes."

She took a long drink of wine, and then refilled her glass with the last of the jug. She held it by the neck and waved it at the waiter, who promptly replaced it.

"So then I didn't go out of the apartment for days. I wouldn't even talk on the phone. Finally, on Sunday, I went to mass. I sat in the back. I confess, I held a mirror in my hands as I prayed, to see if praying for others would improve my appearance."

"Did it work?"

"No. I found that when I prayed for someone that I didn't really care about—for example, I prayed that our doorman would find a wife who owned a laundry—the prayer had no effect. The only time prayer seemed to help was when I prayed for someone I genuinely cared about, someone that I truly wished good things for. But I quickly realized that there were very few people I cared about."

"Still, you found that it was possible to improve your appearance."

"I thought so at the time. I thought, for a while, that I had discovered the secret to regaining my beauty—I just needed to think charitable thoughts, do good deeds. I volunteered at a homeless shelter, visited sick children in the hospital, organized fundraisers, and took part in prayer vigils. I was a Florence Nightingale, for a time."

"Did you grow more beautiful?"

"No. All I accomplished was to slow the progress of my ugliness. Are you familiar with the word, *schadenfreude*?"

"Pleasure derived from other's misfortunes?"

She nodded. "I found that for every good deed I did, I would inevitably have one or more uncharitable thoughts, often the schadenfreude of watching a haughty woman splashed by a passing cab, or a driver on cell phone clipping the curb with his tire. No matter how hard I tried to stifle my thoughts, they would return to schadenfreude as soon as I lost my focus."

We sat silently for a few moments.

"Go ahead," Rebecca finally said. "I know you don't believe me. Tell me about my sister, the good things that have happened in her life. Watch my face."

Megan responded, slowly, one story at a time. Her mother's marriage, her dad's promotions, the first painting she sold, her sister's gymnastics success. Megan could not see any change in Rebecca's face.

"Now tell me of their misfortunes."

She watched her aunt closely as she said, "My boyfriend left me three months ago after he found out I was pregnant. I had an abortion, the priest found out, and now he won't let me take communion. My father threw me out of the house. Mother said I was white trash, just like her sister Rebecca."

Her aunt's face grew a little more wrinkled, the sores widened.

"Schadenfreude," Rebecca said.

"Is that why mother hates you? For what's in your heart?"

"For a long time I believed the blackness was in her heart, not mine. But lately, I've come back to the belief that our hearts must be as similar as our faces were. Is that what you came to find out? If a malign nature is in your blood? If there is something you can do about it?"

Megan nodded.

"Then you've come a long way for nothing. I tried to run away from it, but I carried the hate with me. I still have it." She pointed to her chest.

"What can I do?" Megan asked, staring at the candle on their table. "What can I do, if it's already too late?"

"I drink," Rebecca said. "I watch happy television. I read nothing but elementary school books about happy boys and girls doing happy things." She spat out the words.

"What about your soul? Did you promise the devil your soul?"

Aunt Rebecca closed her eyes and gripped the edge of the table. "He said I didn't have to. He said I would understand why, soon enough."

"Understand what?"

She opened her eyes. "That my soul was already his. He trusted schadenfreude, he said, more than any promise."

They sat in silence for a while, sipping their wine, staring at the uneaten food. Finally, her aunt asked, "I can see your mother in your face. Do you take after her?"

"That's what I came here to find out," Megan said. "I hope not."

"Perhaps I can help you with that. Tell me what you think of our waiter."

Her aunt studied Megan's face intently as she replied.

BUM DEAL

BARRY W. OZEROFF

I would rather be home with my crying wife, but that cannot be. Instead, I am hugging my knees in a sleeping bag under a makeshift lean-to. I am in the woods in the midst of one of the nicest cities I have ever seen, but I am not alone. Sinister denizens of the dark stir quietly around me; their souls as black as the night, and I am afraid.

You've probably never heard of the Springwater Trail, unless you're from Portland, Oregon. But even if you call this aqualand home, what you probably don't know is that your favorite hiking path is really a microcosm of our fair city. In fact, it could probably be declared an actual subdivision. I'll get to how I came to be living out here in a minute, but first there's some stuff you need to know.

My name is James McPhee—Jimmy—and I am a Portland cop. Yes, a cop. I've been doing this job for the past fifteen years. If you saw me, you'd never figure me for the heat, on account of I'm only five-four. But if you think that's small, you should see my wife; she wouldn't top five feet if she was standing on her toes. Dawn has the smallest hands I've ever seen on a woman. I got a son, James Jr., who outgrew me by the time he was eleven. He took third in the state in varsity wrestling in his junior year, so you can figure I'm pretty proud of him.

I've worked every precinct in this town, but my favorite has always been Central—downtown, to be specific. There's this place downtown called Pioneer Square, where every weirdo that Keeps Portland Weird hangs out. It's like a zoo, only without the cages. I call it The Twilight Zone.

Pioneer Square is an open block in the middle of downtown that smells like feet. It is surrounded by trendy coffee shops and stores, but in reality, it's Portland's steamy underbelly. It's inhabited by transients, weirdos, homeless, criminals, and runaways, and those are just the *good* ones. In Pioneer Square, I've met thirteen-year-old prostitutes in ultra-miniskirts and CFMPs, and dealt harshly with their forty-year-old boyfriend/pimps. Pioneer Square after dark is a menagerie, and I got to know well all the beasts who hang out and live there. It's like I have a natural affinity with them all; street Elvises, leather-clad spike-haired punks, mumbling bag ladies, and smelly old men living in cardboard boxes.

Mental illness and disease run rampant among these parasites of the city's bowels, but still, I can't help but call them friends. Go figure, but I actually care about these people. Take Sparky for instance. Here's a guy who sits unmoving from sunup to sundown on the corner of SW 6th and Morrison every day with a lampshade on his head. Nobody knows where he disappears to at night, but there he is bright and early the next morning. Then you got The Kapellmeister, dancing his way around downtown conducting an imaginary orchestra and yelling at them in German. The Jackhammer is another Central Precinct staple. He's an old Santa Claus-looking shlump with a beard yellow from cigarette smoke, who can often be seen frantically masturbating in various locations in the downtown core area. There are hundreds more like them, and every day it's something new. I love working down there; their mental illness holds a real fascination for me. It makes me thank God that my own kid has a good home and all of his marbles.

I actually read up on mental illness and applied what I learned to my buddies in The Twilight Zone. They started calling me The Caring Cop, but you know what I found out? There wasn't a damn thing I could do to really help them. The system has chewed them up and spit them out, and places like Pioneer Square are the spittoon. Still, they manage to thrive on their own, in a way. They have their own society, a big, self-perpetuating culture. And they're not just confined to The Twilight Zone, either. The Square is just the gathering point. Most of them live in city parks and bike trails, which means most of them live right out here on the biggest of them all, the Springwater Trail.

As liberal a town as Portland is, it still considers its homeless population to be a nuisance. Yeah, I know not all of the transients are mentally ill. Lots of them are criminals, and some are on the run from the police, and that gives society the excuse to harass them all. The wanted guys use their hidden camps as hideouts and bases for criminal activity, and all of 'em are in violation of camping, littering, and waste-dumping laws, so there you have it. The Homeless Problem. Blah blah blah. Look, most of these folks are just down-and-out; seriously screwed up, and could really use a break.

But the party line is they're a problem, and we all know how to solve a problem. So, in a kneejerk reaction to a random killing that happened on the trail, the Police Bureau forms this new unit called the Trail Enforcement Team, or TED for short. The idea is the TED guys patrol the trail and parks on a full-time basis using ATVs and off-road motorcycles, citing the "residents" for their various violations and generally seeing to it that they get moved along—a euphemism for shaken down and harassed. Christ, where the hell are they supposed to go? Knowing some of the knuckle-draggers that work in this outfit, I figured my peeps on the trail were in for a rough time, so I get this bright idea. Who would be better suited to work TED than the Caring Cop?

I was the first to put in for the job, and not surprisingly, I was the first selected, and of all the stuff I've ever done for the Bureau, TED was more to my liking than anything else. That's what I thought when I signed on for the four-year assignment, anyway.

I noticed right off that TED was to concentrate on the Springwater Trail, and that Pioneer Square was not mentioned in the operations orders. The city was going after them where they live, and where all the dirty work could be done outside of the public eye. That's typical of the way Portland does this shit. Anyway, the biggest part of my new job was riding the trail seeking out and contacting its residents.

Trail transients are different from Twilight Zone transients. These guys seem to take better care of themselves; they don't smell as bad, and maybe have a little less mental illness than their cousins downtown. Other towns along the trail, places like Gresham, have been actively enforcing transient related laws for years. Its all minor crap, stuff like illegal dumping, unlawful camping, and violating park hours (being a city park, the trail technically closes at sunset, which is kinda funny, seeing that that's when most of the action out here is just getting started). All of it is bullshit misdemeanor crap.

After I got the TED job, I spent the next two years riding motorized vehicles past signs that say "No Motorized Vehicles," and dealing hands-on with the transients that call the trail home. Most of them nested in the woods around Powell Butte and east, including the five mile stretch through Gresham. Gresham PD had been pushing the transients our way, and now we were pushing back, and the poor bastards who were caught in the middle didn't know which way to go.

These transients, they intrigued me. November through February can be downright fucking brutal on the trail—cold, windy, sideways rain—but still, the transients hardly ever go to a shelter. For the most part, they actually *chose* to live out there in the weather. Working TED, I came to love these guys in a way, and honed my left-coast liberal bleeding-heart attitude about them. Not the assholes on the run from the law, mind you; I love busting those guys. But with the rest, it became harder and harder for me to do what I was supposed to.

Along with my partner, Officer Raymond Gunn (no kidding, his name really was Ray Gun), I rode the trail glad-handing legitimate users while at the same time hunting down the transients, ostensibly to move them along or bust them, but really looking to get them the help they needed. We would follow their little footpaths off the trail, tracking them down to their hidey-holes and hidden camps. These varied from the elaborate—multi-story dwellings powered by stolen car batteries, stereos, and electric lights, to the pathetic—a soggy, moldy sleeping bag rolled out on the bare ground. But they all accept each other for who they are, and even get together in the evenings to play cards and shit. There's a lot more to these guys than holding will-work-for-food signs on freeway exit ramps.

Once we found a camp, it was our job to post a twenty-four-hour evacuation notice, give the occupants a reference sheet listing job programs, counseling centers, and homeless shelters, then follow up in two or three day's time to enforce the evacuation order. If they were still there, or if they were frequent fliers, then we were supposed to write them up for anything we could think of and eighty-six them from the trail. Then we'd call in a county jail work crew to haul all their stuff off to the dump.

Ray liked the enforcement part of the job the best. He used to tell people that TED stood for Transient Eradication Detail, and he loved to trash their camps; pepper-spraying their bedrolls, cutting the lines holding their tents up, shit like that. I honestly think Ray would have burned them all on sight like Colonial witches if I hadn't been there to stop him.

Me, I always gave our clients two or three notices, because it was hard for 'em to pack up an established camp and move deeper into the woods, which was basically their only choice. Lots of times I never returned to follow up. I seen too many guys walking away in stunned disbelief, looking at their last remaining possession—a $5,000.00 ticket for unlawful camping and illegal dumping. Maybe it was technically right, but damn it, it just wasn't *right*.

Not all the transients are guys, or even adults, for that matter. The girl transients have it pretty bad out there. Rapes and sexual assaults are to them like getting a traffic ticket is to anyone else. It's a real bitch when it happens, and you know it'll probably happen again, but at least it's not an every day thing. I mean, look at this. You got vulnerable mentally ill females, which makes them prime victim material anyway, and they live unprotected among a bunch of sexual predators in a place with no witnesses. How can you help but feel sorry for them?

Hardly any of the sex crimes ever get reported, but almost every female transient I ever spoke with has her own horror stories. And then you got the kids, which are the worst. Little kids, black with dirt and grime, shivering outside in the cold, shitting in the woods, never getting a bath, with no clothes and no toys, eating garbage scraps covered with ants; they got no school or friends, their parents are whack jobs.... It made me sick then, and it still does now.

After a couple years, I couldn't take it any longer, and begged out of the assignment. When I first hired on, I would beat the crap out of people for disrespecting me, and now I'd become a frickin' bleeding-heart liberal unable to enforce the law. But that's what they did to me, these transies. Hey, it is what it is, you know?

Well, it goes without saying the Bureau wasn't too happy with me for not completing the assignment. I was taken off the trail and reassigned to patrol, this time out in East Precinct. By now I'd been with Portland for fifteen years, but unlike many of my peers, I had a decent family life. My wife and I were still together, and though my kid had his share of problems—he'd just come out of drug rehab—we'd kept pretty close. Like every other parent, I wondered where he was when he wasn't at home, but he managed to stay in school and didn't get into too much trouble, so I counted my blessings instead of bitching about my misfortune.

With about five years to go before pulling the pin, I figured it was a good time to put in for sergeant, and planned to do so at the next opening. But little did I know that I was about to get the assignment of a lifetime, something even better than a promotion.

I will never forget the day that started that particular ball rolling. It was a regular day, with bullshit paper calls, a family beef or three, and a lot of boredom.

Around 2030 hours, a call came out of a man down on the Springwater Trail about a half-mile east of where it crosses 122nd. No TED guys were on duty, so they sent the call to the rest of us. I was writing paper in the parking lot of a strip club on Powell when the call came, and was the first to arrive. In fact, I was alone on that scene for the first few minutes, and I've gotta say it was one of the worst I'd ever seen.

It was a homicide. Now I'd seen a lot of homicides in my career, but this was a kid, and those are always the toughest. Strangely enough, I recall very little about this particular one. What I do remember is that the kid was in his late teens, and he'd been sliced to ribbons. There were defensive wounds on his palms and forearms, and more across the head and face. It was a particularly gruesome scene, with tons of blood and gore, and the coup de grâce was a savage slice across the neck. Someone must have called the kid's mother, because she showed up at the scene just before I left.

This was very unusual. Normally we never let relatives into a crime scene, but somehow this kid's mom got in. She was hysterical, and I remember fighting with her to get her away from the body. Despite being a petite woman, she held me in a death grip, and beat me with tiny little fists like it was my fault her kid was dead. It screwed with my head, dealing hands-on with the mother like that.

Not long after the mother showed up, I was taken away, whisked off to police headquarters without explanation in a patrol car whose clueless driver was under strict orders from the top. They ushered me directly into a hastily-arranged meeting with the captain of the Detective Division and the lieutenant in charge of undercover operations.

In this meeting, I was briefed on a very secret operation. The long and short of it was that a group of five teens had been making videos they call Bum Fights. It started out where the kids would give transients liquor and money in exchange for getting them to attack and fight one another, and all of this was videotaped for YouTube. I remember the days when it was clunky videotapes of cops Rodney Kinging bad guys. Now it's cell phone videos of bums beating all but Jesus out of each other.

Well, the Bum Fights had somehow changed to the teens taping themselves beating transients just for the glory of getting the videos rated on YouTube, and now the transients had begun fighting back. Somehow, they'd found out who was doing this to them, and were systematically going about killing the kids involved. My victim, the kid from the trail, was the third one to turn up dead out of the original five Bum Fights group. Three down and two to go.

My assignment was to go deep undercover as a transient, live among them on the Trail, and find out who was doing the killing. And I had to do it before they got to the last two boys on the list. Nobody was worried about me being recognized, because it had been a couple of years since TED, and the crowd out there changes so much. If I was successful, there would be an automatic promotion to sergeant for me.

My wife broke into hysterics before I was even done telling her about the mission. She wouldn't stop, and her crying kept me up all night and drove me nuts. I left at around three that morning, unable to take the sound her constant wailing, and found myself wandering the streets at oh-dark-thirty, wondering exactly where to go and how to start my assignment.

I picked up my duties in the obvious place, at the scene of the kid's murder on Powell Butte. I felt a strong bond with this place, and knew the area well from my days in TED. The faces may have changed, but the lay of the land certainly hadn't. I remembered every footpath and hidey-hole out there, and had no problem finding the new ones.

By the time that first night rolled around I had taken over an abandoned campsite at the end of a hidden footpath about a quarter mile east of the butte, and like I said earlier, it was scary and lonely, but kind of exciting, too. It was mid-September and the weather was still nice, but I knew it wouldn't stay that way for long. My first week out there was downright enjoyable, except I began to learn firsthand what it felt like to go hungry. I wanted to be as authentic as possible, so I didn't bring any money or food with me, and I learned real quick where I could get scraps or even a free meal.

I began hiking every day to a church a few blocks north of the trail on Eastman Parkway out in Gresham, where for the cost of listening to the Good News of Jesus Christ, guys like me could get a decent hot meal.

Pretty soon I got to know the other homeless guys on the trail and became fast friends with them. My closest neighbor was a guy of about my own age named Rags Doolittle, who spoke endlessly of Vietnam. Rags' campsite had bent-over saplings tied down all around it that looked suspiciously like booby-traps. You didn't want to fuck with Rags. I didn't talk about the murders, waiting as long as I needed to gain the trust of my newfound contemporaries.

A couple weeks after setting up camp, Rags asked me to go downtown with him. His kid had a place there, and that's where his VA checks came. I was glad for the chance, because I needed inroads into the downtown crowd, and by now I was skuzzy and smelly enough to fit right in with them. Neither of us had any money, so Rags and I hopped the MAX train for the ride downtown.

I had a very close call at the Gateway transit center with a Tri-Met cop I worked with in East a couple years back named Trahn Nguyen. I was about to bail to avoid a confrontation when Trahn began staring at me like he knew me, which he did. Fortunately, the sight of a Vietnamese police officer set Rags off, and he began yelling at Trahn, telling him if we hadn't gone overseas to fight for dinks like him, there's no way he could be a cop in this country. This was good for me, 'cause Trahn wasn't about to put up with that shit. When he turned his attention to Rags, I slipped out the door and disappeared.

That close call reminded me that nobody knew I was out here, and if I was going to succeed with my mission, it had to stay that way. In fact, the Bureau was way too enthusiastic about trying to find the murderer. It was obvious that they were looking for someone on the trail; ever since they placed me out here they'd been positively flooding the area with uniformed cops. To say they had stepped up Springwater Trail patrols was a serious understatement. Cops were everywhere, talking to every transient they could find, and avoiding them for the obvious reasons became harder and harder.

One time, when my guard was down, I got stopped by the police. Fortunately, it was a rookie I'd never met before, and the kid was so dumb, he didn't even know what he was looking for. Instead of asking me who'd been killing children, he asked me if any *police officers* were living out here. Imagine having things that bass-ackward! I still hadn't had any contact with my handlers and wasn't about to initiate it through this guy, because it was obvious he didn't know his ass from a hole in the ground. But I knew the Bureau'd be in touch with me soon, I was sure of it. My job was to keep a low profile, learn what I could, and wait for them to contact me.

During the course of the next month the weather turned, and with it, I developed a persistent runny nose. It was nothing I couldn't handle, so I put up with it. Back when I was doing TED, I was always amazed and a little disgusted with the snot that would congeal in the beards of these guys out here, but now I understood it. When the weather turned cold and rainy, nothing could be done to stop it. It's not like you had Kleenexes, or that you could keep them dry even if you did. Pretty soon you were as unaware of the snot as you were of your own smell, and you got used to the salty taste of your mustache when you ran your tongue over it. No big deal.

Though they hadn't contacted me yet, I knew my supervisors were keeping tabs on me. They sent people to check up on me, but there was this unspoken agreement of silence between us that we all honored. The contact agents looked like ordinary citizens walking or biking the trail, and we would exchange glances, holding eye contact long enough for them to know that I was okay, and then they would look away. This might sound a little strange to you, but that's the way deep cover contacts work. Those boys' lives depended on me keeping my cover.

I was starting to make real progress on the investigation by this time. A dude named Bull Thomas, a long-time transient who lived at a place called The Swamp near Main Park in Gresham, was an ex-con and part-time meth cook who I suspected was heavily involved. He talked openly about the murders, and even alluded to a conspiracy among transients, but I think he was beginning suspect the police might have fielded an under-cover operative, and I didn't feel comfortable pressing him for details.

The investigation was starting to go places, and so was I.

᳄

WELL, OCTOBER HAS turned into November, and now I have a persistent cough that won't go away. I've thought of making direct contact to get some antibiotics, but I'm very close to getting the goods on Bull now, and I can't afford to blow that. The subject of the murders had come up between us, and he's told me that the job isn't finished yet, but soon will be. I think Bull is the ringleader in a vast, far-reaching Transient Conspiracy involving literally hundreds of assassins disguised as transients. When he fully trusts me, I think he's going to recruit me into the network.

In the meantime, news of my success has indeed reached the bureau. Lately, I've begun finding coded instructions on things designed to look like discarded trash. My mission has been expanded, and I am not just to look into who killed that poor child, whose crime scene comes back to me in nightmares *every fucking day*, not just when I sleep, mind you, but also during my waking hours and I don't know why but it is really starting to bug me and I can't get the sight of that young man and his hysterical parents out of my mind...

IT'S NIGHTTIME NOW, and pouring. A 7-11 big gulp cup I found yesterday carried an embedded message that the transient network is really an Al Qaeda terrorist organization, and national security hangs in the balance. The cup was color-coded red, which means the threat level has been raised. The responsibility upon my shoulders is staggering and still, the sight of that dead boy and the anguish of his parents haunts me. Also, I now have to deal with a conspiracy of those among my peers who want to see me fail, who are spreading ugly rumors about my family; that my own son was...*is, IS*...a Bum Fight kid, and it is becoming increasingly difficult for me to remain focused on the mission.

I HAVEN'T SLEPT in days. My cough isn't my only malady. I've also developed a pretty good fever, but the medicine they tried to give me at the church was actually poison. Word of my assignment may have gotten out, and I suspect the church people are on the terrorist watch list. I'm eating out of garbage cans now, and my life is in jeopardy on several fronts.

EVERY DAY, I go to the spot where that heroic teenager died to receive orders from his spirit but all I see is his mother screaming and crying and breaking down in uncontrolled hysterics and beating me with tiny fists so like my wife's and I quite literally feel her pain all the time now every moment of every day for what man could survive the sight of his only son so cut apart lying there on the unforgiving ground surrounded by oceans of his own blood without going crazy and I can't get the picture out of my mind which is why it is so important for me to stay out here and do what I am doing until the mystery is solved because I am a police officer and a federal agent and the President is interested in my work and the fate of America lies in my hands and, and, and, and, and...

And my wife is *still* crying and I *deserve* to be beaten with tiny fists and James Jr. won't talk to me any more and its all starting to unravel and...

What are those flashing lights? Are they the police, or are they transient assassins *dressed* as police? This is no ambulance—it could be an Al Qaeda car bomb, and my arms are strapped to the bed! Oh my God, I, I think my cover has been blown.... *James...talk to me, James.... Tell me what to do...*

QUEEN'S GAMBIT

BOB FREEMAN

"Death is the veil of Life, and Life of Death; for both are Gods."
Aleister Crowley

Father Rainey stared into the pernicious night and not for the first time questioned his faith. It came with the territory. As the ecclesiastical liaison to the Chicago Police Department's Occult Crimes Taskforce, he saw more than his fair share of human depravity. This night's horrors were no different. Lighting a cigarette from a crumpled pack in his great coat, he exhaled the twisted knot that had sought to put a stranglehold on his stomach, releasing it into the chilled October air.

"Never easy is it Father?"

The priest turned to meet the face of Detective Andrews, the thirty-something Mick with the face of an angel but eyes that were as dark and as cold as any lost soul you'd ever chance upon. Andrews was a man who had seen too much in too short a time. It wrecked his marriage, alienated his children, and introduced him to a dependency for alcohol that was slowly killing him. Once Rainey would have cared. Those days were long gone. It came with the territory.

"Easy?" Rainey responded. "No, I suppose not."

"The boss wanted me to get your general impressions of the scene before CSU tears into it," the detective said nonchalantly. He was fumbling with a silver flask and taking a nip. A little bump, Rainey thought. It was something to keep the hands steady in front of his superiors. Everyone leaned on some kind of crutch. The priest's own nicotine-stained fingers were a testament to that caveat.

"Self-styled Satanists," Rainey lied. "Teens perhaps, maybe a little older. Typical influences. LaVey, rock and roll, and B movie horror flicks."

"You think?"

"You don't?" the priest fired back, eyebrow cocked to give the impression of seriousness. Rainey had been playing this game far longer than Andrews,

"The way they carved up that girl..." the detective began. He took another swig of cheap vodka. "I don't know, Father? Just seems a little more...organized. And a hell of a lot more vicious."

"One over-zealous member," the priest answered, trying to lead the detective from his line of deduction. "I'd bet next Sunday's collection plate that the rest of the hooligans shit themselves when the knife came out and actually drew blood." Rainey tossed his spent coffin nail into the bushes. "One sociopath playing at Satanism with a bunch of misfits, Detective Andrews. Nothing more."

"Alright," Andrews said with a nod of the head, "you're the expert."

Rainey removed another cigarette from the confines of his coat, lit it, and took a long drag while watching the detective depart. It was better this way, he thought. No sense in starting a panic. Not yet anyway. He flipped up his collar against the wind and strode confidently away from beneath the shadow of St. Paul's. If this night was going to start making sense, he needed to see a man about a horse.

TWO

RAINEY STEPPED OUT of the Yellow Cab on the corner of 93rd and Blackstone in front of the dark Victorian that set nestled in a copse of ancient ash and oak. Time had taken its toll on the Star & Garter, but its reputation alone drew the knowledgably curious, as well as the serious student of the esoteric. The priest knew that if he were to unravel the mystery that was born this night, born upon a bloody Catholic altar, the road to understanding would begin here. He made his way across the uneven walk, climbed the porch stair and knocked upon the faded door.

"Do what thou wilt is the whole of the law," a frail man, bent and twisted, welcomed.

"Love is the law," Rainey responded, finding the discourse distasteful. "Love under will." The traditional Thelemic greeting was required to gain entry and each time he was forced to say it, he felt that a little piece of his soul were dragged into Hell.

The attendant took the priest's hat and coat and hung them within the coatroom, just off the small foyer. The priest waited impatiently for the old retainer, eager to put this night's dark work behind him. With a wave of a withered hand the old one directed Rainey toward the Drawing Room where the sounds of animated discussion emanated.

The room was filled with a magical blend of exotic aromas. Three men sat in Elizabethan chairs drawn together in a semi-circle about the fireplace. The stream of smoke from their pipes mingling with the cedar logs in the hearth; it was a scene that could have been cut from the eighteenth century. Their period dress was perfect in every detail, as were their accessories. A fourth gentleman, the proprietor of the Star & Garter, stood above the others, a cryptic tome held in his well-manicured hands.

"Rubbish," the largest of the three seated gentlemen bellowed, "there has never been an exact Thelemic equivalent to the Middle Pillar Rite as conducted by the Golden Dawn."

"Surely you'd agree, Kline," another responded indignantly, "that the vertical and horizontal enchantments of Reguli *seem* to be a form of it."

"Feh," the large man huffed, "then why is Nuit attributed to Kether in the vertical enchantment? I know, I know "lady of the stars", etc., but in the Star Ruby, Nuit is used in the North and attributed to Earth. In Reguli, Nuit is again found in the North but attributed to Air, while Kether is traditionally associated with the fifth element of Spirit."

"That would lead one to believe," the third man, a bookish twenty-something who had probably not grown his first beard, sat forward and stated, "that the vertical enchantment component is to be conceptualized from a solar perspective."

Rainey shook his head. "Excuse me, gentlemen," he interrupted, "but who says that Nuit is equivalent to Earth in the Star Ruby? In the original version of the ritual, as found in The Book of Lies, the direction of North is attributed to Water."

"Father Rainey," the proprietor said, turning to greet the priest, "welcome to the Star & Garter. It has been too long."

"Indeed, Mr. Buckland," Rainey responded, accepting the hand offered, "it has been *far* too long."

"What is this about the original version of the Star Ruby?" Kline demanded.

"Oh, Father Rainey is quite correct," Buckland replied to the larger man's query, "Around the same time that Crowley wrote Reguli he edited the Star Ruby. It makes sense that the elemental directions follow the same scheme."

"It's interesting to note that in both versions of the Star Ruby," Rainey added, "the position of the guardians stays the same."

"But that would mean," the young scholar mused, "that they are not elemental."

"Precisely," the priest quipped, impressed by the young man's deduction.

"As always, Father Rainey," Buckland said, placing a hand on the priest's shoulder, "you are a fount of wisdom. Come...let us talk. These gentlemen can continue their discourse without further interruption by us. We have some catching up to do."

The youngest of the three men rose and offered a hand to the priest.

"My thanks to you Father," he said with a soft boyish voice, "it is rare to be in the company of one so well versed in the esoteric. I am in your debt. You have given me much to think about."

"I am glad that I could shed some light on your discussion, Mister...?"

"J'Adoube...Andre J'Adoube, Father. And it my pleasure to make your acquaintance."

"The pleasure is mine," the priest responded. "God be with you."

"Now, if you'll excuse us," the host interrupted.

Buckland led the Father through a side door and into a dimly lit office, a mahogany presidential desk the room's centerpiece. The walls were lined with bookshelves filled with aged and worn tomes that gave the room that peculiar smell usually relegated to used bookstores with poor ventilation. Father Rainey loved it. The priest paused before the desk and lifted a framed picture from its resting place. It was of Buckland and a pretty young woman with strawberry blonde curls framing a pale but content face.

"She would have turned thirty four this past winter," Rainey said, replacing the picture to its rightful place. "Not a day passes that I don't mourn her."

"But no prayer for her at Mass," Buckland spat. "All she ever wanted was to be buried at St. Mark's, near the rose garden."

"You know the rules, Richard," Rainey said calmly. "The Church is very strict when it comes to matters of suicide."

"She was your sister," Buckland whispered.

"And your wife," the priest added, placing a comforting hand on the man's shoulder. "If I could have changed it, I would have. I would have buried the report, but...there was so much press coverage. It was out of my hands, and you know it."

"Of course, Father," Buckland conceded, sliding into the over-sized executive chair and drawing a cigarette from a silver case lying on the desk. "What's done is done, right? She rests now in hallowed ground...just not the hallowed ground of her choosing." Sitting up straight and clearing his throat, he gave the priest a half smile. "Now, what would drag my brother-in-law out on a night like this and after so long?"

"I have something I want you to look at," the priest answered.

"A case?"

"I just came from the crime scene." Rainey withdrew a digital camera from his pocket. "Download these pictures and we'll have a look."

Buckland took the camera and attached a cable into its USB port and, calling up the Photo Editing software on his PC, began the download. Before the blue-white glow of the monitor, Richard Buckland was introduced to the scenes of this night's earlier horrors, played out in a surreal slideshow presentation.

"Is this St. Paul's?" he asked, transfixed by the images on the screen.

"Yes," the priest answered.

"Okay." Buckland activated recording software and spoke into the microphone attached to the left of the monitor. "We have a young woman, early to mid twenties with red hair. Not sure if the carpet matches the drapes as she is devoid of pubic hair. Mock crucifixion pose, laid out across the altar...ring and middle finger missing from both hands, and a number six carved into the left palm. There are vertical and horizontal lacerations from a sharp knife or scalpel on the torso, the chest bisected with, I believe, three crossing cuts. There is an angular cut from right shoulder to left breast. Two parallel cuts of unequal lengths on the stomach. Looks like... hmmm, is that an inverted patriarch cross?"

"My thought exactly," Rainey answered, watching over Buckland's shoulder as the images moved slowly across the screen, over and over again, in a diabolical loop.

"And the coins on her eyes? The resolution's not clear enough for me to make them out."

"They are a pair of Vatican 10 lira, tail up, mint year 1923." the priest said, turning away. "They are masking the fact that the victim's eyes were removed."

Buckland closed the program.

"Alright, Father," he said, "I'll bite. What is it I'm not seeing?"

"This," the priest said. He produced a white handkerchief from his pocket and handed it to Buckland. The occult scholar slowly unwrapped the object and set it upon the desktop, kneeling on the floor and espying it intently.

"What have we here?" Buckland mused. Before him was a ring, silver with a narrow band that broadened to a crest face with a stylized chess piece, a knight, within a unicursal hexagram. "A Knight of the Order?"

"A Knight of *what* Order, Richard?" Father Rainey asked. "The symbology escapes me."

"I'm not at all surprised," Buckland said, intent on the ring. "This was found with the girl in the photos?"

"In her, actually," the priest responded. "It had been left inside her vagina."

"Devilish," Buckland said. He picked up the ring and peered inside. "There's an engraving on the inside of the band."

"I'd not noticed," the priest said, curiosity piqued.

"*Tota Mulier Sexus*," Buckland recited.

Rainey translated the Latin phrase in an instant.

"The whole of woman is sex."

THREE

WITH A GOTHIC swagger the Scottish Rite Cathedral cut an ominous visage against the Chicago skyline. It was a testament to the Masonic ideal, masterfully wrought and stylized with the Craft's eye for tradition and divine excellence. Father Rainey was well aware of the animosity between the Brothers of the Sign and Seal and the Catholic Church. There was certainly no love lost between them, but this? No, the good Father was certain that even the Holy See would be appalled at what had befallen the handful of Craftsmen this night.

Rainey felt as if someone had punched him in the gut. The look Detective McFarland had given him indicated that he'd have volunteered to deliver the blow, but a madman with black magick on his mind had beaten him to it. There were two crime scenes in as many nights with enough mumbo jumbo and bad mojo to write a dissertation. Tonight's scorecard tallied eight thirty-second degree Masons with their throats slit and an eviscerated redhead that was the spitting image of the previous night's victim.

Someone was leaving a calling card. Someone wanted him to know what he was up to and he wanted him to know it was big.

The Father unwrapped the object hidden within the bloodied linen that had been culled from the latest altar victim's private parts. It was a ring, very much like the one found in the St. Paul victim. The stylized crest of the unicursal hexagram framed a different chess piece however. Within the magical symbol was a bishop. A thousand thoughts raced through the priest's mind. Knights. Bishops. Sacrifice. Eight Freemasons.

"Eight pawns?" he whispered.

Rainey fumbled for his cell phone and called the only person who would understand any of it. He paced impatiently, his stomach in knots. The priest cast furtive glances at the detectives who were milling about the crime scene. He needed privacy. "Come on," he muttered as he made his way toward the Apprentice Chamber. "Damn it, pick up." He slipped inside just as the person on the other end answered his call.

"Do what thou wilt is the whole of the law."

"Richard, it's me. We have to talk."

"Frank, what it is it? You sound like you've seen a ghost."

"Not a ghost, Richard. The devil. I've figured it out. Well, most of it anyway."

"What are you talking about?"

"It's all an elaborate gambit, a chess match," the priest said. "Our killer is using deflection and sacrifice to place himself in the ideal position for his Endgame."

"Alright, Frank, slow down. You're scaring me."

"There's been another ritual murder. Eight Freemasons and a girl on their altar," Rainey took a cigarette from his pack. "And Richard, she's been brutalized in an almost identical manner as last night's victim—the mock crucifixion, the missing fingers, the evisceration, the carved number six in the palm."

"You said in an *almost* identical manner. There were differences?"

"The differences are the key, Richard," the priest continued. "Tonight's victim was left with eyes intact, but her ears were taken. There will be another murder tomorrow night, the third and final move of our perpetrator."

"How can you be so sure?"

"Because he is arming himself." Rainey paced again. " The eyes so that he can see evil, the ears so that he can hear it... He has inscribed two of the three sixes he needs to make his personal Mark of the Beast." The priest lit another cigarette off the one he had smoked to the filter. "Tomorrow he will make his final sacrifice, a rook I'm sure, and he'll take the woman's tongue."

"So the bastard can speak evil. Damn it Frank, we're getting too old for this shit."

"I need your help on this, Richard."

"Of course, what's a brother-in-law for? I'll put a pot of coffee on and we can talk it through. How soon can you be here?"

"Within the hour," Rainey said. "And Richard..."

"Yeah Frank?"

"Scratch the coffee and have a bottle of whiskey ready. It's already been a long night, and it's hours before the dawn."

FOUR

"RICHARD," RAINEY DEMANDED, "it's time for you to tell me the rest of the story. You referred to these Rites as being a part of the lexicon of the Order of the Spire. I need to know as much about this Order as possible. I can find no reference to them in any of the Church's archives or on the Vatican database."

"It's like I told you last night, Frank," Buckland said, "these guys are like ghosts. But I'll tell you what I can."

The two men were sipping whiskeys before the fire in the Star & Garter Drawing Room. Richard Buckland had ushered out the few patrons who were taking advantage of the Club's esoteric camaraderie after his former brother-in-law had called. When he answered the door, he almost regretted his invitation to help with the case. The priest wore his distress like a comfortable old coat, threadbare from years of intimate contact. It unnerved the host of the Star & Garter to see him this way. Rainey had that same vacant stare that he'd worn at Mary's funeral service so long ago. The Father had interred his sister that day, but Richard had said goodbye to his wife and best friend. He swallowed the rage as it threatened to swell up inside him. Not now, he thought. Duty called.

"The Order of the Spire reached their height of power in the late nineteenth century," Buckland continued. "They were rivals with the other prominent Orders of that era, the Golden Dawn, AMORC, the Theosophical Society. The difference was that they were shadows. They secreted themselves within the Freemasons, a clandestine inner circle networked throughout the world, but especially in Europe and here in the States."

Rainey shook his head and took another long drag off of his cigarette. "The Masons were pawns."

"The very nature of Masonic Society made it the perfect hiding place," Buckland agreed.

"You said they were rivals. In what sense?" Rainey asked.

"It takes a special sort to walk the path of a magician, as you well know. All these groups were vying for the same pool of initiates. The difference was that the Order of the Spire was far more secretive...and they had so much more to offer. They had stumbled upon the very heart of esoterica and their Master was not of this Earth."

"They all claimed connections with Secret Chiefs and extraterrestrial intelligences," Rainey said. "What made the Spire so different?"

"That part's simple...they weren't full of shit."

FIVE

"SO, WHAT DO you think, Father? Did we draw the short straw tonight?" Andrews asked as he took another sip from his liquor flask.

"I'm not really sure of anything anymore, Detective," the priest bemoaned. Hidden within the dark recesses of the alley neighboring the derelict Kilgore Institute he worried over his tarnished faith. Would God stand with him tonight, or was he but a boogeyman, a tale to frighten children into behaving? He didn't know the answer, and that frightened him more than the threat of the real and palpable evil that they lie in wait for.

Rainey was left wondering if he had made a terrible mistake. He and Richard had worked into the wee hours of the morning on their predicament. The third and final sacrifice would take place this very night, of that they both were sure. As near as they could deduce, based on the considerable knowledge shared between them, there were at least half a dozen probable locations for the final act in this madman's passion play. Rainey had suggested that McFarland divide the OCT into two man teams, positioning them throughout the city at these locations.

Rainey and Andrews were staking out the remains of the Kilgore Institute on the city's north side. Its rich history was one marred by death and darkness. Buckland had been confident that the killer's Endgame would require an ample supply of ectoplasmic energy for success, and the Institute's reputation surely fit the bill.

In its earliest incarnation it had played host to a chapter of the Theosophical Society, but the leaders of the group were jailed on fraud and embezzlement charges and a wealthy financier bought the place and transformed it into the very home of the Chicago Blues and Jazz scene. Cryptically called The Black House, the club offered up a stage for the talents of men such as Robert Johnson and Son House. It was within those walls that the Devil's music thundered and the stigma never left. Murders, disappearances, overdoses...it was spoken of in hushed whispers by those that called the streets of Chicago their home. Dark things brewed within its walls they said. After the club closed its doors after one too many scandals, it was put on the auction block. The house was a thing of beauty and there was no shortage of people clamoring to purchase the home, but none stayed long. They either fled in fear or were carried out in body bags. There was no peace within its malefic space.

Enter Malcolm Kilgore. A prominent businessman from Indiana, Kilgore was obsessed with the occult and purchased the aged Victorian intent on establishing a research center whose purpose was to quantify the mystical experience. In 1969, on Halloween night, a fire took the lives of Kilgore and twelve of his researchers. There were no survivors. What had transpired that night had been the subject of much debate in esoteric circles. Some claimed that the Prince of Darkness himself had been called forth and that he consumed the practitioners for their foolishness. Still others claimed that they had merely bartered for an immortal existence in another realm. Regardless, the Institute had become a stain on the very heart of the Windy City.

Father Rainey paced nervously. Just being within the shadow of the damnable edifice robbed his heart of courage and his already fragile faith was teetering on the brink of ruination as surely as the construct that loomed before him. The priest had already consumed a half pack of cigarettes and was about to light another when a shrill scream cut through the night.

"Did that come from inside the Kilgore?" Andrews asked, knowing full well it had. Rainey watched the detective's dull eyes spark to life, sobering in an instant. "Fucking hell."

"How did they get past us?" Rainey muttered, his heart firmly in his throat.

Andrews drew his Beretta and chambered a round, flashing a wink at the priest before he slid out of the alley and toward the steps leading up to the Institute's gaping maw. Rainey started after him, but the detective lifted up his hand to halt the Father's progress. A shake of the head told Rainey to wait in the alleyway while the detective allowed instinct and procedure to take over. The priest watched as the detective entered the vile derelict and then it settled upon him like an oppressive weight. He was alone.

Seconds crawled. Minutes passed like hours. Father Rainey was out of his element. He was not a man of action; he was a man of learning. He was a man of...faith. No, he thought, that didn't ring true, did it? His faith had been gone for a long time. It lay broken and shattered at the feet of his late sister. He had prayed with her and Richard as the cancer ate at her. She was a pious young woman, who loved the Lord more than she loved herself. Her life was one of good works and devotion to the Church. When she chose to end her pain and suffering, more for her husband's sake than her own, it had tore Rainey apart. The Church's stance on suicide only compounded the problem.

A shot rang out, reverberating through the damp and narrow alley. Adrenaline and trepidation merged to overwhelm the priest. He fumbled for another cigarette. He was down to his last. He lit it and exhaled slowly, trying to calm his nerves, but the coffin nail had no chance of alleviating the churning inside the Father's gut. He crept forward and ascended the ruined steps to the Victorian's skeletal remains.

"Andrews," he called out.

He took a slow drag off his smoke.

"Andrews," he called again, more forcibly this time.

Silence? Or not? Was there a whimpering noise, the sound of scuffled footsteps on hardwood...was there the sounds of quieted movement?

"Detective?" the priest called once more. He swallowed hard and took a final hit from the spent cigarette and discarded it into the street. "There but by the grace of God..." he muttered as he entered the Kilgore Institute.

SIX

EVEN AFTER MORE than thirty years, the stench of burnt timber was present, like a phantom odor floating across time and space in an attempt to draw you back to a night of death and chaos. Father Rainey made his way gingerly across the weathered floor, punctured here and there by treacherous holes in the tortured pine. Moisture dripped from above, a ravaged roof serving as but a meager stop against the elements.

Rainey crossed the threshold and through the foyer, past the parlor and into the Great Room. Large and ill-lit by a punishing wound overhead allowing moonlight to bathe down on the scene before the priest. His eyes slid past Detective Andrews who sat on the floor and leaned heavily against a sturdy pillar, his automatic still clamped firmly in his mouth. The blood splatter and gray matter punctuated the moment. There in the center of the room, was the object of Rainey's attention. Like a macabre centerpiece, evil had taken root and welcomed the priest with open arms.

"Andre J'Adoube," Father Rainey said, amused in the way that madmen often find humor in the oddest of situations. The youthful figure, robed in golden magical attire, stood on a raised dais, a crimson tressed victim sprawled out before him in sacrificial splendor.

"J'Adoube," Rainey said again, this time with a hint of disgust. "How could I have been so blind?" The priest strolled forward, a combination of shock and awe overwhelming him. "J'Adoube is a chess term. It means "I adjust".

"See, that's the trouble with you scholarly types, Father," the magician said, "you learn everything from books and sometimes books are wrong. You are quoting the popular take that J'adoube is French, but I know you're familiar with the language and I know that you would agree that there is no such word and no such translation, and yet you cling to the popular reference because of its wide acceptance, even when you should know better."

"I believe that just may be the central theme to this evening's revelations," the magician continued. "J'adoube, by the way, is derived from Old English and means 'Shut the fuck up'."

"Good Lord," the priest exclaimed, "what are you playing at? Are you a madman?"

"Madman? It is all laid out before you, and still you do not see," J'Adoube barked. "Tota Mulier Sexus!"

Father Rainey watched as the magician loosened the belt about his waist and allowed his robe to drop. The magician stood naked above the eviscerated corpse, writhing serpentine in mock ecstasy. Rainey was stunned, looking upon the magician's pale flesh. The magician was...a woman.

"I am the Black Queen of the Night," she cried. "I am the Mother of Abominations, the Unholy Vessel Incarnate! I am Life and Death, Sex and Magick! I was, I am, I will forever be!"

"Dear God," Rainey mouthed.

"Still clinging to that tyrant, Frank?"

Father Rainey turned slowly to face the voice that came from the shadows.

"Richard?"

Richard Buckland stepped from the tenebrous recess, cloaked and cowled in black. He moved with an arrogant gait, like a conquering general across the Rubicon. His left hand wrapped passionately around an elaborate wand while his right weaved arcane symbols in the air.

"Richard, why?" the priest moaned.

"You know all too well 'why', Frank," Buckland spat. "It's time to repay God's love and compassion. He took her away from me and then denied her. He will soon see the error of his ways."

Behind them, the female mage began chanting, her serpentine dance a magical undulation that stirred the Father's manhood. He was repulsed and enchanted, and he hated himself for it.

"Watch Father," Richard called out, forcing the priest's attention to focus on the gyrating sorceress. "Watch as the Moonchild comes forth! Our Rite is nigh complete, and you have been brought here to witness the beginning of God's Fall!"

Rainey watched in terror as the woman's stomach began to swell, bulging unnaturally, her cries rising up into the night sky that peered down through the ruined roof. Before his very eyes, a child, somehow, was growing at an unnatural rate, racing from magical conception to birth in a matter of minutes. The priest spat bile and swooned before the preternatural perversion of all things holy and wondrous.

"It comes!" the woman screamed. She reached between her legs and drew forth a child from her womb and with a deft hand, cut the umbilical chord with an athame, surely enchanted by the darkest of magicks.

Buckland came before her and took the child and, dipping his fingers into the vaginal blood of the sacrifice laid out before them, painted an inverted cross upon the child's forehead.

"Satan be praised," Buckland said, looking upon the infant with reverence. He lifted the child over his head like an offering to unseen spirits and then lifted his voice even higher, "A new day dawns!" he bellowed. "God is dead! Satan reigns!"

"No, sweet Lord in Heaven," Rainey muttered. "No, God, please..."

"Bow, Priest," Buckland commanded, "bow before the Master of the World, for his name is Abaddon and his rule will be one of unfettered abandon!"

Father Frank Rainey dropped to his knees, broken and drained. A man of faith, he had seen it ripped from him only for it to be rekindled by a whimpering babe born of hate and vengeance.

"Richard, please," the priest begged. "You can't."

"I can, and I have...the Kilgores are far more than any of you have fathomed. They have shown us the way, and I shall see their dark work fulfilled."

Father Rainey crossed himself, kneeling beside the body of Detective Andrews, whose frozen expression tore at the priest's soul. "Forgive me, my son," he muttered.

"You know what they say, Frankie," Buckland said, turning to look up at the woman who had just given birth to the Anti-Christ and smiled, "Payback's a bitch."

"That it is, Richard," Rainey choked. He ripped the gun from Andrews' hands and began firing. Thundering lead tore through the stunned magicians' bodies. J'Adoube pirouetted from atop the makeshift altar, riddled with bullet holes, the hellish babe dropping onto the charred floor.

"Frank, what have you done?"

The priest limped toward the crippled body of his brother-in-law.

"God's Will."

Father Rainey fired point blank into Buckland's face then turned to the crying babe on the floor beside him. It looked so innocent...so alone.

A final gunshot reverberated throughout the ruins of the Kilgore Institute.

WITH THE BRIGHTNESS OF HIS COMING

JASON M. WALTZ

"Forgive me, Father, for I know what I do."

Sam drew the serrated edge through the priest's throat with deliberate slowness, spraying blood across the chancel railing and upon the altar. The sudden wetness snuffed the vigils of several candles and splattered the figure suspended above the retable.

He eased the deflating body to the floor, the struggled suctions of the dying man's inhalations loud in the empty cathedral, magnified further within his mind. Sam averted his eyes from the body in his arms and studied the crucifix, squinting at the glisten of the holy man's blood spatter on his Savior's petrified form. He flinched when the body shuddered; cringed while its heels drummed the steps in a frantic chase for breath; grunted with exertion when its legs straightened in spastic reflex and thrust one foot through the chancel latticework. He shied from contemplating the dreadfulness of such a solitary death, and raised his chin to avoid seeing the reciprocating thought he knew resided within his victim's eyes. *No one should die like this!*

Yet Sam no more controlled his actions than did a marionette.

Sam never knew what triggered his actions, or when they'd occur. He didn't know if their subsequent results were symptomatic of his overloaded synapses failing under sensory assault or just due to a temporary nervous disorder brought on by exhaustion. Nor could he tell if it was simply a posttraumatic stress induced by the intermingling effects of the sputtering candle light, the pungent scent of fresh and darkly glinting blood, and the rhythmic final wheezes of the priests.

A dull thought pressed against the inside of Sam's skull, seeking acceptance. *It doesn't truly matter what the cause is.* Whether he watched life stir in those agonized limbs, saw those dejected shoulders lift with ragged intakes of breath, or heard the rending of flesh as each massive hand pulled itself from its nail, the same outcome transpired each time. It never mattered if he witnessed the Christ-figure remove Himself from the cross or if Christ just suddenly materialized in front of Sam. All that mattered was Christ rose again every time Sam obeyed.

Sam stepped back, allowing the dead priest's fall to continue unimpeded as the oversized Christ descended from the cross, and wondered where he was this time. No doubt inside another of those old cathedrals, the massive, castle-like structures that took man a century to build and God the blink of an eye to immolate. These ancient strongholds of religious indoctrination possessed many things in common, not the least of which was their ostentatious displays of Christ's suffering. They could be relied upon to hold the necessary larger-than-life effigy mounted above the central altar, sheer size making it the most grotesque one in the edifice. That had always been his only directive.

The Christ's eyes rolled and spasmed until finally settling in their sockets slightly askew. A glance from the eerie orbs jolted Sam's perception. Something indefinable yet always the same had been not quite right with each of the previous resurrected Lords—and this one was no different. The ravages of torment and death didn't flee His now-living body, just became more fiercely etched into the flesh, His strange skin bronzed but lacking vitality's hue. *Living* connoted things not present. *Animated* more accurately described that which stood before Sam Vestreemen now. Christ wore His body like an uncomfortable suit improperly cut. More than reverence kept Sam from looking directly at Him whenever possible.

Throughout it all, Christ never uttered a sound. He just looked in Sam's direction, cocked an eyebrow, and Sam's body lurched into action. Somehow Sam just knew what he must do. This was the fifth resurrection Sam had enacted in as many weeks and, if events remained consistent, on as many continents. So far, he'd been in Argentina, Denmark, Mozambique, and New Zealand.

That first time, in La Plata, had been a nightmare of an experience.

He'd come to his senses on a pew in a sanctuary he didn't recognize. He'd stumbled out into the dead of night in a city he didn't know. Without a clue as to his whereabouts, Sam walked the streets, entered the first open establishment he found: a nightclub. Thumping music, gyrating crowds and the heavy prevalence of liquor disguised his disorientation and it didn't take long for someone to classify him a drunken tourist and push him into a cab—minus the cash in his jeans. The cabbie demanded to know his destination and Sam, patting his jacket pockets in frustration, found his passport and an airline ticket with a 7:50 AM departure. Four hours later.

Sam sat in a mindless stupor at the airport until someone dropped a stack of morning papers next to him and started hawking them to passersby. After several minutes, the noise of the gathering crowd penetrated his trance and Sam learned there'd been an atrocious murder during the night. One glance at the front page and he recognized the facade of the cathedral he'd run from. He choked and almost began hyperventilating. The drone of the boarding call finally rescued him, its insistent summons penetrating his horror and propelling him unto the airplane.

There hadn't been any difficulties returning home. Sam's car was in the airport 24-hour parking, neighbors had gotten his mail, and his checkbook revealed he had paid for the ticket months in advance. Everyone acted as if his absence had been a planned trip and welcomed him back. No one mentioned a homicide at Catedral Inmaculada Concepción in La Plata, Argentina, but a search online divulged the truth. Sam read how early-morning parishioners discovered a priest horribly murdered and hung upon the crucifix behind the church's high altar. Investigators had no suspects and presented no explanations for the mysterious absence of the Christ that had been on the crucifix. Theologians worldwide could only offer guesses at how such an integral component of the solid icon could be separated from it.

Sam didn't sleep for five days in an effort to remember what had happened. When he finally did succumb to sheer exhaustion, he next awakened in Vor Frue Kirke Copenhagen, bloody knife again in hand. Sam departed that city before the newspapers came out, but another online search back home disclosed a new homicide in another cathedral. Once again, the ravaged crucifix no longer held the immortal symbol of the Church and the theologians could only speculate. As before, Sam's absence surprised no one.

The next week it had been Mozambique, followed last week by Christchurch, South Island. Now here he stood, in yet another cathedral.

While there had never been any indication how long this would go on, nor how many times he would kill a priest, Sam reasoned he had figured out what was happening. He came from a healthy religious background and still recalled the majority of what he'd been taught as a child. He grew up attending Sunday School and studying his catechisms, so Sam felt he had a decent comprehension of the Bible. He knew the usual trope, about the Devil and demonic possessions, about the rapture and tribulation, about the number of the Beast and the return of the King. Sam just never reached the point in his life where faith superseded knowledge. He counted on belief rather than conviction, understanding rather than application.

He was certain a demon could not inhabit the holy body of the Lord Savior, even if man had crafted it from wood or stone or metal. Sam might not understand everything he experienced right now, but he sure could recognize the significance of certain things as foretold in Biblical prophecies. The classic warning of God's impending return—wars and rumors of wars—had been present for some time. The dearth of a godly society ensured a rebirth of Sodom and Gomorrah—the twin cities God's wrath burned from the face of the earth once before. The way Sam figured things, it was high time the Lord came back to exact some more of His judgment.

No, even though Christ still hadn't spoken to him, Sam Vestreemen didn't require any explanation. He knew seven was God's perfect number and he knew there were seven continents. He'd been on four of them already, and Sam would wager his IRA he now stood on a fifth. Sam could spot a pattern when he saw one, and this was a sure thing in his mind. It seemed he'd been called by God to lead the way for the return of His Son—a modern-day John the Baptist. So what if Sam didn't belong to the Catholic congregation, everyone knew corruption filled the Church. Jesus Himself had been considered an outsider, so having another clear the path for Christ's second coming seemed about right. After tonight, there'd be only two more pilgrimages before the final manifestation was fulfilled.

Sam wrenched his wandering thoughts back to the present and marveled at the dual consciousness he could now maintain. It was disconcerting, being two different people at the same time. One the puppet of mortal flesh doing its unknown master's bidding, the other Sam's bodiless spirit barely tethered to the alien reality within the chamber. It hadn't been like this in the beginning. At first, he'd just been blindly obeying, oblivious to his other half, his soul.

The circumstances of the first two holy homicides were beyond his ken—he remembered nothing before his dazed journey through La Plata, and Denmark's Church of Our Lady was only a bloody haze. He did "wake up" in Maputo, however, part of him coming to his senses in time to witness the awkward Christ stagger toward the aisle. Sam had struggled against the mysterious hold controlling his body and mind, but there hadn't been any lessening in the power exerted over him. Whatever kept him enthralled vanished only with the specter.

In the Christchurch Basilica during the fourth excursion, Sam again became aware of his surroundings, this time mid-throat slicing. He fought furiously to free himself, straining to prevent his hand from finishing its heinous act. There had been a slight weakening in the anonymous control, but his fingers wouldn't release the knife and Sam couldn't halt its ripping force. Only after the killing stroke did Sam's spirit manage to snap free of the external force.

While a sliver of Sam's cognizance lingered within his mortal body, trapped in the macabre performance with this theophany, the remnant of his awareness—his conscious self—was expelled when he became host to the nameless occupant. Locked in a disembodied isolation, cut off from his physical form, and unable to communicate or interact with anyone, Sam observed transpiring events with a separation completely foreign to his normal persona. No matter how he raged, Sam remained impotent, relegated to a role as phantom spectator. This frightened Sam even more than the necromantic furor around him.

A crushing hopelessness descended on Sam, exposing his personal help-lessness. Tears of frustration welled as he watched his body jerk through motions over which he had no control. Motions now familiar but still as puzzling as the first time he'd performed them. The reborn Christ stood in the chancel, feet straddling the altar, allowing the blood and water seeping from His side to wash across those prayer lights still burning. Many blinked out, shrouding the death-rebuking deity in robes of darkness. Some candles flickered, flared, fought back, their flames burning darker red. Old-blood red. Those were the ones Sam watched his hands pick up and carry to the central aisle, the ones placed in designated spots.

His body was an automaton of divine purpose, cycling between altar and aisle, delivering each votive candle with measured steps. It never stumbled, never lost its balance bending and placing each votive in precise, equidistant positions until a design stood complete. The priest's pooling blood—dripping from the chancel steps and spreading in a slow creep across the floor of the nave—recoiled upon contact with the closed pattern. Sam watched in fascinated horror as the blood attempted to flow back up the chancel steps to its source.

The faintest sense of apprehension tickled Sam's consciousness, a feathery touch of invisible fingers trying to turn him about. The eerie sensation of someone reaching out for him, an unseen presence seeking his attention, distracted him from the fleeing ichor. He shifted uneasily, glancing about for the source of the uncomfortable feeling. Sam could almost hear his name insistently repeated, the monotone boring into his brain.

He did hear his name.

Sam's soul looked about, seeking the voice. He scanned the sanctuary, noting his static body where it stood poised for instant action outside the diagram, the vacant look on his face belying the leap of his heart at every call of his name. Unfamiliar motion in his peripheral vision drew Sam's interest: the head of the undead god jerked and shuddered in strange rhythm. Sam witnessed a panoply of emotions war upon the anguished face. He stared, wondering what troubled his Savior, and watched Him step into the vaguely familiar pattern.

The repositioned candles blazed, their eruption leaving dazzling white spots flashing before Sam's ethereal eyes. The glare of the flash silhouetted another figure within close proximity; Sam identified the peculiar outline as a pentagram; he recognized the odd cadence of the Lord's head bob. Sam flinched beneath the sudden flare and in dawning confusion—because of the symbol on the floor, because he knew the new arrival, because the jerk and shudder had matched the tempo of the voice calling Sam's name.

The figure had visited Sam's kill sites before. Sam first noticed it at the cathedral in Maputo, but it hadn't done much more than hover high up near the apex. Now that Sam considered it, it had appeared about the same time he'd begun to cut his spirit free of enslavement. It must have followed him from Mozambique, for Sam had seen it inside his home twice since then, no more defined than before. He had ignored it, assuming it a residual hallucination from his experiences. He'd seen it in South Island as well, stronger, but still he'd ignored it.

Now it seemed to gain strength from his stare, accumulating mass and shape, finally defining itself. The shadowy form beckoned Sam closer, its gestures calm yet emphatic. He couldn't see the being's face, but Sam sensed its lips moving, knew it spoke. Close to reading its lips, a flash of movement in the corner of his eye snatched his attention away. Sam turned and watched his possessed body jerk into motion again, heading toward the altar and the dead priest.

Prior to tonight's revelations, Sam had not considered himself a very godly man. In fact, he had rarely considered it at all. Religion had its place, all right—to be there when it was needed. *If* it was needed. Sam believed in the existence of one God and His counterpart, Satan. He believed in a heaven and a hell. Sam even believed that to avoid the latter he needed the help of the former. He admitted to being a little fuzzy on the faith part of the equation, but Sam expected he knew enough about it to matter. He recognized it as a universal truism that God moved in mysterious ways, no sense in disputing that.

Very mysterious ways. And if those ways required Sam Vestreemen's helping hand, well then by God, He'd get it. Even if certain things weren't making much sense to Sam any longer. Despite certain things not making much sense at all.

Sam refused to think much about the five priests he'd personally delivered unto their eternal rewards. He knew there had always been sacrifices made to gods, and the Bible itself contained numerous martyrs' stories. He shunted the startlingly strong memory of pounding heels aside, forced himself to think about other things. Sam trusted all would be explained someday. It wasn't his place to dispute God's chosen path of return.

Further motion from his incorporeal visitor caught Sam's attention. Eyes aslant, he discovered the most perfect profile he'd ever seen. Sam blinked, allowing his vision to adjust to the oblique angle, and marveled at the entity's delineating features. The golden hue of its flesh discouraged any shadows while it remained muted enough to reveal the purest of countenances. As he'd implicitly understood instructions since the onset of these excursions, Samuel Vestreemen realized he now stood in the presence of God. The one and only God.

An unexpected hope surged within his breast. Samuel marveled at this abrupt need, then fell prey to a terrible suspicion. If this latest presence spoke true, who was *that*? Samuel glanced at his erstwhile Christ and in sudden clarity truly saw him for what he was.

Dawning comprehension crumpled Samuel's spirit and drove him to the floor. His stomach seethed with the gnawing guilt that assailed it, his lungs labored beneath the weight of shame that pressed upon him. Almost catatonic with horror, Samuel saw himself across the aisle, a slight stain of blackness standing with bloodstained hands gleaming in the shadow of the larger and deeper well of darkness towering above him starkly defined by heaven's sterile glow. There was no denying the wages exacted by his sins—not with the body of the priest laying there, the sound of five sets of drumming heels pounding through his memory, the sticky residue of warm blood clinging to his hands. Samuel identified each of them in the cold light of perfection and discovered his belief in hell hadn't been nearly strong enough. The knowledge he'd kept secure in his mind for all these years finally penetrated his heart, and Samuel knew beyond all doubt that death and eternal damnation loomed before him. Despair overwhelmed him, for only the sinless God could save him now—the same God before whom Samuel stood beside an imposter.

Samuel staggered on the chancel steps, disoriented at the surprise return to his physical form and the roar of anger that burst from the manmade Jesus. Lack of balance and the slipperiness of the priest's viscous discharge spilled him backward to the floor of the nave. He landed with a thud and the sound of shattering glass. The impact drove Samuel's rediscovered breath from his lungs and slammed his head against the aisle floor. Fog threatened to fill his brain until the sharp pain piercing his left shoulder dashed it away.

The pain brought with it a lucidity he regretted instantly. Blinking away tears, Samuel confronted the ungodly brute's cruel face within inches of his own. Gnashing incisors snapped a single hand span from Samuel's nose and fetid breath hammered him, pounded at his faltering resistance, splintered his barely remaining innocence. A cold malevolence Samuel hadn't felt before now emanated from the beast and wound its way into Samuel's mind, wedged itself deep into all the cracks and crevices of his soul. A living presence, its palpable hunger attacked him with razored teeth and chewed at the edges of his essence.

It hurt like hell.

Samuel shrieked, the excruciating pain ravaging the very marrow of his being. The bestial visage split in malefic grin. Hellfires deep in the black sockets beneath the crown of thorns bored into Samuel's eyes, eager to consume the dawning hope within his heart. Samuel's tongue dried up as his voice fled, dribbling a pitiful whimper across his lips with its departure.

No doubt remained that both devil and hell existed.

A thump inside Samuel's chest rocked him and he almost passed out. Another thump accompanied by the sound of a knock shook him from somewhere within his chest cavity. A flurry of blows had him convulsing across the floor, banging his head upon tile and pew in rapid succession. He closed his eyes, praying it was all a dream, knowing it was not, willing himself to slip into unconsciousness.

"Samuel. Samuel."

Several times his name rang out before Samuel realized he wasn't hearing voices despite the disorientation threatening his consciousness. He caught his breath and waited for the next call, felt it with the next thump, and traced it to its source deep within his black and withered core. Once again, Samuel found himself disembodied and able to exist without mortal restraint. Only this time he traveled in a darkness so deep he could not see his trembling hand before his very face. This time, he knew where he was—and felt trapped, terrified. Samuel shouted out against the devouring blackness and swung his hands about him.

His words bounced back into his face and his hands slammed against rough walls. Samuel slapped at them with open palms, scratched the wooden surface with fingers clawed and desperate. Panicked and frantic he beat at the walls, dreading yet willing the next battering thump to shake them. It came and did, bringing with it a throb of sound strong enough to send him to his knees. He fell, his hands trailing down the wall before him until colliding with cold iron. He snatched his flesh from the bone-numbing chill and gasped at the familiar feel. A door knob. A way out.

Samuel fumbled with the knob, ignoring the ice-crusted surface slicing into the meat of his palms. It took two hands to twist the protesting metal, the blood from his shredding fingers warming it, melting away the hoary rime. He tugged at the heavy barrier, sobbing at his slowness. "God!" he wailed. "Help me!" He swung the door open and stretched forth a hand

...and dropped it limply to his side, cowering beneath the glare of holy scrutiny that shown into his heart. "You don't need me. You shouldn't even want me," he mumbled.

"I am Truth, Samuel. The Truth is in Me and I am in the Truth. Can you trust in Me?"

Samuel nodded in mute acknowledgment, his silent weeping holding his tongue hostage. Of course Truth was in Him and He was the Truth. He was the One and Only Way. Samuel's mouth struggled to form the word, struggled to create the sounds of the name burning like a sigil branded in his mind: Jesus.

Samuel Vestreemen finally believed what he'd known all along. He rejoiced in the novelty of such immediate salvation, relaxed in his new-found faith. Briefly. Though it paid immediate spiritual dividends, it did not extricate him from the dangerous position he was in.

Samuel blinked and reality returned, found him impaled by the fiend's horrific glare. It crouched over him, lips curled back in vicious sneer, a long string of acidic spittle a movement away from drooling upon him. Sudden understanding flowed across the thing's face and it moved, reeling back like a furious canine brought short against the end of its leash, pent frustration and rage released in a dread roar. The drool fell.

Samuel failed the first test of his trust.

He recoiled.

The instant Samuel wavered in his faith, the beast stretched for him, the bleeding hands of a crucified Christ transformed into wicked talons. There could be no denying its demonic nature now.

"Sweet Jesus!" Samuel cried out, his voice faltering in unfamiliar prayer. The creature growled and flinched away, renewed its strike once the last syllable sounded. Samuel licked dry lips and hurried his mantra, the name of Jesus tumbling off his tongue in desperate entreaty. The next utterance enacted spectacular results, slamming the demon aside while staving off its attack. Samuel coughed and sang out again.

Each repetition of Jesus's name bent the knee of the battling fallen angel and an invisible lash opened gashes across its body. Each repetition washed a fount of the true Savior's blood across Samuel's black sins—though it was several moments before Samuel sensed these equally impressive results within him. He called anew upon the name of the Lord, his lips spread in a grim smile despite the cough that followed. The wracking cough that followed that stole his smile and doubled him over. Gasping for breath, Samuel wiped the back of a hand across his lips and stared at the black phlegm that covered it.

His stomach churned and heaved then heaved again. Something lodged in Samuel's throat. Tears burst from his eyes at the searing pain and he gagged in violent reaction, every thrust of his throat muscles propelling the object ever upward. Faint from lack of oxygen, his mouth distended beyond all normalcy, Samuel pressed his thumbs into his own jugular and forced the obstruction free. One final spastic heave spat a chunk of gore from his mouth and left him weeping on the floor. He looked in agony at the sodden mass, recognizing it for what it was—a black placenta of lies and disbelief, its severed umbilical cord crimson with Christ's cleansing blood.

"Thank you Jesus." Samuel rolled onto his side and watched the battle's finish from the ground, mumbling Jesus's name without cessation.

The false Christ had shrunk and it continued to lose a piece of its alarming guise with every blow. Every strike sloughed more black strips from the walls of Samuel's heart and he spat each one out, grinning weakly at their bitter taste knowing seeds of faith took root in the fertileness left behind. The rampaging beast that once resisted with calculated intensity was now reduced to reckless ferocity. Realizing it could not escape and seeking only survival, it twisted about to face its tormentor head on.

Samuel gaped at the awesome disparity. Unadulterated golden light streamed from his left, clearly declaring the identity of its foul counterpart. Pure radiance faced stygian depths and subdued them. The more confident Samuel grew in belief and prayer the brighter shone God's splendor until both litany and light filled the sanctuary. The charged air crackled and became a living thing, individual strands ferreting out and consuming all trace of hell's intrusion upon the mortal realm. One strand cleansed the altar in a flash of radiance; the dark red flames of the cursed votives vanished in another. One erased the pentagram, while another snatched the bloody knife and made it dance in midair. Samuel stared at it, dreading what might next happen.

Once each strand completed clearing its chosen path, it wound back upon itself and hastened toward the hovering weapon, whipping past Samuel in such a blur of living light that he was forced to close his eyes against the vibrant beauty. Each successive charge stirred up winds that enveloped and buffeted the no longer consecrated icon. Samuel choked on the simmering air and opened his eyes, squinting against the glare. He stared in awe at the glowing weapon of liquid light the knife had become. It quivered in the air, the fearsome winds of the growing tempest pent behind it. A pause the duration of a single heartbeat allowed him to see the word *Truth* etched upon its elongated blade—then the gale sent it hurtling toward the monstrous fiend. The sword struck with a thunderclap and drove the charlatan from its gruesome vessel.

The skin of the impostor's body, stripped of its man-made shell, roiled and smoked beneath the light's savage caress. The demon's roars turned to squeals as its lips peeled back in horrified rictus—then in one swift convulsion it caved in upon itself, its mouth spreading wide and swallowing its own head, the crown of thorns shredding its throat as it was pulled inside out, the entire being crumpling as if in the grip of a mighty fist. Then it was no more.

Though still smothered in the dark of predawn night and despite the inconsistent illumination provided by the sporadic candlelight, Samuel saw that the church had gained a pristine quality absent at the onset of his visit. Even as the heavenly glow of his Lord's coming subsided, Samuel saw things more clearly. He knew eternal darkness pushed against the boundaries of his sight; knew it would always push, aggressively and impatiently awaiting its turn.

"Many false gods will come before you."

Samuel jumped, then collapsed to his knees and bowed his head, only to come face-to-face with the slain priest. Tears coursed down his cheeks as he sought an answer. It was hopeless. No words came. He felt as if he, too, sank into that pit of damnation into which God had cast their foe. He flung his hands up in a survival reflex, lifted his face in supplication to the face of God.

"My God, what have I done? Can You ever forgive me?"

Samuel Vestreemen discovered the security of his salvation when he felt the hand of God stretch out and cover him. Samuel felt himself shielded from his despair, brought forth from his misery. He heard God's voice from within his heart.

"It is finished." Samuel closed his eyes in ecstasy and reveled in the joy of sure knowledge. "This day, Samuel, you will be with me in paradise."

His eyes lurched open and he watched with dismay the fading of the Lord's presence. He blinked, and the light of Heaven was gone, replaced by the light of the morning sun strained through stained glass windows. Samuel studied the dance of the colored sunlight speckling the altar and empty chancel steps, then smiled and raised his head. The vigil lights were renewed, the blood removed, the cathedral transformed. He smiled in childish delight.

A hand fell on his shoulder and Samuel lurched to his feet, staring at the white collar. He felt the man's fingers tighten and heard his sharp intake of breath. A pause, then, "Are you in danger, my child? The Church can offer you some shelter, but tell me, who is that has harmed you?"

Samuel recoiled from the priest's warm exhalation, but he couldn't pull his eyes from the man's face, the intimate details of which were forever engraved in his memory. Concern furrowed the priest's brow and his hands sprang forward to steady the reeling Samuel.

"How long have you knelt here?" the priest asked. "If it is hope and peace you so earnestly seek, you've come to the right place."

Samuel's eyes bulged and he gulped for air. His mind felt thick and he could barely hear the rest of the man's speech over the beating of his heart. Cold sweat erupted across his body.

"In a world as troubled as ours, it is easy for the Evil One to lead a man astray." The priest gestured upward with his right hand, his head and eyes following his own movement. "Only by keeping our eyes on Him—" The holy man's voice cut off in a strangled gasp and his fingers spasmed, digging painfully into Samuel's bicep.

"The crucifix! Our Lord's body is missing from His cross!" The priest's voice fell into a whisper, his reverence evident in its very tenor. "It's a miracle."

Samuel's eyes had begun to rise, begun to follow the priest's outstretched hand, when they fell upon the left side of the man's neck, just where the priestly collar dipped at the juncture between neck and shoulder due to the raised opposing arm. They froze on the exposed edge of livid pink tissue.

Tears streamed down the priest's cheeks and he let go of Samuel to raise both his hands in worship. With sudden urgency, Samuel clawed at the man, knocking his left arm down and snagging his collar in grasping fingers and ripping the cloth away until baring the entire jagged scar that ran across the man's throat.

Sudden pain exploded in Samuel's chest and his left arm went numb. A cloud of darkness dropped over him like a shroud.

With a snarl, the priest whirled on him, his once smiling features replaced by the leering face of Samuel's former demonic patron. "You'll not escape that easily!" A sickening sensation filled Samuel's stomach and bile rose through his esophagus. He thought he heard echoes of wicked laughter, but he couldn't be sure over the amplified rushing of the blood through his temples. He tried to choke out an answer, instead snorted and gagged on the bitter fluids robbing him of his remaining oxygen.

Samuel yanked at his own shirt collar, tried to take a deep breath, and keeled over. Tears welled in his eyes, the severe pain in his chest more than he could bear. Just before he landed on the floor of the nave for a third time, Samuel heard the now familiar voice. Even as his heart burst and his neck slammed against the front pew Samuel's face relaxed into the first peace-filled smile of his life.

THE HOUSE OF ABANDONED CHARACTERS

MARIANNE HALBERT

Paul jumped onto the page, and immediately experienced a sudden sense of vertigo. The scene swam before his eyes, and then settled into focus.

He was standing on a stone path. Ahead of him, the path led to the front porch steps of a mansion. The word *antebellum* came to mind. It was white, with black shutters flanking dozens of windows. Sturdy pillars lined the wrap-around porch. Glancing behind him, Paul saw the path ended at a wrought iron gate. Past the gate was a dirt road that seemed to go on for miles in either direction. He could see other homes sparsely strewn across the horizon, but none appeared to be within a comfortable walking distance. He faced forward and made his way toward the house.

Wisteria and Spanish moss draped the live oaks which bordered the path. The smell of jasmine filled the air. Magnolia and azalea bushes lined the front porch. Paul knew he'd never been here before, but each step felt so familiar. As though he had laid each stone by hand. As he ascended the steps, he felt he'd carved each wooden plank, driven in each nail with the sweat of his own hands. *Where am I?*

He could hear voices coming through the screen door. There was no wind to carry them. He was about to knock, but suddenly didn't feel it necessary. *Do you knock to enter your own home?* He pushed in on the screen door, and it creaked, but gave easily. The room he entered was bigger than he had imagined. It looked like a saloon. A mahogany and brass bar spanned the left side of the room. Tumblers, shot glasses, Pilsners and more were lined up in orderly fashion in front of a mirrored wall. He picked up bits and pieces of various conversations from the groups seated at tables around the room. As he stood in the entryway, dumbfounded, a large redhead grabbed him by the arm.

"Over here, sweetheart, we've been expectin' y'all."

He didn't quite feel like he was part of a "y'all" but he let himself be led to a round four-seater table. The redhead pulled a chair out for him, and he took it.

"What can I getcha to drink?" Before he could answer, she was pouring him a draft behind the bar. She set it down in front of him, and plopped down in another chair. An elderly gentleman in a tweed vest and suit was seated at a third chair. Across from Paul sat a young woman. For a moment, all he could see was her blonde hair, in loose waves, draped over her face. *Her eyes would be like the double sapphires his mother wore, the natural blush of her cheeks echoed the rose petals that climbed the garden fence...*

The redhead spoke up first.

"The first five minutes are a bitch. Wait until you get your land legs, you'll be alright. Name's Lula Slye, this here's Evan Cushing." The elderly gentleman gave a nod. "And across from you is Susan Curteledge."

The blond looked up and he saw that her eyes *were* sapphire blue, her cheeks blushed like rose. Those eyes held *the promise of tears, an ever-present melancholy,* but the mouth smiled. "Pleased," she said.

Paul found it difficult to turn away from those eyes, but he did. Addressing Lula, he asked, "Where am I?"

"Well, sweetheart, that's a doozy of a question. You are in the land of Vegas Coleman."

That name struck a chord.

"Coleman...why do I know that name?"

The old gent spoke up. "Isn't it obvious? He created you. Invented you. Authored you as it were. We all sprung from his cerebral cortex, ergo, at some point we all develop an awareness of his subconscious. Once abandoned, we come here, and eventually absorb some of his mind's inner workings. Not that it does you much good. We are what we are, never to advance. Fortunately for some of us," and at this he cast a disparaging glance at Lula, "some of us were created more advanced to begin with."

"Oh, blow it out your southern wazoo," she responded.

Paul still felt the disorientation that hadn't left him. "Abandoned? Created? Is this a cult, a church?"

The blond opened her mouth, hesitantly. "No. Coleman is a man. An author. He's published some novels, a few short stories. Sometimes he creates characters that don't . . . fit in. With his idea for the final product. Or his editor's. Those that fit in exist for eternity in his mind, and the readers'. Those that don't fit in—"

"Get dumped here," Lula finished. "Those first nights he laid awake, thinking about me, were unforgettable. It was like falling in love."

Susan shot her a glance. "What would you know about falling in love?"

"Give me a break, sweetcheeks. Just because it wasn't written in, doesn't mean it wasn't a part of my backstory. When I was still a svelte brunette before his agent suggested he make me a more colorful character. Damn re-write."

Susan got up in a huff and walked up a wide flight of stairs near the front of the room. Paul felt compelled to follow her, but sensed that his answers lay here at the table. He hadn't touched his beer. He was about to ask Lula another question when two men came up to the table demanding another round. At least he thought they were men. They had human form, but were just gray shapes. Faceless. They gestured and emitted a mumbling sound.

"Duty calls." Lula went to the bar and proceeded to fill a dozen shot glasses.

Paul turned to Mr. Cushing. "I'm sorry, I know I seem confused, but I think I may have amnesia, or a concussion or something." He looked toward the gray men. "I'm seeing things."

"No, young man, your eyes do not deceive you. When a character is so woefully underdeveloped that they aren't even given a name, or more than a mere sentence, there is nothing on which to base individual characteristics. The *waitress* who dropped off lunch at a table, the *driver* of a car that sped past, the *group of soldiers* seen from a hillside. One sentence plot devices that never really take form. When they are cut out of a story, they come here, as we all do, only they remain pitifully foggy."

Paul's chest tensed. *Don't panic.* "Is there a phone I can use?"

Dry eyes studied him. "And just who would you call?"

"Well, I don't know. 911? Or my girlfriend? I think I had a, well she may be just a friend."

"Cruel. He hadn't decided yet had he, when he discarded you?"

Lula sat back down and set a full shot glass in front of herself, and another beer in front of Paul, even though he hadn't touched the first one.

"So is it coming back yet?" she asked. "You know, I was the first abandoned character in this house. That's why I get the clearest picture of all the new ones before they arrive. You were just how I'd pictured you, the dark hair, smooth skin, the glasses, thin build." She looked him up and down, a flirtatious grin spreading across her face.

"You don't know me." Paul was shaking. "You're all suffering from some mass hysteria, you all believe you're characters, but I'm real. I'm a man!"

Mr. Cushing stood up and pulled out a cigar. "A man with no past."

"That's not true. I'm from Hoboken, New Jersey. My parents died when I was young, but I have a brother."

Lula drank her shot, then tilted her head toward him.

"A brother? As in you have specific memories of sharing a room, generally pissing each other off, or as in he had a brother..."

"I have a brother. As in—" He couldn't keep from saying it, and somehow he knew it was in their heads already. His voice was hollow when he spoke. "He had a brother who lived out west."

Lula and Mr. Cushing exchanged a sympathetic glance.

"You might try the poker table in the corner," Lula said. Paul looked at that table, and saw it surrounded by a group of the gray men.

Paul had heard enough of this. He stood, rattling the table, causing the drinks to slosh. He turned to run out the front door, but a sense of dread stopped him. He thought of Susan, and ran up the stairs she had taken earlier, hoping to find solace in her eyes. When Paul reached the landing at the second floor of the mansion he saw a young couple.

"Have either of you seen Susan Curteledge?" he asked.

The girl turned to him. "She's probably on the balcony. That's where she goes."

"The balcony?"

"Keep going up the stairs to the top floor," the boy said, grinning. "Follow the ballroom to the back of the house. You can't miss it." The boy turned back to the girl and tickled her waist. Paul ran up the steps, to the sound of giggles fading. The steps seemed to go on for several flights, but eventually ended, opening up into an enormous room. Chandeliers hung from the ceiling. Paul's eyes were drawn upward, taking in the crown molding. Tapestries lined the walls. At the far end of the room stood an exspanse of windows and French doors, revealing a lone figure on the balcony. The boy was right. You couldn't miss it.

Paul's footsteps echoed throughout the grand ballroom as he crossed the high polished hardwood floor. He opened a door, and stepped on to the balcony. Susan was standing by the railing, looking out over a vast landscape. She turned when he called her name. Her eyes held that same sad expression, as though feelings were welling up inside her, she just couldn't quite let them out.

"I was told I'd find you here," Paul said. The balcony was expansive, but it felt intimate just then.

Susan sighed. "Most of Coleman's characters prefer the saloon, or the bedrooms. I'm one of the few he created who prefers a solitary existence."

"Not you too. Those weirdos downstairs don't really have you convinced you're a character, do they?"

"Paul, you've been here long enough now. You should be coming to that realization."

He said nothing, just stared at her.

"You need proof?" She walked toward the far end of the balcony, where a telescope stood on a tripod. She beckoned him. "See for yourself."

A queasy feeling settled in his gut, but he approached her. He leaned slightly, and put his eye up to the telescope. At first it was a blur, but he adjusted the focus.

"What the—"

He jumped back, away from the telescope, as if it had bitten him.

"Don't be afraid," Susan said, surrender in her voice. "They are far enough away. None of it can hurt you."

"What *was* that?" When he'd looked through the lens, out on the horizon was the tip of the ocean. A schooner, and something else. Tentacles.

"That's Adventure Avenue. Turn the telescope to the southwest, you can see the haunted castle of Horror Hollow. Southeast lies Sci-Fi Circle, complete with flying saucers. There's a smaller balcony on the north end of the mansion, from there you can view Western Way and Detective Drive."

This was too much. But Paul couldn't help himself. He gingerly approached the telescope, looked doubtfully at Susan, then brought his eye once more to the lens. He didn't know how many minutes passed, but what had looked to the naked eye like a concentration of dark clouds became a perpetual lightning storm over the haunted castle. He then swiveled the telescope and watched men on the ship battle a ferocious sea creature. He spent the most time mesmerized by the UFO battle taking place over the farmland off Sci-Fi Circle. When he had seen enough, he stood back, silent. Susan said nothing. Finally he had processed enough to speak.

"Where are we?" he asked, resignation in his voice.

"Mainstream, USA."

"Don't you mean Main Street, USA?"

"Mainstream, as in literature. You won't see any strange monsters or elves in the house of Vegas Coleman."

Paul approached the railing, gripping the top of it with both hands to steady himself.

"How long have you been here?"

"I don't know. Time loses its meaning here. We don't progress, so there really isn't much to look forward to."

"Have you ever visited any of those other places?"

Susan gasped, horrified. "No, of course not. We can't leave here. Can't go beyond the gate."

"Why not? Has anyone tried?"

"No, but," she shivered, "I've walked along the live oak path. The closer I get to the gate, the stronger I sense it. I'm certain—going past the gate would mean death."

"Based on a feeling?"

"How would you know? I'm trying to help you adjust, and all you have to give in return is ridicule?" Her lower lip was trembling. She flung open the French doors, and disappeared into the ballroom. Paul could hear her footsteps, running away. Away from him.

He followed her. When he got to the first floor, he scanned the saloon. Susan was up at the bar talking to Lula. As Paul approached them, Susan turned away from him.

"Lula," he said. "What do you know about what lies beyond the gate?"

She laughed, a hearty, full bodied roar. "Susie-Q here told me you were asking about that. You can't go out there, Sugar. Nobody goes past that gate."

"But *why*?" Paul insisted.

Mr. Cushing walked up stiffly, puffing on his cigar.

"Because we exist here, in the land of Vegas Coleman. Beyond that gate lies the creations of other minds. We simply could not exist elsewhere."

"I might have to admit he created me," Paul explained, "but that doesn't mean he controls me. Especially now that he's abandoned me. I decide who I am and where I go."

Mr. Cushing responded in a dismissive tone.

"Young man, who you are remains static. You can no more change your characteristics than dear Susan here could force a tear to fall from her eyes or than Lula could be anything but a sailor-mouthed, whiskey-swigging, ample-bosomed barmaid."

"Hey, leave my bosoms out of it," Lula scolded.

"No," Paul said. "He may have written me as a beer man, but I'm, I'm actually fond of," and he scanned the bottles along the mirror. "Gin. Lula, a shot of your best gin, please."

She raised one eyebrow, but poured the shot and slid it across the bar to him. He gripped it, not really knowing if he was a gin man, since Coleman never had him drink any. He lifted the shotglass and stared at Mr. Cushing, defiant. Paul downed the shot. He coughed once and set the glass on the bar. They were all holding their breath, when a smile spread across Paul's face.

"I *am* a gin man."

"Impossible," Mr. Cushing challenged.

Lula was staring at him. "What is that, on your chin?"

Did he dribble some of the gin? Paul rubbed his chin and felt...stubble.

There was fear in Susan's voice. "You don't have a beard. You're clean-shaven. Always clean-shaven."

Paul looked at himself in the mirror behind the bar. A sense of euphoria spread through him.

"You see? We can re-create ourselves. We determine our destiny. And we can go beyond the gate."

"Coleman has sometimes expressed that the stories write themselves. The characters tell him where to go next," Lula said. "I always thought that was just humble author hogwash."

Susan was trembling. Paul took her by the arms.

"Susan, I'm walking through that gate. And if you'll miss me, and you want to cry, you can shed a tear. Your eyes don't just have to hold the promise of tears, they can make tears if you want them to."

"No!" She pushed him away.

"And Lula, you can be that svelte brunette if you want to be," and he jumped up on the bar, planting a kiss on her lips, "but don't lose your charm."

He hopped down and clapped Mr. Cushing on the back.

"And Evan my man," Paul said, gently taking the cigar from the stunned old gent, puffing twice before handing it back. "I know you are too fond of yourself to want to change, but you can be anything, anything you want to be. As for me," he shouted to the crowd in the room, "I'm an explorer!"

Paul burst out the front door and leapt down the steps to the stone path. He was practically skipping along when he heard a commotion behind him. Lula's southern drawl sounded panicked.

"Paul, wait!"

He stopped and turned. Lula was running toward him, with Susan and Mr. Cushing close behind.

"This isn't your destiny Darlin', it's a re-write."

He felt some of his joy falter momentarily. "A what?"

Even Mr. Cushing seemed genuinely disappointed.

"I'm afraid she's right Paul, it's the only logical explanation. Coleman apparently is making you more 'manly' and pulling you back into the novel. On the bright side, odds are that young lady will turn out to be more than just a friend."

"I am not a re-write! I'm changing because I'm deciding who I really am. And I am going out that gate to explore the world."

What happened next would become legend in the house of abandoned characters. Some speculated Paul ceased to exist. Others were certain he would exist forever in the lastest Coleman novel. And a quiet majority hoped against hope that Paul overcame the odds. Overcame the physics of characterhood. They hoped that he became real, and they imagined him out there somewhere. Exploring the world.

Evan Cushing stood stoic, motionless. Lula Slye held one hand over her ample bosom.

Paul ran the length of the path, the wisteria and Spanish moss waving goodbye as he went. When he got to the gate he turned and waved. He was a different Paul than the one who'd arrived here. Taller. More muscular. His hair tousled, sporting a five o'clock shadow. And he was a gin man. A broad smile spread across his face. The confident smile of a man who knows exactly where he is going, and can't wait to take the next step. He pulled open the gate, and walked through it.

As Paul vanished, a single tear escaped from Susan's eye and ran down her cheek.

THE OFFICE OF SECOND CHANCES

D. S. CRANKSHAW

"You're too late, boy," the crazy old man yelled, shaking his knife at Daniel. Droplets of Tasha's blood splattered the ground.

Daniel's hand slipped from the rock and he nearly fell. On the floor of the cavern below lay four of the madman's followers, groaning in the torchlight. They hadn't been competent fighters. Daniel regained his hold and continued grappling up the cliff face. On the ledge above him, Tasha remained bound between the rock columns. Blood trailed down her cheek where she'd been sliced by the old man. But as she struggled against the chains, the madman brandished his knife near her face.

Wanting to distract him, Daniel yelled, "If you're hoping for a virgin sacrifice, you're about a month too late!"

"Dan!" Tasha stopped struggling and scowled at him.

"A virgin? Pah!" the madman spat. "The Glorious Lord of Devastation would never accept such a pure sacrifice. He hungers for a woman who is neither mother nor virgin. That's why we chose her."

"How could you know?" Tasha turned her scowl on the old man.

"Oh, I have very good sources. And the rumor's all over your high school."

"Dan!"

Daniel heaved himself another couple of feet up the rock incline. "What? People ask questions, and I'm a terrible liar." Of course, most people had believed they were doing it long before it actually happened, but he hadn't lied then either. He'd just let people believe what they wanted to.

The madman peered down at him. "Now that the sacred blade has been wetted with her impure blood, His Glorious Lordship shall consume her, body and soul."

Daniel hoisted himself upward. "Why couldn't you just off yourselves, like every other freaking doomsday cult?" As he finally gripped the edge of the rock shelf, the madman stomped at his fingers. Daniel caught the foot with his free hand and yanked, sending the old man falling backwards. Then Daniel scrambled onto the ledge and sprang to his feet, but the madman lay unmoving, his head cracked against a stalagmite just outside a ten foot circle of runes surrounding Tasha.

Daniel ran to her and hugged her. "Are you all right?"

"I'm fine. Where's Johnny?"

He pulled back. "If you want, I can leave and you can wait for him to rescue you."

"If you're going to be that way, just get these things off of me," she said, rattling the chains. "The old guy has the keys."

"Keys?" Daniel noticed the manacles had old-fashioned locks. Stalking over to the unmoving madman, he quickly patted down the old creep until he found three large iron keys. As he did so, a tremor shook the floor. One by one, the runes began to glow red.

"What's going on?" Daniel asked.

"Whatever it is, it can't be good. Hurry up!"

He tried the keys on her left manacle. By the time it opened, half the runes were blazing.

"Where'd he get these things?" Daniel asked, staring at the keys. "Some S&M store? They look new."

Tasha flexed her free hand. "I'm more worried about the fact that he has two more sets. Come on, get the other one off and let's go."

As Daniel reached to unlock the other manacle, the remaining runes flared and the floor beneath them vanished. Daniel threw himself at Tasha, wrapping his arms around her waist as they fell. She was jerked to a stop by the manacle holding her right wrist, but he slid down her body until he fetched up against her sneakers. Once he dared open his eyes, he could see that they were in a pit whose circumference matched the circle of runes. The smooth walls disappeared into darkness below, while Tasha dangled just beneath the lip.

Daniel called, "Can you pull us out?"

"Are you kidding? You try doing pull-ups with someone twice your weight hanging on to your feet."

Daniel wrapped one arm around her ankles, reached up, and groped along her jeans for a better grip.

"Hey!" Tasha protested. "Hey! Watch where you're putting your hand!"

"Trying not to fall, here!" He grabbed hold of her belt before her squirming knocked him off, and her jeans slid down two inches before catching on her hips.

"I swear, if you pull my pants off, I'm going to slap you!"

"If you'd said that earlier, we wouldn't be in this mess."

"I did say it earlier, but you kept on begging like some damn puppy."

"Just give me your hand and help me the rest of the way up."

With her free hand, Tasha reached down to help Daniel up.

"Hey kids!"

They both looked up to see a blood-smeared face grinning down at them. The madman lay at the edge of the pit, his knife in one hand and his iron keys in the other. His bulging eyes looked ready to fall out of their sockets.

"I thought you had the keys," Tasha hissed at Daniel.

"I dropped them when the ground opened up and swallowed us," Daniel said. "Sorry!"

The cultist wasn't paying attention. "Isn't this wonderful? His Glorious Lordship is claiming his sacrifice. Your impure soul will provide the fuel he needs to break free and consume the world."

"You bastard!" Tasha yelled. "Let us go!"

"Hey, that's just what I was thinking." He reached down and inserted the key into the shackle's lock.

"Wait, no, don't let us go!" Tasha slapped awkwardly at the old man with her still manacled hand as the cuff sprang open.

As they plummeted into the pit, Daniel heard a deep and distant voice laughing.

❧

DANIEL OPENED HIS eyes, and blinked at what he saw. It looked like a doctor's office, down to the beige carpeting and windowless white walls hung with framed prints. He sat in one of a dozen identical chairs lined up against the wall. Across from him a young receptionist sat behind a large desk, typing at a computer terminal. She looked Asian, with cotton-candy-pink hair framing her round face.

"You're here," she said around her chewing gum. "I have your forms, Mister, um"—she looked down at a clipboard—"Mister Garret. You have to fill them out before you talk to Ms. Farlin." The receptionist wore a nametag labeled "Janet" on her leopard print blouse.

"What happened? Where's Tasha? Is she okay?" As he spoke, Daniel ran his hand up and down his left arm to find the bone in one piece. He could have sworn he felt the bone snap as he collided with the pit's wall as he fell. How had he survived that? In fact, he would have expected some scrapes on his palms just from all his rock climbing, but his hands were undamaged. Even his jeans and T-shirt looked to be in better shape than he remembered.

Janet pushed the clipboard and its stack of paper across her desk towards him. "If you want to help her, you need to fill out these forms. Sir."

"Where is she? Is this a doctor's office?" He looked around, hoping to see some sign of Tasha.

"This is the Office of Second Chances, sir. Here's a pen, so you can get started."

Daniel rose and plodded to her desk, picking up the clipboard and pen before returning to his seat. The clipboard did not hold insurance forms for Tasha. Instead, the hefty stack of pages all asked about him. Name, age, race, sex, eye, hair, and all the other standard questions covered the first few pages, and they were already filled out in alarming detail. "21% Anglo-Saxon, 17% Celtic, 15% Nordic, 12% Latin, 11% Slavic, 9% Sioux, 5% Arabic, 4% Shaigiya, ..." he read aloud. "What am I supposed to fill out?" he asked the receptionist. "It looks like you know more about me than I do. And what does this have to do with helping Tasha?"

"Just skip to the fifth page," Janet said, without looking up from her computer.

Daniel turned there to find few questions and many blank lines. He read the first question out loud: "Describe, in your own words, the circumstances leading to the destruction of the world." He scowled. "What's this crap about the end of the world? Is this some sort of joke?"

Janet looked up this time. "You haven't been here before, have you? Sir. Maybe Ms. Farlin should explain things to you. Just take the forms and go back to her office." She motioned down a hallway to Daniel's right.

He frowned at her. "If this is a joke, it isn't funny."

Daniel got up and tramped in the direction she had indicated. End of the world? It had to be a joke. What kind of doctor's office was this?

One of the doors down the hall stood wide open, the name "Emma Farlin" on its nameplate, so he peeked into the room. It was all very orderly, with matching books, on matching shelves, on either side of a round plaque on the wall. The plaque depicted a knight charging a dragon, and encircled the image with the words "Bureau of Heroism." A desk stood in the center of the room where a middle-aged woman in a dark suit sat perusing some papers laid out on its surface. Her brown hair was tied back in a bun, which gave her a severe look when coupled with the narrow glasses perched on her nose. There was no computer on this desk.

The woman peered at him over her glasses. "Ah, Daniel. Please, come in." She came around her desk, briskly shook his hand, and pointed toward a chair. When she had returned to her seat, she said, "My name is Emma Farlin. I've just been reviewing your case."

"My...case?" He remained standing.

"Yes." She picked up one of the papers. "I think I see what the problem is, but if I could just take a look at the forms you've filled out—"

"What the hell is going on here?"

She looked up. "I beg your pardon?"

"What happened? Where am I? Where's Tasha?"

"Didn't the receptionist explain this to you?"

"No, she just gave me this, but it didn't make any sense." He shook the clipboard in her direction. "Is this some kind of joke, or...something?"

Ms. Farlin sighed. "I should have known. Janet doesn't like explaining things to newcomers." She set down the sheet of paper. "So what do you want to know?"

"Well, how am I still alive, for one? That fall should have killed me, and I'm not even hurt."

"Ah, good, an easy one. The answer, Mr. Garret, is that you're not still alive. You're dead."

"I'm dead?"

"Yes. What was your next question?"

"But if I'm dead, how am I talking to you? You're not telling me this is Heaven, are you?"

"Not exactly."

"Is it...is it Hell?"

"Of course not," she scoffed.

"But then where am I? And where's Tasha? Is she dead too?"

"Yes, Tasha is dead. So are the cultists who were in the cavern with you, everyone else you've ever met, and the whole rest of the world. That's why you're here."

"The whole world?" Daniel began trembling and had to sit down. "That isn't possible, is it? How...?"

"It *is* possible because *you* failed to stop the cultists from releasing a Class 6 Sealed Evil. Let's see." She sifted through the papers, picked one up and studied it. "Using an Ancient Artifact we haven't yet classified—that knife they cut Tasha with—the cultists conducted a ritual designed to release the Flaughner, a being which the pre-human civilization called the Trofnac Sovereignty believed to be the God of Destruction. The Trofnacoi had sealed it away in a standard Transdimensional Prison, properly rated for Class 6 Evils."

"The Flaughner? Sounds like someone coughing up phlegm. No wonder the cult guy just called him the Wonderful Master of Destruction or whatever."

She looked up, her lips twitching. "Yes, well, the whole Trofnac language was like that." Returning to the paper in her hand, she continued, "The cultists' ritual opened up a hole in the Flaughner's prison, allowing them to send Tasha to their god. And you as well, although that was unintentional. Once it had consumed Tasha, the Flaughner had the power to invert the portal so that it could pass through, and as you might expect of a portal inversion on that scale, the results were cataclysmic. It ripped the Earth apart. In a few centuries, all that will be left is a new asteroid belt between Venus and Mars. Those who survived the initial wave of destruction were killed by the Flaughner himself. The Trofnacoi didn't call him the God of Destruction for nothing." She looked up with a slight smile. "There is a bright side, however."

"How can there possibly be a bright side to the end of the world?"

Ms. Farlin's eyes widened. "Because this isn't how the world's supposed to end, of course. The end of the world has been scheduled since its inception, and we don't just let some Sealed Evil, Class 6 or even Class 9, end it prematurely. That's why the Bureau of Heroism has a Department of World Saving: to make sure that whenever someone tries to destroy the world, there are heroes to prevent it."

"You mean this isn't the first time?"

"I thought you had television in your time period. Haven't you ever watched it? Someone's *always* trying to destroy the world. Mad scientists, alien invaders, ancient evils, what have you. There's no lack of people out to annihilate the Earth."

For a moment Daniel just stared at her. "You're crazy. All that stuff on television is crap. You want me to believe it's for real?"

"It is for real. World-threatening dangers are a fact of life. Most people can't accept that, so they tell themselves it isn't true and then make up stories about it. They have to acknowledge it somehow, you see, and as long as they can pretend that it's all make-believe, it's safe. None of the details of those stories are right, but they do reflect the greater truth that there is always something threatening the world, and always a need for a hero to save it. Where they get it wrong is in thinking that the hero always succeeds. In real life, sometimes the plucky comic relief isn't plucky enough, the wise old mentor isn't that wise, the cryptic clues are too cryptic, or the ragtag band of heroes just can't manage to overcome their differences. For whatever reason, there are times when the heroes don't have what it takes to save the world. Considering that the odds are always against them, it's inevitable that probability will catch up."

"Then what?"

She shrugged. "Then the world gets destroyed. Six thousand, seven hundred, and twelve times at last count."

"That can't be true."

She paused, a small frown touching her lips. "You're correct. Six thousand, seven hundred, and thirteen, counting the events of this morning."

At this, Daniel just stared at her.

"Don't look so concerned. It's not the end of the world." She paused and frowned again. "Well, it is, but we can fix it."

"Is there someone else I can talk to?" Daniel asked.

"No, I'm afraid that I'm your Corrections Agent for this incident. As I said, the world has ended many times. That's why the Office of Second

Chances exists. When things go wrong in the World Saving Department, we fix them."

"You can do that? Even *after* the world's ended?"

"Time doesn't mean the same thing to us as it does to you. As soon as we figure out what went wrong the first time, we can go back and change it."

"You mean you'll send me back in time?"

"No. While *we* can go back in time, you can't, not without causing a Time Paradox, and don't get me started on how often a Paradox has destroyed the planet. Or more. What we will do is alter your past, so that from your perspective, everything went right the first time, and you'll never have ended up here. You won't remember a thing."

"So I'll forget all of this?"

"Since it never happened to you, there'll be nothing to forget. Of course, we do make a copy of your memories in case you ever come back. We find that things go much more smoothly if you remember our procedures next time. Frankly, though, we'd all be much happier without our repeat clients clogging up the system, so let's try to avoid that, shall we? For now, why don't we begin by getting your forms filled out?"

"That will save the world? And Tasha?" Daniel asked.

"It will help us figure out what went wrong, which is the first step."

He spent what felt like hours filling out the forms Janet had given him, answering questions that ranged from inane, to impertinent, to repetitive. Several pages asked about his love life, and three different questions instructed him to list his flaws: personal, heroic, and professional-slash-academic. Emma Farlin explained the difference. She read that page after he finished it, like she did for all the others, and handed him a fresh copy of that sheet and asked him to try again. Lying about his homework was a personal flaw, she noted, not an academic one, and she instructed him not to forget to mention his temper. At this point, he had lost it one too many times to plausibly deny that he had a problem with his temper. Each time he got angry, she would calmly explain that his anger was not helping to save the world. When he complained that they were wasting time, she just said that time had no meaning here. He would have shaken his watch at her had it not stopped as soon as he arrived.

As she finished perusing the last page, she picked up her pen and a legal pad. "Let me just clarify a few things."

"Okay..."

"How did you locate the cult's lair in the first place?"

"There was a map in the van."

"The van?"

"Yeah, this ugly grey monstrosity, about as inconspicuous as a flashing neon sign. I was searching the neighborhood for the crazies who took Tasha when I found the van abandoned in front of an all night diner. I knew it was the right one when I found Tasha's purse inside. There was also a print-out from Google Maps, which led me to the cave."

"The Flaughner cult's hideout was listed on Google Maps?"

"No, but you can see the cave entrance pretty good on the satellite pictures. It was circled."

"That was sloppy of the Cryptic Clues Office. It's hardly cryptic at all," she murmured as she jotted something on her notepad. "How did you know to look for this van?"

"John told me. He was there when the crazies took Tasha, walking home from school with her. They roughed him up pretty bad, but no one believed him when he said Tasha had been kidnapped by a madman ranting about sacrifices, driving around with a bunch of other lunatics in a big grey van. The police thought John might have been behind Tasha's disappearance, so they took him into custody. Not that I'm a big fan of John's, especially now, but I know he cares about Tasha almost as much as I do, so I went looking for the van he described."

"Hmm-mm." Ms. Farlin finished up her notes and put her pen down. "I believe that makes things clear. As I suspected, this looks like a case of Genre Mismatch, which means that the Department of Heroic Calling screwed this one up quite thoroughly. Someone assigned a Class 2 Arrogant Martial Artist to a Class 6 Sealed Evil, with dire consequences."

"I don't think I'm that arrogant," Daniel protested.

Ms. Farlin picked up Daniel's forms and shuffled through them. "You claim to be the best in the world at an obscure martial art called, uh..."

"Dao Long. And I am the best. I've won international competitions!"

"Uh-huh. In any case, it's just a category. And while I'm sure you're very good, this sort of call should have gone to a Class 4 Destined Hero. At the least! You never should have gotten involved in this mission."

"Never gotten involved? But those crazies kidnapped my girlfriend!"

Ms. Farlin pursed her lips while flipping through more of her papers. "Did they? According to our records, you and Tasha broke up last week."

"How could you—?" He stopped himself before he could say more, folded his arms, and slouched in his chair. "Well, your records are wrong."

"Hmm, it says here that she's been hanging out with this John fellow, and accepted a date with him shortly before her kidnapping. It does appear that you two are no longer an item."

"She just needed her space!"

"If you say so." Ms. Farlin gave no sign that she believed him. "Maybe we should move on. To be honest, it looks like the Office of Victim Designation messed up here too."

"Victim designation?" Daniel sat up straight again. "You mean you guys are in charge of the villains, too? So what, you set up the end of the world and then try to save it? You're crazier than that old guy was!"

"Please calm down, Mr. Garret. We are not 'in charge' of the villains, as you put it. The Department of Villain Management has the delicate task of influencing the villain's actions without interfering with his free will. The Offices of Victim Designation, Cryptic Clues, and several others all fall under their purview. They cannot alter the villain's intentions, but they can use chance and coincidence to give the heroes openings."

"Oh, okay then." Daniel wasn't certain that he understood, but it sounded reasonable when she put it that way.

"As I was saying, it would have been better if Victim Designation had found someone connected to a more appropriate hero, but even if it had to be Tasha, that's no excuse to try to shoehorn you into the hero role." She peered at him over her glasses, her head tilted in thought. "Though I suppose that you could qualify for Sidekick."

"Sidekick! And who was supposed to be the hero? John?"

"No, not John. The Class 4 Destined Hero, of course. Although Class 5 would have been better, of course, but as long as he didn't have to fight the Sealed Evil itself, Class 4 would have been sufficient. So why don't I talk to the Department of Heroic Calling and see who's available? I'll put in a good word for getting you Sidekick status. I think I have the proper forms for you to fill out here." She pulled open one of her desk's drawers.

"No."

"No?" She paused.

"No. As long as Tasha gets kidnapped, I go and rescue her."

She grimaced. "Director Davis of Victim Designation is notoriously stubborn. Bob would never admit that he was wrong, so there's no chance that he'll change the victim just because *I* ask. So I'm afraid that it's going to be Tasha no matter what we do. But tell me, why do you have to be the hero?"

"Because I, uh..." Daniel couldn't admit the real reason he wanted to be the one to rescue Tasha. How could she prefer John over him if he saved her life? "Because I don't trust anyone else to do it, okay?" That much was true enough. And it sounded a hell of a lot less selfish than risking the whole world to try to win back a girl. "Look, I almost reached her in time to prevent this whole end of the world thing. Why would you want to risk messing with that? Just make sure I get there a little earlier and I'll get it right this time."

"You're serious. You do realize that there is no Office of Third Chances, right?"

"Don't tell me you've never failed, in all those six thousand something times. What happens if your hero doesn't get the job done the second time?"

"In that case we send it along to the Department of Intervention in the Bureau of Destiny, but I don't think we want to have them deal with this matter. They've been known to drop a meteor on the villain to stop him. It's effective, but it's terribly anticlimactic, don't you think? 'Then a rock falls on the bad guy and kills him. The end.' Oh, and it does tend to result in a lot of collateral damage. The DoI's mandate puts no limit on that, so if it takes destroying a city to save the world, that's what they'll do."

"Oh," Daniel said. "We don't want that to happen, then."

"No we don't. But all right, let's say that instead of fixing the Genre Mismatch, we give *you* the second chance. What do you need?"

"Just get me there five minutes earlier."

"That's not good enough. Even if you get there earlier, the villain could rush through the ritual and still complete it before you could stop him: it's not all that complicated as long as he has the Ancient Artifact. Are you sure you don't want to be the Sidekick? I could probably find a Magical Girl for this situation. You might even make Love Interest in that case. I can't promise Happily Ever After, but a Class 3 Romance shouldn't be too hard to arrange."

"I've got a girlfriend!"

"Are you sure? Our records are usually right about this sort of thing."

"I'm sure." He needed to come up with a way to not just make sure he succeeded, but to also convince Ms. Farlin that he would. Somehow, he didn't think asking for ten minutes would be enough. Just when he was about to ask what made a Romance Class 3, Daniel realized that the answer was obvious. "Tell me how that ritual works again."

࿓

AS DANIEL TURNED from the old man's body, the keys to the manacles in his hand, a tremor shook the floor. One by one, the runes in the circle around Tasha's feet flared with a red light. "What's going on?"

"Whatever it is, it can't be good. Hurry up!" Tasha urged him.

Daniel rushed to her side and began trying the keys on her left manacle. After the first two keys failed, he started to worry. Almost half the runes now glowed a fiery red. The cavern rumbled, causing him to lose his balance and nearly stab Tasha with the last key. But the tremor subsided moments later and he fit the key in the lock. The manacle snapped open.

"Where'd he get these things?" Daniel said, examining the key. "Some S&M store? They look new."

Tasha flexed her free hand. "I'm more worried about the fact that he has two more sets. Come on, get the other one off and let's go."

As Daniel reached to unlock the other manacle, the rest of the runes lit up all at once. They both froze, waiting for something awful to happen, but the runes gave one brief burst of light and then sputtered out.

"What was that all about?" Daniel asked.

"I don't know and I don't ca—Watch out!"

Daniel spun just in time to catch the madman's hand, stopping the knife an inch from his face.

The old man's eyes shown white in his blood streaked face, and spittle flew from his gap-toothed mouth. "Why isn't it working? It should be working!" He wrestled free of Daniel's grip and danced away. "I carved the runes. I said the words. I wetted the knife with her impure blood."

"Who are you calling impure, you dirty old man?" Tasha snapped.

"Why you, my dear. My disciple heard them talking about you at that school. That's why we chose you—a virgin wouldn't work at all."

"They're saying *what* about me? Dan!"

Daniel, who had been busy judging his distance from the old man and his knife, was suddenly worried that he was standing too close to Tasha. He edged away, trying to guess how far she could move with one wrist still shackled. "Uh, sorry? I embellished a little. All guys do."

"I'm going to kill you!" she spat.

Daniel was just beyond the range of Tasha's kick, which was good, because the madman, his eyes now rolling in their sockets, began to scream, "No! I called His Glorious Lordship. He's expecting a sacrifice. He'll be furious!" He raised his knife and charged.

Pivoting on one foot, Daniel raised his other leg and thrust it out in a side kick. The force of it caught the old man in his chest, and he stumbled back to the edge of the shelf. His foot found empty air, his arms windmilled for balance, and then he tumbled head over heels down the steep incline all the way to the cavern floor.

"Is he...is he dead?" Tasha asked.

Daniel peered down at the broken body. "Yeah, I think so."

Tasha hesitated, then gave a sharp nod. "Good. Now unlock my wrist so I can strangle you."

Turning back to Tasha, Daniel tossed her the keys. "Now, Tash, don't be too mad. I didn't tell people we had sex; they just assumed that we had. All I did was let them believe what they wanted."

Catching the keys, she fumbled at the lock. "And that's supposed to make me feel better?" She got the key into the hole and turned it with more force than was necessary, popping the manacle off her wrist. The cavern rumbled again, causing small fragments of rock to fall from the ceiling and a jagged crack to split the circle of runes in half.

By the time they had regained their balance, Tasha's anger had been replaced by fear. "Do you think he was right? About his god being mad at the lack of a sacrifice?"

"Let's not stick around here and find out," Daniel said, starting toward the shelf's edge.

"Why are you going that way? Let's take the easy way." Tasha pointed toward a dark tunnel which opened up at the back of the shelf.

"The easy...? Where did that come from?" Daniel looked from the tunnel to the rock cliff he had had to climb to get up here.

"It was here the whole time. I was wondering why you came up the hard way." Tasha ducked into the tunnel and Daniel followed.

It circled around in a slow descent. The low ceiling brushed Daniel's head, and he kept imagining the walls collapsing in on them in the event of another quake, but they emerged onto the cavern floor without incident, finding themselves near the body of the old man. The angle of his neck made it obvious that he was dead.

When the next tremor struck, they ran for the exit. Two more quakes sent them stumbling into the walls and pelted them with small stones and massive amounts of dust, but they emerged into the mid-morning sunlight as the last and strongest one hit. The thunder of rock was deafening, and a cloud of dust exploded into the open air, blotting out the sun and covering everything with a fine layer of grit. Dirty, bloody, and tired, they staggered forward until they found clear air and sunlight. Daniel sank onto the grass, coughing to clear the dust out of his lungs, and Tasha collapsed beside him.

"So I don't suppose you'd be interested in getting back together," Daniel said. "Seeing as how I did just rescue you from certain doom."

"You're lucky I'm even speaking with you, considering what you told everyone." Then Tasha's tone softened, "But you did save my life, so I guess that kind of makes up for it. Almost. Thanks for coming after me." She leaned over and kissed Daniel on the cheek.

"That's it? I save the fair damsel and have to settle for that?"

"Hey, don't complain to me. Fair damsels like myself are supposed to be modest. A kiss on the cheek is the limit as far as rewards go. Look it up, it's in the contract."

Daniel chuckled as he lay back and closed his eyes, the grass tickling his cheeks and the sun warm on his face. "I guess it'll have to do."

THE FIELD OF BLOOD

KIM PAFFENROTH

The morning was still cool when the old man started digging, but the spring sun was bright and the day promised to warm quickly. All the more reason to finish soon, rather than let it drag out into the afternoon. He wasn't young enough anymore to toil in the midday sun, and the physical condition of his charge this morning would not improve with heat, either. After hacking at the hard earth with his shovel for a few minutes he looked over at her—a tight package of middling-clean cloths, lying under the one tree in the small cemetery. He'd had to carry her up here, and even though she was quite light, it had been a good deal of work. Still, it would be nothing compared to digging the hole for her. He could make it slightly smaller because of her size, but it would still be hard digging down far enough. He'd seen what happened if they weren't buried deep enough, and he would avoid that for any of his charges if he could, but especially for one so young. Bad enough to be buried in a potter's field without a name, she didn't need to be dug up by dogs at night and have pieces of her strewn all over the valley. Besides, they said that the spirits of those so treated could be very unpleasant to those they thought responsible for their degradation, and he more than half believed such stories.

He got down to digging. Hard, long heaves of the dry clay flew over his shoulder till he was up to his knees in the little hole. He stepped out and went to stand in the shade for a few moments and rest. The cemetery was a particularly decrepit one. It was on a slight hill, and the winter rains carved little gullies through it. He had built little barriers with stones and wooden planks to try to control the water flow and erosion, lest they uncover a hapless occupant. There was one scraggly juniper that gave the place the barest hint of life and hope, and helped with the erosion. But the meager tree also made part of the plot unusable; he couldn't bury anyone close to it, for its roots made it too hard to dig there. Yet, all its pitiable sadness and inconveniences notwithstanding, the place had been a boon to him. The wealthy could be quite beneficial to some in the funeral business —those who sold the aromatic spices they used to embalm the dead, and the professional mourners who would set up a steady and shrill wail at the funeral. The rich would buy a tomb that would last for centuries, and each successive generation would be laid in the same earthen nooks or shelves in it, while the disintegrated remains of the previous occupants were swept up and put in little ossuaries. Too efficient, with not enough new digging to be of much use to him. For a humble grave digger such as himself, the poor turned out to be more reliable and profitable. He had been thrilled when this little plot of land had been set aside as a burial place for the unidentified and unmourned, and he had been hired as its caretaker. It meant a tiny but steady salary for keeping the place from washing away and repairing the little wooden fence around it. He also got a small extra fee every time he buried someone there, like today.

"Hello, old man," he heard off to his right. He looked over to see a much younger man stepping into the shade of the tree and grinning at him. It hardly seemed the place or occasion for grinning, but this particular young man looked as though he frequently enjoyed jokes or riddles that others found inappropriate or disturbing. His eyes had a mischievous, slightly unsettling twinkle to them. His hair and beard were very red, a few shades brighter and much shinier than the dull, russet-colored cloak he wore.

With the instincts of a person who had lived all his life surrounded by crime and poverty, the old man quickly sized up this visitor to determine whether he offered any opportunity for advancement, or any threat. His evaluation immediately came up as inconclusive, for the young man seemed simultaneously too casual, too cheerful, and too mysterious to be either an ordinary criminal, or a possible benefactor. But one always had to be careful, so the old man addressed him with deference. "Hello, sir."

"What are you doing in my little field this morning?" the young man asked cheerfully, but it did not seem as though he meant it only as a joke.

The old man took a step back. "Yours, sir? This sad field belongs to the city."

The younger man laughed. "Oh, don't take me so literally, old man. But really, how does a city own something? I gave them my money, that I'd earned, and they bought this field with it. Doesn't that make it mine? I bet there are a few dusty old bricks in the city wall, paid for with the money they take from you in taxes, and I think you should go and visit them sometime and make sure people appreciate your contribution. Put your initials on them or something."

The old man looked sideways at him, but decided to keep up the bowing and scraping. The poor couldn't afford such eccentricities as this young man displayed, so he might well be rich and worth placating. Though his clothes were non-descript, they weren't outwardly tattered or worn out. "Well, sir, I have heard that the man who helped pay for this field was a very great and generous man, a real patriot who defended his people from corruption and scandal, and who donated his money, but wished to remain anonymous."

There was laughter again at this, but it seemed more of a snigger at something the young man found slightly offensive as well as amusing. "Oh, really? That's very funny, because I heard that he was a great scoundrel." He leaned closer and grinned again. "Which do you believe, friend?"

The young man's intentions were still impossible to intuit at this point, so the old man tried to be evasive and noncommittal. "That's not for me to say, sir."

"It's not for you to say what you believe? Oh, my, then who is to say what you believe, if not you?" When it was obvious the old man couldn't respond, the young man laughed again and continued. "Well, enough about such vagaries. What are you doing here this morning?"

The old man looked down and realized the tiny, wrapped body was behind him. He stepped aside and nodded towards it "Burying her, sir."

The young man looked at the bundle. "Who is she?"

The old man shrugged. "A street child, they said. Begging, stealing, probably selling herself, even though she was so young. And then she got sick and died."

The younger man frowned. "That's sad, don't you think?"

"Oh yes, sir, very sad indeed."

The younger man tilted his head and raised an eyebrow. "Kind of makes you angry at God, doesn't it?"

The old man lowered his eyebrows and frowned. "Well, sir, I don't know about that. I don't know if God had anything to do with it. She just died."

The young man's eyes flashed, and his smile was more of a sneer now. "What, my friend, does God have to do with, if not with the death of this innocent little child? Do you think He has something more important to attend to?"

He was getting way too agitated and making the old man nervous. "Sir, really, it's not right to say such things. Really, I should just get back to digging, so I can finish burying her."

He'd never seen anyone move so quickly. The old man had been leaning lightly on his shovel, when the younger man suddenly sprang forward and kicked it away. Thrown off balance, the old man gave a small gasp of surprise, and staggered to his left. With both his hands, the younger man shoved him out into the bright sunlight. The old man was blinded for an instant, and raised his hands to defend himself and to shield himself from the bright sunlight. "That is the one thing you will definitely *not* do this morning, old man," the young man hissed.

Recovering from the sun's glare, the old man could see that the young man had pulled out a short-bladed, but exceptionally evil-looking knife and now held it in his left hand. The implement was not at all shiny, but dull, grim looking, and practical—the kind a fish-monger or tanner would use in his bloody work. Oh, God, he was a criminal. Or worse, one of the *sicarii*, those crazed religious zealots who went around killing people to foment revolution. The old man considered running, but the speed his attacker had just displayed made him think that futile. A much better strategy to stay and plead. "Please, sir, I meant no disrespect. Please, sir, don't hurt me."

The young man's expression softened slightly, and he dropped his left hand to his side, so it was no longer immediately threatening. "No, I won't hurt you. I'm sorry, I just get very angry sometimes. Especially at God. Do you know what that's like?"

The old man was babbling what he thought the other man wanted to hear. "Oh yes, sir, absolutely. Everyone feels that way sometimes."

The young man was calmer, but he hadn't let go of the topic at all, but just came at it from another side, and more calmly. He raised his eyebrow again. "Oh? I thought you said it wasn't right to say such things?"

Panic again filled the old man. "No, sir. I mean, it's not. I mean, it's not right to say them, but everyone feels them, anyway."

"All right. That's a better answer. More honest. What, exactly, makes you angry at God, old man?"

His mind raced. He wanted to give the right answer, but the questions were so unexpected and unnerving, and the stranger seemed exceptionally attuned to detecting deception. And getting angry at it. "I don't know, sir. I don't know!"

The young man put his left hand behind his back and extended his right hand, palm forward, in a placating gesture. "It's all right. Don't be so frightened. I need your help, but first I need to know what makes you angry at God. Here, I'll start. I just said this little girl dying made me angry at God. Now you tell me something that makes you angry."

He really tried to think. "I don't mind being poor. And I've never been sick my whole life. Neither has my wife. We have a good life."

"And your children, old man? Haven't you seen them sick? Or maybe even some of them died, like this little girl?"

The old man looked down, ashamed. "We don't have any children, sir."

The young man nodded. "And that makes you angry at God, doesn't it?"

"Yes, sir."

"Very angry?"

The old man swallowed and nodded. "Yes, sir. Not all the time, but sometimes I see someone else's children, or a street child like this one, and I feel so lonely and helpless and angry. And we prayed for one, sir, we did. All the time."

"Hm-hmm. You prayed. But God didn't change His mind."

"No, sir, He didn't."

"But you do think God does change His mind sometimes?"

He'd never thought of it that way before, but the way he'd been led to it, he could see now that that was the inevitable conclusion, if one believed in prayers and bothered to say them. "Well, yes, I suppose He does."

The young man smiled, and some of the playfulness and humor had returned to him. "Good. So do I." He leaned back on his heels and looked up at the sky. "You see, once God was very angry with me. And now? Well, I like to think, maybe, not so much."

The old man again thought of running, while the other man was distracted, but still wasn't sure he could make it. And besides, the young man didn't seem so frightening now. "Well, that's good, sir."

The younger man looked at him, still smiling. "Yes, it is. Now, I said I needed your help."

The old man tensed, but knew he had to play along. "Yes, sir, of course, whatever you need."

"Good. Now, come over here." They both sidled up to the tiny grave that had been dug, the old man hanging back as much as possible. With that same uncanny quickness as before, the younger man brought his knife up in front of himself and grabbed the blade with his right hand. His jaw tensed from the pain as he gripped it tightly, and blood started to run down the hilt and through his fingers, dripping down into the hole. He jerked the knife down, and blood really started flowing from his wounded right fist.

The old man froze in place with shock at this self-mutilation. "Oh my God, sir! What are you doing?! Stop it!"

The younger man stuck the knife in his belt. "They call this the field of blood, old man. It was looking a little dry and dusty to me, so I'm just helping it earn its rather morbid name." With his left hand, he grabbed his right arm at the elbow, and ran his left hand down to his right wrist, like a woman wringing water from a wound-up piece of laundry. The blood gushed out between his fingers and dripped in an almost steady stream down into the hole in the ground. When he was satisfied at the quantity with which he had wet the grave, he got a rag out of his pocket and wrapped it around his right hand to quell the bleeding. "Now put her in it," he said quietly.

The old man was terrified. "Sir, it's not deep enough to bury her."

"I told you that you are *not* going to bury her this morning. But you are going to put her in that hole."

"All right." The old man slowly shuffled over to the little bundle, picked it up, and laid it gently in the dust, which was now painted with darker splotches.

"Now, let's go stand under the tree again. It's way too hot out here." They moved into the tiny patch of shade. He wagged his left index finger at the old man. "I had a friend who could really do this. I mean, a lot of style, panache. Made it look so easy. And it'd only take a minute." He smiled again and shook his head. "Me? It's always so messy when I do it.

Everything I do is messy and out of sorts and frightens people. It takes so much longer, too. Are you very patient?"

"Oh, yes, sir, very patient, or so people tell me."

The young man frowned and shook his head. "Not me. Never was. I especially never liked this whole waiting around for the Kingdom of God thing. But, you're right—one should be patient. Now, old man, pray."

"Sir?"

"Pray."

"But, sir, shouldn't you pray? You said you knew how to do this. Whatever it is that you're doing."

"No, that's what I need you for, friend. I'm unclean, impure." He tapped his left temple with his finger. "It's my noggin. I told you—I get angry so much. And so impatient. So many unholy thoughts. But you, you barely get angry at all, and you're calm and patient. It'd be better if you prayed." He then tapped his chest. "Besides, a prayer comes from the heart, and yours is not only cleaner than mine, but only your heart knows what it's felt, what it needs, what to pray for."

"For what, sir?"

"You said you were angry with God? Pray that you might not be so angry. Remember all the hurt you felt, all the disappointment, and ask God to heal it." His voice had become so soothing, like the water in a brook, or the wind in the leaves. He took two steps back, away from the old man. "Close your eyes and put all that before your mind, and at God's feet."

The old man's eyes went wide at first at the suggestion of closing them with this apparently deranged man around, but his voice and demeanor were now so calming, and the old man saw little choice but to go along with him, so he cooperated in closing his eyes. The soothing voice continued, softly, almost like a chant, and in a moment he really couldn't make out the words, even though it continued. Instead, he pictured his wife, very vividly, how much she had cried over the years at their childlessness. He felt the smoldering anger within him flare brighter, that terrible but impotent little flame he'd carried for so long. And more than anything else, he hated the anger, he hated himself for feeling it. He just wanted it to go away. He wanted to rush home and hold her and never feel anger again, but only the joy that he felt when she was happy. He wanted that so, so much, and that was the form his "prayer" took, if it was even right to call such an emotional and inchoate state a "prayer."

His reverie was intense and overwhelming and seemed to last a long time, though in reality it may have been only a few seconds. His eyes fluttered open, and he saw a little girl sitting on the ground by the grave he had dug. A pile of middling-clean cloths lay beside her. She took the hand that the younger man extended to her and stood up. "I believe there's been some mistake," the younger man said with his peculiarly soothing tone. "This little girl was terribly sick, and it made her fall into a deep sleep, so that everyone thought she was dead." The young man led her towards the older man and presented her to him. "But see, little girl, this wise, old gentleman was very careful and observant and he saw that you weren't really dead. It's almost like a miracle from God, isn't it?" He had to put the girl's hand into the old man's, they were both so confused and overwhelmed. He looked at the old man with his raised eyebrow again. "Well, if you believe in such things, that is."

The old man couldn't make words, but only looked, open-mouthed, back and forth between the girl and the red-haired young man. But the girl gazed with a desperate kind of awe at the old man and whispered, "Yes, of course I do. I prayed for one all the time."

The young man smiled and turned to walk away.

"Sir?" the old man stammered. "Thank you. But will I see you again?"

"Oh, no, probably not." He shook his head not exactly sadly, but wistfully. "God often doesn't change His mind, friend, and I only come around when I think He might. I'm afraid that for most of the bundles you bring up here, He wouldn't, and we don't want you to get all disappointed and sad again. It seems as though you've had quite enough of that." He grinned again, playfully and somewhat mischievously, the way he had when he had first walked up. "Now you have to go home to your patient wife, I believe."

The young man walked away quickly, as though he were slightly embarrassed to be around people who showed him gratitude, and instead wished to return to the darker, colder, but more familiar parts of the city, and of his own heart.

SMALL ACCIDENTS OF GOD

VIRGINIA HERNANDEZ

The first time I noticed one, Mama and Wade were picking corn and I was playing in the creek. Wade took really sick out of the blue and it was just when his coughing fit started turning him colors that I detected the shadowman. I wanted to tell Mama about him, but something told me it was best to pretend I hadn't noticed.

A puff of black leaked out of the shadow of a big oak and curled around my brother's face. He choked on a bubble of phlegm and tried to talk through belches of spit and snot. I couldn't tell if he could see the shadow creature or not, but I wondered if something didn't change he might actually die.

I ran to my brother and put my body between him and the tree the shadow was creeping out of. A shiver ran up my arms as I touched the black, but the smoke scattered while my brother took big gulps of breaths in between snivels and hiccups.

Mama screamed for me to get help and I hightailed it to Hattie's House of Hair as if the very dogs of Satan were nipping at my heels, which at the time seemed possible. So I didn't much mind moving myself far away from the forest's shadows, fast as possible.

With all the running I do, I probably should've been the boy instead of Wade. I'm not saying that God made a mistake; Pawpaw says God can do anything except blunder. Lord knows I wouldn't want to be a boy, as I find them disgusting, but I gotta figure if I'd originally come out that way, sweat and grime would be less bothersome and body noises more fascinating.

My family needed a healthy boy. I knew it and did my best to give them close to one as possible. Maybe God missed those signals, but they haven't gotten past me. Memaw would pop my jaw for saying that, I'm not saying God messed up my family, He just didn't think it all the way through.

First off, my name is Bobbi Jo. Who goes naming a baby Bobbi Jo, unless they really aim on a person of the male persuasion popping out? Especially when there are so many lovely girl names. I'm particularly fond of Melanie—as in Hamilton from *Gone With The Wind*, which is one of several books I've read at least ten times. Now that particular name expresses every lovely female characteristic known with just the simple saying of it, as does the name Olivia, the name of the actress that played Melanie in the movie. Both are perfectly marvelous girl names, of which I would have been thrilled to have either. I would say I like the name Scarlett, but she was such a mouthy woman, and that's what I'm trying hard to avoid. I'm afraid having a name bold as that would've given me too much sass. Memaw says I have plenty of that with the plain old name Bobbi Jo.

Not that she says that to my face. Only in a round-about way, which is more lady-like, I suppose.

I've never had the heart to tell her I'm twice as mouthy in my head as I am out loud. I can't help but think if they'd named me Melanie, this wouldn't be a problem.

Second, I have a list of chores that would make plenty of boys squirm. I cut pig teeth and tails, am frequently called upon to wash down after-birth in the farrowing house, notch ears and give shots. The list could go on. I'm not complaining, mind you, because I don't like being inside that much anyways, unless I've got an especially good book, but my chore list ain't exactly girly.

To top it all off, when Daddy wants to relax and talk, he takes me fishing. I'm not even saying I don't like sitting by the pond with a cane pole and a soda, but such stereotypical boy rituals lend heavy weight to the idea I should've come out with different parts, and I don't think God minds me saying so.

Sundays were different though. Any other day of the week I'm all for helping God out, but on Sunday, I'm all girl. For one thing, Memaw wouldn't have it any other way. The idea of me showing up to church in anything but my Sunday dress makes me shudder. Memaw says only white trash hussies would think about entering the house of God in anything less than their best, so I'm careful to always act like the lady God accidentally made me on Sundays.

There was a time when I thought the birth of Wade would ease the pressure to make up for not being a boy, but then we found out he was sick and I knew it would be a life-long duty because Mama and Daddy won't be having any more children after Wade. Even if he hadn't been born ill, I wonder but if they wouldn't have considered stopping because he's such a pain.

Take the afternoon he got so sick. I was playing in the creek because Wade didn't fetch me from the house when Mama called. He knows good and well I like to help Mama pick the corn, but he was the one up there searching for the good ears while I sat at the house with nothing to do. I finally got to wondering where they went and wandered down to the corn field left with nothing to do but throw rocks in the creek. Then not only was I told to run, not walk, to the beauty shop, but I also knew without a doubt that when we had that corn for supper, I'd end up with a weak ear of corn because Wade doesn't take the same care I do looking for the healthy ones.

He'd ruined my day and my supper.

There's maybe nothing I hate more than having to run to town. It's not that far, but running ruins the pleasure of the trip. I like moseying to town, but I'd have to run to town a whole lot less if we'd just get a phone at the house. Mama agrees with that, and she's not even the one that has to do all the message toting, but Papa says he likes that no one can reach him at night. "If they need us bad enough, they'll come get us."

Easy for him to say, he's not the one doing the running.

On a hot summer day when the Florida air settles over you like stinky hog's breath, scurrying off to town is the last thing on your mind. But the heat of the day mixed with the panic in Mama's expression kept my feet moving. I ran so fast I barely even had time to consider the meaning of the shadow being, but I knew enough to figure bad things held store for my family. I think Mama felt it deep down, too, but I didn't think she knew the shadows lived.

There was no doubt in my head that no matter how hot it was that night, I'd be sleeping without the fan. Anytime I really want to know what the adults don't want me to know I have to do a little creative listening. I was not gonna miss what Mama and Daddy talked about while they thought the children slept that evening. I had to know if Mama witnessed the shadow attack Wade.

It's truly amazing how much I've learned just laying awake in bed at night.

For instance, that's how I learned about Mary Beth Widner, one of the girls in the teen class at church, getting the Spirit last month. I never had been one to pay much mind to the goings on in service until I heard Mama remark to Daddy about Mary Beth getting the Spirit at such a tender age. I don't know exactly what that means, but something about the way Mama sounded made me want her to say it about me.

Then I started to notice how everything seemed to be looking up for the Widner girl. She came to service that very next week in a new dress and I overheard Mrs. Gaskin saying that the Widners sure did know how to raise good children, even though I know for a fact that Bo Widner is as mean as a sow is lazy. Maybe the Spirit changes everything about you, even your good for nothing brother, which is something I could really use.

Somewhere between the creek bed and the beauty shop the realization hit, might've stopped me cold in my tracks except I couldn't risk Mama hearing I didn't run the whole way. I knew how to keep the shadowman away and help out with my own brother situation.

There wasn't but one thing to keep disaster from having its way with my family.

I was gonna have to get the Spirit.

&

WHEN I OPENED my eyes Saturday morning, two things hit me right away. One thing for sure, Mama had let me sleep in – it was bright outside. When that happened it was usually because she let me stay up late, which told me she knew I'd been eavesdropping the night before. Second thing, I had already missed any decent cartoons. Only thing on this late was Richie Rich and Super Friends and I wasn't going to even bother turning on the television for that. Wade thought they were terrific, but I preferred the same ones I'd been watching for years.

I rolled back over, tugging the covers back over my head just in case the shadows turned to people in my room. After I bored myself to tears and couldn't breathe under there anymore, I got up and went to the kitchen for a bowl of cereal. A note on the fridge told me what I'd already guessed. Mama took Wade into town with her grocery shopping and if I wanted to I could come on in to town after I woke up.

"Walking to town again." But I ate my breakfast quick because I knew Saturday was my best bet for getting Mama to spring for a candy bar so I wanted to catch her before she left the grocery store.

I went back to my room to throw on some clothes, again slightly annoyed at the walk ahead of me. If there's one thing having a sick brother will do for you, it'll get you lots of alone time. Sometimes I just wished he could do something as simple as take a walk into town with me. I couldn't see the good in having a younger brother to boss around if you can't ever get him out of your parent's sight.

Besides, there was plenty of stuff to show the little creep on a walk to town, if he'd keep his mouth shut and listen. What Wade never seemed to understand is how to take advantage of the wisdom of my ten years. He just kept on making the same mistakes over and over. Most of 'em I could've spared him.

I turned from our drive onto the dirt road and commenced the familiar trek into town.

At least I wasn't running. No matter how fast I wanted to get to town, I still took the time to notice the small creatures along the way. I figure if God's going to take the time to create something so strange as an armadillo, you ought to slow down long enough to look for them just so you could tell Him one day you thought He was clever. God's got way more of a sense of humor than people give him credit for.

Now I knew there were more than God's creatures in those woods.

Front of my mind that day was figuring out how I was gonna get the Spirit come Sunday morning 'cuz I didn't figure the shadowman would leave me much time. I may not have understood much, but I knew enough to assume that whatever he was, God could whip him. Since I hadn't paid much attention to what goes on in services, I didn't really know what my first step should be for getting the Spirit on my side, but I figured following Memaw's list of do's and don'ts must be a good place to start. Course that was gonna be hard, what with the list being so long and all.

My biggest worry was what was going to happen if I couldn't figure it out. Since I had pretended not to see it the day before, I thought I saw it longer than most folks. It floated like black fog from shadow to shadow and seemed particularly interested in my brother. And although the little booger gets on my nerves, I've no intentions of handing him over to the likes of the boogey man.

Coming into town, I hopped up on the sidewalk headed for the Piggly Wiggly when I noticed I was coming face to face with Hester Davies. We made eye contact and I lifted my head in a small greeting, but knew better than to engage in any conversation with the likes of her. Memaw would have a sure fire hissy fit if she ever heard tell of me hanging around with trashy girls. Wasn't all my figuring just for keeping me from turning into a girl like that?

I got enough lecturing from Memaw. No sense bringing any new issues to bear. It was all I could do to navigate the waters of the subjects I already messed up regular like.

If someone was going to cause Memaw to go off on another tangent about the glories of avoiding white trash, it wasn't going to be me.

When I found Mama and Wade in the grocery store, I wasn't surprised to find him acting like a baby. Even the very forces of Satan being after him couldn't keep him from conducting himself in the most spoiled manner. The two of them were in the frozen food section debating which flavor ice pops to bring home. Wade dead set on the expensive ones. Last time Mama had given in, but if Wade had the sense God gave a flea, he'd know you don't push for the expensive ice pops. Especially when Hell's just nipped at your door the day before.

But more disturbing than watching Wade fling himself around like a toddler was noticing just how many regular shadows there seemed to be in the grocery store.

"Hey, Mama," I said. "Whatcha'll doing?"

"Hey, baby," Mama said, shutting the freezer door with her hip. She wasn't missing the opportunity to distract the little monster, that's for sure. She wasn't ever missing a chance to divert Mr. One-track-mind.

And I wasn't passing by a chance to show my devotion to the family woes, so I pointed up to the cheapest ice pops on the shelf. "I think we should get these."

I looked over at Wade and let him know with my eyes there was a real lesson to be learned. Of course, he wasn't paying attention. He'd already found a spot under the grocery cart and pretended to be a race car driver.

We didn't have a lot to say as we finished up the rest of the aisles. Mama didn't want a bunch of kids interrupting her thoughts while she was figuring on how to feed a family with no more than what we've got.

When the products turned to cleaners and charcoal, I decided the outdoors called and asked to go. I supposed that particular Saturday wasn't really the day to hang around and see if I could hit Mama up for a candy bar, anyway. I really had more important things to do.

I walked outside into the boiling heat and balanced myself on the edge of the curb all the way to the end of the parking lot. No doubt my poise was improving. I could've kept steady without wobbling all the way across town if the curb hadn't ended.

By the time I finished up gliding across the cement like an elegant tightrope walker, Hester Davies was two stores in front of me on the sidewalk. There wasn't gonna be any avoiding conversation this time. Just when I'd worked up the gumption for an innocent how're you, C.J. Milton stepped out of his family store, with a couple of shadowmen tailing him. I was shocked to realize there was more than one. Then I wondered if he was about to have his own coughing fit. If it meant death was on his trail.

If there's anyone in this town I'd like to see picked off by smoke creatures, it's C.J. Milton. He thinks just 'cuz his daddy owns the antique shop he's hot snot. Every Sunday they saunter up to their spot on the third row. I don't think I've ever seen his mama wear the same dress twice. I wonder how a woman could have that many different dresses. I suppose they must be something special for attaining God's blessing in such a mighty way, but C.J. hadn't done a thing to deserve those gifts yet, far as I could see.

C.J. walked right over to Hester and blocked her way without an excuse me or pardon. "What're you doing on my daddy's sidewalk?" I froze to the spot as I pretended not to notice the shadow caressing C.J.'s cheek.

I wouldn't take that kind of lip from such a twerp, but Hester just looked down at the ground. "Sorry," she said and kept walking. She had the courage of a beat dog.

My scorn for that boy overcame my good sense. "I don't see no names on that sidewalk, C.J. Milton." I went over and put myself right between him and the Davies girl without even thinking. I swore I smelled sulfur.

"You mind your own business, Miss High and Mighty."

"You're one to talk." It wasn't clever, but it was the first comeback that came to mind.

C.J. smirked. He knew it wasn't my best work. "No one was even talking to you Baby Jo Tisdale."

Hester shrank away from the exchange, but I grabbed her arm, pulling her forward. "You don't have to get off this sidewalk, no matter who you are. Don't one single soul own this sidewalk. It belongs to the town. That means everyone, no matter what family they come from."

C.J. rolled his eyes. "You think I don't know that, dummy?"

"You would know dumb," I said. "What with you being the King of dumb." I grabbed Hester's arm and linked it in mine, just like we were the best of friends. "Come on, Hester. Something around this place stinks." Then I turned and walked off down the sidewalk with her.

As soon as we were out of sight, I dropped her arm. "Why'd you go and let that little fancy pants talk to you like that?" I sat down on the bench in front of the hardware store and picked rocks out of my right tennis shoe treads.

"People talk to me like that, Bobbi Jo," she answered, as if it was the most natural thing in the world for people to treat their neighbors poorly.

Right at that moment, I didn't want to be lumped in with those lots of people. "That don't make it right."

"I guess not. But I'm used to it."

I started examining my left tennis shoe treads real careful. "Still, C.J. ought to know better than trying to kick people off the sidewalk, even if you are..." I faltered a little, not having meant for that part to come out loud.

Hester raised her eyebrow and finished my sentence. "A Davies?"

"Uh, well, you know," I sputtered, feeling foolish.

Hester smiled, looked at me as if she understood exactly what I'd meant. I waited for her to say something else, but she didn't. Just let me stew around in my own awkward moment.

I decided right then and there, that if I was ever gonna get the Spirit, I was going to have to start examining these moments a little more carefully. As far as I could tell, no harm had come to me or my reputation by spending a moment with Hester. I wondered if Memaw knew what she was talking about.

Next thing I knew, Mama yelled at me from the Piggly Wiggly parking lot. "Bobbi Jo Tisdale, you get yourself over here right now."

I held up my finger, telling Mama to wait. I placed my hand right on Hester's shoulder and looked her straight in the eye. "I've gotta go," I said. "But I was just thinking. You know, everybody's got their trials in life to overcome. I got mine, you got yours. Well, I haven't seen any better place than church to lay down your troubles. Far as I can figure, you and me just need the Spirit."

Hester smiled. "That's a good word, Bobbi Jo," she said softly.

I turned and ran toward Mama. Surely I was one step closer to the Spirit. Nothing makes the Spirit happier than spreading the Good News.

THAT SUNDAY MORNING I woke up with fresh enthusiasm for going to the house of God. I couldn't think of anything but how special it would be to hold the very presence of the Spirit right in my body. I just knew I'd wield the power to keep the shadow people away from my family. It was a mystery to me, but surely I'd know what to do when the time came. I knew without a doubt, after practically living out the very parable of the Good Samaritan the day before, the Spirit would be looking for me at church that day.

I put on my pale yellow dress with the lime green stripes and smoothed my hair down as best I could. Of course, getting my hair to cooperate was like expecting Wade to sit through a Sunday service without picking his nose.

I stepped out into the hallway to see if Mama would help me with my hair when Wade walked by with a big wad of chewing gum in his mouth and half a package left to go. I couldn't help but notice his shadow seemed bigger than it should.

"You know good and well you're not allowed to have that first thing in the morning," I said. "Mama's gonna skin you alive." We both knew that was a lie, if ever there was one. Wade hadn't had a whipping since the day he came home from that first trip to the hospital, no matter how bad he needed one.

He stuck his tongue out at me. "Mama's more likely to spank you for letting me have it," he said back, all sassy.

I reached over his head to grab the rest of the gum when he took out the wad in his mouth and threw it right in my hair and made his escape.

I started chasing the little fiend. "Why you little..."

He ran into the living room and jumped the sofa. I couldn't reach him, but I could keep him cornered there. He was already struggling to breathe from just that little run. "You threw that in my hair, you little brat."

"Bobbi Jo," Mama screamed from the other end of the house. "You will not use that word in this house. You know better than to chase your brother around this house. Come here, right now."

Wade's triumphant grin would be short lived. When I showed Mama what he did to my hair, we'd see how long that smirk stayed on his face. I held up my hair with gum in it, showing I had proof he was at fault and gave my own little smile of victory. He looked worried for a second, then he ran off. Probably trying to get as far away from Mama as possible. Maybe those brains of his were finally starting to kick in.

I walked into Mama's bedroom and held up my hair. "Look what he did."

Mama started picking the gum out. "Good Lord, child. What on earth did you let him get gum for?"

I let out a huge huff. "Me? He already had it. I was trying to take it away from him. Geez. How'd this end up being my fault?"

"Watch that sass, young lady. I swear, child, if you're ever going to make something of yourself, you've got to learn to control those impulses of yours. You hear me?"

"Yes, ma'am." I waited until she got the last bits of gum out then sulked back to my room. He didn't even get in trouble for having the gum.

When I get the Spirit I can almost guarantee I won't have any trouble controlling my impulses and I'll always know just what to say to make sure Wade pays for his trespasses.

When we got in the car headed for church I didn't even look at Wade, even when he tried to give me one of his quarters to put in the offering plate. He was just going to have to learn that such treachery was not to be paid off with a measly quarter. Plus, he couldn't stand it when I wouldn't look at him.

Halfway through Sunday school it started to storm outside. I could hear the pitter patter of the rain as the drops hit the tin roof on the church building. The wind started whipping up frightful strong, but I wasn't worried. I liked the idea of such dramatic weather for what was sure to be a spectacular Sunday service.

I almost couldn't get through Mrs. Polly's lesson on the feeding of the five thousand. I was squirming and jiggling. I couldn't seem to help myself. It was the first time I couldn't wait to get to the preaching hour. Usually I dreaded having to stand up, sit down, sing a song and listen to the preacher go on and on. I didn't understand a thing he was yelling about, either. One time I asked Mama why the preacher was always so angry. She said that wasn't anger, it was righteous indignation at the state of affairs in our nation. I figure it's something along the lines of the way I feel when I get in trouble for Wade putting gum in my hair. I sure hoped the unnatural power of a sick child would be diminished by the authority of the Spirit.

And on this particular Sunday, I couldn't let anything interfere with my ability to get the Spirit. After the hour dragged by, I hopped up and practically ran to the sanctuary. Practically, but not quite. I thought I might better practice controlling my impulses before I got the Spirit so He'd be more likely to cooperate.

I walked right up to our regular pew and took my place in the middle. I really wanted to sit in the aisle, but knew that was where Daddy'd be sitting.

As I was waiting for the congregation to fill in the rest of the spots I noticed, up at the front, one of the smoothest looking men I'd ever seen in my life. I knew right away he had to be a preacher because of the way his hair looked, all high and slicked back. He was laughing it up with some of the holiest women at the church and they were just as charmed as they could be, I could tell all the way from the middle of the room.

He worked the sanctuary, going from pew to pew with a hi and a how're you. I guessed he must've been someone fairly special with the way people were gushing all over him. I could see why all the church folks were cooing at him, but from the moment I noticed him, the shadows around the room swelled and jumped and I wondered just why those beings were even allowed in a holy place like our sanctuary. Surely that had to be another of His accidents. Why the shadow people seemed so fascinated with the preacher was what I wanted to know.

Mama slid in next to me just a couple of minutes before the service started. "Lookie there," she said. "That's Brother Dwayne T. Prescott. He's going to be preaching revival this week."

That seemed like good news to me, even if the shadows danced around him. Maybe they themselves were fascinated by the hand of God. If the Spirit was ever going to be visited upon me, revival was the best time for it to happen. Jesus, God and everyone had to come down for revival. Every night of the week, too, although Pawpaw said he didn't see the need to go every night just because the preacher said we required extra God that week. Pawpaw said he found God himself plenty every week of the year and he didn't need to quit farming early just to go up to the church building every night of the week. Of course, Memaw showed up every night of a revival, Bible in hand praying for his backslidden ways.

That preacher sure was shucking corn that day. Never have I heard such eloquence on the subject of the Holy Spirit of God. I knew he was preaching right at me, too. He noted how the ground shook and the people were changed on the day of Pentecost. And although I was mightily distracted by the shadows for a while, soon their obvious delight with the visiting preacher somehow made me listen all the harder.

I was so caught up in the sermon that I figured Jesus himself might just walk through the door to hear him.

So when the door swung open half way through, I sure startled. I turned around right along with everyone else to see who was walking in. I was expecting Jesus, but was equally amazed to see Hester Davies. Every shadow creature in the house dashed to the back door and I could've sworn Hester shrank away from them.

Brother Dwayne stopped for a moment as Hester slid into the back pew. I smiled a little and gave a tiny wave. You'd have thought Jesus really did walk in from the reaction that bubbled up from that congregation. I've never heard so much whispering about one person showing up for Sunday service in all my life.

I patiently waited for the Spirit to take me in light of the true fruits of my evangelizing sitting right on the back pew. I listened to every word and tried to decipher their meanings the best I could. I wondered if there was something more I should be doing, so I closed my eyes. Mama elbowed me and told me not to sleep in church.

When the sermon came to a close, no one could've been more shocked than me. Nothing had happened in my soul. I set to thinking about what I had done wrong, what could've made me unworthy. I looked to the back of the church at Hester. What if Memaw was right and fraternizing with trash just made me unclean. I quick wondered if I shouldn't beg forgiveness.

Hester waved at me from across the room and I just couldn't see how being nice to somebody should be something I needed to ask forgiveness for. After all, I had suggested the Spirit might help her, and here she was. Couldn't be anything bad in that.

Then I looked down at Wade sleeping on the pew and realized it was probably his fault. I had chased him across the house and messed up his breathing and now I was going to have to wait another week. I vowed to stay as far away from him as possible the coming week so as not to mess up my chances for a pure visitation next service.

As everyone shuffled out of the church I noticed Hester was waiting for me at the back pew. I looked to the front of the church and, sure enough, Memaw was eyeballing me hard. But with my confidence shot since I wasn't leaving full of God, all of a sudden I had to get out of there. I just knew if I had to pretend not to see the smoky beings for one more minute I'd lose what little breakfast I'd had. All of a sudden I was truly scared. Why hadn't I been more frightened before?

I got a little panicky, I have to admit. I started flailing my arms around in front of me and rushing for the door. Last I noticed, Memaw was talking to the visiting preacher, but kept looking at me with a distinct look of confusion and displeasure.

I didn't want to seem rude to Hester, but was breezing right by her when she reached out her hand and pulled my arm. She put her face as close to my ear as it could get without actually touching my brain and whispered, "You see them, too, don'tcha?"

"I FOLLOWED THEM right in there," she said when we got outside. I dragged her to the brightest spot I could find, which wasn't easy in light of the fact that we'd just had a storm.

I turned and punched her arm. "Don't you know nothin'? You can't say you see them out loud. You can't let them know you see. I thought you came to the church 'cuz I invited you yesterday afternoon."

"Well, that was real nice of you Bobbi Jo, but I don't belong at no church. I was just wonderin' where all them shadows was going."

I hit my forehead 'cuz I was truly shocked at the absurdity, but also for dramatic flair, I must admit. "They are *not* something to follow, Hester, they're something to *avoid*. I've been spendin' all day tryin' to get the Spirit just so I can figure out how to quit seein' them. Hell's bells!" I hit myself in the forehead again when I recognized my big mistake. "Now see whatcha made me do. God'll probably' dock me a whole day for cussin' and it'll be that much longer to figure this all out."

Hester wasn't listening. "Didya notice how they just seemed to love that preacher man?"

I just stood there looking like a wide-mouthed bass gasping in dry air. I couldn't believe them evil things mesmerized her.

Just when I was trying to work up really profound words of wisdom to steer her onto the narrow path, the front door of the church turned dark and started pouring out black shadows. They scattered as they hit the outside, lurking in the shade of trees and bushes.

Following right behind them was Brother Dwayne T. Prescott. And Memaw. And half the ladies' Thursday night fellowship group buzzin' round him like flies to road kill.

Memaw spotted me with Hester right away. "Bobbi Jo! Get over here and meet the preacher right this second."

Hester grabbed my hand. "Take me. I need to meet him, too."

My day flushed straight from visions of glory to damnation. I felt sure that instead of dragging her to Jesus, I was about to introduce her to one of Satan's front men. Surely the Spirit would frown on that.

Memaw glared at me when I walked over attached to Hester.

I pulled my hand out of her grasp and stuck it out to shake the preacher's hand. "Nice to meet you, sir."

But instead of grabbing my hand, he picked up Hester's and clutched it in both of his. "So nice to meet you, young lady."

I suppose Memaw and the other church ladies must've figured that the preacher reaching out to the wayward sinner made it okay because just as soon as he spoke to Hester, women who wouldn't share the sidewalk with her just started fawning all over her.

"This is Hester Davies, Brother Prescott," Memaw said. "She's visitin' today with my granddaughter, Bobbi Jo."

I flashed the evil eye to Memaw just so she'd see I noticed she called Hester by her name instead of calling her trashy girl. I'd never seen Memaw so accommodating to a sinner.

The preacher just couldn't seem to rip his eyes off that Hester. He kept holding her hands in his and nodding. And she just kept letting him. To tell you the truth it made me uncomfortable. The old ladies surrounding them started staring at one another. I reckoned the last thing Hester needed was a whole bunch of biddies gossiping around town how she'd seduced the visiting preacher.

I grabbed her arm and pulled her toward the church. "Come on, Hester."

Just then my parents and Wade came out the church door. He started hacking up his innards and every shadow being in the yard went slithering to the church wall behind him, skipping and leaping for joy. I felt sure if they'd had faces their grins would be eating up their whole countenance.

Hester turned her attention away from Brother Prescott to my brother. "My, Bobbi Jo, would ya look at that."

I ran to my family. "Mama, we gotta get him away from here." But no one was listening. Everyone was gathering around Wade telling him to breathe and Papa jumped in there and started whacking him on the back. That's about the only way to get all the stuff in his lungs loosened up but it looks just awful. Looks like my daddy's beating him.

NEXT DAY, WITH Wade in the hospital and Mama crying all the time, I set to figuring what those shadows had to do with my brother and the visiting preacher. Grown-ups didn't seem to know they followed him around, so I reckoned it was up to me and God. I didn't suppose I was the best partner but considering no one else knew there was a job to do, He'd have to be happy just having somebody.

Scared as I was, I still made my way to the hospital 'cuz that's where I'd seen the most of them at one time, outside of that morning at the church with Brother Prescott. When we first rushed Wade to the emergency room after church, I could hardly look around the place there were so many of them. I just put my head down and cried. Everyone assumed I was grieving over Wade, but really I just couldn't bear to see them all.

But this time I wasn't going to cry. I decided I was gonna watch and figure them out.

I walked into the front lobby expecting a flurry of shadows. One or two of the shadows in the room flickered in the corner of my eye, but other than my imaginings it looked like any ordinary lobby in a regular office.

The receptionist looked up as I walked in. "Well, hello there, Bobbi Jo," said Mrs. Wilcox. "Isn't it so sweet of you to come look in on your brother?"

I nodded my head. "You have no idea how worried I am about him." Really, she had no idea.

"You're just nice as you can be. You tell him I said hey and get better."

I pushed the elevator button for Wade's floor. "I will, Mrs. Wilcox."

Just when I started to wonder if maybe I wasn't gonna get a chance to see any, the elevator doors opened onto Wade's floor, the critical care area. The bright hospital lights cast short shadows, but there was no mistaking the activity in those shadows. Dark shapes slithered from wall to wall, dancing in and out of rooms. Nurses, doctors and orderlies walked down a macabre hallway full of chilling phantoms only I could see, their insubstantial threat invisible to the adults around me.

I approached room two hundred and paused right outside the cracked door as I noticed a dozen of my new mischievous foes shoot toward the room. A mother leaned over the bed of her young son, wiping his brow with a cloth, silently weeping much like my mother. The familiar refrain, known only to the family members of sick children, flowed from the room and sang in my own heart as my eyes caught hers.

Just when I got to wondering why so many of the shadows converged on the touching scene, a loud monitor beeped and the chaos began. Several nurses rushed into the room, followed closely by doctors demanding the mother remove herself from the room.

The more frenzied the room, the more raucous the shadowy organisms grew. So much excitement over a young boy's distress made me pause to scrutinize. Then it dawned on me they weren't so much causing the grief as they were *feeding* on it. Almost as if the more anguished someone was, the more they bloated with nourishment. The creatures swamped the room. In just minutes there wasn't a dozen, but several dozen. They ping-ponged back and forth between the room with the dying boy and his mother standing in the hallway, praying as she watched the doctors work.

I turned and walked toward my brother's room when I heard the machine in the room quit beeping and fall to the steady hum I figured meant the boy lost his fight. I didn't want to be there to watch them waltz and rejoice around the mother's misery.

And I'm not ashamed to admit I was awful relieved to notice not a single shadow moved in Wade's room.

❧

WHAT WITH WADE momentarily safe, I decided to head home and see if I could rustle up my own dinner. Any time Wade's in the hospital, I'm pretty much on my own. Papa and Mama spend lots of time at his side and I mostly fend for myself.

I figured Memaw was my best bet for an easy something to eat. Often times she'd sneak me out a couple of dollars from her tip money at the beauty shop. When I popped my head in the door I heard them all carrying on about the revival preacher.

From under a dryer I heard, "That sermon was just about the best I've heard."

Memaw paused her comb at Mrs. Whitefield's crown. "And did you..." she stopped and looked at me in the doorway. "Well, Bobbi Jo, come right in here and tell us your impressions of Brother Prescott. It's always refreshin' to hear a young person's point of view, isn't it ladies?"

Of course I knew I couldn't just pop up and tell those ladies I figured he must leave a pretty wide trail of misery everywhere he went in light of all the dark creatures swarming round his person, but I figured I might could just drop the slightest hint I wasn't too sure about his intentions.

I leaned on Memaw's sink and acted like I was thinking real hard. "Well, I guess he sounded alright, but I don't guess I learned anything I hadn't already heard sittin' in ya'll's Sunday School classes."

I congratulated myself on figuring out how to say I didn't think he was all that great *and* kiss up to the church ladies. Sometimes I amaze even myself, frankly.

Memaw was not impressed, so she flashed me the mean eyes and said, "Bobbi Jo, you mightn't know fresh words from the Spirit if the Lord Jesus himself came down from above and delivered them. You must learn to tune your spiritual radio in, darlin'."

The ladies all shook their heads at me, confirming for Memaw that I was not picking up the spiritual frequencies flying through the air. I debated telling them all about what I was tuning into, but didn't figure they'd believe me and if they did, maybe they'd decide to take me to that preacher for a good old-fashioned exorcism.

Quick thinking got me out of that tight fix. "You're right, Memaw. Maybe I'll sit by Mary Beth Widner on Sundays. Maybe that'll help."

Conversation turned right to the virtues of Mary Beth and they forgot all about my lack of discernment where Brother Prescott was concerned. I nodded and smiled at all the right spots, wormed a couple of dollars out of Memaw and headed toward the Burger Shack for a little dinner.

Just as I turned the corner toward the burger place, my eyes caught movement over near the church. I didn't figure on there being anyone there 'til just before seven when Brother Prescott would be starting the revival services, but what I saw was a massive movement of shadows toward the church's back shed near the cemetery. The best thing I could do, in order to learn more, was follow the dark.

I forgot my growling stomach and headed for the church shed. I wondered if the shadows would be interested in a wounded animal or broken down lawn mowers, 'cuz that was about the only thing I could figure would be in there. Just to be on the safe side, I climbed up on a crate to peep in the window.

The shadows were working themselves up into a frenzy and I knew something bad skulked in that shed. I could make out Hester backing up into the corner, surrounded by dark shapes, and somebody standing in front of her. Her face said she'd decided those shadows weren't quite as fascinating as they'd been yesterday. Fast action was what was called for.

Before my brain could catch up with my body, I hopped off that box and opened the door to that shed. "Hester, did I see you come in here?" I yelled out, as if I didn't know she was in there. Her expression changed from panic to relief the minute Brother Prescott spun around to see who'd broken in on their conversation. The shadows in the room dashed back to their rightful places on the walls and floors. As they dispersed, I could tell their glee was gone, they pouted in their corners.

"Well, hello there. Bobbi Jo, isn't it?" He reached out his hand to take mine and I politely shook his clammy hand.

I looked past him. "Hester, I've been lookin' all over for you. You know you're late meetin' me at the Burger Shack." I looked over at Prescott and smiled. "I never know where I'm gonna find this girl."

"I just saw her come in here myself and got curious," he agreed, glancing over my shoulder. "I'll leave you two ladies to your burgers. Hope to see you tonight up at the revival." He took off mighty fast, followed by all the minions, and I knew right then and there seeing the shadows move wasn't all bad. After all, just then the ability had saved Hester from something horrible. Maybe I didn't need to get the Spirit after all, maybe He'd been with me the whole time. Like Scarlett O'Hara, I set my mind to think on that another day.

Hester grabbed me by the shoulders and wrapped me up in her arms. "Bobbi Jo, I've never been so happy to see anyone in all my born days."

"I gather that from all the squeezin'," I said as I slunk out of her grasp. "What were you doin' in here with him?"

Hester exhaled through her nose quickly, and in that huff of breath I knew. "I wasn't hearin' the gospel preached, that's for sure. He's a bad man, Bobbi Jo. A really bad man."

"I tried tellin' you that when you were so fascinated the other day with the you-know-whats. They're bad, too, Hester." I glanced around the shed to see if any of them were still there. "Let's get out of here."

We walked outside and I pulled her to the sunniest place in the graveyard. "Now I've been studyin' on them for two days and from what I can tell, they don't hurt anybody, they just feed on sorrow. Not that I wanna place a bet on that theory, but I'm startin' to think it's a blessin' we can see 'em."

Hester couldn't relax. She kept looking around as if expecting to disappear into one of the shadows cast by tall gravestones. I touched her arm and she swung around to look at me in a panic. I read in her eyes a long story, only it wasn't the kind I was used to hearing. Mama put me to bed with happy endings and hope. Hester's narrative disheartened me and for some reason I thought back to the mother of that little boy in the hospital.

Hester leaned in close and whispered. "You may be blessed, but they'll get me in the end, Bobbi Jo. I'm surrounded by nothin' but sorrow."

She turned and ran out of the church yard, past the sanctuary and on down the dirt road I knew led her home.

I DON'T KNOW anyone else who sees them. I break up their good times whenever I get the chance, but Hester's the one I really worry about now. Ever since that preacher left town, seems like she's got more than her fair share of the shadowmen tagging along. I do my best to bring her a little peace and joy so as to disappoint them away, but it's like she said that day. Hester looks as if she's drowning in sorrow and they just can't stay away from her.

In several years I will read of her death and wonder if I could have done something more to rescue Hester. Until then, I still manage to work up wonderment that I get to glimpse into another side of this world. I guess God figured since He messed up on that whole boy/girl thing, He better give me a little extra something to fight with. Every once in a while I've gotta step out and break up a little shadow party. Sometimes I'm scared. Sometimes I wonder why there are Hesters in this world. Mostly though, I just give God a nod for coming up with the idea of letting me in on the secret.

He is clever, I'll give Him that.

9TH WARD

JERRY GORDON

Momma used to always tell me that Jesus was black, but after the water poured in over those levees, I had to wonder. It seemed to me that Katrina answered the prayers of an awful lot of rich white people. It may have washed away my sins, but it took everything I cared about with it.

These days there's nothing worse than being a black kid in the 9th Ward of New Orleans. You feel about as welcome as a gangster rapper at a Klan rally. Never mind the fact that I finished my freshman year of high school first in my class, now I'm the reason white people lock their doors at night.

If you're wondering what happened to the old 9th Ward, the one you saw on TV after the hurricane, it's long since gone. Sure, the redevelopment plan made room for a few of those poor black folks you saw clinging to the rooftops, but after years of being scattered across the fifty states like refugees, most of them took the money and left New Orleans to the greedy developers.

With the reconstruction almost finished, the streets are beautiful. Every house is huge. Every car is shiny. It's like someone swallowed the neighborhood I once knew and vomited Disneyland in its place. Everything's a little too perfect, a little too clean. It's not even my neighborhood to hate anymore. I'm just an inconvenient reminder of the past.

"Hey Charlie! Why weren't you at football tryouts today?"

The sound of Woody's voice caught me off guard. Even the white kids at school jumped when they heard him coming. Hanging out the window of his buddy's Land Rover, he started in on me again.

"Hey jackass! I'm talking to you!"

"S-s-s-s-stop making f-f-f-fun of me you t-t-tub of shit! You know I'm t-t-t-t-too small to play!"

Woody's size might have been an advantage on the football field or in the cramped hallways at school, but out here in the open, my scrawny legs gave me the edge. I'm not saying I could make the track team or anything, but I don't stutter when I run. The second that door started to open, I took off.

He chased me through half a dozen yards before I ran between the plastic lighthouses that marked Mr. Bishop's invisible fence. Woody yelled something at me between gasps for air, but I couldn't make it out over the bark of the German Shepherd snapping at my feet. That dog was half an inch from tasting my black ass when the radio collar sent him yelping.

I didn't have to look back to know that Woody stopped chasing me. If I could barely make it across that yard, he'd get eaten for sure. A bully only respected one thing, and that was a bigger bully.

Before Katrina brought Woody to my neighborhood, I took my daily beatings from a kid named Toby Montgomery. What Toby lacked in size, he more than made up for in pure rage. He'd cut you rather than punch you. And if you were dumb enough to punch him back, you'd wake up in an ambulance. When the hurricane ripped Toby's house to pieces and flooded the 9th Ward, I thought God had answered my prayers. Turns out, my nightmare was just beginning.

You see, my parents died when the levees gave way. They left the house early that morning, after the hurricane had passed, and went into the streets to help people. They told me to stay home and take care of Grandma. They promised me they'd be right back. I waited and waited, but I never saw either of them again.

By the time I got back to our old house I had just about melted the tread off my shoes. The notice on the front door said it was condemned, but I had long since pried the particle boards away. Now that the court battles were over, ours was the last of the old neighborhoods to be demolished. Everyone at school said this part of town was cursed, but they were just scared of what New Orleans had once been.

Several people did die on my street, that much is true, but the idiots at school didn't have the decency to treat it like a cemetery. They liked to get drunk and sneak into the condemned houses late at night, scare their rich girlfriends. To them, it was a big amusement park, a street flooded with haunted houses.

As soon as I pushed the front door open, Woody and his buddy came barreling around the corner in their Land Rover. I waited long enough to flip them off as they skidded to a halt in front of my house. As far as I was concerned, they could yell at me all they wanted from the outside.

The house didn't have any power, but the windows were still barred and the deadbolt worked. I locked the door behind me and grabbed the gas lantern out of the kitchen. No reason to stand there and listen to Woody's crap, so I headed down to the basement.

My old room was...not much of a room. Before the levees gave, I had a cool racecar bed and a bunch of books and comics and even an old computer. It couldn't do much, but I still loved tinkering with it. All my books and comics rotted in the same water that ruined my bed. I never did find that computer. After it disappeared, I had to resort to putting my adventures down on paper like this.

I lit the gas lantern and plopped down on a pile of my grandma's old quilts. The handmade blankets were in the attic when the water hit and had somehow managed to stay dry. They smelled like my family, and that meant more to me than anything.

Curling up next to the lantern, I pulled out a worn copy of my favorite paperback. I stole it from the library today, hoping to lose myself in a world full of vampires. I wanted to be a legend like Robert Neville. So what if my vampires were rich and white? I wanted to turn my house into a fortress and spend my days hunting the evil bastards who taunted what was left of my life.

Unfortunately, the pounding at the front door refused to cooperate with my delusions. I could hear Woody slamming his whole body into it. Since the neighborhood was scheduled to be flattened next week, I didn't expect the cops to come along and stop him.

Putting the book aside, I got up and reached behind the door for my baseball bat. I had wrapped it in some barbed wire from an old construction site. The flood washed away the blood caked on it, just as it washed away the body of Toby Montgomery. Nobody missed him much. Another black kid lost in the flood.

I thought God broke the levees to save me, to wash away Toby's body and my sins with it, but I was wrong. He let me live so he could punish me for what I had done. I killed Toby, who spent the better part of his life torturing me, and for that God took away my family. He drowned the only people who ever loved me. And now that Toby was gone, Woody happily took his place in my waking nightmare.

With my bat in hand, I didn't have to take Woody's crap, but part of me thought I was supposed to do just that. Maybe I should walk upstairs and take the beating I deserved. Then again, maybe I should walk up those steps and show him what crazy really looks like.

Robert Neville wouldn't let himself get lured outside by the vampires, but maybe I would. Running my fingers along the barbed wire, I could still see Toby falling to the ground. The pool of blood that formed around his head was huge.

I heard the door coming off its hinges, but I didn't move. I just stood there, at the bottom of the steps, thinking about all that blood. Hurried footsteps screeched to a halt in front of me.

"Jesus, Charlie! Put the bat down! The haunted house thing was funny last night, scaring the girls and all, but it's over. You're the captain of the football team, man. Stop walking around like some kind of possessed retard."

I hated Woody and everyone like him. Now was no different than before the flood. "H-h-h-how many times do I have to tell you. I'm n-n-n-not Charlie!"

With a swing of the bat, Woody dropped to the ground. I chased his friend into the kitchen and knocked his legs out from under him. The bastard kept pleading for *Charlie* to stop. I thought he'd give up on the joke after the second or third hit, but he never did.

At least when the police come to arrest me, I won't have to listen to their crazy stories anymore. People will leave me alone now. They won't tease me about being rich or playing football. And no one, I mean no one, will try to tell me that the poor black kid who lived here died in the flood.

Dropping the bat on the kitchen floor, I went downstairs to my grandma's blankets and prayed that God would come and wash me away.

RUNNING TOWARD EDEN

JASON BRANNON

The church was a quaint white building with a nice green lawn. It had the customary stained glass windows depicting the miracles of Christ, a small metal cross atop the steeple, and a gravel parking lot filled with assorted pickup trucks, dirty station wagons, and the standard fare of minivans. Organ music filtered from the open doors like warmth from an oven.

A drooping apple tree knelt in the church's front yard like a sinner searching for redemption. Bruised and rotten fruit dotted the ground, waiting for the birds to eat their fill. A little blonde girl sat on the steps with a bushel of the rotten apples from the tree, rolling them down slowly one at a time. Something was wrong with her. Retardation of some sort perhaps. A small unkempt cemetery flanked the sanctuary. A few of the graves were adorned with silk flowers. Most hadn't been attended to in years and were covered with weeds.

All in all, it was a typical church, a thumbnail sketch that could have come from any of a dozen states in the Deep South. The only thing that wasn't typical of the scene was the fenced-in corral behind the church and the cages.

Nobody really seemed to pay the corral much attention. They all knew what it was for, what it held. To them, it simply contained another facet of their religion, just as the cups they used for the Lord's Supper contained the symbolic blood of Christ. The symbolism, however, ended with the grape juice that filled those cups. What lived inside those cages behind the church was real. It was the source of true miracles.

And a miracle, after all, was the one reason they came to the Church of the Crucified Nazarene in the first place.

The crippled staggered up to the church, bracing themselves with crutches. The sick hobbled in, supported by members of their family. The blind walked uncertainly, hoping that the steps leading up to the sanctuary hadn't moved since the last time they came to be healed. Despite their infirmities, the needy all wore their masks of hope. For many of them, this was their last chance.

"You're nervous," Becca said, clutching Connor's hand for reassurance.

"Why wouldn't I be?" Connor said, pulling away from Becca. "I know what kind of things go on here." Without thinking about it, he massaged the lump in his cheek. At one time, the lump could have easily been a wad of tobacco. Not any more. Now it wasn't just something he could spit out and forget.

"This is going to work. I promise," Becca said. "And I know this isn't the most conventional way to do things, but keep an open mind about it." Although it was clear by the look on her face that she was optimistic, the words themselves held just a little too much false hope for Connor's liking.

He watched the parade of freaks march up the steps to the church and wondered if they were just as deluded as Becca. Surely, they all didn't think that God was going to miraculously heal them.

"I don't think I want to do this after all," Connor said as they started up the steps.

"This is a church of faith," Becca reminded him. "I've seen things here that you wouldn't believe. God can take that cancer away if you'll just let Him."

"I'm not religious," Connor said. "Never have been. Why would I expect to waltz in here and be healed when there are devout believers who have spent years praying without result?"

"Because I have faith even when you don't."

"Places like this make me uncomfortable. I can't promise that I'm going to stick around once things get started. All those people shouting and clapping and speaking in tongues makes me feel weird."

"Well, having your cheek rot off could be a lot more uncomfortable. Don't you think?"

"I've got a question for you since you've got all the answers," Connor said as they took a seat at the rear of the church. "If faith is the key to healing, why aren't you healed? You've still got all that scar tissue, and it doesn't seem to be going away. You may have all the faith in the world, but you still can't have children."

It was clear Becca didn't like the question but knew she had to answer. "God is not a genie who grants wishes," she said. "It's not that simple. Sometimes tests of faith aren't instantaneously rewarded. I'll be healed eventually. God won't let me down."

"I couldn't have said it any better myself," a booming voice said from behind them.

Connor turned and found himself staring at the tallest man he had ever seen. The man looked to be in his sixties with thinning white hair and deep set eyes that looked like bits of coal. There was a certain electric intensity about him that made him seem like one of the old prophets from the Bible. Moses perhaps. Or Abraham.

"So this is the Connor I've heard so much about," the reverend observed. "Did he come to be healed? Or is he just curious about what we do here?"

"I've got cancer," Connor said. "In my jaw. I guess that's what too much tobacco will do for you. I've been chewing since I was thirteen."

"Be careful," Webster said. "Your sins will always find you out. The body is God's temple and should not be abused."

"I'm sure you've haven't always been a saint," Connor said defensively.

"My sins aren't the ones in question here," Webster said. "You're the one whose transgressions have manifested themselves through affliction. But it doesn't matter. Whether you know it or not, you've come to the right place. Faith is what this church is built on, and soon the cages out back will be opened for your infirmity."

"Care to elaborate?"

"A doctor always goes to the source of an infection," Webster replied. "You wouldn't amputate an arm to save a leg, would you?"

"I don't understand what you mean," Connor confessed.

Reverend Webster smiled and shook his head knowingly. "Of course you don't. Let me try to put this in terms you can grasp. Man hasn't always sinned. There was a time in the beginning when men and women were perfect. This would be like a body being free of infection. Then the serpent tempted Eve and the virus was released into the world. Your affliction is evidence that you've sinned. To rid you of the affliction we go to the heart of the sin. We go to the tempter himself and beseech him to take the temptation away. With that goes the sin and the sickness."

"If you say so," Connor said, still puzzled.

Reverend Webster nodded and checked his watch. "You'll see in a few minutes," he said.

The chattering in the sanctuary was soon quieted by lush textured chords from a pipe organ.

"Brothers and Sisters, I'm glad you're here," the Reverend said from the pulpit. "But even more, God's glad you are here. He's happy for an opportunity to manifest His power and show you that He's the supreme authority over everything, including death. God is a merciful and all-powerful God. But He's also a bit picky. Sin is an abomination to The Father, and He refuses to look upon it. That's where the distance between you and heaven comes from. That's also why you've come here today. To rid yourself of sin and the physical manifestations of it."

The room was a chorus of amens and hallelujahs set to the tune of "Victory in Jesus." Connor glanced over at the woman seated at the organ and thought to himself that she was probably the most normal looking person in the room. Then he noticed that she was missing both legs from the knees down.

"Is there a man among us who hasn't sinned?" Webster asked. "I think I can speak for every one of us when I say that we've all fallen short. Yet sometimes we take that for granted. We pass each other on the street and overlook the obvious afflictions that are outward manifestations of the wrongs we've committed. Sometimes it takes a newcomer to bring the truth full-center again."

"No," Connor whispered as he realized what was coming.

"Take this young man, for instance," Reverend Webster said, pointing at Connor. "He was a slave to tobacco and now he has a tumor on his jaw. Pretty sufficient reminder, if you ask me. But has God not promised us that there is a chance for redemption? Has He not given us sufficient means to erase the past? I say that He has."

On the reverend's cue, several rough looking farmer-types in bib overalls stepped out the side door of the sanctuary. Connor instinctively knew where they were going.

The cages....

Until now, he had only suspected what was being kept there, but the return of the farmers confirmed his every fear. The snakes writhed in their hands, eager to strike.

Connor didn't know much about snakes, but he knew enough to realize that they were poisonous and could very likely kill him with one bite.

"Since the beginning of time," the reverend said, "the serpent has personified evil. By placing our faith in God, we can overcome that evil and control the hold it has over our lives."

"I'm outta here," Connor said, rising up from the pew as one of the farmer-types held out a three-foot cottonmouth to him.

"Take it, brother," he said. "Show God how much you believe in Him."

"Get away from me with that thing," Connor stammered. "I'm afraid of snakes."

"We're all afraid of something," Webster chimed in from the pulpit. "That's where having a strong set of beliefs comes in. Go ahead. Take the serpent. Grab evil by the throat. Trust that God will keep the snake from striking. That kind of faith is the only thing that will ever heal you."

"Please," Becca pleaded. "Take it, Connor. Do it for us."

Connor looked at Becca, saw the tears streaming down her face, and knew that she truly believed this was the way.

"I'm not doing this," he maintained. "I'm sorry."

Becca's face hardened. Her eyes went cold. "Fine," she said. "Your cancer. Not mine."

The fact that Connor had declined the serpents simply meant that there were more of them for the other fanatics in the congregation. The lady sitting behind them took a snake in each greedy hand and began to dance. Her eyes rolled back in her head, and the pins holding her tightly wrapped bun in place came loose, spilling her hair around her shoulders and down her curved back. The snakes squirmed in her tight-fisted grip.

Connor backed away from her. "Let's go," he told Becca.

"I'm not going anywhere," Becca said.

Connor sighed. "You're riding with me, and I'm leaving."

"I'll get a ride," Becca said.

"Fine," Connor said as he slipped out of the pew. "Suit yourself."

He barely got halfway down the aisle when two of the farmer-types that had helped bring in the snakes parked themselves in front of the doors.

"You need God," one of them said. "And you're not leaving until you find Him."

"Let me out," Connor said.

"No," the other said, pulling a Buck knife out of his overalls. "Not until this is done."

Connor didn't want to start a fight that he knew he would lose. As calmly as he could manage under the circumstances, he found a seat on the back row and tried to quell his rising temper.

Soon everyone, Becca included, was handling snakes. The church was a frenzied house of flailing limbs, fluttering eyelids, and angelic tongues. The steady percussive sound of rattlers provided a subtle backbeat to all of the chanting and strange words that were floating through the air like the feathers of fallen angels. Connor kept checking the door to see if Reverend Webster's thugs were still there. They were.

"Brothers and Sisters," Reverend Webster shouted from the pulpit. "We face evil everyday in all its guises. Some of our trials are small and readily handled, like these serpents. Others aren't so small and require the force and prayers of a church like ours. Since the beginning of time, the world has been a battlefield of opposing forces. Good versus evil. God versus Satan. And why is this so? Why is this a problem for us? The answer is because we were born into sin. The root of our problem goes all the way back to the Garden of Eden where Eve was tempted."

"Our sins can control us," Webster continued. "Or we can control them. Our sins are like these snakes. We can release our grip on them and hope they won't be a problem any longer. That's the exact moment they will come back to bite us and doom us to eternal hell. Or we can be proactive and kill the evil in our lives before it has a chance to ruin us. Faith, of course, is the key."

The reverend motioned to one of his congregation, and the little girl with blonde ringlets joined Webster on stage. Webster kissed the little girl on the top of the head and made her face the crowd.

"No," Connor whispered.

"This is Virginia," Webster said as his congregation continued to dance and to tempt fate. "She's been sick for a very, very long time. Was born that way in fact. But I would venture to say that she has more faith than anyone in this room and triumphs daily because of it. Let her be an example to us all."

The little girl readily accepted two writhing cottonmouths and held them up for everyone to see.

"Ssssssssnakesssss," she said in a long, drawn out voice.

Connor stood up with the intent of helping the little girl, "And what was her sin?" He felt two hands clamp down on his shoulders. The deacons glared at him and showed him their tobacco-stained teeth.

Realizing that he was a prisoner here in this church, Connor sat down and watched in horror as Virginia lost her grip on one of the cottonmouths. The serpent hissed and sank its fangs into her. It was only a matter of seconds before her eyelids fluttered and she fell to the floor in the grip of a massive seizure.

"God won't let anything happen to her," Reverend Webster explained. "Our faith will guide her through."

"She needs to go to a hospital," Connor shouted. His voice was buried beneath the din of so much shouting and praising.

"Hospitals," Webster said, spitting the word out. "Why are people so quick to dismiss God in times like these?"

"God invented common sense so we wouldn't pick up snakes that are poisonous," Connor said.

"Do you believe in God?"

Connor swallowed hard. He wasn't sure what kind of answer would be satisfactory here.

"I believe in a higher power, yes."

"But do you believe in God?"

"I'm not sure."

"Do you believe in Satan?"

"I believe that there is evil in the world."

"If I could prove to you that Satan exists, would that lead you to believe in God?"

Conner was nervous, he noticed men moving closer to his pew. He didn't know how to answer.

Webster smiled and motioned to his deacons. "Open the Penance Pit," he said.

"No," Becca said, snapping out of the trance-like state she'd been in. The snakes squirmed in her fists. "Don't put him in there."

"I'm trying to save your boyfriend's soul," Webster said.

Becca didn't seem quite so nailed to the cause anymore. She looked at Connor with tears in her eyes. It was enough to make him uneasy and a little scared.

The deacons did as they were told and began moving some of the pews around. Although he hadn't noticed it before, Connor realized that there was some sort of trap door set into the floor of the church.

"Don't worry," Webster said as one of the deacons raised the door to reveal a pit full of snakes. "I'll send Virginia in with you to protect you from Methuselah."

Connor started to run, but several men grabbed him and manhandled him toward the pit. It wasn't much of a fight, and he soon found himself cast into a room full of dark slithering shapes. As promised, Victoria was thrown in with him. She trembled and twitched as the snake's venom raced through her veins.

The last thing Connor saw before the door was closed was Becca peering over the edge at him and Webster's leering face.

☙

THEN DARKNESS.

Connor tried to remain calm and keep his wits about him, but it was a difficult thing to manage with so many snakes slithering over his legs, up his arms, and across his chest. He wanted to scream so badly but refused to give Webster that sort of satisfaction. His only hope at this point was that Becca had finally come to her senses. Maybe she was going to get the police.

Amazingly enough he hadn't been bitten yet by any of the snakes, but he knew that one wrong move could change that. Hesitantly, he reached out his hand, hoping that Victoria was nearby. He could hear her ragged breathing and knew that she wouldn't last long.

"Let me out," Connor shouted. His voice was drowned out by a rousing rendition of "At the Cross."

Snakes hissed all around him, and Connor felt sure that one of them was about to strike as he reached out for Victoria. Yet, he didn't feel the sting of fangs.

Only the tenderness of Victoria's skin. The skin was cold and clammy to the touch, still a little sticky from the apples. For a moment, he was certain that she was already dead. Then she spoke to him.

"Methuselah will be here soon," she whispered to him in the darkness.

"We need to get out of here," Connor said.

"A serpent tricked us into sin. A serpent can take it away again," she said in sing-song.

It took Connor a moment for the significance of that to truly sink in. "You mean that allowing yourself to be bitten by these serpents is your way of repentance."

"Methuselah can heal you."

"Who is Methuselah?" Connor asked.

But Victoria didn't reply. Instead, she lapsed back into unconsciousness.

Thin slats of meager light filtered in through the cracks in the door above them. Connor squinted and tried to get a better idea of his surroundings, but one of the pews was quickly shifted back into place, effectively blocking out what little illumination there was.

In those brief seconds before he was plunged into complete darkness, Connor had observed that a set of tunnels actually branched off from the Penance Pit, snaking off in different directions. He had absolutely no idea where any of them could lead, but reasoned that one of them might offer some form of escape.

Thankful that he hadn't completely given up tobacco altogether, Connor pulled a lighter out of his pocket. He flicked the lighter and gasped at the moving, undulating mass of snakes that were squirming beneath his feet.

"Jesus," he gasped as he looked around for Victoria. Strangely enough she seemed to have disappeared. He scanned the nearby tunnels for any sign of her. There was no possible way that she could have gotten up and staggered out of here in her condition. No doubt the cottonmouth's poison was already firmly entrenched in her system and debilitating her minute by minute.

There was no place else she could have gone. Unless...

Connor eyed the mass of snakes in front of him and caught a brief glimpse of white in their midst. Victoria had been wearing a white dress. The snakes moved around enough to show him another glimpse, this time of Victoria's pink skin.

The lighter went out, and Connor used the brief respite to gather his courage. This poor little girl couldn't climb out of her situation without help. Her parents had brought her here and forced her into this lifestyle, ignoring the dangers. And now she was covered in hundreds of venomous snakes and on her way to succumbing to the cottonmouth's bite.

"Faith," Connor said, spitting out the word like something rotten. This little girl had possessed faith and look at what it had gotten her. Maybe Becca had gone through something similar as a child. Maybe that's why she didn't consider this bizarre or bent in any way.

Realizing what he had to do, Connor flicked his lighter again. Adders, racers, king and bull snakes slithered across his boots and each other. Connor shook his leg lightly to discourage one from crawling up the leg of his jeans. A rattler hissed at him, angry that it had been disturbed.

Carefully, Connor reached his hand into the working mass of serpents. The snakes parted for him, and he found Victoria's ankle easily enough. Snakes fell off of the little girl like old scales as he hauled her out. Her skin was clammy and cold to the touch.

In the church above, the congregation was singing "Shall We Gather At the River."

The song made him think of water moccasins. He shuddered and tried to put the thought out of his mind. It was a difficult thing to do when he felt snakes slithering all around him.

Once Victoria was completely out from beneath the moving wave of serpentine flesh, Connor shook her slightly, in case some of the filthy creatures had found their way into her clothing. A black racer and a dark brown snake with black stripes fell out of her dress. Satisfied that he had gotten rid of them all, Connor threw the little girl over his shoulder and took a close look at the tunnels, hoping to spot something that would tell him which way to go. A faint reddish glow emanated from one. Hoping that it was the last fading rays of the sun, Connor chose that direction and carefully tiptoed toward the tunnel.

Several snakes struck at him as he walked over, around, and sometimes on top of them. Their fangs were made harmless, however, by the steel-toed workboots that he wore. Knowing that his luck would eventually run out, Connor hurried into the tunnel, breathing a sigh of relief once he realized that there were no snakes this far up. Yet there was something that made him pause.

"It can't be," he said as he surveyed the enormous skin. It must have been twenty-feet long and five feet wide. A snake would have to live a hundred lifetimes to grow this large. Methuselah, he remembered. The name would certainly fit.

Instinctively, he turned back toward one of the other tunnels only to find that a veritable army of snakes had fallen in behind them, blocking their way. Connor thought about chancing it but decided against it when a line of cobras rose up and began to spit venom in his direction.

Victoria shuddered in his arms.

"Just hang on a little bit longer," he said to the unconscious little girl. "We'll be out of here before you know it."

"The exit's this way," a husky voice whispered from the opposite end of the tunnel.

"Who's there?" Connor asked.

"A friend," the voice said. "I'll show you how to get out of here, but there's something I need from you first."

Connor knew this was a trick of some sort, but there was no other way out. He was stuck down here with the snakes and whatever or whoever this was.

"What's the deal?" he asked.

"Give me your sins," the voice instructed.

"I don't understand," Connor admitted.

"You obviously weren't listening to Reverend Webster when he explained the nature of sin and how it manifests itself in physical deformities and maladies."

"I heard it. I just didn't believe it."

"Come a little closer," the voice instructed. "You'll believe soon enough."

Connor flicked his lighter again and noticed that Victoria's eyes were rolling back in her head. He gritted his teeth in frustration. There was no other choice. He walked deeper into the tunnel, following the reddish glow.

"You've got what I need," the voice said.

"Who are you?" Connor asked.

"I'm known by many names," the voice whispered. "These people call me Methuselah."

"What should I call you?"

"How about Father?"

Although it was clear that the voice was devious and full of deceit, it was also alluring in a strange sort of way. It reminded Connor of stories he'd heard about sirens luring sailors to their deaths. This voice had that same magnetic quality to it.

He had already prepared himself for the fact that Methuselah was a snake and a big one at that. What he hadn't prepared himself for was the origins of this particular creature. The serpent sat there at the end of the tunnel, coiled and alert, its eyes looking like rubies.

"Where did you come from?" Connor asked. "And how are you able to speak?"

"Where do any of us come from?" the serpent replied cryptically. "As for how I'm able to speak-think about it. I've been around a very long time."

"I'm not very good with riddles," Connor admitted.

"Maybe if I offered you an apple, you would realize who I am. Adam and Eve certainly would."

Connor gasped. "Impossible," he said.

"Not true," Methuselah responded. "Give me your sins, and I'll show you."

"Why do you want my sins?" Connor asked.

"It's what I live for," the serpent admitted. "Without sin, I would have no reason for existing and would die."

"Where does faith come in?" Connor asked, trying to play it cool even though he was panicking inside.

"I'll heal you and show you the way out."

"Are you Satan?"

The serpent laughed.

Methuselah opened his mouth to reveal a set of fangs as big as butcher knives. Connor screamed, but it was too late to protest as the snake's fangs drove into Victoria's limp body. Methuselah's laughter was the last thing he remembered in the cave.

WHEN HE WOKE up, he found himself back in the church, surrounded by the curious. Becca was fanning him furiously with a hymnal.

"Are you okay?" she asked.

"Have you conquered your sins?" Reverend Webster asked.

Victoria was in the first pew with a rotten apple, she was going to eat it. Conner tried to stop her but noticed she looked different. The abnormal facial structure and outward signs of her retardation were gone.

"I told you," Becca said as tears streamed down both cheeks. "I told you to have faith."

"Praise God," Reverend Webster shouted as he handed Connor a serpent.

This time Connor didn't shy away from the snake as he had before. Instead, he reached out to take the serpent from Reverend Webster. Victoria stood up and threw one of her apples to him and he had no choice but to catch it. Connor expected the apple to squish from rot, but it was completely whole.

VIRTUE·S BLOOD

ANNA D. ALLEN

Vienna, November 1759

"Madame von Reichstadt?"

A voice in the darkness woke Tessa.

"You're late for Mass."

Tessa opened her eyes to see Maria, her aunt's maid, standing at the edge of the bed, a single candle illuminating the cold room.

"At this hour?" Tessa groaned.

"I'm sorry, Madame," Maria said, "but Madame von Golling goes every morning."

As a guest in the house, Tessa would abide by Aunt Sophie's wishes. Sophie Princess von Golling had been kind enough to take her in. Mass was the least Tessa could do.

Tessa threw the heavy covers off and climbed out of the bed.

"Teresa," Aunt Sophie called from down the corridor, "God is waiting."

With Maria's help, Tessa dressed and hurried to meet her aunt.

"Teresa, my darling." The old woman held out her arms. "Still in black, I see," she said, embracing Tessa, as they had not seen each other the night before when Tessa arrived. "Just because your husband died doesn't mean you have to die as well."

Once appropriately bundled against the cold, Sophie took Tessa by the arm and led her out into the darkness of the courtyard where a closed carriage waited. Leopold, Aunt Sophie's manservant, helped them into the carriage, and then climbed in himself, closing the door behind him.

As they rode through the city, Tessa looked out the windows. Without a trace of dawn in the dark sky, people moved through the dark cold streets—men and women setting up stalls in the market and delivering goods to households near the Hofburg. The carriage continued on, and the houses and shops gradually became poorer until the carriage came to a medieval church.

"This is our chapel," Sophie smiled.

Despite Sophie calling it a chapel, it towered over the surrounding buildings. To Tessa, it seemed more like a small cathedral, albeit in need of much repair, its parishioners comprised of the poorer subjects of the Empire.

"Why here?" Tessa asked.

"It's easier to be pious when everyone isn't gossiping about what everyone's wearing or doing. There's much more time for that in the evenings." Tessa noticed a twinkle in the old woman's eyes.

Leopold helped the ladies out of the carriage and fell in behind them as they entered the church, which Tessa discovered was dedicated to Saint Martin. The two ladies walked arm in arm through the crowd. With no pews or chairs, everyone simply stood throughout the nave and faced the altar.

"Is it always crowded?" Tessa whispered to Sophie.

"Just in the mornings," Sophie replied, "Most of the day, it's empty."

Tessa lowered the hood of her cloak and raised her black lace scarf over her head, yet went no further in the removal of her cloak or gloves, as the church was barely warmer than the darkness outside. She looked up to the altar to see the priest arriving. As the priest spoke and the ceremony went on, Tessa stood next to Sophie until her feet ached and she longed to sit. But at last, Communion came, the priest saying the Latin words over the Sacrament.

Eat...For this is my body.

Next came the wine.

Drink...for this is the chalice of my blood....

He called the faithful forward. At last, Tessa had a chance to get off her feet, if only for a moment. She helped her aunt to kneel before the altar and then knelt herself. The priest stood before them and held up a piece of the Host.

"*Ecce Agnus Dei...,*" he said. *Behold the Lamb of God, behold Him who taketh away the sins of the world.*

After Tessa received Communion, she wandered to a side chapel where she discovered a statue of the Virgin surrounded by hundreds of burning candles. The chapel was almost warm here. She removed her gloves and lit a candle for her dead husband. Kneeling, she crossed herself and then prayed aloud, her voice a whisper.

"Angel of God, my guardian dear...."

In the midst of her devotions, she felt a coldness drift into the warmer air of the chapel. A draft from a window or opened door, she reasoned. Yet the chill moved, slowly enveloping her entire body, beginning at her feet and gradually moving over her skirts, up past her waist, over the mound of her breasts, along her arms and neck, and covering her head. Despite her cloak and layers of clothing, the coldness reached deep down within the folds of material, as if consciously searching for her body securely wrapped within. At last it touched her skin and moved along her flesh, caressing, reaching....

Tessa opened her eyes and looked up, the coldness, suddenly and completely, vanishing. But now, she sensed someone watching her. Out of the corner of her eye, she glimpsed a shadow move near one of the massive columns. She quickly turned to follow the movement, and briefly, she saw a pale hand resting against the column, a figure just beyond in the shadows, but nothing was there. Just empty air. A trick of the candlelight, perhaps.

Tessa stood up, her hand holding on to the prie-dieu for support as she leaned forward just a bit to peer around the column and into the shadows. Suddenly, she felt a warm hand covered her own. She jumped, crying out, and turned to find the priest standing beside her.

"Merciful Heaven, Father," she said, her heart pounding.

"My apologies, Madame, I did not mean to startle you." Then he smiled.

Tessa smiled also, catching her breath.

"It's quite alright," she said, withdrawing her hand and clutching it to her chest, "I didn't realize you had finished."

"Yes, a moment ago," he said, "I'm Father Julien. Madame von Golling asked that I find you. She said not to hurry."

"Thank you."

Father Julien motioned toward the prie-dieu. "Do you have any special need?"

"No more than any other soul. I lit a candle for my dead husband."

"I understand,"

She was sure he did not—an arranged marriage to a man with adult children, a man more friend than a lover, a man she dearly missed.

"I shouldn't keep my aunt waiting." As she moved to leave, the priest stopped her.

"Might I have a word with you?"

"Of course."

"I feel the need to warn you...." He hesitated before continuing. "An... Angel of...Death dwells in this Holy House from time to time. I have never known him to harm anyone, but his mere presence can be most frightening. I have never seen him, but I've felt him watching me, just beyond the shadows."

"Perhaps that is what I felt," Tessa said, "I thought someone watched me." She pointed to the darkness beyond the column.

"Then you understand," he said, "Please, don't let his presence frighten you."

"I'll try not to," Tessa said, "My aunt is waiting."

"Of course."

Tessa rejoined her aunt outside.

"Don't worry, my dear," Sophie said as Tessa reached her, "your grief will become easier to bear in time. Who knows...perhaps you'll find love again."

"Yes, Aunt Sophie," Tessa replied, taking her arm. She glanced back to the chapel and saw Father Julien standing in the doorway, a worried look on his face.

Outside, while still dark, the sky grew brighter, faint light on the horizon. As Leopold helped Sophie into the carriage, Tessa turned and looked back toward the church. Under a tree along the church wall, a man stood staring at Tessa. With the ever-brightening sky, she saw him clearly, despite the distance, as if he stood next to her. He was tall, a long dark cloak covering his body down to below his knees, with only his hunting boots visible beneath. His well-shaped head was void of hair, except for a blond trace above his ears, and even that was cut close to his scalp. His face was a deathly white, yet handsome, with a strong jaw, aquiline nose, high cheekbones, and thin eyebrows. The blue eyes gazed out at Tessa and drew her in. She felt his eyes bore into her body, penetrating deep, and piercing through her very soul. Her heart pounded, and she opened her mouth to breathe, but found she could not catch her breath. Part of her wanted to scream. She closed her eyes, her eyelids hot and heavy, her cheeks flushed.

"Madame von Reichstadt?" Tessa heard Leopold say, his voice far way.

"Leopold!" Sophie shouted, "She's about to faint!" Tessa felt Leopold put his arm around her to support her. Opening her eyes, she looked back to the pale man standing under the tree, yet he was gone. Nothing remained to indicate he ever stood there.

With Leopold's help, Tessa climbed into the carriage and sat beside Sophie.

"There, child," Sophie said, pulling Tessa close and patting her hand, "all you need is food and rest."

Leopold climbed in, closing the carriage door behind him as the first ray of sunlight fell over the horizon and touched the church and all of Vienna.

∾

SOPHIE PUT TESSA to bed.

"I'm so sorry, my dear," Sophie fussed, pulling the blankets up around Tessa, "Had I been thinking properly, I never would've taken you to Mass today."

"It's quite alright," Tessa assured her.

"Arriving so late last night, after days of traveling, I should have been here to greet you."

"You didn't know when I would arrive."

Sophie took the breakfast tray from Maria.

"Now don't worry about anything. Once you feel better, we'll start making the rounds. We'll get you some new clothes, and soon you'll be the talk of Vienna."

"Aunt Sophie," Tessa protested.

"It's settled," Sophie continued, pouring a cup of chocolate and handing it to her, "So eat your breakfast, get some sleep, and I'll check on you later." With nothing more to be done, Tessa simply obeyed.

Tessa slept most of the morning and awoke to play cards with Sophie. Lunch interrupted them, but the games and gossip continued afterwards into the evening, until ending with dinner, after which, Tessa said goodnight.

During the night, as Tessa slept beneath the warm layers of bedcovers, she dreamt someone crept into her room....

A cold wind blew outside, pushing against Tessa's bedroom window and rattling the panes. The wind became frantic until at last, the latch gave, and the window flew open. The sheers and curtains parted with the gust, but then the wind subsided, a grey mist entering. It hovered over the floor, drifting across the room to Tessa asleep in her bed. It forced its way between the bedcovers and enveloped the sleeping woman, covering her bare legs, moving over her arms, and leaving no part of her body untouched by its cold caress.

In her sleep, Tessa felt a pair of hands touching her, the hands of a man. One hand moved slowly up her leg, the fingers lightly stroking her skin, until coming to a rest at her waist. Another hand tenderly brushed her hair away from her face, lingered on her cheek for a moment, then moved down to her neck. Tessa felt cold lips press against her own lips, but no breath. Trailing down to her neck, the cold lips never lost contact with her warm flesh, only stopping at her pulse. The lips parted, Tessa's heart pounding beneath their touch. She arched her back, and the hand at her waist slipped under her body to the small of her back. A moan escaped from her lips, and she opened her eyes.

The room was empty, the window well latched, the curtains closed. She was alone. Tessa stood up, went to the window, opened it, and looked out into the night. Before her, all the city slept. Nothing stirred. Shadows filled the streets. Darkness covered the houses.

Tessa touched her neck, the sensation of the lips still lingering there. She closed the window and went back to bed, while in the street below, a shadow moved.

❧

THE NEXT MORNING, Sophie went to Mass alone. When Tessa awoke, she discovered three new dresses waiting for her.

"I stopped by Frau Kaufmann's," Sophie explained, "Baroness von Solden ordered several dresses and couldn't pay for them. The Baron gambles. Did you sleep well?"

"Very well, except for a strange dream," Tessa replied, her hand touching her neck as she remembered the lips.

"Then you feel better?"

"Much better."

"Good. The Countess Harassowitz is having a party tonight."

Tessa did not wish to go. She did not want to wear one of the formal dresses before her. They were too bright given her status. Tessa did not want to be around people. But seeing that Sophie truly wanted to go, Tessa agreed.

"Wonderful," Sophie said, "Now, I think you should wear the pink...."

Tessa paid no attention. Instead, she stared at the window and thought of the man in her dream—the way his hand rested on her waist, the way his mouth lingered on her neck. She never felt his body, just his hands and lips, and she wished she had not opened her eyes, that she had let the moment continue, that she might have experienced....

"I normally go to Confession on Wednesdays," Tessa interrupted her aunt. "Do you think Father Julien will hear my Confession?"

～

THE DAY WAS damp and dreary, the sky grey. Removing the hood of her cloak, Tessa found the church empty, the light dim. She made her way to the confessional, the skirts of her new dress trailing along the stone floor. She entered and waited for the priest. She soon heard him enter on the opposite side.

"Bless me, Father, for I have sinned," she said, "It has been a week since my last confession."

"And how many sins could one such as you acquire within a mere week?"

"I beg your pardon?"

"Tell me what you have done which requires confessing."

"I had a dream."

"A dream?" He sounded amused.

"I dreamt a man was in my bed."

"I see. What happened?"

"Nothing. I woke up."

"My dear, it is not necessary to confess dreams."

"It isn't?"

"Of course not."

"But my old confessor...."

"Your old confessor was probably some poor old fool whose only pleasure in life came from hearing the sins of his fellow man."

"Do you really think so?"

"Of course," he said then asked, "You are recently widowed?"

"Yes."

"How long were you married?"

"Fifteen years."

"And your husband, how did he die?"

"He was old."

"A young woman such as yourself married to an old man. No wonder you have such dreams."

"I've only had one dream," she corrected him.

"Of course, but it's to be expected given that you have been loved by only one, and him an old man. You have no children?"

"Our only child died at birth...early in our marriage."

"And after that? Your husband was too old?"

"He..." she hesitated, not wanting to reveal her private life to a stranger, but something made her want to answer his question, something in his voice she could not resist. "Yes, he was too old."

"Have you any other sins to confess? Please, do not say you had an angry thought."

"Then no, I have no other sins to confess. What is to be my penitence, father?"

"There is none for there is no sin in your dream."

"But I enjoyed it, and I keep thinking about it."

There was silence, the priest saying nothing for a long while.

"Well, that's different then," he said. "Here is your penitence. Go out and find yourself a lover."

"What?"

"Come back when you have more substantial sins."

"I don't understand, Father. Are you telling me to go out and sin?"

"I am telling you to go out and live. Go to parties, drink wine, laugh. Let yourself be wooed by some handsome young man. Allow yourself to be swept away. Perhaps you'll find happiness. Perhaps children."

"Father, I don't think...."

"That is your penitence."

Then he was gone. She left the confessional, quite flustered by what had been said. She stood there for a moment adjusting her dress when she saw Father Julien coming toward her from near the altar.

"Madame von Reichstadt," he said, smiling, "are you here for confession?"

Tessa looked at the empty confessional. Someone else, not Father Julien, had heard her confession.

"Are you all right, Madame?" Father Julien asked.

Tessa took a deep breath, attempting to compose herself.

"Someone was..." she stammered, pointing at the confessional.

Father Julien looked at the confessional then back at her, realization on his face.

"The Angel of Death?"

"I don't know." But Tessa believed it was that dark angel. She ran past Father Julien to the Chapel of the Virgin. She knelt, crossed herself, and prayed.

"Angel of God, my guardian dear...."

THAT NIGHT, TESSA wore a silk dress with embroidered pink flowers, but she did not like it. The bodice laced very tightly, and besides leaving little room to breathe, it lifted Tessa's breasts to the point of scandal. One wrong move and all would be revealed. Laughing, Sophie assured Tessa that everything was tucked in nice and tight. Tessa felt like a trussed chicken plumped up to show off the breast while tucking the legs neatly away.

The Countess Harassowitz lived near the Hofburg. All lit up in the glow of candlelight, the house seemed the grandest Tessa had ever entered, filled with fashionable people.

Everyone stopped and looked as Tessa and Sophie entered the room. Smiling, Sophie scanned the room, nodding in greeting to several of them.

"Madame von Golling," a man said coming to greet the new arrivals. He took Sophie's hand and kissed it. "We missed you last night. Wolfgang didn't have a partner." He turned to Tessa.

"And what have we here?" he said, smiling, "You must be Madame von Golling's niece, Madame von Reichstadt. *Enchanté*." He took Tessa's hand and kissed it, his wet mouth on her hand much too long.

"Baron von Solden," Sophie introduced to Tessa.

Tessa felt his eyes linger on her cleavage.

"Oh, look," Solden said, much too loudly, "she's blushing. I think we've found ourselves a virtuous woman. Someone get me a ruby."

Everyone laughed as Tessa blushed even more.

"Madame von Golling," Solden said, "I'm shocked that you'd bring such an innocent into our midst. She'll be devoured. But don't worry, Madame von Reichstadt, I'll keep a close eye on you." He put her hand on his arm. "Come, I'll introduce you to everyone."

"Don't worry," Sophie whispered to Tessa, "he can't afford another mistress."

Thus went the evening. Sophie played cards while men of all ages offered to bring Tessa a glass of wine, a plate of fruit, or some sweets. Some offered to show her about the great house. Others invited her to visit them at their country houses. Each held her hand as he spoke with her, and when she rid herself of one, another took his place.

As the evening passed, Tessa grew tired, although Sophie seemed full of energy. Baron von Solden offered to take her home. Tessa hesitated, but Sophie assured her that Solden was safe given his finances. Yet when she and Baron von Solden reached the courtyard, another man waited there, one of her admirers, Baron von Helck.

"Monsieur," he said, "I am going in that direction. I can take Madame von Reichstadt. Your wife might miss you."

Tessa sensed Solden's annoyance, but he smiled and asked Helck, "You wouldn't mind?"

"Of course not," Helck replied, "provided the lady doesn't protest." He smiled, his dark eyes staring at her. "I'll be a perfect gentleman," he continued, putting his hand on his heart. Tessa hesitated. Aunt Sophie had assured her that Solden was quite harmless. Helck, however, part of a pack of potential suitors, seemed more interested in new blood rather than Tessa in particular. As she decided to return to the party, the skies opened up, a torrential rain pouring down.

"Quick," Helck shouted, opening the carriage door, "Inside."

Before Tessa could protest, Helck placed his hands about her waist and lifted her into his carriage. He quickly followed, closing the door behind. As the carriage drove away, Tessa glanced outside the window at Solden looking satisfied in the rain.

Tessa sat back, Helck sitting opposite her.

"What an unfortunate turn in the weather," he smiled.

"It looked like rain all day," Tessa countered.

"Really? I hadn't noticed. I sleep quite late and then spend most of my day in bed. I rarely leave the house before dark," he said, "This is very early for me to return home, but I have a pressing need."

"I pray I'm not keeping you," Tessa said, leaning forward to look out the window.

"Not at all," he smiled, "In fact, you might be able to help me in the matter."

Tessa realized they were no longer near the Hofburg but heading away from it.

"This is not the way," Tessa said.

"I thought we'd stop by my house and dry off," Helck said, his voice smooth.

"Please," Tessa said, "Just take me to my aunt's."

"I don't think you understand." He moved to sit next to Tessa and took her hand. He was very close, and she tried to back away from him, but the carriage was too small.

"I think that we should get to know each other," he said, taking one of the ribbon ties of her cloak and pulling it, "In private."

The cloak slipped, revealing cleavage. "We could be very close," he said, brushing her breast with his fingertips.

Tessa slapped him, but he just laughed. Before he could do anything else, Tessa opened the carriage door and jumped out into the rain and darkness, only to fall as she hit the ground. She scrambled to get up and ran down the street. Glancing back, she saw the carriage stop, Helck jumping out.

"Tessa!" he shouted, "Come back. You'll get lost out here." He ran to catch her.

With her heeled shoes and lengths of skirt, Tessa made little progress. Her cloak slipped and fell to the ground, but she did not stop to retrieve it. She heard Helck getting closer, and she rounded a corner to escape, promptly running into a cloaked man standing there. She hit him with such force that she fell back onto the ground. Tessa attempted to get up, only to slip in the rainwater just as Helck rounded the corner.

The man stepped over her, his long cloak brushing her, and he grabbed Helck. Helck screamed, and Tessa thought she heard a wolf's growl as the man threw Helck against the opposite wall to fall unconscious to the ground.

The man turned, holding his hand down to her. Slowly, Tessa slipped her hand into his, and he pulled her up off the ground.

"Are you alright, Madame?" he asked, his voice warm.

"Yes," she lied, tears coming to her eyes, "I'm fine." Drenched, her new dress stained with mud, her hair falling about her, she realized that not only had she lost her cloak but also one shoe, never noticing in the mad dash.

"Here," he said, taking off his cloak and wrapping it around her. He disappeared around the corner and returned a moment later with her cloak and lost shoe.

"Thank you," she said, taking them from him, the heel of the shoe broken, "I am in your debt, Monsieur," and for the first time, she looked up at his face, the same face she had seen in the churchyard—only no longer pale despite the rain washing over his hairless head.

"I've seen you," she managed to say.

"Yesterday." One corner of his mouth turned up in a half-smile. "At Saint Martin's. I pray this man is no kin of yours?" He motioned to Helck.

"No." She stared into the stranger's blue eyes. "He's an acquaintance of my aunt's."

"I've seen him about. He is not a gentleman. You should be careful with whom you associate. There is all manner of danger in Vienna."

"Yes, you are right. He caught me at a moment when I was unaware."

"If you would allow me to escort you home?"

"Thank you, Monsieur." Tessa looked about. "But I've become quite lost and don't know which way is home."

"Yesterday, I saw you with Princess von Golling."

"My aunt. I live with her."

"Then have no fear. I know her house well." He offered his arm to her.

"Forgive me, Monsieur, but your name?"

"My apologies. Christophe de Valois. And you, Madame?

"Tessa von Reichstadt."

"*Enchanté*, Madame," he said, bowing slightly.

Helck moaned.

"We should go." Christophe took Tessa's hand, placed his arm about her, and hurried her down the street.

Making their way through the darkness of the city, the rain pouring down, Tessa limped along with Christophe's assistance, the broken shoe in her hand. After a while, she stopped.

"I'm sorry," she said, leaning against a wall, "I must rest for a moment."

"Are you alright?"

"Yes, just very cold." She lifted up her skirt to reveal her stocking foot soaked and covered in dirt. Without another word, Christophe picked her up in his arms and carried her.

Arriving at Aunt Sophie's, they discovered the house filled with candlelight and several carriages in the courtyard. As Christophe carried Tessa up the front steps, the door opened, Aunt Sophie standing there with Leopold and several men.

"Teresa!"

"I found her in the street," Christophe explained, then motioned inside the house, "With your permission."

"Of course," Sophie said, stepping back, "bring her in." With that invitation by the mistress of the house, Christophe entered.

"In the salon." Sophie pointed the way. "There's a fire there."

As Christophe carried Tessa into the warm room, she could hear Sophie thanking the men for coming and dismissing them. Christophe set her down on the divan before the fire. Kneeling before her, he took hold of her foot and pulled her shoe off. Then he removed her stocking. Taking the other foot, he began to remove her other stocking, this one covered in mud, when he glanced up at her. Tessa stared at him, a surprised look on her face.

"Your forgiveness, Madame." He stood up. "I forgot myself." He stepped back.

"You have done me a great service tonight, Monsieur Valois," Tessa said, "I am grateful."

"Teresa, my dear child." Sophie returned and sat next to Tessa. "I'm so sorry. I saw Monsieur Solden turn you over to that monster Helck, but you were gone before I could act. I have no doubt the two arranged it. Can you forgive me?"

"Let us not talk of it. I am safe," Tessa assured her.

"You are only safe because of this kind gentleman." Sophie turned to the stranger. "Monsieur?"

"Valois. Christophe de Valois. And I am happy to be of service to Madame von Reichstadt."

"It is most fortuitous that you were out," Sophie said.

"Yes, indeed," he replied.

"I'll have a room made up for you." Sophie called to Leopold. "Put Monsieur Valois in the *chinoise* room."

"That won't be necessary," Christophe said, "I must be on my way."

"No, Monsieur Valois," Tessa protested, "You are as drenched as I am. You must be very cold. Please stay until morning."

"I'm afraid I cannot. My cloak?"

"Oh yes, I'm sorry." Tessa smiled as she pulled it off and handed it to Christophe.

"Thank you," he nodded to Tessa then turned to Sophie, "Madame."

With that, the stranger departed, leaving Tessa wondering how he came to be out on such a night.

TESSA SLEPT UNINTERRUPTED by dreams. On waking, she learned the city talked of nothing but Tessa's abduction by Helck. Countess Harassowitz refused to see him when he called, despite his always being welcome when her husband was away. Reports of the incident even reached court, with rumors of his impending dismissal as a hunting companion to the Empress's second son. Everyone agreed the incident would ruin Helck.

Tessa chose to stay in, spending the day doing needlework and reading her Prayer book while Aunt Sophie played solitaire. In the evening, she retired early, still worn out by recent events.

That night, Tessa dreamed again.

Although the night was cold, the wind did not blow, the windowpanes did not rattle. A man stood in Tessa's room, near the window, in the shadows. How he managed to get in, she did not know.

"Who are you?" Tessa asked, sitting up. He came to her bedside and sat down.

"Shhh, my love," he whispered, placing his hands about her waist. Tessa could not see his face in the darkness, but it was close to hers, and she felt his warmth.

"Who are you?" she whispered, unconsciously putting her hands on his arms.

"One who has waited so long for you." He leaned forward to kiss her.

"No," she pulled away.

"But this is only a dream, Tessa," he purred, "It isn't necessary to confess your dreams."

"A dream?"

"Yes. You are asleep. You are alone. I am just a creature of the mind, a part of you that emerges only with the darkness."

She felt her head falling back, her body relax, as his hand moved up her back, gently lowering her down to the pillow.

"There is no sin here."

She struggled to keep her eyes open. Part of her drifted away, yet she still felt him beside her, his arms holding her, his mouth on her cheek. She felt no breath, only the warmth of his skin against hers. He rubbed his cheek against hers and lowered his mouth to her neck. "Forgive me," he whispered, his lips brushing her neck. He shifted his weight onto her, his arms holding her tight so that she could not move. Tessa felt a sharp pain at her neck, and she moaned.

"Shhhhh," he said, caressing her face with the back of his hand. "I will not take much."

Tessa moaned again, drifting off into oblivion.

❧

"TESSA?!"

Tessa opened her eyes to see Aunt Sophie standing over her, the room bright with sunlight.

"What time is it?" Tessa, very groggy, tried to sit up, but she felt weak and fell back to the pillow.

"It's mid-morning," Sophie informed her, "You do not look well, Tessa."

"I'm just tired," Tessa said, "I didn't sleep well."

"I can see that." Sophie sat down on the bed and, holding Tessa by the chin, turned her head to the side.

"What have you done to your neck?"

"What is it?" Tessa touched the spot and felt pain. She sat up, Sophie handing her a mirror. There, Tessa saw the small gash on her neck—a bruised puncture wound crusted over with dried blood. "I've scratched myself. In my sleep, I suppose."

"However you got it, you look quite peaked. You have not been eating enough."

Tessa lay back down as Sophie left to order breakfast. She felt so tired, and except for the strange dream, she had slept so deeply. She did not understand any of it, most of all the man in her dreams. Perhaps whatever person had heard her confession days before had been right. Perhaps she simply needed companionship. She decided to discuss it with Father Julien.

⊱

SEVERAL HOURS LATER, against Sophie's wishes, Tessa went to Saint Martin's. She arrived to find the church deserted. However, she heard voices somewhere within, only she could not understand what they were saying.

Walking down the nave through beams of sunlight, Tessa heard the voices get louder and knew they came from the Chapel of the Virgin. Taking another step, she saw Father Julien with a man. Tessa stood unseen behind one of the massive piers.

Father Julien stood in the chapel doorway, the other man with his back to Tessa. When he turned, she saw it was Christophe de Valois. She leaned close to the pier so he would not see her. Christophe moved from the south aisle out into the nave, Father Julien following him. Christophe stood in the shadows before the shafts of sunlight pouring down from the great windows high above. He remained still for a long time, as if gathering up the courage to make a great leap. Slowly, he stretched out his hand before him and held it in midair. Then without warning, he thrust his hand into a beam of sunlight, only to have it burst into flames. Tessa screamed, Father Julien looking over at her.

Howling like a wolf, Christophe fell back into the shadows, Father Julien, as well as Tessa, rushing toward him. Christophe clutched his hand close to him, the flames replaced by smoke. Christophe stumbled into the chapel and, writhing in pain, crumpled to the floor.

As Tessa reached the doorway, Father Julien turned to her.

"Madame," he said, "you mustn't...."

Tessa ignored him, stepping inside the chapel yet going no further toward Christophe. Father Julien went past her and over to Christophe.

"Let me see your hand," he said, about to lay his hand on Christophe's shoulder. But then Christophe turned on Father Julien, growling and revealing the two sharp fangs in his mouth.

The priest fell back, pulling out his crucifix and holding it before him in protection. Christophe laughed.

"Your trinkets have no effect on me, priest."

"Put it away," Tessa ordered.

"Madame," Father Julien said without lowering the crucifix, "get out while you can."

"We're not in any danger," she said, stepping forward. Christophe looked up at her for the first time.

"Don't you know what he is?" Father Julien shouted at her.

"Yes," Tessa said, "and if he wanted to harm you, he already would have done so. He could have killed me last night in my bedroom."

Tessa looked down at Christophe.

"It was you, wasn't it?" she said to him.

"I'm sorry." He lowered his eyes. "I thought it would change me."

"You fed on her?" Father Julien did not hide his disgust.

"No..." Christophe began, "I just...."

"You just needed a little," Tessa said, repeating his words from the night before. "And it was you in the confessional, too."

"Yes."

"He preys on the innocent, Madame," Father Julien said.

"I do not prey on the innocent," Christophe countered. "I am a predator, but like a wolf, I do not attack the strongest of the herd. I feed on the sick and dying. I feed on the criminals. In a city such as this, I am well fed."

"You feed on living creatures," Father Julien said.

"And are you so innocent, priest, that you can judge me? What was your dinner last night? A bird? What about your breakfast this morning? A piece of pig? All of us feed on living creatures. The only difference between us is that I drink only the blood while you feed on everything, even sucking the marrow from the bones. So do not presume to judge me."

Father Julien stood up and stepped away from Christophe.

"Why do you dwell in my church?" he asked.

"Your church, my crypt," Christophe replied, "I paid for it four hundred years ago so that I might have a place to sleep."

"How perfect," Tessa said, "Darkness, even in daylight, and no one would disturb you there."

"Exactly."

"So why did you seek out me?" she asked.

Christophe was silent for a long while, and then spoke.

"'Who can find a virtuous woman...'" he whispered the ancient words, "the Sybil said that to me long before the Hebrew was translated into Latin. I went to her seeking a cure for my affliction. That is all she said to me. So I have been searching ever since."

"The Sybil?" Father Julien asked, "You are Roman?"

"No, I am Swiss. I was there before the Romans even arrived."

"You are that old?" Father Julien asked.

"I don't know. I can't remember. I can't even remember my real name. I would think I'd been this way forever, but I remember being a child playing in a field of sunlight." His voice trailed away, seemingly lost in his search for the memories.

"Why did you seek me out?" Tessa asked again.

"I thought you were that virtuous woman," he replied, "I thought when I drank your blood, it would cure me and I could walk in the sunlight again, grow old and die, sleep in my crypt forever. I was wrong. You aren't the one."

"Whatever made you think I was?"

"I was travelling one summer night to Munich. I happened to pass by your house. The bedroom windows were open, the candles all alight, and I looked in. You were on the bed with your dying husband, and I saw the way you used your body to pillow him, cradling him in your arms, all the while reading to him. I could hear your words—Molière."

"Franz loved comedies," Tessa smiled.

"I sat there all night listening to you," Christophe continued, "I barely made it into your cellar before the sunlight hit me. I watched you every night until he died and every night after that. I believed you were the one, but then you moved on, and I lost you. I came to Vienna to figure out how to find you. Imagine my joy when I saw you that morning enter this church where I sleep by day. I knew you were the one, the one who would end this curse. Why else would God send you here to me?"

"That is why you put your hand in the sunlight?"

"Yes. I spent the morning praying here. I asked God to forgive me of all my crimes, even though I cannot remember them all. I thought I felt His grace. I thought I was cured. I was wrong. God has abandoned me."

Tessa sat down on the floor next to him.

"Let me see your hand?" she said, holding out her hand to him.

"It is nothing." He showed his hand to her. There was barely a mark on it, just a little redness. "See, it's almost healed. Even the pain is almost gone."

"Why don't you go back to your crypt?" Father Julien asked.

"I can't," Christophe replied, "the sunlight keeps me away from it. I'll have to stay here until nightfall."

Christophe looked at Tessa, the scarf around her neck hiding the wound.

"I'm sorry I injured you," he whispered.

"You saved me from Helck," she replied, "Had you asked, I'd have freely given you my blood. It would've been a small sacrifice, especially knowing it might have cured you."

He reached up and touched her cheek.

"I still can't believe you are not the one," he said.

"I'm sorry," she said, taking his hand and kissing his palm.

"I have a favor to ask," Christophe said.

"What is it?" she asked.

"I need to sleep," he said, "but here, I am exposed. I fear for my safety...."

"You needn't worry," Tessa interrupted, "I'll stay here and watch over you until darkness."

"Were it anyone else, I would not trust them. Only you."

"Come," she said, opening her arms to him, "rest against me. Close your eyes and sleep."

"I will dream of walking in the sunlight with you," he said, and he lay in her arms the way her husband had on those summer nights.

For a long while, Tessa sat there on the floor and held Christophe in her arms. She could not tell if he slept because once he closed his eyes, he seemed dead, his body making none of the usual movements of a sleeping person, and he had no breath. Tessa finally concluded he must be asleep, so she carefully moved out from under him and gently laid him on the floor. Then she made her way over to Father Julien in the doorway.

"Tell me how you happened upon him?" she whispered, sitting next to him.

"He was praying here in the chapel," Father Julien explained, "The moment I saw him I knew who he was. I asked if I could be of service to him. He begged me to absolve him of his sins. When I asked him to confess his sins, he refused, saying they were too many. I could not give him what he asked of me."

"He has been alive since before the time of Christ. How can he remember all his sins? Can you remember the sins of your childhood, sins you know you committed but were absolved of long ago?"

"He is a demon."

"He is a soul in need. The church requires that you help him."

"But his crimes...."

"You cannot refuse a man absolution because of the nature of his crimes. He is repentant. That is enough." She sat back against the wall and looked over at Christophe sleeping.

"No wonder he cannot break the curse," she continued, "when even the church refuses him God's help. I do not think God would abandon him as easily as you do."

"I am just a man."

"And so was he, once upon a time."

They sat in silence for a long while. Tessa looked back at Father Julien, his head lowered with shame.

"We must find a way to help him," she said.

Father Julien nodded slightly.

"I will do what I can for him," he said, looking up at her.

"All I ask is that you do for him what you would do for any other repentant soul," Tessa said, "Nothing more."

❦

THE MOMENT THE sun disappeared beneath the horizon, Christophe opened his eyes, Tessa reading her prayer book beside him.

"Good evening," she said, closing the book, "or does one say 'good morning?'"

"I don't know." He sat up. "I've never awakened next to someone."

"Do you..." she hesitated, "need...?"

"To feed?" he finished her question, "No. Like all cold-blooded creatures, I can go a long time without feeding."

"How recently did you..." and again, she could not finish the question.

"Several nights ago."

"I'm sorry, I didn't mean to intrude."

"No apologies necessary," Christophe replied then asked, "Where's Father Julien?"

"He had some manuscripts to look through."

Christophe stood and held out his hand to Tessa, the hand he had burned in the sunlight, now perfectly healed. Tessa took it, and he pulled her up.

His blue eyes peered down at her, and she could see the longing in them, just as she felt the longing within herself, but then Christophe looked away.

"I'll see you home." Without another word, he led her from the chapel, into the great emptiness of the church, and out into the darkness of the world.

❦

"MONSIEUR VALOIS," AUNT Sophie said as Tessa, led by Christophe, entered the house, "once again you've returned my most precious gem to me. How can I repay you?"

"The pleasure has been all mine, I assure you, Madame."

"You'll stay and dine with us, then?" Aunt Sophie asked.

"I'm afraid I cannot tonight."

"Oh, what a pity. Perhaps tomorrow night."

"I must be off." He turned to Tessa. He took her hand, brought it to his lips, and kissed it. "Do not expect to see me again," he whispered, "and do not come looking for me."

"No."

"It is the only way," he said. He kissed her hand again and left without another word, tears forming in Tessa's eyes.

~

THAT NIGHT AS Tessa slept, Christophe sat on her window ledge and watched her all night. Just before sunrise, he quietly slipped inside, kissed her, and left.

~

"LOOK," AUNT SOPHIE said as Tessa came down that morning. Sophie held a large bouquet of lilies.

"They just arrived," Sophie continued, "Imagine. Flowers in the dead of winter. They're for you." She handed a cream-colored envelope to her niece. "Perhaps they're from your Monsieur Valois."

"Perhaps they are," Tessa smiled, and opened the note. Perhaps he had changed his mind. She read the single sentence. *I know what he is.*

"Throw them away," Tessa ordered.

"What is it? Who are they from?"

Tessa handed the note to Sophie.

"I know this hand," Sophie said, "It's Helck's."

"Helck," Tessa said, the realization of his words sinking in. She remembered the growl when Christophe attacked Helck in the street, that one unchecked moment when Christophe revealed his true nature while protecting her. Helck had seen what Christophe was.

"I don't understand," Sophie continued, "What does he mean? Who is he talking about? Teresa?"

But Tessa was not listening. She knew Christophe was in danger, and she prayed Helck did not know where he slept.

"Maria, my cloak," Tessa called.

"What is it, Teresa?" Sophie asked.

"Christophe is in danger," Tessa said, "I believe Monsieur Helck intends him harm. I must warn him."

"But what can you do?"

"Very little, I fear." Tessa took her cloak from Maria. "But I must try."

"Where will you go?"

"Father Julien will know," Tessa whispered, "Tell no one."

❧

"CHRISTOPHE!" TESSA RAN into Saint Martin's. Emptiness echoed back. "Christophe!" Behind her, she heard one of the wooden front doors close. She turned to see Helck standing there.

"I never suspected he had the audacity to hide in the house of God," Helck said, walking toward her.

"I...I...don't...know..." she stammered, knowing he would not accept her feigned ignorance.

"Don't play the fool with me, woman," he said, grabbing her arm and holding tight until she cried out in pain. "Now tell me where that demon sleeps."

"He's not a demon."

"He drinks blood to achieve immortality. He feeds on us mortals."

"You only want him because he bested you."

"Because of him, I am ruined. I've lost my position at court, none of my friends will see me...all because of that demon. Now, where is he?"

"I don't know."

"He sleeps in darkness. Where in a church is it darkest?" Helck asked, looking around, "The crypt, of course. How appropriate."

He dragged her across the nave to the steps leading down to the crypt, Tessa struggling to break free of him.

"Christophe!" she screamed, "He's coming to kill you! Christophe!"

Helck pulled out a knife and held it to her throat.

"Another word, and I'll slit your throat," he whispered, his hot breath on her neck. With one arm around her neck, he dragged her down the steps. He opened the door, the hinges creaking, and daylight spilled into the darkness. He stepped inside, pulling Tessa with him. She saw nothing, and the further they went, the darker it became. She sensed the stone floor beneath her feet and smelled damp decay. Suddenly, several candles came alight all at once, as if by their own accord. Before them, at a short distance, stood Christophe.

"Is that better for you?" he asked, an open casket behind him, "You nearly walked right into me." Tessa glanced around. While there were coffins in several recesses in the walls, it was nothing like she had imagined. The walls were white and clean, the floor well swept, and not a cobweb in sight.

"I pay for the upkeep," Christophe said, apparently noticing her reaction. "Would you like a tour? A famous prince is over there, and a crusader is right here."

Helck said nothing. The three of them just stood there and stared at each other, the two men sizing each other up.

"Well," Christophe said, "what are you going to do? You could just walk out of here. I promise I won't come after you, but any harm to the lovely lady and I will devour you before you finish. Or are you foolish enough to think you can kill me?"

"That sounds good to me," Helck said, "Of course, once I kill you, I'll take care of her too."

"So then, how are you going to kill me? Fire? Better not. You'll burn down the whole church around you. Stake through the heart? You could throw holy water on me."

Helck held up a crucifix before him.

"Or a crucifix."

Helck pushed Tessa away from him, sending her falling against the wall. In his other hand, he held a wooden stake, its point sharp. Before he could use it, Christophe rushed at him and knocked both the stake and the crucifix out of his hands. Christophe grabbed him, and sank his teeth into his neck. Helck screamed, thrashing at his assailant. Tessa looked away. When she looked back, Helck lay dead on the floor, no trace of blood anywhere.

Christophe came over to where Tessa lay against the wall and, sitting down, took her into his arms.

"Are you alright?"

"Yes, I'm fine," she replied, "I'm so sorry. I didn't realize until it was too late that he had tricked me into revealing where you were."

"If you had not screamed when you did, I might not have awakened in time, and he would have succeeded in killing me."

"What will you do with the body?"

"I'll hide it in a coffin," he said. "You should go home."

"No, I want to stay with you."

"It's impossible."

"There has to be a way to lift this curse. I cannot believe God would've brought us together only to separate us forever."

"Nothing will break this curse, not even a virtuous woman."

"Please let me stay with you."

"You can stay until nightfall. Then I'll take you home, but we cannot see each other again."

"I'll find Father Julien and ask him to send word to my aunt and tell her all is well."

Tessa ran past Helck's body and out of the crypt.

"Father Julien," she called, but there was no answer. She searched through the church, first the vestry, then the Sacristy. She began to go out into the cloister beyond when she noticed the wine. The communion wine.

"*Agnus Dei,*" she whispered. For a moment, she stood silent, the words of Mass and their significance echoing through her mind.

"*Agnus Dei,*" she cried out even louder. "Father Julien. Christophe."

"What are you shouting about?" Father Julien asked, entering the Sacristy.

"*Agnus Dei,*" she smiled.

❧

IN THE CRYPT, Christophe knelt before Father Julien, Tessa kneeling beside him.

"Bless me Father for I have sinned," Christophe began, "this is my first confession. I have killed thousands, and while I killed the dying and the condemned, it was still murder. I do not remember their faces. I do not know how many there were. But I ask God's forgiveness."

"You have God's forgiveness. I cannot, however, find any penitence to give you. I suspect God has already given it to you."

Father Julien made the sign of the cross over him and spoke in Latin.

Father Julien held up the cup of wine and said, "Drink, for this is the chalice of My blood.... Behold the Lamb of God, behold Him who taketh away the sins of the world."

Father Julien held the cup so that Tessa could drink from it.

Next, it was Christophe's turn to drink. He put his lips to the cup and drank as Father Julien said the words.

"May the Blood of Our Lord Jesus Christ keep your soul unto life everlasting. Amen."

"Amen," Tessa repeated as Christophe drained the cup. Father Julien took the cup away, both Tessa and the priest watching to see what would happen. Tessa held her breath and waited for Christophe's reaction.

Christophe gave a sudden cry. Clutching at his chest, he fell onto the floor.

"Christophe!" Tessa shouted, kneeling next to him.

"It burns," he screamed, reaching for Tessa as he writhed in agony.

"Oh, God, help him,"

Christophe's screams filled the crypt and echoed throughout the church. Tessa grabbed his hand, and he held it so tightly she wanted to scream. His body convulsed, his legs shook, and his free hand clutched Tessa's skirt. He threw his head back, screaming. Then, it stopped, and Christophe lay still on the floor, his eyes vacant.

"Christophe?" Tessa shook him. "Christophe?" Then she saw his chest move and heard the sudden gasp for air.

"Christophe?" she said again.

"I'm breathing," he whispered, then coughed. They were short shallow breaths, and he struggled for each one, but he was breathing.

"Yes," Tessa smiled, tears flowing, "you're breathing."

"Can you get up?" Father Julien asked.

"I think so." Christophe struggled up with Tessa's help.

Leaning against Tessa, Christophe made it to the door and stood there for a moment. He took a step forward, up the steps and into the church, yet still in the shadows. Letting go of her hand, Christophe took a step away from Tessa and stood on his own, shafts of sunlight just inches away. He reached out to Tessa, took her hand, pulled her close, and together they stepped into the light.

BALLAD OF WOLVES AND ANGELS

MICHAEL MEDINA

Antioch City, mid-December...

The cacophony of police and ambulance sirens had eventually faded. *All* sound had faded from his ears. Nothing existed outside of his own thoughts. His partner, Jiana, stood behind him, but he did not realize it. He was lost in the past, dwelling on a memory that would never go away. The police lights danced silently across his face.

Red. Blue.

Red. Blue.

He was sitting on a wrought-iron chair on the outdoor patio of the *Seven Days Café*, elbows resting on knees, hands clasped together. A black leather cord coiled itself between his fingers. A silver cross dangled at the bottom. It rotated in the bitter breeze. He watched it rotate. He watched it sway side to side.

The corpse splayed on the street before him was a man. Perhaps twenty-nine or thirty. The dead man clutched a non-descript plastic shopping bag to his chest. The contents of said bag included various sex toys, three pornographic movies, and a vacuum wrapped blowup doll.

James Samuel Vega found this disturbing.

Had this happened a few months ago, Vega would have leaned over to his pretty blonde partner and whispered some kind of joke to lighten the mood.

Not anymore.

This was the second time he had watched a man die with all his disgusting secrets laid before him for the world to see.

It wasn't funny. Not when the first man to die was Vega's friend.

Not when Vega had been the one to kill him.

He felt it in the pit of his stomach, the haunting feelings of his last hunt, and now this body heralded the next one.

&

Twenty minutes ago....

LUNCH IN THE café was a good distraction for both James Vega and Jiana Lyman. They sat across from each other in a booth. A large paned window documented the hustle-and-bustle of Antioch City's holiday rush. Vega was thankful for the reprieve from the all-too-regular drama of being a federal bounty hunter. Recent events had weighed heavily on the both of them, but time had its ways of healing, and on days such as this Vega found it a bit easier not to focus his thoughts on what had happened to him and Jiana just a couple of months ago.

Jiana was glad for it, too. Vega hadn't been as easy to talk to since the last mark they had hunted. Killing one of his best friends was a silent torture for him. She could see that. He hadn't talked about it since, but she could see it weighed on him. His quiet stoicism was gone. Now he seemed burdened, introverted, not so sure of himself.

Sure, he was coming around, but he wasn't ready to talk about it. And that's what Jiana needed from him most of all. She needed him to talk about it because *she* needed to talk about it. Things had gone horribly wrong that day.

And because they went wrong she had been forced to kill people. She had never killed anyone before.

It hurt. It wasn't like the movies. There was no glamour to it. She was never so naïve as to believe it would be easy, but the feeling was beyond anything she could have been prepared for. Bad guys or not, they were dead now. First she felt guilty, then she felt empty, hollow. It was like there was nothing left inside with which she could hold herself together. She was crumbling mentally, emotionally. She was only eighteen years old. She wasn't ready to deal with this.

Oh well. Bottle it up, girl. For Vega's sake.

She sighed to herself, then looked down at her chocolate milkshake with its mountainous whipped-cream topping. Three golden tresses fell across her face, each of them tipped with a row of beads: one red, one white, and one blue. She hooked them behind her ear and lifted the glass to her lips, coming back up with a white-tipped nose.

Vega looked at her and smiled. The sight reminded him of how young she still was. It could be easy to forget with all of the responsibility she had so willingly taken upon herself in this job. "Why don't you use the straw?" he asked, his voice quiet, with a sandpaper tone that only sounded friendly to Jiana.

"It's too thick. I'll be here all day," She replied in a soft southern accent that stood in stark contrast to his voice.

"Then don't order the whipped cream next time. "

"I'll pretend I didn't hear that." Jiana smiled as she licked the spoon clean. "Hey, I forgot. Tech called. Said he's staying with his family till after New Year's. That means it's just you and me in the apartment."

"Won't be a problem."

"Don't go trying to take advantage of me while we're alone," she playfully warned.

"Also won't be a problem," he replied dryly.

Jiana's big chestnut eyes searched around the room as she helped herself to another spoonful of chocolate and whipped cream. Her glance settled on something outside. "That gets on my nerves."

"What does?"

She pointed her spoon at the window, indicating a fresh-off-the-assembly-line yellow and black Ferrari. Vega turned and noticed the license plate on the front. *M-N-Y, M-K-R.*

"Money Maker," Jiana said. "So annoying. Betcha' his daddy gave it to him."

Vega smirked and turned back to his lunch. "Touchy, aren't you?"

"I guess he couldn't fit 'I'm a Total Douche Bag' on there."

"T-T-L, D-S-H."

"What?"

"T-T-L...D-S-H."

Jiana mouthed the words thoughtfully. Then, "Ha! Rock on!" They both laughed the subject off. While the mood was reasonably light, Jiana thought she might take the moment to broach an awkward subject. She turned her eyes to her plate, poking at her food with her fork. "So, uh, I've been thinking about, you know, taking on another hunt. It's been a couple of months. I thought we should get back in the game."

Vega shrugged. "Sure. Why not?"

"Really?" Jiana felt he conceded too easily.

"You're right. It's been too long. Our last payoff won't last forever." He tilted his head to the Ferrari outside. "Can't all be natural money makers."

"Speak of the devil." Jiana lifted her chin to the window.

Vega turned for a look, saw the Money Maker walk down the opposite sidewalk, then jog across the street to his Ferrari, shopping bag in hand. Vega noted where he had been shopping. "Forbidden Fruits."

"What's that?"

"They sell adult movies and...other stuff."

Jiana crinkled her nose and shivered. "Ew!"

Vega chuckled at her, shook his head. Jiana returned his smile...

And then the window exploded.

Glass rained down upon Jiana, followed by the familiar *crack!* of gunfire echoing through the city streets. She slammed flat onto the booth, arms covering head. "Vega!" she cried out. She cursed herself for not bringing her gun with her when she left the apartment.

More gunfire.

She dared lift her head from the seat. Vega was kneeling in the booth, gun drawn. He yelled something, but Jiana was too distracted to understand.

More gunfire from the street.

Vega pitched his head to one side as a round hit the windowsill. He returned fire.

"Vega!" Jiana called to him.

But Vega's focus was outside. He took in the scene: black car, two gunmen, one driver. The first gunman had sprayed a barrage of gunfire from the front seat, striking the café, the rich man and his Ferrari. By the time Vega had turned to the window the rich man was already falling against his car and sliding to the pavement. The second gunman exited from the backseat, stepped brazenly up to the rich man and put two rounds in his head.

"Stay down!" Vega vaulted the windowsill and charged the street. He put two rounds in the windshield of the assaulting car, hitting the passenger and prompting the driver to speed away, deserting the assassin still standing on the street. "Freeze! Federal Bounty Hunter! Drop your weapon!"

The assassin made no movement. He stared Vega down. He waited.

Vega could see it in his eyes just before it happened.

The man dove for the back of the Ferrari as he turned his gun on Vega.

They fired at the same time. They both missed.

The assassin blindly fired from behind the rear driver side of the car. Vega sprinted for the front passenger side, jumped, slid across the hood on his seat, and fired as he came up on the opposite side.

Pop! Pop!

The gunman caught two in the chest and fell.

The sound of screaming pedestrians was distant in Vega's ears. He kept his gun fixed on the dead assailant as he slowed his breathing. He walked guardedly up to the hit man, knelt beside him and checked for a pulse. Nothing. Searching him, Vega came up with a bloodstained photograph of a young African-American girl. On the back it read:

Praze Manning
8 yr. old
Highland Valley Apartments, 26e
D'Avien Manning

Vega furrowed his brow, eyes transfixed on the face of the little girl. He thoughtfully stroked his heavy five o'clock shadow.

When he started for the café he looked down and saw the rich man on the ground beside his prized Ferrari. Vega didn't check his pulse. He already knew the grim truth. Red and black brain matter flowed from the man's temple. His eyes stared off, lifeless and askew. Even in the throes of death one hand clung tightly to his shopping bag.

All kinds of unspeakable items had spilled from it during the violent encounter. They stirred up memories Vega would rather forget.

"Hey, partner." Jiana had sidled up to him and placed her hand on his upper arm. "You okay?"

"Yeah."

Jiana noticed the picture Vega was holding. She took it, studied it, front and back. "What's this?"

Vega holstered his gun and walked back toward the café. "They're going to kill her."

৵

AFTER GIVING HER statement to the police, Jiana had instantly dialed her employer at the Guild of Federal Bounty Hunters.

Vega had seated himself on a wrought iron chair on the patio of the café. His cross necklace had broken at some point during the confrontation. He held it clasped in his hands, watching it sway in the chilly winter breeze. Try as he might, he couldn't push away the memories of his old friend, of the last time he had to draw his gun on someone. It just wasn't going to go away.

He looked back up at the scene. Traffic had been cordoned off in record time. Both bodies had been covered, but still strewn on the street were the reminders of the victim's dirty secrets, and the unsettling thought of what he had been thinking about just before he died.

The medical examiner was squatting over the gunman. He stood and approached Vega, "Busy?"

"What do you have for me, Bob?"

Bob first handed him a photocopy of the front and back of the Praze Manning photo that he had run off in the ACPD mobile lab. Then he showed him a photo of the gunman's corpse. "You recognize him?"

"Should I?"

"Jiana didn't either. They call him *El Vaquero*. He's a contract killer employed by Javier Dominguez. Know *him*?"

Vega did. "Dominguez deserted the Salvadorians years ago. Branched off into drug trafficking and extortion. "

"And he's been their mark ever since."

"The *Mara Salvatrucha* never were the forgiving types. But what does Dominguez have to do with our depraved Money Maker?"

"His name was Evan Mathis. But to answer your question, Mathis pissed 'em off, plain and simple."

Vega nodded. It was a common enough explanation.

"Hey, Vega," Bob said. "Good work today."

"Thanks."

Bob returned to the crime scene. Vega turned to find Jiana still on the phone. She held up a finger to indicate she needed just a few more moments. When she finished she told him, "That was the Guild. They granted us the contract and investigative authority on this Dominguez guy. He's been a federal skip since he broke away from the Salvadorians."

"That's good." Vega stood up, tucked his necklace into his pocket, and said, "Well, back to work."

He seemed quiet, even for Vega. Only Jiana could notice the subtleties of his demeanor, but she could definitely tell what was on his mind. "Hey, Vega. You up for this?"

"Yeah. Why wouldn't I be?"

"I don't know. It's just...."

"I'm fine, Ji. Let's get to work."

"You sure?"

"I said I'm fine." He walked off toward his car, and Jiana followed.

"What about your statement to the police?"

"I told them to reach me at the Guild."

They got into his car. Vega pulled the copy of little Praze Manning's photo from his coat pocket and reread the address.

Jiana asked, "We're gonna go find her?"

"It's a start. If nothing else we need to warn her parents."

"Did you tell the police?"

"They said they'll look into it. But that's not good enough for me. By the time they get around to it, it could be too late."

Jiana knew she shouldn't have asked, but she did anyway. "And what if it's already too late?"

He said nothing.

"Vega?"

He threw the car into gear and pulled out onto the street. "We'll figure something out."

༄

THE HIGHLAND VALLEY Apartments were little more than a single brownstone public housing project copied over and over again for two blocks in south Antioch. Paint had long ago chipped away along all the windows and doors until there was nothing but a drab gray speckled with the former colors.

Scaffolds lined one side of the face. Weathered plastic tarps swayed ghostly from the tops of the skeletal structures that had long ago broken their promise of renovation and fresh paint. Broken out windows betrayed the location of those apartments that were no longer livable. The rest were not far behind.

Vega and Jiana walked the hallway, keeping watch for apartment 26e, noting the brazen graffiti and torn away patches of wallpaper present up and down both sides of them. The walls reverberated with the thrum of some bass-heavy music at the opposite end of the hallway.

Vega said, "Remember, whoever this D'Avien Manning is he has an eight year old girl. Until we know his involvement in the hit try not to make him feel threatened. Him or his daughter. If he just happens to be a caring, uninvolved father—which isn't likely—he may close up if he feels we're putting information before his daughter's safety."

"Which we're not."

"But he doesn't know that. Based on this environment he may not be trusting of just anybody who comes to his door. Based on his possible criminal connections he also may not trust federal agents. In either case, don't intimidate him."

"Didn't know I *was* intimidating," Jiana remarked.

"You've been known to have your mood swings."

"I already told you...*that* was an accident."

"Sure." They came across 26e. Vega knocked.

The peephole darkened. A woman's voice said, "Who is it?"

Vega held the small gold badge around his neck, followed by his ID, up to the peephole. "Federal agents, ma'am. Bounty hunter guild. Just a few questions, that's all."

A pause. Locks clicked from within, and the door opened slowly.

A heavyset African-American woman stood there wearing white shorts and a tan tee shirt so over worn that it was nearly see through. A scarf held back wiry, unkempt hair. "Can I help you?" she asked.

"We're looking for D'Avien Manning."

Her eyes went downcast, and she sighed. Not sad or relieved. Frustrated. "What did he do now?"

"Nothing, yet. Is he here, ma'am?"

"D doesn't live here, by God's grace."

Vega noticed her left hand, free of wedding ring. He ventured the question anyway, to coax her into opening up. "You his wife?"

"Sister. Desiree."

"Desiree. I'm James Vega, this is Jiana Lyman. Do you know where D'Avien lives? It concerns his daughter, Praze."

Desiree's eyes shot up to Vega's. "What about Praze? What's wrong?"

"She may be in danger."

Desiree's chin stiffened. Her plump cheeks started to tremble, and then she broke into tears and sobs. She eventually wiped her eyes, trying to compose herself to some small extent. She asked, "Is it that Salvadorian he's been hiding from?"

Vega didn't say anything. Jiana followed his lead.

Desiree swung the door wider, motioned for them to come inside. The apartment was sparse and worn down. Well kept by Desiree, but very minimal: cheap furniture, a decades old television. A small plastic Christmas tree was lit up in the back corner. No presents. The three of them sat at a Formica table that was bare save for a single chipped coffee cup and an open Bible.

"We're sorry for this," Jiana said. "We just want to ask a few questions."

Desiree wiped tears from her eyes. She cleared her throat. "No, no. I understand."

Vega folded his hands on the table and leaned forward. "Ms. Manning, what can you tell us about the Salvadorian? Do you know his name? Where to find him?"

"Everybody knows his name. Javier Dominguez."

"And how do you know D'Avien is involved with him?"

"He told me. D has always been a sorry excuse for a man. Been in and outta jail since he was twelve. Every hustle is gonna be his next big payoff, he promises. Always trying to convince me and Baby Girl that everything's gonna be alright. Just one more score."

"Baby Girl? You mean Praze."

Desiree fell silent at the name. She nodded. "That man needs to understand that all she wants is her daddy. She don't need nothing else. All he doin' is draggin' her down with him. Just..." The tears started to come again. She slammed her hand on the table.

"Auntie?" came a little girl's voice from the bedroom. The word sounded like *Annie*. "Auntie? Did Daddy come?"

"No, baby. Not today. Just some friends."

Little Praze Manning poked her head out of the bedroom, wary finger in her mouth as she eyed the two strangers.

Jiana caught Vega's eye. Her expression was as curious as his.

"Come on, Baby Girl," Desiree said, waving her forward. "Come say hi."

Praze shuffled barefooted over to Desiree, hugged her aunt, and said, "Auntie Des, Daddy ain't comin' over today?"

"No Precious. This is James and Jiana. They're friends of Daddy."

"Hi," Praze said softly.

Jiana held out her hand with a big warm smile, and Praze took hold of it. "Hey, darlin'," she said to the little girl. Praze smiled, saying "Hi," again.

Desiree patted her on the head. "Praze, honey, can I talk to Mr. Vega alone, please?"

"Uh-huh." Praze started toward the bedroom, still holding Jiana's hand.

Jiana motioned after her. "Is it okay if I..."

Desiree said nothing.

"I'll leave the door open."

"Well...okay."

Jiana followed after Praze, who was quick to strike up conversation.

"She's usually so shy," Desiree noted to Vega.

"Jiana has a way with kids."

"She seems young."

"Too young. Makes me feel old sometimes."

That earned a smile from Desiree.

Vega cleared his throat. "So, tell me about D'Avien."

"First, tell me why Praze is in danger."

"Javier Dominguez is angry with D'Avien over something. I don't know what. But whatever it is it's not just enough for him to kill D'Avien. He wants to go after those who are important to him."

A trembling hand went to Desiree's mouth. "Oh my God."

"There may be good news, though. The fact that he's not out to kill D'Avien tells me that your brother has something he wants. That means that until he gets it he may only want Praze as leverage. I was hoping you might tell me what D'Avien has been up to. What is it that Dominguez wants from him?"

"Me and Praze got nothing to do with him. He's a criminal. Always has been. I got away from him 'cause I didn't want Praze growing up in his shadow. All I know, he called me up day before yesterday telling me he got in some trouble, but not to worry. Said he'd fix it, but then he always says he'll fix it. Ain't seen it happen yet. I don't care, though. So long as he leaves us be."

"So Praze lives here all the time?"

"Since the last time D went to jail. He wanted to be father of the year in the beginning, but it didn't last. Now all D does is make promises he don't keep. Keeps saying he'll pick her up and take her out for the day. Usually something 'comes up,' whatever that means."

"And her mother?"

Desiree sniffed sarcastically. "That ho's in jail right now."

"Where can I find D'Avien?"

"Can't help you there. He's off work already. He ain't been going home 'cause they'll find him there. Don't know where he's been hiding out. He's still going to work though. He said he can't afford to miss any more days. They'll fire him. If you want to find him, check his job tomorrow morning."

"Where's that?"

"Iroquois Shipping Co. He goes in to work at seven tomorrow morning."

"I appreciate this, Desiree."

She nodded, went quiet for several long seconds. "Look, I know I talk bad about D, but he's still my brother. Just...well...take care of him, will you? I don't want nothing bad happening."

"I will," Vega told her earnestly.

Praze sat Jiana in a chair at a small, bare desk in the only bedroom the apartment had. Praze sat on a worn out mattress that lay on the floor. No bed frame. Also no second mattress. Jiana figured that Praze and Desiree had to share.

She also found that she was very cold. The apartment had no heating. It came as no surprise to her in a place like this, but the sight of Praze wrapping a too-thin blanket around her little shoulders broke her heart. "Um," Jiana tried to start. "So, are you excited about Christmas?"

Praze shrugged her shoulders, lowering her eyes.

Jiana folded her hands in her lap, hunched her shoulders to make herself smaller. She found it often worked to help children feel more at ease. "Anything special you want?"

Again, a shrug. "We don't really do much for Christmas. Me and Auntie Des do some cooking and watch some Christmas movies, but she don't really make a lot of money. She works extra hard so she can buy me stuff, but I know she gets tired. When she asks me what I want I just tell her to cook something good, 'cause that's something she's real good at. We have lots of fun when we cook together. It makes her feel better."

Jiana could not tear her eyes away from the pretty little girl before her. She couldn't imagine that she was only eight years old. Praze's words rang in her ears, and something deep inside of her began to hurt. Jiana drew her off of the bed and sat Praze in her lap.

Praze hugged her. Jiana wanted to cry.

"Is daddy in trouble?" Praze asked candidly in her small voice.

"No, darlin'. Why would you say that?"

"Well, Auntie Des says y'all are friends of his, but daddy ain't got no friends, especially cops."

"Actually, we're trying to keep him out of trouble. Do you know where we can find him?"

Praze shrugged. "He usually calls me after work, but he didn't today. He's supposed to take me out for the day tomorrow, but lots of time he changes his mind." Praze went quiet, deeper in thought than any eight year old should ever be.

The phone rang.

"Daddy!" Praze was off Jiana's lap and to the phone.

"Praze," Desiree called out. "I'll get it."

"Let me talk to him." Praze's little voice was overly excited.

"I will, precious, just let me talk to him first. Okay?"

"Okay, okay. But hurry."

Desiree went into the bedroom to answer the phone.

Vega stood in the doorway. "You have speaker?"

She nodded.

"Put it on. Find out where he is."

Desiree pressed a button, spoke, and waited. D'Avien Manning's voice came over the speaker. "It's me, Des."

"Where are you?"

"Don't worry about that. I'm laying low. I won't be back at the crib for a few days at least, so don't worry if I don't answer there. Let me talk to Praze."

"Why haven't you been answering your cell?"

There was no response. *I'm avoiding you,* Vega gathered. "Just let me talk to Praze."

Desiree nodded to her. "Daddy?" Praze began.

"Hey, Baby Girl."

"You coming to get me tomorrow?"

"I don't know. I've been kinda busy. I'll try."

"No," she scolded. "You promised you'd come get me tomorrow. We're supposed to go out."

"I'll try, Baby Girl. For real this time."

"You promise?"

"Yeah, yeah."

"Don't forget, okay?"

"Yeah. Look, I gotta go. You be careful, and listen to Des, alright?"

"I will. Be careful, daddy."

"Yeah, I will."

"I love you..."

Click.

All was quiet. Praze paused, then slowly hung up, not getting the response from her father that she was hoping for.

Desiree sighed in anger at her brother, and returned to the living room. Vega somberly watched the poor little girl for a few seconds, and then followed Desiree to ask more questions.

Praze looked up and smiled at Jiana in a way that failed to cover up her embarrassment. Praze was simply too young to express how she was feeling. It was always easier to cover up the hurt with a smile.

Jiana could relate to that. So could Vega. That was their problem, she knew.

It was always easier to cover up the hurt.

Desiree had gone to the kitchen, turning her back on Vega, still too frustrated with D'Avien, and too scared for Praze, to speak about it any further. Vega placed his hand on her shoulder. He could feel her trembling. She sniffled, wiped her eyes, and turned back to him. "I'm sorry for that, Mr. Vega. Sorry I couldn't be more help."

"You helped plenty, trust me. And, thank you."

"I guess it's in God's hands now."

Vega nodded. "It always has been."

"I'm just so scared for Praze, and for D. I pray for them both."

"It'll work out. You'll be free of this soon. I promise."

"Thank you."

Vega led her to the door as he got ready to leave. "You should go to a hotel until this is resolved. May be a few days, but we want Praze safe."

She shook her head. "We can't afford that, Mr. Vega. But we'll manage. We'll figure something out."

"What I meant was, I'm going to put you two up in a hotel. I'm not letting them hurt Praze."

His resolve brought a welling of tears to Desiree's eyes, and she steepled her fingers over a smile of appreciation. She patted him on the cheek. "You're a good man, Mr. Vega."

Vega gave a melancholy smile and shook his head. "I wish that were true."

Desiree nodded in rebuttal. "It is."

WHEN THEY LEFT the apartment building the late afternoon horizon had faded into a cloudy golden-purple canvas.

It hadn't taken long for Desiree to pack up the few essentials they owned for their stay. Vega had loaded all of it into his trunk. He watched as Praze gave Jiana the tightest bear hug she could manage and then climbed into the back seat. He handed his keys to his young partner. "Access my Guild account and make sure you take out enough money for the hotel and at least a three day stay."

Jiana's stare shifted quizzically between the keys and Vega's eyes. "Why are you doing all this?"

"It's the right thing to do."

"I know...but—."

"Just do it, Jiana."

She paused, then "Okay. But...what about you?"

"I'll catch up with you later."

"Vega, wait."

"What?"

"It's...well, it's Wednesday. Why don't you...I don't know. Why don't you go back to church or something?"

Vega stared out thoughtfully at the street, deliberately not making eye contact with her. "I'll catch up with you later," he repeated, then turned away.

Jiana grabbed his arm gently. "I'll go with you, if you want."

He smirked. "Thought you didn't buy into all that fuzzy-wuzzy religiosity."

"I never said that. But I know it's important to you, and...well, I guess it just bothers me that you don't go anymore."

Vega sighed. "I might," he said, and walked off down the street.

Jiana watched him leave.

She knew he was lying.

∾

VEGA HAD TURNED off his phone. It was after ten o' clock when Jiana finally found him. She had received a call from Shannon, owner of the *Seven Days Café*, saying that he was at the *Shorty George '37* jazz café. Shannon met her at the front door. Jiana hugged her. "I'm glad you weren't at work this morning."

"That's what James said when he called," Shannon answered in her native British accent. "I'm just glad nobody was hurt. Scary thing, it is, to have your patrons shot at."

"How is he?"

"I could tell something was bothering him when we spoke. I heard the music in the background and knew exactly where he was. I wanted to come speak with him. We haven't spoken since he last came to church...the day Roddy died."

Jiana nodded. Shannon didn't know the truth. She didn't know that Vega had killed him.

"Could you talk to him, Jiana?"

"I've tried," she shrugged helplessly.

"I know it was hard for him to find out what Roddy had done. He was concerned about the church youth group."

"Understandably."

"You know he was their youth pastor before Roddy, didn't you?"

"Who? Vega?"

Shannon nodded. "You wouldn't know it by seeing him now." A smile came with Shannon's memories of it. "But, oh how they loved James. He inspired them to do so much good."

Jiana couldn't resist a smile herself. "I can't see it. Vega just seems so...."

"Scary?"

"Maybe that's not the right word. He's still a great guy."

"Deep down he's the same James he was back then. It's just the outside that's changed. He carries more burdens, and it's hard for him to let go."

Jiana thought about that. She sighed. She knew the burden of taking another's life. "I'll talk to him."

They parted ways. Going inside, Jiana found the dark café's booths and tables packed. An older black man on stage blew out his rendition of a Dizzy Gillespie classic on the trumpet.

Vega was in the corner booth at the back, just like he always was. She walked over and sat across from him. He never looked up at her.

He didn't say anything, either.

Neither did she, for at least three minutes. A waitress came over to Jiana, but she waved her away.

Vega was cradling a mug of some hot beverage. He took a sip. "Is Praze safe?"

"I arranged for a police guard at the hotel."

"Good."

"You ready to talk, Vega?" *Might as well make it quick.*

"About what?"

"About Roddy. About you going back to church."

"What do you want me to say? Roderick Darlington was a pedophile. He fell in with a cartel selling child prostitutes. They all resisted arrest, they all died. He just happened to be one of them. What? Now I'm supposed to go back to church, remind everybody that their beloved youth pastor turned out to be a child molester, and then say 'Oh, by the way, because he did all of this I blew his head off'?"

"It wasn't like that."

"Wasn't it?"

"He knew he was caught. He was going to kill himself."

"Maybe I should have let him."

Jiana shook her head. "You don't mean that."

Vega didn't reply.

The music on stage changed to a soft, almost melancholy saxophone solo. Jiana recognized it as Vega's favorite.

Ballad of Wolves and Angels.

Alone at night, when Vega thought she was asleep, he would sit quietly, read his Bible, and listen to that number over and over again. Jiana never asked him why. "I think you know why you killed him."

"There were a few reasons, I guess."

"Because of the youth group. You thought they might have been victimized. You took it personally because they used to be your kids."

Vega locked eyes with her. Silence.

"Why didn't you tell me you used to be their youth pastor?"

"Wasn't trying to hide it."

"It makes a difference, doesn't it? Did you choose Roddy as your replacement?"

He paused. "Yes, I did."

"And you'd feel responsible if something had happened to them."

"Don't psychoanalyze me. Maybe some people just deserve to die." Vega placed a generous tip on the table, set his mug on top of it, and left.

Jiana followed him outside. "So that's it? After all we've been through, that's all I get?"

"That's all there is."

"You killed your friend, Vega. Don't pretend that it's okay."

Jiana could see the pain in his eyes. It was there on the threshold, boiling just beneath the surface. She expected an outburst, but Vega's next words came softly. "Why do children keep suffering for the sins of adults?"

Jiana didn't have the answer, and it scared her that he didn't, either. "You once said that God will always put His people where He needs them most. Children will always be in danger. Maybe you're just supposed to be there to stop it."

Vega's jaw was trembling. "I didn't ask to be a killer. I didn't ask for any of this."

"Well who the hell does? But don't forget, you *did* kill Roddy. It was your call. It sucks, I know, but would you rather have seen him blow his own brains out? Would that really have been any easier?"

"You didn't shoot him. You don't understand."

"I do understand. I was there, remember? He wasn't the only person to die that day. I killed my share. They may have been prostituting children, but they were still human beings."

"You did what you had to do, Ji."

"That doesn't make it better!"

"What do you want from me?"

"I want you to talk to me about it! I want you to tell me where I go from here. You used to have all the answers. I want...I want you to be strong again. I need you to help me through this." Jiana's voice cracked with emotion. The tears started to flow freely now. "I'm eighteen years old, Vega, and I've *killed people*! I can't keep pretending like everything's okay. I understand it's painful for you, but I need you to be strong because I can't deal with this on my own and I'm falling apart!" She took a deep breath, wiping her eyes. She gave up. "You know what? Just forget it. Sorry I brought it up."

Vega watched as the pain she had concealed broke forth before him. Then he knew that they would have to be there for each other. "Jiana?" he said. "It's going to hurt for a while. But...I'll always be there to help you through it."

Jiana looked at him sadly. She stepped forward and threw her arms tightly around him. She buried her tears in his chest.

"I'm sorry," he told her.

"It's okay."

They stood there silently for a while. She didn't want to let him go.

After a time, Vega reached up and stroked her hair. He smiled as he said, "Crybaby."

"Shut up," she said. She giggled through quiet, cleansing sobs.

❧

THE NEXT MORNING, Jiana awoke to the chime of her cell's alarm clock. Her hand fumbled blindly around her nightstand until she found it and shut it off. Unburying her head from under her pillow, she sat up, fighting off the groggy early morning. She slid into some blue shorts, tugged at the wrinkles of her matching camisole, and pussyfooted into the hallway.

Vega's door was open. When she sidled up to the door she found Vega seated by his desk, hunched over a gun clip, feeding bullets into it. The metallic *scrape, click, scrape, click* of each round punctuated the silence. His Bible rested on the edge of his bed, indicating to her that he had been reading it. He turned to find her there, her hair askew and tangled, eyes squinty from the sunlight peeking through the curtains.

"Mornin', partner," she said.

"Hey," he said quietly.

"You're ready to hit Iroquois?"

"Whenever you are."

"I'm gonna take a shower."

"Take your time."

Jiana left him there, alone.

Vega took the clip, slid it into his HK pistol, flicked the safety on, and nestled it into his shoulder holster.

Then he knelt down at his bedside and prayed.

HAROLD ROLLINS, FOREMAN for the Iroquois Shipping Co., led the two bounty hunters through rows and stacks of 18-wheeler shipping crates, chatting them up the entire time, until they arrived at the main warehouse. Rollins snagged the intercom off the wall, "Manning, report to the front of the warehouse! ASAP!"

A minute later, D'Avien Manning was leaning over the railing of the rightmost catwalk above them. He yelled down, "W'sup, Boss?"

"Say, D, the laws is here to see you. Get down here, quick."

D'Avien's face dropped visibly at the announcement. "I-I'm coming'," he stammered.

Rollins snorted, shook his head. "Break room's right over there. Y'all can talk quietly there." He walked out, leaving D'Avien to fend for himself.

D'Avien Manning was the nervous, guilty-as-sin type. He sat hunched at one of the many tables in the break room. His hair was a thick, disheveled afro and the whites of his eyes had yellowed from years of hard living. He looked up at the two hunters, as if expecting them to slap the cuffs on him for something he was most likely guilty of.

They didn't do it.

Jiana leaned casually against the lockers. Vega sat across from him. A look of stone crossed his face as he addressed D'Avien. "What can you tell me about Javier Dominguez?"

D'Avien's eyes shifted from Vega up to Jiana, and back. "Who?"

"Javier Dominguez. Drug and weapons trafficker. Former MS-13 with a penchant for violence and brazen contract killings."

"Name doesn't ring a bell."

Vega pulled out the copy Praze's picture and slapped it onto the table in front of D'Avien. "Then perhaps you know his hired gun, *El Vaquero*—the guy that was carrying that picture as he gunned down some rich pervert in broad daylight."

D'Avien's face was awash in stunned silence. He picked up the picture, studied it, ran his fingers over it. "My baby girl...."

Vega cocked his head to the side. "How's that?"

"My baby girl." D'Avien slumped back in his chair, eyes frantically darting about the room as the truth bombarded him. His voice was barely audible. "Crazy-ass nigga's gonna kill my baby girl."

The picture slipped from his hands, falling, unnoticed, to the floor.

"You want to protect her, Mr. Manning?"

He had fallen silent.

"Do you want to protect her?" Vega repeated.

"Of course I do."

"Then talk to me."

"Who was the guy? The rich guy that got killed?"

"Name's Evan Mathis."

"Son of a bitch," D'Avien hissed through gritted teeth. "I knew it."

Vega motioned him forward with his fingers. "Come on, D'Avien. Talk to me. What was up between Dominguez and Mathis?"

"Nothing. Just another rich cracker that thought his money made him invincible. Rumor was he was heavy into drugs, him and all his rich corporate buddies. He thought he could cut Dominguez out of his own business and got his ass capped." D'Avien pulled a joint out of his coveralls pocket, heedless of what the two federal agents might think of it. He lit it up, took a long drag. "We all saw it coming."

"And how are you involved with Dominguez?"

D'Avien took another drag. He opened his mouth to respond, but didn't.

"We can protect you," Jiana offered.

D'Avien *humphed*. "Not from him. Nigga's been killing with the best of 'em since he was twelve years old. It's what the *Mara Salvatrucha* do."

Vega shrugged. "You can always go back to work and wait to die. We'll protect Praze."

"She deserves better than that," Jiana said. "Come on D'Avien. Why is Dominguez after you? Give us something that can help us put him away."

He was thinking about it. "You *will* protect Praze, right?"

"Yes."

"And Des, my sister. You can protect her?"

"You have my word," Vega assured him.

"She doesn't deserve this. It's my fault. Always has been. That's why she hates me so much."

Vega shook his head. "She prays for you, you know. Asks God to protect you."

D'Avien threw the joint to the floor. He mashed it with his foot. "God doesn't live in Antioch."

"Desiree disagrees," Jiana told him.

"Yeah...that's why she's better than me."

"You want to change that?" Vega asked. "Do something right. Tell me what it was Dominguez had you doing that was so important he needs to silence you."

"Look, man, all I ever did was make some deliveries for him."

"Drugs."

"Most likely, but I never saw anything. It paid enough for me to get by. It's expensive to live here, even in my neighborhood. But here's the thing: he offers me triple the money to drive a truck loaded with cocaine to a big deal he got goin' down with some South American. They both got, like, eight, ten guys—each standing by while they square the deal. With Dominguez is that Vaquero guy you mentioned and some big-ass Mexican called Hector Delapeña. They call him Casa Bell, or something."

"*Cascabel*," Vega corrected. "Rattlesnake."

"Yeah, that. They say he's Dominguez's top level enforcer. Does all his dirty work."

"So what happened with this deal?"

"Don't know. Dominguez holds out a huge brick of white to the South American so he can check it out. All of a sudden they start yelling, going off about something in Spanish, and next thing I know, the deal goes all to hell. People start shooting. The South American shoots Dominguez, hits him in the hand, and Dominguez blows the nigga's head off. I hit the floor boards."

"Then what?"

"Dominguez opens the passenger door of the truck, throws in a bag of money and the cocaine brick, and then pulls a gun on me, like he's gonna carjack me or something."

"How much money are we talking about?"

"About a hundred G's."

"So he pulled a gun on you. What did you do?"

"Me? *Shee*-it! I hit the pedal and run like hell. Dominguez was climbing in and fell out as I took off."

"Taking the money and the shipment with you."

D'Avien held up his hands, "Say, now, I was just trying not to get shot," he placated.

"So where's the truck?"

"I can show you."

"What about the money?"

D'Avien lowered his eyes to the table, mumbled, "Um," followed by something unintelligible.

Vega cocked his head to the side. "What was that, again?"

Something was running through his mind, Vega could see. Finally, D'Avien said, "Look...Do you know what it's like not being able to give your little girl a Christmas year after year? You know how it feels knowing that your sister and daughter are on the verge of getting thrown out on their ass every month because of rent, and you can't do nothing about it?"

Vega shot back, "You know how it feels not to be able to afford that dime sack when you need that high?"

"Come on, man—"

"Look, D'Avien, I know you care about Praze. But ask yourself this: how hard are you *really* trying to put things right for her?"

"Real talk," D'Avien conceded. "I ain't done enough. I know that."

"Then let's start. Let's go get that money. Where is it?"

With some hesitancy, he replied. "At my apartment."

"Then I guess we're off. I'm driving."

A look of defeat crossed D'Avien's face as he followed the hunters to the parking lot. "This is gonna get me killed," he said.

"Maybe," Vega said. "But dying is easy. Redemption is hard. It takes more effort."

"Maybe some niggas deserve to die."

Vega thought on those words. He had uttered similar words in reference to his old friend. Then he said, "We all deserve to die for the things we've done. You...me...but not Praze. Not for your mistakes."

Again, D'Avien said, "Real talk."

THE RATTLESNAKE, HECTOR "Cascabel" Delapeña, had his ways of finding those people Dominguez wanted. He strode confidently down the hallways of the hotel until he found the room occupied by Desiree and Praze Manning. He brazenly approached the two police officers stationed outside the door.

He reached inside his jacket.

The two officers turned his way with welcoming smiles. One of them said, "How's it going, Detective Delapeña?"

"Busy, just like every other day." He withdrew his hand, bringing with it his badge.

"You don't need that."

"Just going through the motions."

"So what can we do for you?"

"The Mannings are needed at the precinct for a few questions. That's all."

"Orders?"

Delapeña provided some forged authorization. The officers allowed him inside.

After a brief conversation with Desiree and a smile for Praze, he had the two of them in his car, headed to D'Avien's apartment where they would meet with Javier Dominguez.

❧

NOT SURPRISINGLY, D'AVIEN'S apartment building was in worse shape than Desiree's. The two hunters followed him up several flights of creaky stairs, bypassing the broken-down elevator.

Vega asked, "So where's the money?"

"There's a panel in my closet roof that comes off. The money and the brick are in a duffel." They were approaching D'Avien's floor. "I'll take you to the truck after—."

Vega paused immediately after D'Avien did. Jiana furrowed her brow, unable to see anything from the landing where she stood. "What's wrong, Vega?"

"Shhh...." Vega waved a warning hand to her. He reached into his coat pocket.

D'Avien just stood there, staring at his front door.

Then came a thickly accented Latin voice. "I see you, D. Who's that with you?"

"Ain't nobody with me, man."

"Don't play with me, *pendejo*! I heard you talking to someone. Come out!"

D'Avien turned a deer-in-the-headlights look to Vega. Vega left his gun hidden and called out "I'm just a friend of D's! I'm coming out!" He locked eyes with Jiana, held a finger to his mouth, and mouthed *Wait here*, to her.

They hadn't seen her yet.

Vega held his hands up in surrender and stepped into view. There were, in fact, two men standing guard at the front door, both brandishing guns and fixing them on Vega and D'Avien. The one who had spoken patted them both down, retrieved Vega's gun and cell phone, and then brought them into the newly ransacked apartment, calling out "Jefé, we have some visitors."

The small living room was crowded. There were four men in the room. Two guarded Desiree, who sat on the couch. Praze was in her lap, terrified, helpless eyes locked on Vega. Another man casually stood with gun in hand beside the fourth man.

This fourth man, Vega knew, was Javier Dominguez. He stood facing the window, hands clasped behind his back, one of them immobilized in a bandage. Dominguez turned, revealing a face heavily tattooed with Aztec symbols from his neck to his cheekbones. His gaze was cold, like a shark circling its prey. "Wait outside, Rodolfo."

"Sí, jefé."

"D'Avien, D'Avien." Dominguez was shaking his head. "Where have you been?"

D'Avien didn't know what to say, so he opted for silence.

"Who is your friend?"

Vega spoke up. "Federal Hunter Vega."

"Ah, Señor Vega." Dominguez tilted his head, indicating the man beside him, "My associate, Hector Delapeña, has told me about you. He's privy to much information as an officer of the law in this...*fine* city of mine."

"Jefé," Delapeña said. "We must kill this hunter. He has many friends in the police."

"*Cayaté!*" Dominguez fixed Delapeña with a glare. To D'Avien, he said "Where is the bag?"

D'Avien shook his head. "Let my family go, first. Then we'll—"

A gunshot!

D'Avien yelled out as he fell to the floor, grabbing the side of his thigh.

Praze screamed.

Desiree held her tightly, whispering "Oh, Jesus, oh, Jesus..."

Dominguez aimed for his head this time, and calmly asked again, "Where is the bag?"

D'Avien stiffened his jaw, and hissed defiantly "Let my family go first!"

Dominguez pulled back the hammer of his weapon.

D'Avien turned his eyes to Praze. "I love you, Baby Girl."

"Wait!" Vega called out. "I know where it is. I'll get it for you. Just put the gun away."

Dominguez didn't put the gun away, but it seemed they had a deal. He turned to one of the men guarding Desiree, and said "Antonio, vaya con el lobo."

"Sí, Javier." Antonio followed Vega into the bedroom.

Vega moved slowly, keeping things calm. He found a small stool in the closet, climbed it, felt around for that piece of ceiling that would come away. He prayed that D'Avien was telling the truth, or they were all dead.

There it was. An exposed board lifted away, and Vega came down with the black bag. Inside were dozens of large money stacks, and the brick of cocaine, smeared with Dominguez's blood.

That was it then. Dominguez didn't want the drugs or the cash. With the blood, the bag, the trail of bodies and the truck D'Avien would lead them to, they could put Dominguez away for good.

This bag was the only reason they were still alive.

Now they were all expendable.

"Is that it?" Antonio demanded.

Vega withdrew a stack of bills from the bag and held it up for the gunman to see. The moment Antonio's eyes went to the stack, Vega threw it in his face. Like a flash of light, Vega grabbed the gun barrel, flicked the safety on, and twisted it, snapping Antonio's finger.

Before Antonio could yell out, Vega struck him in the throat and put him into a sleeper hold from behind. The thug struggled, kicked, fought to make some type of noise, but Vega held him tightly. He had to. If he failed, it was over. For Praze's sake, he held on. He pressed harder against Antonio's neck, jerked, twisted, waiting for that sickening, gut-churning moment...

Crackle...

Antonio's arms stopped flailing, and he went limp. Vega lowered him silently to the floor. He retrieved two guns from the body.

Now what? Being completely honest with himself, Vega had to admit he was making this up as he went along. Whatever he decided to do it had to be soon. He had already taken too long to find the bag. It was going to be dangerous regardless.

Finally he shook his head, checked both weapons, and mumbled to himself, "We'll do it cowboy style."

He opened the bedroom door, kicked the bag into the living room, and stepped out, one gun fixed on Dominguez, the other covering Delapeña and the third man. Delapeña tried to draw his weapon, but Dominguez waved him off. "What is this, bounty hunter?"

"Just a negotiation, *hombre*. Take the bag, leave the Mannings, and walk."

Dominguez snickered. "If only it was so simple, my friend." He flashed a psychotic smile to Praze. "Bring me the bag, *mija*."

"Don't," Vega told her.

Dominguez drew back the hammer of his gun. "Do it."

And Praze reluctantly did. She dragged the heavy bag to him and released it at his feet.

And then Dominguez grabbed her, pressed the gun to her temple. "We'll be leaving now, Señor Vega. Hector, Luis, *vamanos*."

Delapeña was at his boss's side. Praze and the duffel were handed off to him. Luis left Desiree, who came off the couch and knelt down beside her writhing brother.

When Vega looked down at her, Luis prematurely lunged for him. Vega spun, dodged, placing himself behind Luis, so that when Delapeña inevitably fired he killed his own man instead. Vega dove for Desiree and D'Avien to shield them.

Jiana heard the commotion and acted. She was at the top of the stairs, head poking around the corner. The two doormen moved to go into the apartment. "Freeze!" she yelled in a voice too small for the circumstances she found herself in.

Both men turned and opened fire on her. She thrust her weapon around the corner and fired. The exchange went on until she struck one in the chest, and he fell.

Dominguez bolted from the apartment, Delapeña close in tow with a struggling Praze Manning under his arm. With Jiana holding the stairs, they opted for the roof. The final doorman covered their flight and then followed.

"Vega!" Jiana called to the apartment.

"Clear!" Vega turned to D'Avien. "You okay?"

D'Avien cradled his bleeding leg. "Save my daughter, Vega. Save my Baby Girl."

Vega entered the hallway. Jiana moved up the stairs. At the landing she called "Move!" and Vega continued past her as she covered him.

They continued up, floor after arduous floor, unimpeded until the eighth. Jiana jumped when Vega suddenly opened fire from the landing. Without pause he continued up, hurdling over Dominguez's doorman as the body came tumbling down the stairs. The last two flights were passed in a blur of adrenalin, and Vega and Jiana were on the roof.

Their quarry was heading for the fire escape with Praze.

Vega fired and missed. Dominguez dove behind an air-conditioning unit, leaving Delapeña in the open with a whimpering Praze as a shield.

Vega strode forward, gun outstretched, and ignored Delapeña's shouts of "Stop, *cabrón*! I'll kill her!"

He simply said, "Praze, honey, close your eyes."

She did.

Then Vega shot Delapeña in the eye.

"Come on out, Dominguez. It's over." Vega covered Dominguez's hiding spot with his gun, sidestepping to get Praze out of his line of fire.

Praze had frozen in fear. She looked imploringly at Jiana. "Come on, baby." Jiana reluctantly put her gun away and squatted down, holding her hands out to Praze.

Dominguez chuckled in frustration, tapping his gun barrel against his forehead. "Is this how you want it to end, bounty hunter? With that little girl's blood on your hands?"

"I just want one less corpse on my conscience, that's all."

"I swear by the Virgin, bounty hunter, there *will* be one more body if you don't turn and walk away. Which would you rather have on your conscience: my escape or the little *niña*'s death?"

Vega wasn't playing that game.

"We all want something, bounty hunter. You want the girl, I want the money. I'll even throw in a little Christmas bonus for her. Feliz Navidad por todos! We can kill each other later." Dominguez slid closer to the corner of the air unit, beckoning to Praze, "Chiquita, venti aquí. Bring me the money."

This time, the small girl found the courage to turn and walk away from him.

And Dominguez knew his bargaining chip was slipping away.

So did Vega.

When Dominguez leaped, grasping at Praze for cover, Vega caught him in midair with a single shot...a shot he never thought would find its mark. But it did.

Dominguez hit the ground hard, thrown back until he slammed against the escape ladder.

Praze ran into Jiana's arms.

With a cough and a gurgling hack, Dominguez struggled slowly to his feet, hand grasping his crimson neck, blood spurting from it with every beat of his failing heart. He was a man who knew death, could feel death. And he saw his flowing forth in the red between his fingers. He stood tall, defiant, fixing Vega with a cold stare. From his hemorrhaging throat came the words, "Asesino cabrón."

Vega adjusted his aim. "Quizás."

The shot rang out. Dominguez tipped backwards over the escape ladder, falling silently away.

Vega did not exhale until there came the distant thud of the drug lord's body far below.

"What did he say?" Jiana asked as she hugged Praze.

Vega shook his head. "Nothing. It wasn't true, anyway."

❧

Christmas Eve...

DESIREE FOUND THAT same melancholy feeling deep inside that she had every Christmas, but she put on a good face for Praze. She fed Praze a spoonful of stuffing. "What do you think?"

"Mmm...more salt."

"Think so?"

"Yeah."

"Whatever you say, Baby Girl."

A knock at the door announced their guests. D'Avien limped in on crutches with Vega and Jiana close behind. Praze ran to her father and hugged his waist. He bent low and kissed her forehead.

Also with them was Pastor Steiger and six of the church youth group. "They won't stay long," Vega assured. "They just wanted to wish you and Praze a merry Christmas."

Next thing Desiree knew, the six teens were hauling in boxes of presents for both her and Praze. Everything from clothes to toys to appliances and electric heaters. Even two brand new beds. Praze was overcome with excitement.

Desiree was overcome with emotion.

Vega smiled to her, saying, "Just a little something for a few friends."

Desiree wept, hugged Vega, kissed his cheek. "God bless you, Vega. God bless you."

They spent the rest of the night discussing Vega's friend in the church, who could pull some strings to get Desiree and Praze into a better apartment closer to Desiree's job.

And D'Avien...well Desiree knew him well enough to know there was something different about him. Something better.

࿓

PRAZE HAD A busy morning of opening presents tomorrow. The first such Christmas in years, according to Desiree. So they called it a night.

Mostly. Vega and Jiana had returned to their apartment. Vega was out on the balcony, breathing in the cold winter air just as the fresh snow began to fall. It was two o'clock in the morning when Jiana joined him, carrying two mugs of hot cocoa. They sipped quietly for a few minutes.

Jiana said, "I talked to Pastor Steiger. He said you're going back to church."

"In a few weeks, after the holidays. He wants me to address the congregation, tell them everything about what happened with Roddy. I'd just as soon keep it to myself, but he says I don't deserve that. He said I deserve closure."

She nodded. "Are you ready for that?"

"I will be."

"Then I'll go with you." Jiana sighed, thinking about the sound of Praze's excited laughter earlier that evening. "You really gave Praze a Christmas, didn't you?"

He didn't say anything. He didn't like blowing his own horn, but Jiana knew he felt good about it. "You're a good man, Vega."

"The Word says there are none good except our Father in heaven."

"Well, you're close."

He shrugged. "I'm okay, I guess."

They shared a laugh—a laugh that faded into a comfortable silence between them. Jiana had the thought to lean over and kiss his cheek. She considered it, and decided she wasn't quite brave enough for that yet.

The thought of it warmed her cheeks against the snowfall, though.

Vega commented on the redness in her face, and the fact that he had noticed probably made it worse.

Jiana sighed, pulled the three beaded locks of hair back behind her ear. She playfully bumped her shoulder against his arm. After a while she started to hum. She hummed Vega's favorite ballad.

And together they watched the snow fall on Antioch City.

CHANGE OF HEART

BRETT D. MCLAUGHLIN

Terry wondered what would happen if a family in their Sunday best looked up and saw pieces of a broken gypsum ceiling tile hurtling down towards their heads. He imagined they'd scream, or at least gasp, probably inhaling a bit of the snowy white dust accompanying the tile on its trajectory downwards. Terry smiled, unconcerned, and continued pulling on a strand of clear, high tensile fishing wire. He followed the wire with his eyes, from his hands to the greased and oiled pulley three feet above him, mounted to an overhead air duct with super glue, and then back down to a quarter-inch steel hook. The hook was screwed into the top of a ceiling tile, a foot in front of where he lay, the tile resting on a latticework of metal supports. As the wire moved through his hands, the near edge of the tile rose, allowing a shaft of florescent light to enter the crawlspace where he was stretched out.

He pulled until the edge of the tile raised up a full three inches, and then tied the near end of the wire to another hook, this one mounted several inches to his left. He removed his hands and held his breath, making sure that the knot and line would hold steady, that the tile in front of him would stay raised.

Terry slipped the barrel of his matte black M40A3 sniper rifle into the opening he had created between support and tile, cradling the stock of the rifle into his right shoulder. He closed his left eye, relaxing, letting the upper lid sink towards his cheek.

He looked into a Schmidt & Bender PMII scope, ebony black and sleek atop the rifle. The scope was set up Marine-style with a counter-clockwise turning elevation knob which Terry used to bring a dark brown wooden dais, 150 feet away, into view.

Terry's shoulders tensed as the Target stepped behind the dais. He was tall, but not slender. An expensive European-cut suit and custom tailoring could not hide the effect of a steady diet of Sunday lunches, wedding receptions, and funeral wakes. The Target's pace was quick, still that of a twenty-eight year old preacher getting started in Biloxi, Mississippi. The combination of added weight and youthful stride resulted in an aggressive and energetic presence, and his baritone voice rang out, clear to Terry through the auditorium's speakers.

"What was the lesson of Job? Was it that God is cruel? Surely not! Perhaps it was that God *allows* cruelty towards his children. But then, why? Was there purpose in Job's suffering? Perhaps most important of all, can we know what that purpose was? Can we realize the purpose of our own sufferings? Or are we condemned to Job's fate, railing against a God who allows pain without explanation?"

The Target continued, voice rising and falling, legs churning. Terry could feel the energy of the man, understood how a small group of ten had blossomed into the two thousand below. Terry had listened to over thirty hours of recorded sermons from the Target, had catalogued every nuance of his speaking voice, and yet he was still captivated by this live demonstration of the man's personality and charisma.

This is a man that people will follow, thought Terry. *But I suppose that's the problem.*

Terry brought his attention to bear on his scope, on the Target, on the simplicity of being still. His muscles relaxed and his breathing slowed. The first finger of Terry's right hand slid into the trigger guard of his rifle. It came to rest on the trigger, and he exerted the smallest amount of pressure, establishing a solid connection between flesh and fiberglass.

He waited.

THE TARGET'S NAME was Henry Rollings, a conservative Christian preacher. His death would prevent a rising tide of intolerance in the South, and result in the advancement and acceptance of thousands of Muslims and other non-Christian faith-minded people in America's Bible belt.

That's what the man in the dark-rimmed glasses and charcoal grey suit had said, and for Terry Jenkins, that was enough. Terry had learned that to question was folly, to blindly accept divine.

"Timeline is standard: six weeks. Lethal action approved," the man droned. He looked serious, but still a bit bored. Terry supposed the man probably thought the same about him, not that the two would ever speak a word to each other outside of this room. Their acquaintance was limited to a name and a degree of force. Everything else was inconsequential.

THE TARGET PASSED through the circular reticule of Terry's scope rings one time, two times, three...again and again. Terry watched, visualized pulling the trigger, saw his bullet find its mark.

He had four weeks left, four weeks to analyze and plan. The church was a poor option. A murder here would be too public. Reaction would be immediate, and Terry would have lots of exposure during an exit. He already knew it would take seven minutes to stow his rifle, make his way out of the crawlspace without breaking any tiles, climb down the rusted metal access ladder at the back of the auditorium, discard his coveralls and straighten the suit he was wearing underneath, and then mingle with what would be a screaming, chaotic crowd trying to shove their way out of the building.

The only reason to kill the Target here would be to create a spectacle. Spectacles were dangerous, messy, and sensational. Terry preferred a private kill. He slid his finger off of the trigger, and began to disassemble his rifle.

THREE AND A half hours later, the man who called himself Terry Jenkins stepped out of a steaming shower, the rigors of his morning's survey of the Target's church washed off with soap and water. His left hand massaged the back of his neck.

Just because the human body is capable of being still doesn't mean it should have to be, Terry thought. The service had lasted another forty minutes, and it took thirty-five minutes beyond that for everyone to clear out of the large sanctuary. Terry had waited another full hour before moving. He knew that a noise in an empty building was far louder than the same noise in a crowded one. Then he walked twenty minutes to a grocery store a mile away, unlocked and opened the door of a rented 1998 navy blue Honda Accord, and drove eight miles to the Comfort Inn he was standing in now.

Terry wrapped himself in a white towel, and stared into the mirror spanning the south wall of the motel's bathroom. It was steamed, clouded, and Terry saw only the most indistinct of shapes, dark at the top where his short thatch of hair would be. *Appropriate,* Terry thought, *the ghost of a human.*

Terry walked out of the bathroom and into his room. He looked across two double beds, both piled with documents. The floor was naked, though, cheap carpet stained by a thousand feet but clear of papers, shoes, even absent a discarded gum wrapper or stray paperclip. Terry had shoved the dresser and the TV sitting on top of it into the room's southeast corner. The only other piece of furniture was a cheap imitation-wood end table between the two beds. It had a lamp and alarm clock on it, the clock flashing out 4:12 in green neon.

On the beds were manila and brown folders, stuffed with black-and-white photographs taken with a telescoping lens; paper clipped stacks of Google Map printouts, detailing hundreds of routes to the Target's church, his home, his wife's favorite spa, the private schools where his children attended school; scrawled notes next to a tape recorder, minidisk player, and walkman; and his Apple G4 laptop, silver, thin, and lightweight, its blackened screen secured by a password-protected screen saver.

All of this gave the room an odd, surreal feeling. The room wasn't empty, but the hallmarks of life were missing. There were no clothes stuffed into a half-open dresser drawer, no watch or wallet on the end table, not even a crumpled burger wrapper from McDonald's.

There was no razor on the sink, no comb next to the faucet, not even a toothbrush lying in an open toiletries bag. Toothbrush, comb, shaving gel, each in 3 and 4.5 oz containers, stored in a clear plastic Ziploc, and when emptied, taken to a dump 3 miles away and disposed off. When not in use, the Ziploc was stored in one of two black bags lying on the floor of the room's single closet. The bags contained everything Terry had brought to the hotel. Not a single item of clothing had touched the dresser drawers, and Terry drove twenty minutes out of town to do his laundry, every third day, taking a different route each time. When he left, the two black bags would leave with him, although they would be lighter; the papers and photos on the beds would be burnt until only ash remained.

His weapons were in a third bag, this one made of canvas dyed olive green, and stored underneath the wheel well in the trunk of his Honda Accord. He brought the weapons into the room for cleaning and inspection each night, and returned them to the vehicle when finished, early in the morning. Terry knew that a cheap motel room was far more susceptible to theft and burglary than a rented late-model vehicle, and never kept anything in the room of value except for a single pistol, his Heckler & Koch 9mm PS9. He would have a hard time explaining the notes, photos, and laptop, but they were far less damning than the 6" double-edged blade of his Morey MK1 knife or the sniper rifle that were in the Accord.

Terry Jenkins was a ghost indeed.

As he surveyed his research, his notes, his ideas, he planned his next twelve hours. He would reconnect with and follow the Target to his home, ensure that he was in for the night, and then return to Rose Hill Burial Park, Terry's preferred location for target termination. He'd spend three hours reviewing the location, and ensure that no security guards had been hired, no late-night jogger had plotted her new route to pass by the cemetery grounds.

Terry smiled at the irony of using a cemetery as a staging location until his eyes alerted him to something...different. He looked over the room, sweeping his eyes from one side to the other, but did not focus. In his mind, he superimposed the vision of the room he held in memory over the image his eyes provided, looking for a discrepancy.

He found it: something on the far bed, the one closer to the room's exterior door. He refocused and saw a yellow piece of paper, 8 1/2 x 11, lined, ripped from an ordinary yellow writing pad. His body tensed. He sidestepped twice to his right and reached backwards into the closet between the bathroom and beds. He pulled his pistol out of the smaller black bag, raised it to shoulder height, and pointed it at the door in front of him. It was ready to fire, loaded early this morning; instinct guided Terry's thumb to the lever on the left side of the pistol's black steel grip, and he cocked it.

Terry Jenkins did all of this in less than two seconds, in nothing but a towel and a thin film of steam and sweat.

His eyes swept the room again, looking for any other signs of disturbance. He moved towards the yellow sheet of paper. In a non-descript plain black font, four words stared up at him: *Leave the preacher alone.*

Terry lowered his pistol. The sheet was a warning. Otherwise, he'd already be dead.

â

AN HOUR LATER, the room was vacant. Terry packed his maps, pictures, notes, files, and laptop accessories into his black bags, folded his laptop shut, dressed, and checked out. As he left the room, he wrapped two pieces of clear packing tape around the room's door knobs—one on the inside knob, one on the outside—removed the tape, and placed each piece sticky side down on a blank white sheet of paper. The paper went into a FedEx envelope, and Terry was now on his way to drop the envelope off at a local Kinko's. He'd use the self-service stand outside, and by tomorrow morning, fingerprint, hair, and fiber analysis would tell him what he already knew: nobody who could walk into Terry's room undetected, leave the papers and photos untouched, and place a note on top of it all, would leave behind fingerprints or a loose strand of hair.

Terry then drove across town to a Starbucks. He pulled his laptop from one of the black bags in the Accord's backseat, and went inside. He never spoke, even when the college-aged barista with the dyed orange hair smiled and told him how glad she was he'd chosen to come by.

He turned on his laptop and established a WiFi connection using an account paid for by a lawyer in Seattle who had died three months ago. Opened up his email and typed in an address constructed by taking a memorized 16-digit number, adding to it the month of the year, the day of the month, and the hour of the day, and then turning that sum into an alphabetic address with yet another memorized number, this one a cipher. The result looked like nonsense, but would reach his handlers untouched by any Internet Service Provider. All this was done in the space of five seconds, Terry's mind a machine. He typed three words into the message body, and pressed Send:

"Acceleration required. Confirm."

❧

ALL OF THIS was observed, catalogued, and analyzed. The man calling himself Terry Jenkins had their undivided attention.

Henry Rollings had a purpose, and must be allowed to live and continue on the path he was destined for. Once before, they had intervened, and now they would intervene again. Terry Jenkins must be persuaded to stop; the preacher must not die.

❧

EARLY THE NEXT morning, Terry drove from the new motel he'd checked into to a different coffee shop with wireless Internet—Java Joe's this time, one more cheery college-aged coffee brewer with one more awful shade of hair greeting him, although it was a boy this time, not a girl—and checked his email. He had a single item in his inbox with only a single word in the message body: "Confirmed."

Later that afternoon, he received a text message on his cell phone, again with a succinct message: "Evidence Inconclusive." The collected fibers and fingerprints he'd sent off the day before had come up empty, all checked against a thousand databases.

By late afternoon, Terry had no more information on who had left him the note, but had been green-lighted to take down his Target and complete his assignment. Terry's training overrode his concern about the warning he had received, and the part of his brain that wondered about the person who had left that note was turned off, no questions asked. He went to work cleaning his rifle, preparing for the evening's work.

❧

TERRY WAS ONCE more lying still, relaxed, the fiberglass stock of his M40A3 pressed against his body, but this time, the rifle had a 7.62 mm NATO round chambered. Terry had four more rounds six inches from his right hand lined up on a thin square of cloth. His right hand held a small inexpensive directional microphone pieced together from parts he'd bought at the local electronics store. On his left side was the large olive green knapsack he had pulled from the Accord's wheel well, containing additional cartridges and gear. Next to this was his knife. He let himself feel the H&K pistol against his back, pinching the skin above his waist, and then dismissed the discomfort.

Terry breathed slowly and glanced at the black digital watch on his left wrist: 8:23 PM. Rose Hill Burial Park was quiet, dark, and the final resting place of the Target's sister. She had lost a long battle to cancer three years ago. Terry could have recited the time she died, the attending physician, and what color blouse she was wearing when she was admitted. What he didn't learn from medical files, traffic cameras, and newspaper clippings was how deeply the woman's death had affected the Target. This had come from direct observation.

Every evening the Target would come here, although the time varied. Saturday directly after finishing at the church office at 6:00 PM, Sundays much later after conducting evening services, today just after the weekly meeting of the church officers. He would spend ten, sometimes fifteen minutes just staring at her modest tombstone, and then he would kneel. Terry had heard him crying, listening from fifty yards away with his microphone. Why he still wept at a death a thousand days done, Terry could not understand, but he did know that this was an opportunity. During this ritual, the Target was motionless, alone, and vulnerable.

Tonight, the Target would die directly above where his sister was buried.

Terry heard a low hum ahead and to his right, recognized it as the sound of a car approaching. He turned to see a navy sedan turning off of the asphalt of Grand Boulevard and into the parking lot of the cemetery, eighty yards northeast of his position.

The Target parked his car and stepped out, dark against the twilight, a black or perhaps navy suit with a dark tie and white shirt. The effect was a pale round head floating above a patch of white, eerie but well suited for a graveyard. The man walked through the cemetery's open gate, a four foot high white metal fence that enclosed the grounds. The fence was quaint and somehow suited to the near thousand unmoving occupants in Rose Hill Burial Park. Terry couldn't hear the Target's footfalls, but knew it would take the man several minutes to arrive at his sister's tombstone. Terry collected himself, reviewed his protocols, and prepared his mind and body.

❧

THE TARGET APPROACHED his sister's gravesite, and Terry turned on his microphone.

"I don't understand. Is there nothing more? Is this all I have to look forward to?" The Target knelt, and Terry wondered at the massive dry cleaning bill this man must incur, night after night pushing grass and dirt into the knees of his expensive pants.

"I'm just not sure I can—" The Target kept talking, but Terry was no longer listening, at least to the kneeling man in front of a tombstone half a football field away.

Terry had heard something else, and his body reacted before his mind had time to process the new sound. He dropped his microphone and rolled to the right, away from the sound, over the cartridges and cloth he had set out, tucking the rifle into his body, and reaching for his pistol with his right hand.

He felt dirt kick up onto his face as he rolled, and knew the sound his body had reacted to was one he had heard before: someone had fired at him, and they'd done it from far enough away that only the thin *phhhtttt* of a cartridge passing by had penetrated his ear canal and reverberated against his ear drum. The dirt on his cheek was from the shot burying itself into the ground, kicking up soft black sod along the perimeter of the graveyard where Terry was positioned.

He kept rolling. The shot had landed closer to his knapsack than to where he had been positioned, suggesting a poor shot—*or*, he thought, *a very good shot intended to miss.*

He stopped his roll with his belly to the ground, two feet from where he had been lying. He planted both hands palm down in the dirt and pushed up. He was on his feet instantly, bent forward and low. He began to move, back towards his original position, grabbing his pack and knife and listening, expecting the next shot. He glanced to his right, saw the Target still in front of the tombstone, and considered moving in.

Foolish, he thought. His mind had already done the math, estimating angles and distance, and he knew that the warning shot—already he had determined the shot was a warning, a more serious version of the yellow note in his motel room—had come from a position closer to the Target than he was, and elevated, at least ten feet.

I head for the target, I'm an easy shot. Terry knew he was at a disadvantage. It wasn't retreat, it was survival.

Ten minutes later, Terry was over a mile away, breathing hard but still calm and in control. He had left only four cartridges and a nondescript mustard colored cloth.

And the slug. What I'd give for that slug buried in the ground...

Terry knew better than to return tonight; he had read the thrillers, knew that they were full of reckless chases and testosterone-driven killings separated only by chapter numbers, but his work was more patience and monotony than anything else. He would return to the cemetery in the morning.

Just as he had known there would be no fingerprints, though, just as he had known the shot was a warning, he knew when he returned there would be no buried bullet, no rag with a tiny bit of oil residue from where four NATO cartridges had lain...he was equally sure that the tiny hole where the warning shot had entered the earth would be covered and invisible.

THEY DIDN'T NEED FedEx or cryptic email accounts to know who Terry Jenkins was. They knew his real name—as well as every alias he had ever used—and his employer, and they knew he preferred Navy-issued weaponry and historical biographies. They knew not only the instant he was born, but also the instant he was conceived.

And now, they knew that he was more determined, that they had given him his chance, and he had refused it.

Above all this, they knew the importance of the preacher. The utter disaster that would result from his death now, before his purpose was accomplished. That left only one thing unknown: *what to do with Terry Jenkins?*

TERRY HAD RISEN two hours before dawn, returned to the cemetery, and found just what he expected: nothing. No spent bullet, no patch of freshly turned dirt. Not even an oval of disturbed grass marking the spot he had occupied the night before, where he had almost killed the preacher, where he had almost been killed himself.

Now he sat alone in his motel room, thinking about yellow pieces of paper and warning shots. The beds in the room were piled with the same papers and photos, and Terry had been through it all again. Every note, every clipped photo, every file on his laptop; it was all examined for a reason that this Target's life should be spared.

But Terry knew only one course of action: aggression. Pursue and attack and persist. The Target's charisma, a warning note, even a bullet screaming by his left ear, did not change this. They were a concern, an obstacle to his assignment, but they could not overcome his training and single-mindedness.

Throughout his deliberation, Terry's hands clenched and unclenched. His heart was beating faster than normal, and his brow was furrowed. Terry Jenkins was angry.

৵

THE PREACHER SPENT every Tuesday morning visiting the local hospital, spending a few minutes with patients on the non-critical floors.

The Target, Terry corrected himself. *Not Rollings, not the preacher, but the Target.*

Terry felt his anger rise and fought it. He was used to danger, combat, even being shot at. But being toyed with was something else. Emotion had no place in his line of work; it crippled a man, made him susceptible to suggestion and paranoia and worse, compassion. And what value did this Target have, his life over any other? The idea required that one life be valued over another, that there was more than chance behind life and death and everything in between.

Terry tried to relax as he walked towards the hospital. He had parked a half mile away but was now within sight of Mercy Health Center. The complex was enormous, a main hospital and five medical buildings. He walked towards the main building, through a parking lot, then passing a conference center and the towering granite entrance to the physician's offices. He adopted the fast pace of a doctor, ignoring the sculptured bushes and fresh-cut flowers that lined the sidewalk. The gait matched his clothing, khaki slacks, a pressed pinstriped blue shirt, a bold yellow and navy striped tie, and an American flag pin. Over all of it was a white surgeon's coat with the hospital's logo stitched in navy blue on the left front pocket.

Terry had his hands in the coat's pockets, the fingertips of his right hand brushing the coated grip of his 9mm pistol.

☙

"HE'S STILL COMING." *It was a statement, not a question.*
   "Yes."
   "And you think he will keep coming? No matter our warnings?"
   "Yes."
   "Would he be receptive to us?"
   "He might. His has become...emotional."
   "Then go. Convince him that the preacher must be spared."

☙

TERRY WALKED DOWN a hallway of the hospital's second floor, the cancer ward. On each side of him, doors opened into rooms of patients, many quiet or sleeping. He was on an open ward, but most of these patients would die here, assaulted with chemotherapy and radiation. Everything was white and sterile, as if the brightness would deter death.

With each circuit of the floor, Terry glanced at the elevators and stairwell, and then continued on. When the preacher appeared, Terry would follow him. The preacher would step into a room to say an encouraging word to a patient, promise him that better things were waiting for those who believed in...something more. Terry would step into the room, and shut the door. He would pull the trigger of his 9mm twice, once for the preacher and again for the patient turned witness. The patient's monitoring gear would sound, and Terry would walk out as nurses ran in, just another doctor rushing through the chaos. Twenty minutes later, he'd be driving out of Oklahoma City.

Then maybe he'd stop feeling so angry.

Terry turned left again, into the next hallway. He heard the elevator sound ahead, and quickened his pace. Around another corner, and he saw the preacher step out. He was wearing a light gray suit, white shirt, yellow tie. Hair immaculate, black shoes mirror-bright and clear; a small silver cross pinned on his lapel.

Terry settled into stride fifteen feet behind the large man. The preacher turned towards an open door on his right, and entered. Terry quickened his pace.

He wrapped his right hand around the grip of his pistol. His thumb cocked the gun, first finger sliding into the trigger guard. He was two paces from the door.

Everything stopped.

❧

IF SOMEONE HAD asked Terry what it would be like if time stopped, he would have laughed and described a frozen crowd, hundreds of feet in midstep, ice cream cones melting but never dripping onto the ground, a paper airplane in flight, hanging still in the air.

Nothing could have prepared him for the abyss he found himself in.

When time stopped, so did the light traveling from overhead fluorescents to Terry's eyes. The retinas of his eyes had no information to collect, nothing to reflect onto the rod and cone cells inside his eyeballs. He saw... nothing.

In an attempt to compensate, his brain broadcast the last image it held: an open wooden door along a white hallway, a large grey-suited man half visible in the doorway. The end of a hospital bed, chrome bordering pale blue blankets, and a single naked foot dangling off the end, its mate warm and covered.

The dissonance between his eyes and brain fired synapses, and the effect was that of a computer monitor without a screen saver, burned out from displaying the same image for too long. To Terry, it felt like an army of wasps had settled onto his eyeballs and began to sting him all at once.

His ears malfunctioned, too, still trying to relay all the sounds from the instant that time stopped. The hum of a central air conditioning system, the single high beep of a heart monitor, a nurse's mid-sentence syllable— "Nan—" —all continued on, his eardrum relaying the same vibration to his brain over and over and over.

Terry Jenkins wanted to die.

❧

TERRY HAD NO idea how long this went on; it could have been ten seconds or two millennia. He tried to relinquish his sanity with every passing instant, but never could.

"John." Terry heard the voice, and wanted to weep. The sound with a beginning and end was a gift to his ears.

"John Grason." Terry relished in the sounds, the beauty of the consonants and vowels. Then his eyes widened. The voice was using his given name. That name appeared in print only on a birth certificate locked in an underground vault in Langley, Virginia.

The man who called himself Terry Jenkins and had been christened John Grason opened his mouth and gasped a single word:

"Yes."

The instant the word left his lips, it all changed again. John was back in the hospital, two paces from an open door. Nothing else was moving, the door half-open and the preacher trapped in mid-step. He raised his left hand and touched a finger to his ears. He was surprised that the drums had not burst, that he didn't feel the sticky tackiness of blood on either cheek.

"Our warnings in your reality have gone unheeded. Now you have seen *our* reality."

John Grason turned his head towards the voice.

He saw nothing. Not the hospital walls, not an empty corridor, but nothing; an absence of anything. His eyes slid off the source of the voice, and struggled to focus. There wasn't a dark spot, for darkness was the opposite of light, light turned down to zero on the dial. This was *not-light*, and his brain struggled to comprehend one more unreality, worn from what he had experienced already.

"Leave the preacher alone," it said.

John's anger returned, all at once, replacing his fear and amazement.

"No," he said. Then, louder: "No!"

~

"TELL HIM."

"He will not understand."

"He will. He must."

"And if not?"
"Disaster."

❧

"LEAVE THE PREACHER alone." The thing repeated itself.

"Not so smart, are you? I said, NO!" John willed his eyes to the spot of nothing, resolved to show this thing his determination.

"He must live," the thing said.

"Why do you care? *Why does it matter?*" John knew he was going to die, that this thing could kill him in an instant. But the answers mattered now, more than the assignment itself.

"He will change things that must be changed."

"Yeah, I know. That's why I'm here," John said. He recalled the man in the dark glasses, painting a picture of intolerant America goaded by the preacher, standing frozen a mere five feet away.

"You don't know anything."

"I know I'm going to kill a man, and feel a lot better. Drive out of this town and find the first place I can to drink myself unconscious. Forget about preachers and God and you yanking me in and out of heaven or hell or whatever that was." John summoned his will, and moved. His left leg rose, and then cut through the air; it was like walking in water, an ocean pushing against him.

"Or, you can kill me, and send me right back. I don't care anymore," John said, and took another step towards the open door and his Target.

❧

"TELL HIM MORE."

"Are you sure?"
"Yes."
"How much more?"
"As little as you can. As much as you have to."
"Is the preacher this important?"
"He is."

❧

"HIS DEATH WILL change everything."

John stopped and turned his head. He struggled again to look at a patch of air that his eyes kept sliding off of.

"I get it. That's why I was sent," John said.

"To make sure he does not do certain things." It wasn't a question. John didn't suppose that this thing asked many questions.

"Yeah, you're really catching on, aren't you?" John was tired of the game of destiny. Angry at this thing's arrogance, and at his handler's instructions. Both supposed a world without real choice, or at least one where the big choices were pre-determined. And God; John couldn't leave out God, somehow interested in whether one man lived or died. It all infuriated John, and he returned to what he knew: action.

He stepped into the hospital room. He could see the preacher now. He visualized the pistol firing, then again. Saw two dead bodies. Rehearsed his exit route.

"We are here to make sure he *does* do certain things," the thing said.

This stopped John. He turned one last time, impatient now.

"You want him to *do* these things? Are you kidding me? He's going to tell people they're going to burn forever because they don't agree with his opinions about God!"

"No, he will not," the thing said.

"And you know this. It's all pre-determined." John's voice went flat. Angry and despondent all at once.

"Yes," it said.

"That he *won't* create intolerance. Or condemn people to hell, just because they don't see things his way."

"Yes," it said again.

"What about choice? How can you know *anything* for sure?" John was pleading. Desperate.

"Because we exist beyond you, around you, and Time does not hold the same sway over us. And you believe us because of what you have seen and experienced."

The thing was gone, and the world moved again.

&

JOHN HAD SPUN on his heel, pulled his hands from his pockets, and exited the room. Took the stairs down to the first floor, and left the hospital. Walked to his car, and checked back into his motel.

He didn't unpack this time. John Grason spent the day sitting on the end of a made bed, staring at a stain on the floor's carpeting. He thought about the preacher, and how his eardrums felt when Time stopped flowing, and destiny.

He fell asleep in the same khakis and yellow tie that he wore to the hospital. Woke up, changed clothes, and drove to Rose Hill Burial Park. Stood over a gravestone, and remembered his life before men in suits handed him folders with pictures of people to kill in them.

John ate some lunch, and then drove around Oklahoma City all afternoon. He passed coffee house after coffee house, trying to remember a time when how his hair looked was more important than keeping a bullet in the chamber in case he lost his magazine.

As the sun began its descent, John decided to go to church.

❧

JOHN PULLED UP the same acoustic tile as he had three days before; even used the same wire, the same screw hooks, all reattached and retied. He slid his rifle into the gap again, made sure he had a clear view through his scope.

The preacher was pacing, energy and power pouring off of him. He seemed louder, more intense, urgent.

"So what do *you* believe? Is there something beyond the veil, or is everything that happens to us chance, random acts of entropy and molecular collision?

"Deep in our hearts, do we doubt? Do you hear the whisper of a voice insisting that there is nothing, that we're wrong, that heaven and hell are just cliques, organized to keep your friends in and your enemies out?"

John listened with a new perspective, and thought about a patch of space he couldn't quite focus his eyes on.

"If we're honest with each other, we must admit that our actions betray us. They scream that we don't believe in anything beyond this life. We're worried far more about the price of gas climbing than what God's purpose for us might be. We're concerned more with our neighbor's new car than we are with the state of their soul."

His voice rose, the force of his words palpable to John, lying flat in a crawl space sixty feet up.

"Is there anything outside of our vision, that reflects a greater truth? Or have we been persuaded by bad things happening to good people, by lost jobs or college rejection letters or unending debt...or by the death of a loved one, ravaged by cancer and left to die despite our prayers? Have we decided that God is just a myth, or that He is beyond our understanding and concern?"

John wanted to scream an answer, his anger from the last several days mixing with experience, changing him. There was more, and he didn't understand it, couldn't fathom his choices being known before he made them (or was it after? He didn't know, couldn't hold the problem in his head).

Tell me, he thought towards the air in front of him. *Why is he so important? Tell me!*

There was no horror, no cacophony of sound and light. The preacher simply stopped moving and speaking, and a shouted "Amen!" died on the lips of a zealous congregant.

And just to his left, John knew the thing had returned. His eyes turned away from it, skittering off the non-air, and this time he let them.

"He's speaking the truth, isn't he?" John said. "There is more, and you're part of that?"

"Yes," it said.

"And a God? And, what, some kind of heaven?"

"And hell," it said. "Heaven and hell."

"Then the preacher...he's going to change what people think. That's what this is about, isn't it? Not what happens here, but after."

"Yes."

"He's going to make people believe, people will choose because of him," John said. "That's what this is all about."

"Yes."

"But there must be a thousand of these preachers, a hundred thousand..." John's voice trailed off. Then he understood.

"The preacher...he's going to affect millions, isn't he?"

"Yes."

"So millions of people going to heaven or hell based on, what? Whether I complete an assignment?"

"Yes."

"But I can choose? You'll let me decide?"

"We have to. We must."

"And if I kill the preacher, millions of people won't hear him, won't listen, and millions of people will die and go to hell?"

The thing answered John, and John asked one more question. He received his answer, and then everything moved again.

❧

HE LOOKED THROUGH his scope, watched the preacher pace. And he listened.

"What will you do? Will you act as if this life is just a cruel short joke? Or will you choose to believe there is more, that our existence has a purpose beyond what we can see?"

John believed. He understood. And now the joke was on him.

John centered the inner ring of his scope on the yellow silk handkerchief poking up from the right front breast pocket of Reverend Henry Rollings's two thousand dollar black suit, and exerted exactly 2.2 pounds of pressure on the rifle's trigger. The handkerchief bloomed scarlet, and the preacher fell. He was dead before he hit the ground.

❧

JOHN GRASON WAS driving. Two black bags were in the trunk of his car. The olive green bag that traveled under the wheel well was gone, deposited in the Oklahoma River. John didn't think he'd need what was in that third bag anymore. The car was silent, John replaying his last conversation with the thing from a place John thought of as More.

"And if I kill the preacher, millions of people won't hear him, won't listen, and millions of people will die and go to hell?"

"No."

"But isn't that the purpose? That people need to hear him, and to believe?"

"In a year's time, Henry Rollings will be America's foremost Christian leader. In three years, he will be known worldwide. Millions will listen to him, and be exposed to the Truth. And then he will stop believing; he will give in to the madness of a sister dying before her time. He will decide that God ignored him. Mocked him.

"He will stop believing, and it will be beautiful.

"His faithlessness will be broadcast live to the world, and when he comes running into our bosom, millions will come with him. Hell will fill with the souls of the disillusioned, because this man does not have the strength of his convictions.

"That is why we were allowed to kill his sister.

"That is why you must let him live."

John closed his eyes, rubbed them with his left hand. His right hand was still on the steering wheel of the Accord as it moved north on Highway 77. He wondered if God would understand the choice he had made. He hoped so, but it didn't matter, not really. John believed, and now others would, too.

DANIEL G. KEOHANE
BOX
EDITOR'S CHOICE

Daniel G. Keohane's fiction has appeared in a number of magazines and anthologies over the years, including *Cemetery Dance*, *Apex Science Fiction and Horror Digest*, *Shroud Magazine* (coming soon), *The Pedestal Magazine*, Gothic.Net, and many others. *Solomon's Grave*, his debut novel, is slated for release in 2009 by Edge/Dragon Moon Press in 2009, after being previously released in both Germany (as Das Grab des Salomon) and Italy (as il Segreto di Salamone). An active member of the HWA and SFWA, Dan lives with his family in Massachusetts, where he is always at work on the next novel.

SIOBHAN SHIER
NOWHERE
EDITOR'S CHOICE

Siobhan Shier is an author, artist and horse owner who spends her free time riding out on the trail and attempting to ignore her cell phone. With a degree in Computer Science and a technical background, Siobhan discovered writing stories was more fun then any lines of code. "Nowhere" is Siobhan's first published short story, and is the inspiration for her work in progress: Every Nowhere, a book that challenges the concepts of good, evil, and reality.

M. L. ARCHER
PAINT IT BLACK
EDITOR'S CHOICE

A native of Los Angeles, M. L. Archer wound up living in seven major cities and points in between as the member of a fundamentalist religious cult. One day, the leader of this cult bragged that he so renewed his mind to the Word that he no longer even dreamed. Ms. Archer was reminded of 'The Haunting of Hill House,' where Jackson described the house as insane...because it too never dreamed. This made her realize she was in the wrong place and escaped.

She remains convinced that God can use fiction to reach people, even in the strangest places.

And yes, she plays the violin.

CHRIS MIKESELL
HINKY JENKS
DINER ALUMNI

Chris Mikesell has been a potential Publisher's Clearinghouse winner twenty years running. Since Ed McMahon seems in no hurry to stop by, he has filled the time in recent years writing and teaching English. His poetry, short stories, and satire have appeared in Infuze, DKA (now a part of Mindflights), Raygun Revival, Fear and Trembling, and *The Wittenburg Door*. His short story "In R'lyeh, Jesus Walks"; appeared in the debut edition of *Coach's Midnight Diner*. The opening 30 pages of his zombie novel placed second in the Association of Christian Fiction Writers 2008 Genesis contest.

His writing family, The Misfits, live in Arizona, Indiana, Tennessee, and Texas. He and his actual family (wife: Dina, son: Philip) live in Plano, Texas. His online home is mikesell.blogspot.com.

GREG MITCHELL
FLOWERS FOR SHELLY

Greg Mitchell likes monsters. So much so, in fact, that he devotes a great deal of time to writing about them. When he's not writing about monsters, he can be found with his wife Meghan and their daughter Jo Beth, sharing tickles and lots of laughter. In his Christian Horror series "The Coming Evil", Greg mixes the worlds of fear and faith into an unlikely concoction that could very well spell the unraveling of the cosmos as we know it.

Check him out at www.thecomingevil.com.

MAGGIE STIEFVATER
THE DENIAL

All of Maggie Stiefvater's life decisions have been based around her inability to be gainfully employed. Talking to yourself, staring into space, and coming to work in your pajamas are frowned upon when you're a waitress, calligraphy instructor, or technical editor (all of which she's tried), but are highly prized traits in novelists and artists. She's made her living as one or the other since she was 22. She now lives an eccentric life in the middle of nowhere, Virginia with her charmingly straight-laced husband, two kids, and neurotic dogs. She is the author of LAMENT (Flux 08), BALLAD (Flux '09), and SHIVER (Scholastic '09).

MIKE DURAN
EN ROUTE TO INFERNO
DINER ALUMNI, CONTRIBUTING EDITOR

Mike was born and raised in Southern California, where he lives with his wife and four grown children. In between working construction, he's managed to land stories in places like Raygun Revival, Fear and Trembling, Forgotten Worlds, Alienskin, Infuze Magazine and Dragons, Knights and Angels. His essay, The Ark, recently received Editor's Choice award in Relief Journal 2.3 He contributes monthly commentary at Novel Journey, one of Writer's Digest 101 Most Helpful Websites for Writers. And though his website is named Decompose (www.mikeduran.com), it has very little to do with corpses or compost.

WILLIAM BRIAN JOHNSON
TIM·S HOLY HAMBURGERS

If Brian Johnson were rich, he'd be a profession adventurer; but since he isn't, he chases storms around the Kansas Prairie and writes. Tim's Holy Hamburgers is his third published short story.

TOM BARLOW
SCHADENFREUDE

Other stories by Ohio writer Tom Barlow may be found in *The Apalachee Review*, *Hobart*, *The Duck & Herring Pocket Field Guide*, *Hiss Quarterly*, *Thieves Jargon*, the *Steel City Review*, and other magazines, and the print anthologies *Book of Dead Things*, *Desolate Places*, and *Hard-boiled Horror*. His story "My Daughter of Many Colours" was recently named a Notable Story for 2007 by the Million Writer's Award, and his story "Call Me Mr. Positive," which appears in the anthology *Best of the Intergalactic Medicine Show*, was called "brilliantly sardonic" by *Publisher's Weekly*. Tom is a graduate of the Clarion Science Fiction and Fantasy Workshop and a lead writer for the most visited personal finance blog on the Internet, AOL's WalletPop.

BARRY OZEROFF
BUM DEAL

Barry Ozeroff is a 22-year police veteran who works for the Gresham Oregon police department. A former SWAT sniper and the recipient of Gresham PD's Medal of Valor, Barry is a full-time traffic motorcycle officer and fatal crash investigator. He also serves as the department's lead hostage negotiator and is a crisis intervention officer. For the past ten years, Barry has ridden off-road motorcycles while patrolling Gresham's many parks, trails, and off-road areas. Barry lives in the Portland area with his wife and the youngest three of his six children, and also has two grandchildren over whom he dotes incessantly. Keep up with Barry at www.barryozeroff.com

BOB FREEMAN
QUEEN'S GAMBIT

Bob Freeman is an author, artist, and paranormal adventurer who lives in rural Indiana with his wife Kim, son Connor, and sister-in-law Cassie.

Bob is the author of the novels *Shadows Over Somerset* and *Keepers of the Dead*, and the collection *Widdershins: Dark Prose and Darker Poetry*. His short fiction and poetry has appeared in numerous magazines and anthologies, including *Legends of the Mountain State 2*, *Dark Harvest*, and the forthcoming *Death in Common*.

He is a member of Indiana Horror Writers, Midwest Paranormal Writers, The Aleister Crowley Society, as well as being the founder and senior investigator for Nighstalkers of Indiana, field investigator for ADCI, and the Hoosier State's Doorways Investigation Group liaison.

JASON M. WALTZ
WITH THE BRIGHTNESS OF HIS COMING

Thirty-five plus years spent with his nose in a book has given Jason—besides the alternate personality found at von Darkmoor's thoughts—an insatiable taste for quality reading material. And a crooked nose. Reader of many words, struggling writer of a few, Jason has been a long-time inhabitant of the worlds of fantastical fiction and an eager pupil at the feet of its illustrious members. The man behind Rogue Blades Entertainment, he longs for fiction thick with action, adventure, heroism, and hope. He aims to rejuvenate the world of reading by delivering a shot of adrenaline to every reader, author, artist, and publisher he meets.

MARIANNE HALBERT
THE HOUSE OF ABANDONED CHARACTERS

Marianne Halbert is an attorney in Indianapolis, IN. She has published one short story, "Invisible Fences", which appeared in *Indiana Authors 2007: Inspiration from the Heartland* (New Century Publishing), and her short story "The Last Spectre" will appear in *Dark Distortions II*, due out in 2009. Her writing is a bit ecclectic, as she can't help what pops into her head. Most of her stories seem to combine mystery, suspense, quirkiness, poignance and the unexpected. "The House of Abandoned Characters" is dedicated to Olivia and Chloe, who she hopes will always strive to be the authors of their own life story.

D. S. CRANKSHAW
THE OFFICE OF SECOND CHANCES

D. S. Crankshaw is an Electrical Engineer in Boston. As his job doesn't give him much of a creative outlet, he's found other ways to indulge his writing obsession, including his blog, Back of the Envelope, its associated Storyblogging Carnival, and a writing group he leads at his church. He's previously published short stories in *Aoife's Kiss* and the e-zine Residential Aliens.

KIM PAFFENROTH
FIELD OF BLOOD

Kim Paffenroth is an Associate Professor of Religious Studies at Iona College. His nonfiction work, *Gospel of the Living Dead: George Romero's Visions of Hell on Earth* (Baylor, 2006), won the 2006 Bram Stoker Award. Since then he has been writing zombie fiction, including *Dying to Live: A Novel of Life among the Undead* (Permuted, 2007), and *Dying to Live: Life Sentence* (Permuted, 2008). Check out his Gospel of the Living Dead blog at http://gotld.blogspot.com/.

VIRGINIA HERNANDEZ
SMALL ACCIDENTS OF GOD

Virginia Hernandez, youth minister's wife AND writer/reader of horror, wishes those two things didn't seem mutually exclusive to most church members. She lives in Florida with her three terrific kids and spectacular husband, who have all adjusted to her weird tendencies and reading addiction. She is tired of all the "almosts" in the writing world and is therefore thrilled to have her first short story published.

JERRY GORDON
9TH WARD

Jerry Gordon couldn't figure out a way to be an astronaut, film director and superhero in the same lifetime, so he settled on writing about them. His work has been published in InfoWorld, Indie Review, and the *Midnight Diner*. He recently completed his first novel, *Severed Dreams*, and can be found blurring genre lines at www.jerrygordon.net

JASON BRANNON
RUNNING TOWARD EDEN

Jason Brannon is the author of The Cage, Winds of Change, The Machinery of Infinity, and others. He currently resides in Amory, MS and maintains a website at www.jbrannon.net

ANNA D. ALLEN
VIRTUE'S BLOOD

An award-winning writer, Anna D. Allen lives in western Michigan with too many books and not enough dogs. She recently completed her BSc and MA. Her future plans include cleaning out the freezer and growing tomatoes. She can be found most days in the kitchen or with her nose stuck in a book. Other publications include "Ten Gallons a Whore" in *Writers of the Future* and "Mrs. Kelly's Ghosts" in *Ruins Metropolis*.

MICHAEL MEDINA
BALLAD OF WOLVES AND ANGELS
DINER ALUMNI

Michael couldn't remember having a normal life. Not after he, Vega, and Jiana accepted that very first hunt from The Diner. It certainly didn't involve international crime bosses, drug traffickers, or any flying bullets. But this was his life now.

Michael looked out over Antioch City. He shook his head. "I have a bad feeling about this."

Jiana rolled her eyes. "How bad could it be?"

Vega placed a hand on each of their shoulders. "It always gets worse when you say that."

"So we're not taking the hunt?" she asked.

"Of course we are," Michael replied.

Vega sighed, "I'm going to regret this...I just know it."

BRETT MCLAUGHLIN
CHANGE OF HEART

Brett McLaughlin is a bestselling and award-winning nonfiction author. His books on computer programming, home theater, and analysis and design have sold in excess of 100,000 copies. He has been writing, editing, and producing technical books for nearly a decade, and is as comfortable in front of a word processor as he is behind a guitar, chasing his three kids around the house, or laughing at reruns of *Arrested Development* with his wife.

COACH CULBERTSON
HEAD FRY COOK

It was a dark and stormy night when I stumbled into the Diner, half-drunk on adrenaline and needing a serious coffee fix. It was my usual stop after fighting off the demonic hordes of chaos that seemed to make frequent play-dates in my corner of the world. The same guy who always sits at the counter was sitting at the counter, looking like everything and nothing was wrong. I thought I'd take a seat next to him, like I usually did when the universe stopped making sense.

"Hey, Jesus," I said, "How's the apple pie tonight?"

VENNESSA NG
DINER EDITOR
JESUS VS. CTHULHU EDITION, BACK FROM THE DEAD EDITION

With a coffee in one hand and a pile of manuscripts in the other, I occupy the end stool at the counter. I glance at the other editors behind me scattered throughout the diner, each with their own piles spread before them, red pen in hand, critical eye scanning each word. As I mark up the last correction, a flash of papers thump onto the counter beside me. Then another, and another, and on it goes until the pile is complete, the editors trudging out the door, their job done. I swallow the last cold gulp of coffee and push away from the counter. "Coach, orders up!" I yell as I head out the door. With a satisfied sigh, I let the door swing closed behind me. It was time to reinhabit my own cyber cafes at www.aotearoaeditorial.com and www.illuminatingfiction.com.

MICHELLE PENDERGRASS
DINER EDITOR
BACK FROM THE DEAD EDITION

Michelle Pendergrass loves living in the Boondocks (which also happens to be her favorite song!) with her husband and son, Phil and Zane. They watch Food Network and CMT--Ace of Cakes and Gone Country are their favorites, and for them, there's nowhere better to be than home. Michelle has made pizzas, put paste on billboard signs, waitressed at truck stops as well as high class steakhouses, and she has also led a Convoy (another favorite song!) across the bottom of Texas when she and Phil drove their semi across this great nation. Now she homeschools, messes in mixed media art, prays in color, and sometimes she writes horror stories.

MIKE DURAN
CONTRIBUTING EDITOR
BACK FROM THE DEAD EDITION
DINER ALUMNI - JESUS VS. CTHULHU EDITION

Mike was born and raised in Southern California, where he lives with his wife and four grown children. In between working construction, he's managed to land stories in places like Raygun Revival, Fear and Trembling, Forgotten Worlds, Alienskin, Infuze Magazine and Dragons, Knights and Angels. His essay, The Ark, recently received Editor's Choice award in Relief Journal 2.3 He contributes monthly commentary at Novel Journey, one of Writer's Digest 101 Most Helpful Websites for Writers. And though his website is named Decompose (www.mikeduran.com), it has very little to do with corpses or compost.

MELODY CHAN GRAVES
LAYOUT EDITOR - BACK FROM THE DEAD EDITION
DINER ALUMNI - JESUS VS. CTHULHU EDITION

Melody Chan Graves's short fiction has gained national attention in the *Writer's Digest* Annual Writing Competition, the *New Millennium Writings* Contest, the National Literary Awards at Salem College, and the *Nimrod* Literary Awards: Katherine Anne Porter Prize in Fiction. She is currently working on a literary romance about a time-traveling genie, as well as a linked collection of short stories. Melody works as a freelance graphic designer and technical/marketing copywriter. She lives in Texas with her husband. To read more about Melody and her work, please visit www.melodychangraves.com.

ROBERT GARBACZ
STORY EDITOR - BACK FROM THE DEAD EDITION
DINER ALUMNI - JESUS VS. CTHULHU EDITION

Robert Garbacz, when in his natural habitat, can frequently be seen arguing theology, politics, and art over ale with often excessive volume, haranguing his friends repeatedly with obscure but fascinating facts about Medieval literature, or staring cloyingly into the eyes of his beloved wife Hannah. Unfortunately, his natural habitat is Oxford in the period from 1930-1950. This is a bit awkward for someone born in Tulsa in 1983, but he is studying towards his Doctoral at the University of Texas in Austin and feels this is a firm step in the proper direction. His short story, "The Salvation of Sancho," appeared in the previous Diner anthology, inducting him into this peculiar world of horror, bloodshed, and merciless ravagement of grammatical missteps.

MATT MIKALATOS
STORY EDITOR--BACK FROM THE DEAD EDITION
DINER ALUMNI--JESUS VS. CTHULHU EDITION

While being chased by editors armed with radioactive rayguns, Matt Mikalatos unwittingly stumbled on an underground animal fight club, disturbing a vicious duel between a beaver and an electric eel. The combination of being simultaneously bitten, shocked, and irradiated has given him the proportional strength, powers and agility of an electric beaver eel editor. He is pleased to have discovered a place like the Diner, where he fits in so well. He blogs about his adventures at http://mikalatos.blogspot.com.

KEVIN LUCIA
READER - BACK FROM THE DEAD EDITION
DINER ALUMNI - EDITOR'S CHOICE AWARD WINNER,
JESUS VS. CTHULHU EDITION

Kevin Lucia writes for Shroud Magazine. His short fiction has appeared in *Coach's Midnight Diner*, Shroud Publishing's *Abominations* and *Northern Haunts* anthologies, Snuff Book's anthology *RAW: Brutality as Art*, and Necrotic Tissues' anthology *Malpractice: An Anthology of Bedside Terror*. Nonfiction credits include appearances in Tyndale House's inspirational anthology *Life Savors* and Bethany House's upcoming anthology *Love Lessons*. His first novel, *Hiram Grange & The Chosen One*, from Shroud Publishing, is coming in Spring/Summer 2009. He's currently finishing his MA in Creative Writing and teaches high school English. Visit him at: www.kevinlucia.net.

ADRIAN RIVERO
COVER ARTIST - BACK FROM THE DEAD EDITION

Adrian Rivero is an artist who works primarily in comics. He also works in film and screenwriting. He has made(along with Doug Clarke) a full length film called *The Dead Next Door*. His other projects are the extremely embarrassing and true Thought Balloon Man comic and his samurai epic Tooth And Nail which was first done in screenplay form and he is now developing into a comic. He lives in the San Francisco bay area where he raises his younger sister by himself. He enjoys puffing up his ego in third person and then self-sabotaging himself. Whew.

LaVergne, TN USA
25 March 2010
177133LV00001B/1/P